MW00965251

The Last Templeton

by Mike Morey

also by Mike Morey:

Uncle Dirty
Anonymous

The Last Templeton; Copyright ©2012 by Mike Morey. All rights reserved, including the right to reproduce this book or portions thereof in any form whatsoever. For information, contact the author: moreymichael@hotmail.com

This is a work of fiction. Names, places, characters and incidents either are the product of the author's imagination, or are used fictitiously, and any resemblance to persons, living or dead, business establishments, events, or locales is entirely coincidental.

Morey, Mike
The Last Templeton: a novel / Mike Morey
ISBN 978-1-257-12764-1

Cover design: Augusta DeRooter

Dedicated to Paul Quarrington,
whose advice, wisdom and inspiration made this book possible.

1

It wasn't meant to end like this, with me lying face-down in a cornfield. But here I am, twelve-hundred miles from home, skewered by some very prickly agriculture, and no help in sight. Worst of all, I've left my cigarettes in the car.

Did I mention that I'm dying?

When I turn my head to the right, I can see the car, ten yards away, parked on the shoulder, black against a fading dusk sky. It looks black, but it's really green. At dusk, in silhouette, everything is black, including Harry's head, which is resting against the passenger-side window. As with the car, Harry's blackness is an illusion, a trick of the light. Harry is white. The Pinto, as I've said, is green. Things are never what they seem.

My plan was to adjust Harry's seatbelt after I emptied my bladder in this cornfield. Plans change. My new plan is to lie here and die.

And that's my final decision.

- - -

Don't get me wrong. No one gets through life without an occasional setback, I know that. If Harry were alive, he'd tell you, as he told me so many times, "No one promised you a free ride, kid. There's no rule that says life gets to be easy." Lying helpless in an isolated cornfield, struck down by a weak heart, this could be seen as a fairly significant example of a setback. But the turning point, the crisis that changed everything for me, began three years ago. And like most big problems, this one began small. It started with a little stiffness in my leg.

- - -

I am chief stock boy and heir apparent to the family business: Templeton Hardware.

Isn't it the third generation that destroys most empires? I think I read that somewhere, and I believe it's true. But I'm no roving Playboy, no hard-drinking son in the prodigal vein, gambling away the family fortune. There is no Templeton fortune to squander. I'm of no consequence to heiresses or tabloids.

It was my grandfather who built Templeton Hardware upon the ruins of a devastating depression, and it was my father who, with an unshakeable blue collar ethic, sustained the business through the uncertain Sixties, the recessionary Seventies, the booming Eighties and the transitional Nineties, when independent business once and for all fell out of fashion. Now, at the dawn of a new century, it is my failure to live up to established Templeton standards that will finally sink the family ship.

I am a relatively competent—or at least harmless—stock boy; but, due to an abiding lack of interest in business, I am not equipped to take over the helm from Harry's capable captaincy. I guess I just never cared about hardware as much as I should have. What can I say? We're not all cut out to be captains of industry.

As for the incipient stiffness in my leg, I had no obvious explanation. Confined six days a week to the store (a twelve-hundred-square-foot space on the corner of Woodbine and Gerrard, in an east Toronto neighbourhood that seems doomed to be forever referred to as "developing"), my lifestyle has been largely sedentary. The tedious hours of my workday might be spent hanging grommets on the display case, or marking down a display of gardening tools for an end-of-season sale, or merely leaning on the wooden stool behind the cash register with the yellowing pages of a paperback hovering before my eyes.

(Despite what you may have heard, hardware sales is not a physically demanding trade.)

In any case, I could think of no recent occasion when I might have strained myself in the course of my professional duties. Outside of work, my sleeping patterns remained typical and my diet was unchanged. In other words, there was nothing to explain this mild discomfort. But it persisted, and when it began to spread to my other leg, I knew I had to mention it to Harry—not so much to seek the infinite wisdom that only a father possesses, but because it's natural, I think, to want to share grievances with those closest to you.

I had no one close except Harry; we had only each other.

So. On a hot June morning, with the cicadas already buzzing, and with the stench of the early commuters' exhaust wafting through the open window, Harry and I convened in the kitchen, as we did every day, at seven o'clock. It was our custom to take a quiet breakfast of black coffee and buttered toast, share the various sections of the newspaper, and generally attempt to reserve this time, this first waking hour, as the singular and exceptional hour in our day together in which we didn't annoy each other. It was a tacit understanding between us that we held as sacred, until now.

Out of respect for tradition, I waited until Harry finished eating his toast before I disrupted our peaceful routine. By then he had scanned the headlines, set aside the sports section unopened and made his usual scoffing noises at the preposterous entertainment news. He now lingered over the obituary pages.

"Harry?" I experienced only the slightest twinge of remorse for having molested our sacred hour. Harry's usual look of burbulence hardened into a scowl. He rattled the newspaper and ignored my intrusion. But I felt that my situation warranted his full attention. "Harry?"

The paper fell away, and the old duffer refocused somewhere just over my shoulder. "What is it?"

The irritation in his voice stirred the hairs on my neck. I briefly considered lashing out with some well-wrought bit of sarcasm, but I let the impulse go. This was a serious business; I didn't want it undermined by petty anger, not even *my* petty anger. In a gentle timbre, I said, "I just wanted to mention my leg."

"Your leg?"

"It's been bothering me, lately."

"Your leg."

"Yes."

"Bothering you…"

"Lately."

He looked at me as if a purple goiter had suddenly blossomed on my neck. We were getting nowhere.

"Stiffness," I explained.

"Stiffness?"

"You're just repeating everything I say."

Harry's face puckered. "You're not telling me anything. What are you trying to say?"

"I'm telling you about my *leg*. Do I need to draw you a picture?"

"There's no need for that tone. Show some respect."

I took a time out, lit a cigarette, clouded the air above us. "My leg is stiff, that's all I'm saying. Forget it, it doesn't matter."

"It must matter if you're telling me about it."

"It's probably nothing. Forget I said anything."

He seemed content with that plan, and returned to his death notices.

After pulling on the Rothman's for several silent minutes, I crushed the stub into the oversized ceramic candy dish that accommodated my morning's input of tobacco, and lit a second one. Soon, a satisfying blue haze churned slowly in the stratosphere of the tiny kitchen.

Harry gave a little cough, which was his way of telling me to cool it with the smoke. Three decades ago, he had been forced to take up the habit as a second-hand participant, and was tolerant in his churlish way. As for me, I was what the doctor had once called an "incorrigible smoker," which he assured me was not a good thing. But lung cancer and bronchitis and emphysema, I would soon learn, were dire consequences that I would not live long enough to face.

"Maybe I should see Doctor Nasir," I said, finally.

Harry's response wafted from behind the newsprint. "Hm."

I reworked this into a question. "What do you think, Harry?" The newspaper between us shrugged. "Maybe I should wait until there's pain. So far, it's just a little stiffness."

Harry sighed. "Go see the doctor," he said, giving in, at last, to my persistence.

But I found his lack of genuine concern disappointing. I was his only child—his only living relative, in fact. Even though it was not in Harry's character to be demonstrative, emotionally or physically, I thought he ought to have been slightly more attentive to this potential crisis. That was my opinion. "It might be too late if I wait until it really hurts."

"Go see the doctor," he repeated, this time with a little more feeling.

"It's probably nothing," I said. "He'll tell me it's nothing." I chewed on my coffee and shifted in my chair to confirm the stiffness was still there. "Maybe it's already too late."

The paper dropped noisily into Harry's lap. "For Pete's sake, go see the doctor, and leave me to read in peace."

Another decision successfully dodged. *Thanks, Harry.*

- - -

Dr. Mohammed Nasir was somewhere near the age of retirement, an amiable Pakistani ex-pat who, after a half-century in Canada, was now utterly gentrified. Even his accent was more Oakville than Karachi. He cottaged in Muskoka, invested widely in real estate and mutual funds, took his wife to Las Vegas for a week every February, and was a passionate and outspoken sportsman. He had recently taken up golf, which I took as a sign he would soon be heading out to pasture.

"I don't golf," I said, after listening to him gush for twenty minutes on the value of a proper grip.

"Good-good." The doctor used this phrase as a nervous tic, a senseless, reassuring leitmotif. "Terrific game, Mister Templeton, just terrific. I command you to take it up at once. Fresh air, great exercise..." He was examining my aching leg, so he missed my relevant glare.

"It hurts to walk," I said, hoping to drive home the point.

"Good-good." He fiddled with my limb, working the joints, pinching bits of skin and asking, "Tell me this hurts."

"Yes."

"And this."

"Yes, *yes.*"

He began to make illegible notes in my file. As he worked the pen, I became fascinated with his hair, which was an immaculate helmet of short grey thatch that snuggled his scalp, contrasting his Earl Grey complexion. It was so faultless, I had trouble believing it was real. I resisted a growing temptation to reach out and touch it, shook off the distraction and refocused on the matter at hand. After watching him compose several long paragraphs, I grew impatient.

"Come on, Mohammed. You must have some idea what's wrong." I was reserving a more respectful tone for the moment he delivered a proper diagnosis.

He closed my file with a definitive motion and pushed it to the far corner of his desk, and then smiled at me with his perfect, glowing teeth. He was all charm. "This is a great mystery, isn't it?" The mystery appeared to please him, as if it were a challenge that he took as lightly as he did his wife's modest gambling debts. As if the solution meant nothing to him.

Of course, it did mean nothing to him, but it meant something to me. "I wouldn't be here if it wasn't a mystery."

Once again he displayed his flawless dentition. "Good-good." He replaced the cap on his gold pen and jammed it in his breast pocket, implying further notes were pointless. "I'm going to insist you take a few sessions with the physiotherapist. See if we can loosen things up down there."

Five sessions with the physiotherapist confirmed my earlier diagnosis: Dr. Nasir should retire to his beloved links before someone really gets hurt. The treadmill and stair-step routine did nothing but aggravate my mysterious condition, forcing me to bed for three agonizing days (which soured Harry's mood when he was left short-handed in the store). Once I recovered sufficiently, I hobbled back to the old cracker's office.

"Are you trying to kill me?" I asked, in all seriousness.

Nasir laughed and gave my shoulder a playful push, which sent me reeling in agony. Yes, the stiffness had migrated to my left arm. And after he forced me to accept his earnest apology, I allowed him to prod me in all the same sore places, and some new ones, and prod me further with the same refrain: "Tell me this hurts!"

"Yes, dammit!"

The old bone must go through the motions, and I must permit it because it's the only way to get what I need.

"You require a specialist," he said, the last one in the room to reach this conclusion.

"You think so?" But the good doctor was impervious to sarcasm.

"I command you to see Doctor Pudding," he said.

Doctor who?

- - -

True to her name, Dr. Wioletta Podink transmitted the faint aroma of cocoa butter, and also conveyed a manner as sweet and tempting as a truffle. She hovered over me like a luscious foreign cupcake, touching me here and there with warm fingers of softened butter, asking harmless questions as she investigated my outer shell. "Have you been losing weight?" "Yes." "Have you been feeling fatigued, lately?" "Yes." "Feeble?" "I beg your pardon?" "Have you noticed that it's more difficult to lift heavy objects?" "Oh, right, yes."

"Does this hurt?"

Not anymore. Her touch on my virgin skin was bestirring a masculine grit I never knew I possessed.

"Are you sure? If I'm not mistaken, this should be very painful."

"No, I'm fine."

"How about this?"

In the end, the tears gave me away. And my reward for being so manly and brave during the examination was the unraveling of the "great mystery".

"We'll have to wait for the results of the blood work to be certain, but I believe you may be suffering from Scleroderma."

"What?"

"It's an autoimmune disorder that causes overproduction of collagen."

"What?"

"There is no cure."

"…"

"To put it in the simplest terms, you are turning to stone."

"And that's bad, right?"

"Yes."

In time I learned more about Scleroderma than I would have liked, but when we face our own mortality, we must search the small details for hope. Here are some of the highlights I had to look forward to over the next two to five years: a painful tightening and thickening of the skin; restricted blood flow; failure of the major organs, including lungs, liver, kidneys and heart; loss of hair; heartburn.

Eighty percent of Scleroderma sufferers are women. Statistics are vital to victims. Right off the bat I was a rare case. With a rare disease. Most sufferers degenerate slowly, often over decades; a few seem to experience prolonged remission. I'll say it again: I was a rare case. It was only a matter of time before something essential failed. My immune system was pumping out the collagen with an almost religious fervour.

Three years after I felt the first twinge in my extremities, my left knee locked permanently in place and my neck refused to swivel more than twenty degrees from center. I could stand for only a few minutes before a blunt ache seeped up my spine and spread out like a malevolent, barbed vine.

- - -

And by this slow process of fossilization, as my motor skills continue to degenerate, even the simplest task has now become an experience in transcendent frustration. I will eventually be as helpless as an infant.

Hello, Harry.

2

Harry was sceptical.

But I could hardly blame him. If it weren't for the physical symptoms—the stiffness, the tender areas on my forearms and shins, the headaches—I might have scoffed, too.

"It doesn't make sense," he said. "Who ever heard of someone turning to stone?"

"I think there were one or two cases in the Bible," I said, "but that was probably just divine retribution."

Harry blinked a few times. He didn't approve of religious talk in the house. He then suggested I was inventing this so-called disease in order to escape my duties in the store, until I reminded him I had never needed an excuse before. Which was true. I was not overly endowed with ambition. Harry could only concede the point.

"You should get another opinion. You probably just pulled a muscle."

I knew he was wrong about the pulled muscle, but, in order to get him off my back, I consulted a second specialist, and then a third, both of whom confirmed the diagnosis.

Harry remained entrenched in his denial. "Next you'll tell me you've grown gills and have to live at the bottom of the sea."

Well, I'll take that over turning to stone, thank you. I was eventually able to convince him with a note from my doctor and a leaflet from the Scleroderma Association of Canada.

"Does this mean you can't work in the store?" He had his priorities.

- - -

Three years later, after reading every book on the subject, every leaflet, every article in obscure European periodicals, I was eventually led to a promising prospect, located in the unofficial gateway to the Great White North: Edmonton. At this exotic outpost, optimistic advances were being made in the treatment of my devastating disease—if you can believe Armenian Drs. Abkarian and Vartan, who reported the most recent results in the Marmara Journal of Medicine. According to the article, a group of brilliant scientific minds was developing new drugs that had thus far shown positive results in some test animals, and which now needed to be tested in human specimens. There was a worldwide call for willing participants. For the first time since being diagnosed with this deadly illness, I was given the smallest granule of hope.

I made contact with the facility—which was the research branch of the pharmaceutical giant, Traxco-Meriwether Industries—and put my name on their list of guinea pigs.

For a man given no chance of survival, it was an act of desperation, never anything more than a last-ditch effort to delay the inevitable. But I was relieved to have finally been able to do something, *anything*, to defend myself against this physiological ogre. It's the helplessness that is hardest to overcome. In any case, I had nothing to lose.

Living three years with a death sentence had brought me a certain level of acceptance, if not exactly *submission*, that allowed me to function without being mired in a suicidal depression. I was coping with as much humour as I could muster. Harry was little help to my state of mind. He continued to pretend there was no problem, or at least to ignore the part of the problem that meant my remaining days added up to a very small number. In other words, he didn't want to talk about it. But during this time he also continued to furnish me with the necessities of life, as he had done for more than three decades, without grudge.

Now I had a new favour to ask.

"Where did you say?" That was Harry. With one ear on our conversation and the other on the television newscast, he was getting short shrift from both sides.

"Edmonton," I repeated. "It's in Alberta."

"I know where Edmonton is."

I had my doubts.

"Why do they want *you?*"

I patiently explained, again, that they were keen to have me take part in this round of revolutionary drug testing. Being both male and terminal, I was a rare specimen. "If these drugs work, I might live longer."

The person I spoke to at TMI told me she could offer no guarantee of positive results, and in fact went on at great length about the potential risks of introducing an untested drug to the human body. "That's why it's called *research*," she had said. "We think we know what will happen, but only practical trials will bear that out." On a positive note, she told me her team of gifted scientists was fairly confident that a life extension of anywhere from six months[†] to two years was "not beyond the realm of possibility." ([†]Individual results may vary.)

The main obstacle to my participation was that I had to get to Edmonton. "If you let me borrow the car," I told Harry, "I'll drive there, myself."

"No, that would never work. If you're going to go, I'd have to drive you."

"I can't ask you to do that," I said, with a somber shake of the head. "Not at your age."

"My age? What's that mean?"

I tried to look surprised by his umbrage. "I don't mean anything. It's a long drive, that's all I'm saying."

"It's not so long." His brow furrowed slightly. "How long is it?"

"I figure we could do it in four days."

"Hm."

I had to tread carefully, not seem too desperate. "You can see the Rocky Mountains from there, so I hear."

Harry pondered that, while staring at the flashing images on the television screen. "Never been fond of mountains," he said, finally.

I decided to take a less subtle tack. "It would be a real test of your driving skills."

He looked at me as if I had slapped his face. "My driving is fine."

"Of course it is. That's what I'm saying. You're the expert. No one else can get me there."

"Huh." His jaw set. He hadn't said no, which was a good sign. "Edmonton," he muttered. "Middle of nowhere."

"It's a long way," I admitted, "but we should be grateful that someone out there is trying to save my life."

Harry was sophisticated enough to see the value in any new development that might make his own life easier. My current battery of pills was expensive, and achieved little more than masking the symptoms, but could do nothing to reverse, or even slow, my deterioration. Sooner or later, this disease was going to kill me. I've had three years to adjust to that certainty; any future cure will come too late for me. But for Harry's benefit I didn't want to downplay the hopeful aspects of this treatment. If he was willing to believe I might live another ten years, I was not going to discourage him.

The newscast broke for a commercial. "Seems to me they could just send you the pills in the mail. I don't see why you have to go all the way out there."

"They need to monitor my reaction to the drugs. They'll have doctors standing by, in case something goes wrong."

"What's going to go wrong?"

"Nothing. Nothing's going to go wrong."

"Maybe this isn't such a good idea. Those pills could be dangerous."

"The pills are going to help me. They're just being cautious."

The television commercials ended. Harry watched impassively as American troops patrolled an Iraqi village. "What about the store?"

"Well," I said, with as much nonchalance as I could gather, "we'd have to close the store for a short time. I don't see any way around it."

Harry's lips compressed into thin, bloodless slits.

"It's only for a few weeks," I said.

He scratched his chin, a habit I had always found irritating. "A few weeks," he said.

"October. It's a slow month." I didn't need to inform Harry Templeton of the up-and-down cycles in the hardware business. Better that I simply change the subject. "Why don't you read the brochure? It explains everything a lot better than I can."

Along with the brochure, TMI had also sent a sheaf of nearly incomprehensible legal documents, the gist of which could be summed up as a forfeiture of my right to sue TMI, in the unlikely event I should suffer ill consequences from this treatment. I didn't mention the waiver to Harry.

"They should send you an airline ticket, if they want you so bad."

"That's not part of the deal. We have to find our own way there."

Harry made a disparaging sound in his throat. "What happens when we get there? Where do we live? I suppose they expect us to pay for a hotel."

"They put us up in the university residence."

"The what?"

"Student apartments. They're very comfortable."

"How do you know?"

"I'm sure it'll be fine. You can't expect them to get us a room at the Hilton."

"I don't know what I should expect them to do."

"When we get there they'll pay us a daily stipend."

"A stipend? How much?"

"Fifty dollars."

"A day?"

"Fifty dollars a day. That's what I said."

"*Sheesh*. That's a lot of money just to sit around and swallow pills."

"We'll have to buy our own meals."

"You mean in restaurants?"

"Of course in restaurants."

"How much will that cost?"

"Fifty dollars."

"*Sheesh*."

Harry had a neurotic aversion to restaurants, so I didn't want to linger on this topic, either. "We can give ourselves plenty of time to get there, see some sights along the way. It'll be an adventure."

Harry was picking at a loose thread on the arm of the sofa, a sign he was mulling over the idea. I knew that the driving aspect of the plan appealed to him. To his way of thinking, a man was defined by his skill with machinery; a notion cultured, I suppose, from the manly nature of the family trade—although the culture had somehow escaped me. After a moment of reflection, he said, "The car needs a new fuel filter, and I'd have to look at the tires.

That one in back has a slow leak." I knew his mind. He wanted me to know the range of inconveniences he'd be required to suffer, if he was going to do me this kindness.

"If it's too much trouble…" I said, prodding him to commit.

"I didn't say that. Did I say it was too much trouble?"

"I could always take a bus."

"No, that would never work." Harry didn't believe in busses.

It was time to close the deal. "If you say so. Thanks, Harry." I left a solemn pause, and then I got down to practical business. "I've been studying the map."

I had already spent hours squinting at the Atlas, evaluating various routes and making calculations. The result was the surprising discovery that the most efficient way to cross our fair country was to take a shortcut through another one. From Kalamazoo to Chicago to Saint Paul to Grand Forks, the United States of America would open its gates and permit us passage through its backyard, requiring in return merely that we verify our citizenship and obey their laws to the best of our abilities. After meeting these conditions, we would venture down Interstate-69 to I-94, along I-90, up I-29. From our re-entry into Canada, three inches below Winnipeg, it is a straight diagonal line across the prairies to our destination. I explained the route to Harry.

"I don't see how that's possible," he said. "You must have the map upside down."

I showed him the map, traced the path with my pencil, explained to him the alternate route, over the top of the Great Lakes. "Going through the U.S. takes a whole day off the trip."

"I'll be darned." He scratched his chin at this seeming paradox, and then switched the channel to CNN.

"We'll need passports," I said.

But Harry was suddenly engrossed in the goings-on in Uzbekistan. I interpreted the end of our conversation as assent, and began making plans. I returned the signed documents—the liability wavers—to TMI, plotted a daily driving schedule that would get us to Edmonton in time for the study to begin, encouraged Harry to attend to the Pinto's minor repairs, and crossed my fingers— figuratively, since they would no longer twist in that lucky fashion.

I was signed and sealed. All that remained was to be delivered.

Early on a Monday morning in October, we left behind the smoggy bustle of Toronto and set out for that great metropolitan dot on the western plains: Edmonton.

3

"Here we go," said Harry, a little tremulously, as he steered the Pinto out of the alley and merged into the morning traffic on Woodbine. His fingers tapped the rim of the steering wheel nervously, and I saw his eyes flick to the rear-view mirror, where he watched the shop disappear from view. "Did you remember to turn off the bathroom light?"

"Yes." I tried to ignore Harry's nervous tension, concentrating instead on the horizon ahead. "Stop worrying."

"I don't want to be paying for that light for the next month."

"I turned it off."

"Okay." But his hands twisted the vinyl grip of the steering wheel as if he were wringing thirty years of sweat from it.

A fragmented view of Lake Ontario spread before us, a grey, turbulent mass that looked inhospitable under the drab autumn sky. The morning shadows were diluted by a smoggy haze. To the southwest, a pair of smokestacks smouldered indolently, like massive cement cigars left unattended on the rim of the vista. The road soon curved westward to run parallel with the lakeshore. Ashbridge's Bay Yacht Club drifted by on the left, a cluster of sailboats bobbing in their slips, anticipating the coming winter's hibernation under blue shrink-wrap. The adjacent boardwalk was populated with desultory dog owners and bicycle commuters. Further along, a busy, vivid strip mall, with Food Barn and Burger King and drive-through coffee, stood in garish contrast to the monochromatic lake. I peered through the locked gates of a former film studio that now awaited the wrecker's ball. Beyond that, Mayfield Fitness Centre; Harrison Pontiac; hydro sub-station; all of it familiar, but seeming somehow different, now that we were leaving it behind. The way you look at something you might never see again.

"What about the coffee pot?" Harry was still fretting.

"What?"

"The coffee pot." He was relentless.

"Think of the insurance money, if the place burns down."

Harry's foot lifted off the gas pedal. He was looking for a place to turn around.

"Joke, Harry, joke," I said. "Come on, relax. The lights are off, everything's off, the door's locked."

The old duffer exhaled slowly and steered the car up the ramp, onto the Gardiner Expressway, settling in the slow lane. Before we could achieve cruising speed, which for Harry was predictably below the posted limit, the flow of westbound traffic ground to a halt. We had just driven into the heart of Toronto morning rush hour. Not an auspicious beginning to our historic journey. Thirty minutes later, as we drew even with the Dunn Avenue ramp, we finally overtook a disabled truck that was stalled in the center lane, and were ejected from the jam like a small-caliber bullet into a clear road. *Tally ho!*

I navigated while Harry complained about the other drivers and the poor condition of the highways and the high price of gasoline. Through Sarnia, Flint, Lansing, Charlotte, Lawton, Bridgman and countless unmemorable whistle-stops, I absorbed the new and ever-changing landscape with an open mind. I wanted to appreciate what these new, exotic places had to offer, admire their respective attributes and styles, but I admit it wasn't always easy to foster flattering thoughts.

Harry was uniformly unimpressed by much of what he saw. "Looks like Toronto," he'd say, "only flatter." Not a compliment.

Many times I tried to find something positive to say about a town, in order to keep my own spirits up. "We've passed three fitness clubs, so far. You can't fault a town that's this interested in good health."

"Look at the rust," Harry would say. "Nobody undercoats, these days." His tongue would click in despair of modern times. "Thirty years old and not a spot of rust anywhere on this car." Which wasn't exactly true. The rust on Harry's Pinto was advancing at approximately the same rate at which his eyesight was deteriorating. It was a harmless delusion.

As first mate and navigator, I was determined not to disappoint Harry. I remained vigilant, constantly aware that one inattentive moment could have us off course, lost, rolling into inhospitable territory, forced to ask directions—in Harry's mind a mortifying offence. But my maps didn't fail me, and at dusk on that first day we parked in front of room seven at the Trade Winds Motel. We were just outside Gary, Indiana, four-hundred and ninety miles from home.

But who's counting?

"You know," I said, "Frank Borman is from Gary." We were in a booth at the Denny's restaurant across the street from the motel, where Harry was poking sceptically at the crust of something deep fried.

"Who?"

"Frank Borman, the astronaut. Apollo Eight."

"Huh."

"Remember the space race, Harry?"

"Sure," he said, to humour me. "Exciting times."

"'One small step for man...'"

"What?"

I was doing my best to stimulate the conversation, but Harry was hopeless. He must have been tired after the long day's drive; I was exhausted, myself. "The Jackson Five are from Gary, too."

Harry gave me a vacant look.

"They're a singing group," I explained. "They were popular in the Seventies."

"I don't remember the Seventies."

The conversation dwindled after that. But Harry wasn't off the hook. Our endearingly frumpy waitress stopped by to remonstrate Harry for not eating his dinner. "Those good vegetables you pushing round your plate, son."

Neither of us could quite believe she had just called him "son."

Harry looked more closely at his plate. "There are vegetables in there?"

She spoke to him as if he were four years old. "Sure, lots of good stuff in there. Go ahead and try it." She crossed her arms, resetting the slant of an impressive bosom, waiting for him to comply.

"What are you grinning at?" he said to me, after the waitress had moved on, with her coffee pot and her maternal strictures.

"Nothing. I just have something caught between my teeth."

"Some part of the rat that didn't dissolve in the pot."

"What do you expect for a minimum wage establishment?" If he hadn't been so tight with his cash, we might have selected a better grade of restaurant—perhaps one where the waitress didn't stand over you until you finished your peas. I was too tired to remind the old duffer what a cheap bastard he was.

Back at the motel, we didn't fare much better. Our neighbour in room six turned out to be an insomniac in need of a new battery for his hearing aid. Harry and I lay awake until the wee hours, listening to an unidentified spaghetti western play through the thin wall.

"Karl Malden grew up here," I said, to the dark ceiling. I'm not sure how I knew that.

I heard Harry grunt in the dark. "*Him*, I remember." Harry wasn't a total loss.

Day two: Chicago, Madison, Portage, Mauston, Black River Falls, Eau Claire. We bypassed St. Paul. Didn't slow down for Coon Rapids or St. Cloud or Barrett. At Fargo, another formless motel, another Denny's—Harry was getting the hang of it, finishing most of a grilled cheese sandwich and a stack of coleslaw. We slept well.

- - -

Our third morning on the road was profitable, at least in terms of mileage. Harry flirted with the speed limit, which I found surprising and encouraging. Our mission was time sensitive. It was a matter of life and death, both of them mine. By midday we had covered more miles than my itinerary had planned for. We were ahead of schedule, and I was looking forward to an unhurried repast.

To my everlasting regret, it was I who forced the decision to halt our progress through the desolate North Dakotan frontier and lunch at Uncle Jim's Mexican Fiesta. "I've got a hankering for Fiesta," I shouted from the co-pilot's seat, using jargon that Harry could relate to. *How bad could it be?* I asked myself. *We can't eat grilled cheese sandwiches for every meal.*

I'm not solely to blame, though. Harry should have known better, should have taken his first impression of this rundown shack, fifty miles north of the nearest village and fifteen-hundred miles from the nearest Mexican, and pressed his Hush Puppy down on the accelerator, asserted his alpha status, and reduced this unsavoury temptation to a pinpoint in the rear-view mirror. But while I harangued him about my "hankering," I saw his eyes flit between the empty parking lot and the blank horizon ahead, a vista that promised another hour of driving before the next likely prospect. His foot came off the gas pedal and the Pinto, farting in protest, turned off the highway.

Warped and sagging like a house of wax under a hot sun, the low building hunkered into the landscape, quietly losing its will to survive. It was a relic of a bygone century, a solitary and isolated holdout, seemingly aware its time had passed. As evidence of a previous incarnation, a set of rusty, impotent gas pumps stood guard in the parking lot. In the front window hung the remains of a poster advertising an "amazing" and "shocking" reptilian roadside attraction that appeared to have long ago migrated elsewhere. Inside, in a foyer that had no doubt changed little over the past century, hung the faint scent of some primordial bog, damp, black, cold. Maybe I imagined it.

Harry and I stood inside the front door, shaking off the dust and surveying the dim interior of the restaurant. There were no other customers, which meant either we were early for lunch or there wasn't much call for foreign delicacies in these remote parts. I was about to call out, when someone crashed through a set of saloon doors leading from a back room.

Uncle Jim, presumably—who it turned out was a woman of rare and extravagant obesity. "Howdy," she called, with a mid-western twang that rang with a faint hint of menace, as if we were interrupting some important business.

I put my hand up and returned a little wave, hoping to encourage her to slow down and take care with her movements. I certainly didn't want to be held responsible if she toppled over. "Hello," I said. To my left, Harry sighed.

Because of Uncle Jim's impressive circumference, it was impossible to estimate her age. Her face was under siege by what looked like a heat rash, this in spite of the rather pleasant autumnal temperature. Below the rash hung a yellow tarp, stamped randomly with red and green chili peppers, an expansive and shapeless drape that creaked like dime-store rubber when she moved. Above the rash rose a monstrous synthetic beehive, listing to starboard and threatening to unleash a swarm of angry insects. Her seeming disapproval at our arrival only confirmed my lack of shrewdness in this particular decision, her porcine gaze daring us to make a run for it before it was too late. But Harry missed these signals, and I was too proud to admit defeat and back out the door.

She came to a full stop before us, breathing heavily and quivering from the strain. "How you doin, boys?" she wheezed. "Table for two?"

There was an awkward pause. I wondered if she might be nearsighted. "Two, yes. Thank you."

"Okay, then," she said, not exactly admiring our commitment. "Right this way." She led us past a row of empty booths that overlooked the parking lot and the monotonous plains beyond.

Because of my deteriorating physical condition, I fell behind, pivoting my hips in exaggerated arcs to generate the centrifugal energy necessary to propel each leg forward: the Frankenstein's monster's walk. Despite his advanced age, Harry was spry by comparison. And the beehive, in her entrepreneurial fervour to get us settled in before we mustered the courage to flee, moved with admirable agility. When I realized we were being directed to a cramped side table, beneath a dirty window that overlooked a rusty propane tank, I spoke up. "Could we have a booth?"

"Here we are, boys," said the beehive, openly disregarding my request. She waved a sausage hand over the table and attempted to smile, managing only to make her eyes disappear somewhere beneath all that flesh. After dropping two paper menus on the table, she waddled off to the kitchen to shoo away the rats and stoke the griddle.

I lowered myself into the chair opposite Harry and extended my stiff leg into the aisle. The window was painted shut, allowing no relief from the lingering smell of mould and scorched meat. Hanging over my shoulder was a dying fern with parched tendrils that scratched the back of my neck, while my elbows scraped across the table's flaking red paint. A well-fed bluebottle zigged past my nose and collided with the glass pane, dropped to the sill, buzzing in angry convulsions, regained its composure, and then took a swipe at Harry's left ear before careening off to one of the empty booths.

"Maybe this wasn't such a good idea," I said.

Harry rubbed his tickled ear and scanned the heavily thumbed menu. "I don't know much about Mexican food."

Looking at the menu myself, I could only conclude that this experience would do nothing to change that. "Take my advice and stick with the chili."

Harry had spent his childhood under the influence of wartime rationing and post-depression prudence. He had limited experience with restaurants, and was a virtual novice in the ethnic realm. During the three days since our road trip began, he had developed a budding appreciation for cooking in the short order vein. It was, after all, not much different than the culinary efforts he managed in his own kitchen: pan-fried pork chops, boiled potatoes, green beans steamed until all texture and flavour were purged. After I repeatedly assured him of the stringent codes for hygiene in the food preparation industry (perhaps with more confidence than the industry merited), he began to relax and enjoy having someone else do the work. Now, in Uncle Jim's Mexican Fiesta, the glint in his eye did not bode well for his inexperienced palate.

"Maybe I'll have the Burrito Fiesta Deluxe," he said.

"For God's sake, Harry, have the chili."

"Either that or Jimmy's Yummy Chimichanga."

I gave him a hard look. "I'm not getting in the car with you if you order that."

He ignored me. "It says here it comes with pinto beans."

I grunted.

"*Pinto* beans. Just like my car."

"Both notorious for exploding rear ends," I said. But the old duffer was beyond the range of my sophomoric humour.

"The Jumbo Jim Shrimp Fajita sounds good."

"We're a thousand miles from the ocean. Don't order the shrimp. Why don't you have the chili?"

Harry scrutinized the menu, as if the meaning of life were encoded in its exotic lists. "I don't think chili's supposed to be green," he said, finally.

"It's a special kind of chili. You'll like it."

"Maybe if they have red chili…"

"Well, they don't. They only have the green kind, and it's the only safe thing on the menu. Take my word for it."

"Hm."

I could see I wasn't convincing him. "You'll be sorry."

The beehive emerged from the kitchen, approaching like the leading edge of a lava flow, sandals pulverizing the dirt on the linoleum tiles, chili-pepper tarp sashaying. The bluebottle made another lurching pass at my head, missed, swooped over Harry's right shoulder and dashed himself into one of the front windowpanes, a final act of bravado. Perhaps an omen I should have heeded.

The whiff of Vaseline and decay enveloped our table. "You gentlemen decided?" The sausage fingers held a pencil nib poised over a pad.

I jumped in before Harry could make a foolish choice. "Can you make a grilled cheese sandwich?"

The sausages nearly lost their grip. "Not today, honey. The bread man never showed up."

Harry set his menu down with a flourish. "It says here the Jumbo Jim Shrimp Fajita comes with pinto beans."

"Sure, honey. Everything comes with that."

"Good, good. I'll have that. And a beer."

I surrendered with a sigh and ordered for myself the green chili and a Coke. As the beehive buzzed off, I enjoyed the rare sensation of having made at least one sensible decision, lamenting only that I failed to persuade Harry, too.

But I couldn't be too hard on the old duffer. He was doing me a kindness I didn't deserve by subjecting himself and his beloved Pinto to a two-thousand mile journey that both were too old to endure. His duty to me as a caregiver had extended well beyond the normal burden put upon a parent, his obligation fulfilled long ago. He has fed and sheltered me, has given me employment, has subsidized the expensive medications I've required, these past three years, to remain locomotive, has provided a secure base that I would not otherwise have had. Looking him over, I had to wonder, not for the first time, if he was up to this current task. There was a sanguineous flush to his face and neck that I had rarely seen. Harry had always seemed old to me, but for the first time I saw how old he really was.

Over his scalp crested thick, orderly brilliantine waves, a consistent shade of blue-grey. His chin bore an ashen half-day stubble. He was thin in the way that men who have never been muscular become in old age, sunken around the jowls like a beach toy slowly losing air, arms showing too much bone at the elbows, legs wishboned as if he'd spent his life in the saddle. Having been a short man to begin with, Harry had lost an inch over the years to the pull of gravity and the slow progress of kyphosis. His lemur eyes blinked myopically behind the thick lenses that were as much a natural and familiar part of his face as his nose. But behind the lens was a rheumy sheen that contributed to a dopey septuagenarian veneer, and around his head hung a fog, a fine mist that was almost visible, enveloping him like a protective skin and giving him a fixed air of bemusement.

Sitting under the dusty haze of a sombrero light shade in Uncle Jim's Mexican Fiesta, I thought the old man deserved a better life, deserved a better son—one that might have taken care of him in his declining years, rather than the other way around. Harry was a nitpicker, a nag about the small details, a worrier over the minutiae of daily life, but he never complained about the big things, the important things, and I realized that, in spite of the petty bickering that regularly passed for conversation between us, I had never loved the old duffer more than at that moment. Had I possessed just a touch of supernatural prescience, I might have told him as much. Alas, I kept those dangerous feelings to myself.

The beehive delivered my Coke in a green plastic tumbler (presumably evocative of ancient Mayan custom), the contents hovering near room temperature and wanting for carbonation. Harry's bottle of beer was so cold it immediately began to sweat on the table. The beehive once again vanished into the kitchen, and soon the dining room was insinuated with new, unappetizing smells. There were no Michelin stars in this establishment's foreseeable future.

"If we have a late supper," I said, to Harry, "we could reach the border tonight."

"I don't want to have a late supper." That was no surprise. Harry always took his evening meal at precisely six-thirty, and was disinclined, at this late stage in his life, to alter his routines.

"It won't kill you to have dinner a little later, just this once. We could make some real progress by the end of the day." I realized, too late, I should have waited until after he'd eaten his lunch. The prospect of a late supper would have seemed more tolerable on a full stomach.

Harry pulled a long draught from his beer and removed the foam from his upper lip with a flick of his finger. "I'm not fond of progress," he said.

"Jesus, Harry. We're not discussing the Industrial Revolution. We're trying to get to Edmonton in a timely fashion."

"You don't have to be there until Friday. We have lots of time."

Lots of time is a phrase that takes on new significance to someone who is dying from an incurable disease. And if only the old duffer could have seen one hour into the future, he might have chosen his words more carefully.

"I'm just saying we can get a little further ahead of schedule, bank some time, in case there's an emergency."

"What emergency?"

"I don't know. How would I know?"

Harry inspected his fingernails. "I don't see what your big hurry is."

"I'm not in a big hurry. I'm just setting goals."

Harry snorted. "A bit late for that." His attention wandered from the conversation. After a minute he said, "How about that waitress?"

"What about her?"

"She's some woman," he said, mysteriously. Was he showing manly interest, after all these years? Would I be calling Uncle Jim "Mom" in the foreseeable future? It seemed unlikely, for many reasons.

"She's not some woman," I said. "She's *three* women."

"You don't have to be like that. It's not her fault she's…" There were so many possibilities, he was stuck.

"You're the one who brought it up."

After a moment, he leaned forward and whispered, "D'you reckon all Mexicans are that…*big?*"

I looked carefully to see if he was serious. "She's no more Mexican than you. Did you get a good look at her? She's as white as a ghost, except for the rash."

"Huh," he said, as if he didn't believe me. He took another long pull from his beer.

"Forget about her. We should talk about the schedule for tomorrow."

Harry looked out the window at the propane tank, as if the amount of rust worried him. He had the attention span of a child.

I pressed on. "Tomorrow night we could stop in Saskatoon, if you're too tired to drive."

"I'm not too tired."

"Not now, tomorrow. You're not listening."

"I'm listening."

"Tomorrow. Saskatoon, or straight through to Edmonton. Depends how tired you feel."

He tore his eyes away from the rusting propane tank. "I don't feel tired."

I had to take a pause, count slowly to ten.

Harry drained the last of his beer.

"Don't drink so fast," I said. "It'll go to your head."

"I'm thirsty."

"Have a glass of water. You have to drive."

"Of course I have to drive. Who else would drive?"

He had a point. I possessed a driver's license, for what it was worth, but my reflexes were not what they once were. And even before my debilitating illness gave him a legitimate reason, Harry never lacked excuses to deny me access to the driver's seat of the Pinto. He didn't want anyone else driving his car, the jealous bastard. I tried to shrug, but managed only to strain an obscure muscle between my shoulder blades.

"Did you take your medication?" His tone was accusatory.

"Of course I did," I said, unable to recall whether I had or not. Ordinarily, I would have taken signals from my body, but after three days, folded into the passenger compartment of a compact car, the usual aches and stiffness were compounded by travel cramps. Unlike the old duffer, I had achieved the full masculine height of six feet. It was one of my earliest disappointments to realize that, while Harry doted on his little Pinto, the other duffers in the neighbourhood spent their Saturday mornings waxing the steamship hood of a Chevy Caprice or Crown Victoria, full-size barges with ample leg room for a fully grown male.

We sat in silence a while. Harry twisted his empty beer bottle in the wet puddle it had left on the table. I tapped a finger to the faint beat of a Country & Western ballad that bemoaned the unfairness of life and love from somewhere within Uncle Jim's kitchen. The genre didn't exactly set the tone for a Mexican Fiesta, but somehow it seemed appropriate for the sad restaurant and its two tired and dispirited clients.

Twenty minutes passed before the beehive emerged from the kitchen and delivered two wicker platters that brimmed with what might have been mistaken for components of a botched surgery. The powerful hum of southern spices overwhelmed my nasal passages, caused my eyes to water. Harry, whose sense of smell I had always thought suspect, appeared not to notice the pong; instead, he seemed stunned by the sheer foreignness of his dish. I knew he had no preconceived idea what a fajita was, but this was clearly outside the boundaries of his limited imagination.

"Enjoy, gentlemen," said the beehive. She began to lumber away with an air of someone who has many pressing tasks on the go, but she wasn't fast enough to make a getaway before Harry ordered another beer. "Sure, honey. How about your friend, he want another soda?" She was talking to Harry but looking at me.

"Thank you," I said, "no." Had I been a braver man, I might have surrendered my abstemious ways. Perhaps alcohol was the best way to cope with this culinary experience.

Because of my compromised mobility, eating was a slow and laborious process for me, a bit like trying to run underwater. It required perseverance, plus an extra dash of patience from Harry. Each time I lifted the fork to my mouth, my shoulder creaked, as if someone in the next room were trying to quietly open a door. The previous evening, that sound had disturbed an elderly couple seated next to us at the Denny's restaurant. They had glanced around surreptitiously, quietly speculating in loud whispers about what the mysterious sound might be. They thought that perhaps the restaurant's foundation was unsound, that the roof was about to come down on their heads. They asked for their bill before they'd finished their coffee. In Uncle Jim's Mexican Fiesta, there were no other customers for my creaky joints to worry.

The Jumbo Jim Shrimp Fajita must have been satisfactory, or at least tasteless enough not to offend Harry's bland palate. Within minutes he had polished his platter, scooping up a few straggling pinto beans with the blade of his knife, and drained his second beer. I was having less success. In revolt against the pasty texture of the green chili, my esophagus constricted, and soon my stomach began to show signs of potential mutiny. My mouth refused to produce saliva, and my warm, flat Coke was an unsatisfying lubricant. In the end, I consumed just enough of this unsavoury spread to gratify Uncle Jim and her swarm of agitated bees. (Why I should wish to cause no offence to someone whose second-rate fare and service I—or, rather, Harry—was paying for is a question

I refuse to answer, except to say it is part of my collective Canadian personality to do so; this in light of the glaring fact that I've never had a problem telling Harry all the ways he is capable of offending me.)

"That was good," Harry said, belching indelicately. Now that he was fed, he seemed less concerned about the deteriorating propane tank. But he looked more flushed than ever, and he was perspiring.

"You'd better ask Uncle Jim for a Tums before we get back in the car." I had lived with him long enough to know he wouldn't complain openly about having heartburn; instead, he would sit stolidly behind the wheel and sigh with a slow rhythm that would drub my senses with the cruel persistence of a dripping faucet.

He looked at my bowl. "How's the chili?"

"It's good," I lied. "But I couldn't eat another bite." That was the honest truth.

Harry paid the bill and left a small tip.

"That's less than five percent," I said, counting the pile of coins he'd left on the wet ring next to his plate.

"Mexican food's pretty good," he said, "but it isn't cheap."

"That's not the point. If you enjoyed your meal, which you clearly did, you should tip at least ten or fifteen percent."

To be honest, I didn't think Uncle Jim's Mexican Fiesta was worth the five percent it was getting, but I wanted Harry to understand that such a small gratuity was a deliberate and critical commentary on the quality of food and service. He was new to proper restaurant etiquette, and he was a notorious skinflint.

If anyone should be insulted, he told me, it was he. "As it is," he said, "five percent is highway robbery."

"Less than five percent," I reminded him.

We had been having this argument for three days, and I wasn't optimistic he was any closer to registering the nuances of dining out, but my conscience drove me to persist. If I'd had money of my own, I would have avoided the discussion altogether and provided the tips myself. But I was indebted to Harry for more than his fancy wheels. I was not only broken, I was broke.

And Harry not only paid the bill, he paid the price for his first—and last, as it turned out—Mexican Fiesta.

We emerged from the restaurant, blinking at the harsh midday sun. There was little to see in the landscape surrounding Uncle

Jim's Mexican Fiesta, but we looked anyway, as if we might expect to see an invading army appear suddenly over the horizon.

A waft of stale air came at me when I opened the passenger door, the stench of an old car that had been working too hard. Harry quickly settled in, making fiddly adjustments to his seat, even though it didn't need adjusting, as he was the only one who ever drove the car. Once he was satisfied, he buckled his seatbelt, fired up the motor and began tapping his fingers on the steering wheel, watching me hoist my fossilized leg into the passenger compartment. I looked over at Harry to see how his patience was holding out, and the moment our eyes met, his expression changed. His face clenched like a fist, and he seemed to be trying to formulate words his mouth couldn't articulate, as if he were consumed by an unaccountable rage. The flush in his face turned a vivid shade of magenta.

"I'm going as fast as I can," I said. But his gaze was focused on the distant horizon, and he didn't appear to like what he saw there. Whatever his problem was, it had nothing to do with my slow progress.

"What's wrong?" I asked. "Heartburn kicked in, already?" He didn't answer. I was about to upbraid him, one more time, for ordering the wrong thing from the menu, when his shoulders stiffened and his eyes began to orbit. He slowly arced forward, until the bridge of his nose touched the upper rim of the steering wheel.

I reached over and touched his shoulder. "Harry?"

He made a small sound with his mouth, like an aerator in a fish tank, and then his bowels released, filling the car with a stink that nearly caused me to swoon. I didn't require a second opinion to know he was dead.

4

I remember my birth as if it were yesterday.

How is that? chimes the voice of the sceptic. *Impossible!* Maybe so, maybe no, I answer. Who's to say which memory is real and which is not? Proof is in the remembering. And here is an honest truth: first impressions are always the strongest. I stand by my claim.

Remembering day one: I see the delivery room, as bright and noisy as a carnival, my mother's face faintly blue and utterly still, golden hair circumscribing her like a halo. Her arms lay unmoving at her side, left palm facing upward while the right reached for something unknown. One leg dangling over the edge of the table, the other cocked at a carefree angle. She looked frozen in time, as if caught in the middle of some unfinished business—which, I can now suppose, was the act of delivering me. This was my mother, as I remember her, the first and last time I ever saw her in the flesh.

The scene, as I recall it in vivid detail, could best be described as slapstick, the standard "having a baby" skit, acted out in vaudevillian splendour. All around me was pandemonium on a ridiculous scale, humans in blue hospital livery scuttling here and there, bumping into one another, ducking shouldered planks, skating on fruit peels. Frying pans met foreheads and fingers plunged into eye sockets. And the noise! It was enough to make me pine for my recently vacated womb. Only my pale blue mother was not in a state of panic; she was a model of comportment.

My mother's name was Sara Glynn Valentine until she married Harry and became a Templeton. I learned later that Sara Glynn was dead before the doctor slit her open and plucked me out. I survived and my mother died. That's the long and short of it. Something inside gave out, malfunctioned. In the manufacturing of me, my mother gave too much of herself. We were incompatible from the start, which does not belie the immeasurable love I have for her.

Whether or not she should have been saved by the wealth of medical experience that was present in the delivery room is now, all these years later, moot. It took me a long time to accept that when someone close to you has died under questionable circumstances, casting blame provides no real comfort. Proving malpractice wouldn't have brought back Sara Glynn to me. No degree of retribution could have compensated for my loss.

In defence of those doctors and nurses who failed to save my mother's life, way back in 1961, I understand that they believed her trauma was simply the natural distress of a woman in the throes of childbirth. Her body was engaged with the tidal rhythms of labour, the ebb and flow of contractions, the stress of dilation. Somewhere in there, her heart stopped beating, and by the time the alarm was sounded it was already too late.

Once I recovered from the shock of seeing the real world for the first time, I made my own contribution to the chaos in that delivery room, flailing my arms and legs, making demanding sounds, sending up flares to ignite over this tragic Keystone Cops extravaganza. I was trying to get someone, anyone, to explain to me what was going on.

I would have to wait for answers.

- - -

My survival was declared a miracle, if only a small one in the long history of earthly miracles. The expert opinion was that I shouldn't have lived. I had arrived seven weeks ahead of schedule, and emerged from a corpse. Either fact alone could have made things tricky for me, but combined should have given me long odds. For the weeks following my miraculous delivery, I was incubated through artificial means, hovered over by concerned faces, fed intravenously, and fervently prayed for by local church groups. I did my part, accepting this nourishment with silent gratitude, growing stronger every day, until I was eventually hatched from my glass shell and placed, for the first time, into Harry's tentative arms.

A touching moment, I'm sure—something worthy of a John Williams score—although the extraordinary memory sockets that wired me for total recall of Day One show their limits here; I have no recollection of my first meeting with the old duffer. Nothing. I have only his account of the event to go on, surely a biased view. I'm told that Harry nimbly plucked me from my cradle, held me up to the light by the window, inspected me for flaws, found none, and kissed me on the forehead, declaring me the perfect son. See what I mean? That doesn't sound like the Harry I know; more like Charleton Heston in one of the biblical epics. Well, one thing I learned is that nothing about family is objective, so I suppose I have to take it all in stride. At the least, I was lucky to be alive.

Do I attribute my survival to the practical attention of the nurses and doctors who plugged me in, fed and watered me, dripped nourishment into my angel-hair veins—to, in other words, the Empire of Science—or ought I tip my hat to the Spiritual Kingdom, to those thoughtful and selfless church ladies who thumbed through the silky pages of their prayer books, searching for just the right words to appeal to His capricious nature? I am withholding judgment until the last possible moment. But I can say this much without offending anyone still living who might be responsible for the miracle of my birth: I was an ugly thing, and it was a condition that, unlike with so many ugly children, I did not outgrow. (Did Harry not see it, as he held me up to the light? Apparently not.) Even now, forty-three years later, my appearance is capable of causing an unsuspecting public to recoil in horror. Only the teenagers, who are attracted to all things gruesome, will fall into paroxysms of laughter, which is at least a refreshing change.

I was given a name to go with my dog's-breakfast face: Mavis. *Harry, I forgive you.*

His beautiful and adoring wife had just died, and been replaced by an unripe onion crowned with a tuft of black fuzz. Poor Harry. He must have seen the name on the lapel of one of my nurses, and in the throes of grief could think of nothing else to jot down on the form. Harry had always lacked imagination, having relied on his wife, my mother, to lead him in creative matters.

But I say names are important, and I cast at least some of the blame for my misnomer on those around Harry who did nothing to prevent this folly. Imagine the boy, Mavis Templeton, age eleven, enduring the first week of yet another school year in which teachers and students are forced to acknowledge, with poorly concealed smirks and open taunts, respectively, that I possess a name quite obviously meant for a girl. The faculty, and adults in general, overcame this queer appellation more easily; for the diehard bullies sitting behind me in class or following me across the schoolyard, I could only deflect their derision by spreading a small and harmless lie, which was that I was named after my mother, who died while giving birth to me. That usually shut them up. Even the most heartless tough won't make fun of a dead mother. But it was an annual rite of passage for me, one that left scars.

The humiliation of Mavis Templeton, I should point out, began long before I was thrown to the wolves in the public school system. Yes, because of my miraculous birth, I made the local newspapers, filler pieces, no doubt meant to fill gaps on a slow news day. There I was, in black and white, my hideous onion-face, my meatless bones, my wee clenched fists hovering in the air, my black fuzz, and my girly-name printed below. Three local papers printed photographs, each taken from roughly the same angle, showing off my naked profile as I lounged in the tropical atmosphere of the incubator with tubes pumping the stuff-of-life into my premature body. Those were the days before Photoshop, so my tiny pecker made the shots. Why couldn't I have had a nurse named John? And where was Harry while I was being exploited so egregiously by the fourth estate?

Miracle Mavis! screamed the headlines.

- - -

The story of my life is one of degrees: degrees of success/failure, degrees of happiness/sadness, degrees of love/unlove, degrees of faith. And it is by these degrees, these increments, that I fall on one side of the /slash or the other. Only *faith* is, to my way of thinking, slash-less, such as it is an infinite series of increments, with more degrees than our modern geometry can measure. Even atheism, with its unambiguous rejection, is a degree of faith for what it accepts. The needle on my own faith-o-meter has lately suffered tremors, wavering uncertainly above the mark to which it had once been solidly locked. I've been the wandering sheep, led astray by a crafty wolf and re-educated—let's say brainwashed, to give it its proper cultish context—and then released back into a society I no longer conformed to. A bit melodramatic, you say, but I can attest my skull is crammed with all manner of superstitions and *wooji-wooji* foolishness, most of which I believe wholeheartedly—or at least some of which I refuse to disbelieve.

It wasn't the Moonies or the Hare Krishnas or any Jonestown faction that did this to me; there were no saffron robes or Kool-Aid concoctions involved in the altering of my mind. Rather, it was a non-conspiracy of people and events during my formative years that shaped my warped system of beliefs into a moderately unified theory. And like most brands of faith, mine was founded largely on fear.

Of all the irrational fears I carry from childhood, the gravest is that I will die face-down. A childhood bully once put a knee to my spine, pressed my face into an unkempt flowerbed and educated me on the finer points of death, including—as a passing note, it seems to me—the disquieting assertion that entry to Eternal Paradise was conditional upon facing heavenward at the moment of death. Anyone unlucky enough to expire face-down, he went on to suggest, was doomed to a fiery spiral into Everlasting Damnation. Since I routinely found this bully's brand of instruction persuasive, I could find no reason to doubt him on this point. Even after my mind was expanded by better teachers, I could never quite purge this concept, no matter how preposterous, and it became one of the many random facets that eventually coalesced into something resembling a *faith*.

Since then I have been haunted by grim forecasts of my ultimate downfall. That long-ago engagement with a fundamentalist bully opened a door that my mind could not shut, projecting unwanted visions of the countless and diverse ways I might bring about my doom. In the most recurring scene, I see myself pitching headlong after an encounter with the uneven sidewalks that plague my city; a sudden, magnified view of stale cigarette filters and wads of chewing gum, adorning the gutters like modern art, mingling with the red-black juice of life as it seeps from my cracked skull, a soft-edged circle wipe closing in on the tableau. Or, I see myself standing in a slippery bathtub, aware of the sharp edges surrounding the enclosure, each one ready to pierce my skull if my concentration slips even for a moment— which it invariably does. A mugging in a shadowy side street, a blade opening my gut, down I go into a foetal position, forehead touching the asphalt. There are more, and they are encouraged by my fecund imagination and my agnostic insecurity. I don't want to believe the bully's words, but I can't dismiss them so easily, and this is a sign of my own weakness, not his strength.

Even the media fires my nerves with fascinated dread, CNN's global eye roving with godlike omniscience, flashing images of death from places I've never been, in some cases never heard of, bodies rendered inanimate by guerrillas/police/boyfriends/peace-keeping troops/sharpshooters/unknown assailants/terrorists/rebels/martyrs/skinheads/bullets/knives/car bombs/anthrax/speeding drivers/pit bulls/lightning/avalanches/tornados. My wary eye scans the pixels in search of the *body*; there is a desperate need to see, to know: face-up or face-down?

Every so often, these visions cause me to regret my lowercase faith. Perhaps if I were able to embrace the doctrines of a traditional religion, I might find, if not definitive answers (a failing I perceive in those clubs), at least some measure of comfort, a reassurance that I will not suffer the unspeakable torment of a hell I am not sure I believe in. Instead, I am stuck in the mire of indecision, wallowing in questions that will never be answered; but I persist, clutch my faith like a ratty shawl, drape it around my shoulders and garner what comfort I can.

At night I recline on my mattress *missionary* style—which is to say, flat on my back. Having assumed this somewhat stringent and unimaginative sleeping posture for all these years, I no longer experience the natural itch to roll to one side or the other. I'm made to believe this position encourages snoring, but this "missionary" sleeps alone, so the issue is moot. As I fill my bedroom each night with rhythmic, fricative evidence that there is still breath in me, I dream of the day when I will perish peacefully in my sleep, locked by *rigor mortis* into my final funereal posture, hands laced across umbilicus, chin pointed towards the ceiling. By then, I will presumably have made a final decision regarding my faith.

- - -

Reclined involuntarily in a remote field of harvested corn, I am alone with my dark thoughts. Or not quite alone, because Harry remains in the vicinity, slouched unsociably in the green Pinto; and I also see a pair of crows—blacker than the deepest shadow, blacker than death itself, except for the eyes, which reflect a brilliant light that has no earthly source—lingering on a nearby telegraph pole, watching me squirm in the dirt. And at recurring intervals, a cloud of overwrought gnats descends on me, orbits my head and face, doesn't like what it sees, and permits the westerly breeze to take it off to greener pastures. (Hey, you can't *make* someone like you.)

So, with Harry sulky and silent, with the crows supervising from above, with the gnats coming and going, I use the time to reflect on my name and its significance, now that I am nearing the end of my abridged life.

Here is the thing. From the beginning it was the first half of my signature, *Mavis*, that attracted all the attention, my surname never more than three innocuous syllables fading on the weathered sign over the family store. But it has just occurred to me that I am the *last* Templeton. I have no heirs, and Harry was, like me, an only child. There are no male cousins who might propagate the family name. I represent the bottommost root of a family tree that will grow no more, and somehow the thought makes me sad—even more than the knowledge that I am about to die. But then, I've had three years to prepare for a death that is, I am assured by a team of competent professionals, imminent and inevitable. Second opinions have been sought and third opinions, redundant as they are, acquired. And the real evidence—evidence of an arguably circumstantial nature—speaks to me in my bones, and in my heart. I am no longer afraid, but I will not pass on without taking along a measure of regret.

The degree of failure in my life is measured, I see now, by my procreative track record; or, to be precise, lack thereof. After all, when the big questions arise—why-am-I-here/what-is-my-purpose/...&c.—the answers, if they can be found at all, come not from the philosophy majors who cram the dole queues in droves but from a most primeval source: genetics. Which is to say, I exist for no higher purpose than to *breed*. One can pay lofty fees to get a more satisfying answer than that, but it won't necessarily be true. So here is the simple truth of my life: I failed to accomplish the singular task I was genetically engineered to perform, which was fatherhood. And here is another truth, as hard to swallow as it is to divulge: during my forty-three years, I never once got past "first base." (Enough! No more confessions. My hideous head hangs in humiliation.)

I will ask this question, and expect no satisfying answer: Would my failure have been less complete if I had tried just a little harder? If I had conquered dozens, even hundreds, of women with the gusto of, say, the professional athlete, and still come away empty-handed, still left behind dozens or hundreds of unfertilized eggs, would the judgment against me be any less severe? Maybe, maybe not. Does it matter? Will I be turned away at the Door for this crime against nature? Enough! Time to abandon those questions that cannot be answered.

Let the facts stand. I have never fathered a child. I have never made love to a woman. I have not fulfilled my duty as a man. End of facts.

My lowercase faith has no specific policies on the subject, so I am left to fend for myself. But I will say this: right about now I'd trade my soul to the devil for a post-coital cigarette.

5

After Harry slumped over the steering wheel and died, I shut down. I experienced a blankness of the mind I'd never known before. There was nothing, no despair, no panic, no anger, no emotions of any kind, not even detached curiosity. There surely could have been many questions impressing themselves on me at that moment, and they did come later. Was it his heart? Was it merely coincidence that we'd just left a dubious Mexican restaurant? Was there something I could have done to prevent it? Apply CPR? Pump the chest? A couple of slaps and a splash of water to the face? Had the dark man come for me, and taken Harry by mistake? Perhaps Harry volunteered to go in my place. He was like that; a grumpy, reluctant martyr. But the only thing occupying the space between my ears was a sort of white noise, like the rolling, oceanic surf a child hears when he puts a conch shell to his ear. I suppose it was the faraway hum of the idling engine.

To a passer-by it might have seemed these two men in the old green clunker had both succumbed to the toxic emissions of a faulty exhaust system; and indeed a brown fog rose from the underbelly of the car. But Harry had succumbed to old age, and I was immobilized by shock. With my eyes damp and stinging, I should have switched off the ignition, but the effort seemed monumental, impossible. I wanted to give up. Or perhaps it's more accurate to say the idea to give up came down on me like a great weight, as if gravity had increased tenfold, and beneath that impossible burden it just seemed easier to surrender. I knew that I should take some sort of action, that doing something was better than what I was doing, which was nothing; but that instinct was not supported by coherent thought. I simply stared out at the sloping hood of the car in a catatonic daze.

Time passed, minutes/hours/years, speeding past in the style of cinematic time-lapse photography, boiling clouds scurrying off to other hemispheres, shadows expanding and contracting, a yellow glint arcing overhead on a westward orbit, seconds accelerating until they blended together, became a humming note, increasing in pitch and volume, reaching the acme and then receding, fading in the predictable Doppler manner. Somewhere in there I saw the end of the world, a new beginning…

It was the need for my drug of choice, nicotine, that finally brought me out of my shock-induced trance. With a shaking hand I pulled a Rothman's from the pack on the dashboard, and soon those sweet tobacco fumes were mingling with the creeping exhaust. But the drug, as it worked its way into my system, brought not relief but only a growing anxiety. I realized that, when Harry died, he was facing forward, his eyes level with the bleak horizon, and I couldn't decide where that fit within my face-up/face-down system of faith, my lowercase faith. I wanted to believe he ascended, that looking *forward* was equal to a proper and reverentially heavenward gaze. I needed to believe it because, no matter how many things about Harry irritated me, no matter how many times he implied, in his fashion, that I had disappointed him, he deserved his Everlasting Reward. God knows he deserved it.

I sat a long time in the passenger seat pondering this, until I made the decision to take the optimistic view, to believe Harry was all right, wherever he was. I wasn't refuting my faith so much as expanding on its admittedly vague precepts, permitting these new circumstances to illuminate elements of my doctrine that I hadn't seen earlier, but which must have been there from the beginning.

So, I adapted my thinking and was happy for Harry. At seventy-two, he had lived a life that was, statistically speaking, complete. No one could say he went before his time; although I alone might argue he could have waited two more days, fulfilled his promise to deliver me to our destination. I say, without rebuke, he left me in a bit of a bind.

Now what do I do? I whispered in Harry's ear. But it was no use. The old duffer was officially removed from the decision-making process. He traded in his ticket to Edmonton for a cruise on the Styx. I lit a second cigarette with the first and contemplated my options. The gathering fumes in the cockpit shrouded me in a gauzy haze, an atmosphere conducive to deep thought.

The simplest plan would have been to return to the restaurant, to Uncle Jim's Mexican Fiesta. I suppose a sensible person would have seen that choice as somewhat obvious. Help was only steps away, it would seem. In my defence, let me say this: judged against even the lowest epicurean standards, the establishment would rank poorly. Yes, there might have been a working telephone on the premises, a means to summon emergency personnel (or a priest!), but before I could go forward, I had to ask myself what, precisely, I needed help with. Harry was beyond the reach of medical science, and, unlike me, he was not prone to events of a "miraculous" nature. And besides, I couldn't dismiss that odious canteen as having contributed to Harry's death. It was plausible, to me anyway, that the lunch they served him was in part, if not largely, responsible for pushing his heart to its limits. And I had to wonder how much help a five-percent tip would buy you.

Narrowing down my choices, I considered going back, returning the way we had come. I knew there was a town twenty minutes to the south, a charmless hamlet of tilting, weather-beaten shacks, with lazy dogs molting in the shadows of unkempt yards; a treeless and grassless park that the local teenagers had stripped of anything useful; a rash of forlorn shops (coin laundry, barbershop, Doll-r-ama) comprising the so-called business center, these dodgy ventures infused with the stale resentment of poverty and isolation, a whiff that encouraged passers-by to roll up their car windows and feel protectively for their wallets.

The town was called Withers, no doubt named for its founder—some distinguished old grandee, I imagine, with lush burnsides and a stovepipe hat, a gold fob dangling from his vest—who surely had practical reasons for settling in such an inhospitable frontier. From what I had seen of the place from the cockpit of the car, there were no trees to butcher, no mills sulking in the valley, no cattle mooching at the sidelines, nothing that could be described as industry.

Harry also had failed to see the attraction. As we rolled slowly through the town, he made disparaging chucking sounds with his tongue. "A coat of paint would do this town a favour."

I had watched a bandy-legged geezer in dirty coveralls drop grease-stained rags into a burning drum. Another slow day at JD Auto. "I'm not sure the paint would stick," I said, more to myself.

Whatever old man Withers saw in the place, back in the nineteenth century, has long since vanished. Its primary enterprise now seemed to be a tavern, which shared a plot of land with a gas station. It was hard to imagine the town employed either a sheriff or a doctor, and returning to find out struck me as futile.

In a situation like this—which is to say, an *emergency*—one needs Authority to take charge, give orders, make arrangements, relieve the bereaved of their burden. But if I was going to involve an authority, I couldn't help believing it should be a Canadian one. As I squinted through the cigarette haze at the landscape surrounding Uncle Jim's, I became acutely aware of being in a foreign land, one with potentially strange and exotic customs, with values and laws that were unfamiliar and a little frightening. We Canadians have always claimed to be different from our cousins to the south, although we are often at a loss to define those differences; now that I was embroiled in a crisis on this alien soil, they seemed obvious.

I imagined the complicated bureaucracy involved in retrieving Harry's body from the hands of a foreign government: the endless flow of incomprehensible paperwork, passed along the corridors of the most dull and disinterested offices; a checkmark found to be in the wrong box, a minor slip that leads to delays that leads to phone calls that leads to more paperwork that leads to angry words that leads to political intervention—a last resort, for any sane person; diplomatic negotiations ensue, on our part earnest, on theirs indifferent except to the proper codes of procedure; the inevitable outcry from the Canadian media and ambitious government runts, insincere protests that the "delays in this matter are unacceptable." My ogre's face will alight on television screens, looking glum, eyes cast down to the sidewalk, not a symptom of my despair but a defensive gesture against the photographers' flash. *All I want is to bring my father home...* They will tell me to say this, and I will say it because it is true, but the sorrow in my voice will seem fraudulent to me, simply because they have put the words in my mouth. And in the end, when Harry is finally released from this administrative nightmare, he will be turned over not to me but to my country. Lenses will capture his arrival at Pearson International

Airport, will pursue him through the city streets, record his progress to the funeral home. Thousands of strangers will attend Harry's memorial service, not counting the millions who will get an edited version on the television, a highlight package, as they say in the business. There will be only one family member in attendance: me. I will be obliged to accept these interlopers because this man, the late Harry Templeton, is now public property, handed down from our government like a gift to a public hungry for its leadership to give something, anything, back. After all the scandals and corruption, after raised taxes and lowered services, after breached contracts and broken promises, the public wants something back, and what it gets is Harry.

When it comes to patriotism, the Americans have us beat, hands down. *Ask not what your country can do for you...* But I am not interested in giving Harry to the public. Let the politicos give a few bucks back to healthcare, if they want to throw us a bone, but leave the old duffer alone.

Once the smoke cleared, I propped Harry up in the passenger seat and took the wheel of the Pinto myself. My plan, my carefully constructed plan, was simple: I would get Harry across the border, back on our native soil. After that, my plan became somewhat vague. It was a work in progress.

Given my physical limitations, I probably shouldn't have been driving. And let's be clear: if Harry had still been alive, I never would have had the memorable experience of piloting that classic automotive relic.

The car, which was a shade of green consistent with boiled Brussels sprouts, belonged to Harry in the way that jealous men take possession of their girlfriends. Harry never grew weary of talking about his car in the boastful fashion of a proud lover, full of manly pride and passion. His relationship with the Pinto began in October 1974, and no one but Harry could have imagined this love affair would endure for three decades.

Naturally, it was my view he loved that old tin box more than any inanimate object deserves, to the point of unnatural—even unsavoury—obsession. He spent hours fondling its nostalgic curves with a soapy sponge, painstakingly reaffixing bits of peeling faux-chrome moulding, rubbing into the cracked and blistered dashboard exotic ointments that carried the same lustrous and dubious promise as those European balms that pledged more youthful skin for the aging female population. And his passion for the Pinto was matched only by his unswerving devotion to his wife, the late Sara Glynn Templeton—a devotion made manifest by a brooding reluctance to talk about her, and by his outright rejection of the idea of filling that painful void with a second Missus Templeton.

- - -

Now that Harry has ascended, where he is, one hopes, reunited with his first great love, possession of the green Pinto has passed, legitimately if not yet officially, to his son. Oh boy, I think I'm in love. When I consider my current circumstances, it may well be the shortest romance in history.

6

I steered the car out of the parking lot of Uncle Jim's Mexican Fiesta and aimed us north, in the direction of home. While Harry leaned indolently in the passenger seat, I silently prayed thanks to all the potential gods for automatic transmissions. Before long, a daring (or foolish) hare put my reflexes to the test by scampering across the highway in front of the Pinto, but I passed the test and swerved gently around the reckless animal. And now that Harry was in no condition to complain, I exercised some liberties he surely would have objected to. I lowered the driver's side window, permitting my cigarette smoke (and Harry's excretory pong) to mingle with North Dakota's crisp country air. Harry never liked driving with the windows down, claiming the wind and noise upset his concentration. And speaking of noise, there was music playing inside the car, quite possibly for the first time ever. For three decades, Harry had kept the AM radio tuned to the all-news broadcast. Now I cranked the dial until I found a bearable rock 'n' roll station. *Satisfaction*, I crooned at Harry, over the groove. *Hey hey hey, that's what I say.* He had no opinion on the matter.

Traffic on Interstate-29 was building steadily as we made our way towards the international border. With Harry buckled in loosely beside me, I tried to convince myself he looked like some old geezer taking a nap, but I couldn't help noticing he looked like a man who had recently died. Transport trucks thundered south, striking the car with shockwaves that sent us into an unnerving shimmy. I tightened my grip on the steering wheel and, with each passing transport, grew increasingly anxious. I imagined that, from their elevated cabs, these truckers could look down on us and see, in a flashing instant, that the passenger was unambiguously deceased. I could almost hear the crackle of static across the Citizen's Band airwaves as word spread that some desperado was transporting a corpse in a beat-up Pinto, making a run for the border. *Breaker breaker, good buddy…*

- - -

Only this morning, as we cut a straight line through the uniform terrain east of Fargo, Harry told me he'd once dreamed of becoming a farmer.

"It's the sort of work that requires patience and self-discipline," he explained. "You don't rely on anyone but yourself."

"And the weather," I said.

"The reward is right there, growing in front of your eyes."

"Locusts and ragweed."

"Self-sufficient. That's the thing."

"Couple of John Deere goons sneaking into the barn after midnight to repossess the combine. Sheriff's Deputy supervising the auction from your former front porch."

"Don't be a smart-aleck, Mavis."

I admit he had the temperament for the work, but such dreams were not in the cards for young Harry Templeton.

His parents, my grandparents, were city dwellers, whose poverty extended beyond the monetary to include an utter lack of interest in anything outside the scope of their immediate district. They did not travel. They rarely ventured beyond the boundaries of the neighbourhood they lived in for sixty years. My grandfather never owned a car, and, according to Harry, was in the habit of making disapproving sounds at passing automobiles, those "gaseous rattletraps" that terrorized honest citizens who merely wished to breathe clean air and cross the avenues in relative safety. (Perhaps the senior Templeton was a modern visionary, after all.)

Growing up in a four-room flat above the family hardware store, young Harry couldn't have been further removed from his yearning for the agricultural life. His mother grew tomatoes and herbs on the steaming tar roof, but even that meager garden was off-limits to the boy.

If it hadn't been for the gentle pressure applied by Sara Glynn, my mother, Harry might never have bought a car. If not for my mother, he might never have known the love a man can have for an automobile. Think of that!

I tried to imagine my own life, had the Templetons been third generation cattle ranchers rather than purveyors of hinges and light bulbs and garden hose accessories. I might have inherited fifty acres of prime meadowlands, trod and munched by Grade-A beef. Instead, my destiny is a ramshackle store with a dusty inventory that can no longer compete with the mega-stores in either price or selection. Just to put it in its proper historical context, Templeton Hardware has been a fixture on the corner of Gerrard and Woodbine since the year *Gone With the Wind* premiered at the Uptown, since Mackenzie King was Prime Minister, since Adolf Hitler marched into Czechoslovakia uninvited. It was no longer a going concern.

In the end, Harry was forced to abandon his golden harvest dreams; he took his rightful place at the helm of the family empire he was born into, and resigned himself to his chosen station. Based on historical dynastic tradition, one might expect it would be passed down to his son, by and by. Alas, I may have already mentioned that his son, the over-ripe onion with the girly name, has proved to lack the required acumen for business.

Mavis Templeton's training in the ways of hardware began at an early age; yet, even with this head start, and with a mind that was still malleable, still capable of absorbing new data, with a head, ugly as it was, that was still relatively empty and eager to be filled up, even with all that going for him, it was clear that he…that *I*…lacked some fundamental element, a critical shortage that shut me out of the businessman's lunch. *Two bricks short of a load*, Harry was heard to utter, on more than one occasion, back in those early days. *One head short of a nail.* There was no denying it.

Even during my middle teens, at the pinnacle of my adolescent egotism, I knew Harry was right. And make no mistake: I wanted to please him. It's not as if I had soaring aspirations, not as if I dreamed, like so many sons, of surpassing my father and his small, small world, of validating my existence outside the sphere of his influence and control. I had no plans, for example, to take to the stage—a vehicle frequently used by the prodigal son as a means of retribution against a father whose only crime was success. Nor was I inclined to take up the challenge of competing against him, head to head, man to man. I wanted to learn, wanted to do well, was desperate, as I've already said, to make him happy. But my fingers fumbled with the buttons on the cash register; my knowledge base, regarding the specialized inventory, was shifty and unreliable. The key-cutting machine became my long-standing nemesis. I could never get the hang of it, botching so many jobs, receiving so many complaints from customers whose wives or children or cleaning ladies were locked out of the house because the key I had cut earlier that week had failed to perform its singular function, Harry eventually, and sensibly, banished me from the apparatus, to the collective relief of his customers.

But Templeton Hardware was a *family* business, make no mistake. Harry couldn't afford to replace me with more competent staff; and anyway, such a move would have left me unemployed and unemployable. I was qualified for nothing, and that would have made me a one-hundred-percent burden to Harry, instead of merely poor help.

Come to think of it, I suspect it's just as well Harry didn't become the farmer of his youthful dreams. Imagine the havoc his inept son might wreak from the cockpit of a thresher.

- - -

In an ever-shifting universe, even the most stable empire is finite, and by the third generation, Templeton Hardware was beginning to show cracks in its foundation. Recently, at the end of another day of disappointing sales, Harry dropped an unexpected bombshell.

"I'm thinking of selling."

I had been pushing a broom listlessly across the wood floor, my mind, as always, preoccupied with trivia, so I hadn't fully processed Harry's meaning. "Selling what?" I said, looking up.

"The store." He said this as casually as he might have told me the time of day.

I tried to catch his eye, but he was busy tallying the meager receipts. "What are you talking about?"

"I want to go fishing."

"Fishing?"

"That's what I said."

"What does fishing have to do with selling the store? You're not making sense."

He seemed to consider the question. "It's just a thought."

"Well," I said, "that's some thought!"

"I'm just thinking about it."

"So you've said. Don't you think you ought to discuss it with me, first?"

"I am discussing it with you. That's what we're doing."

"We're not discussing it. You just announced that you want to sell out. That's not a discussion. A discussion would be where you ask me what I think of the idea."

"Okay, Mister Smartypants. What do you think of the idea?"

"It's a terrible idea. I can't believe it would even cross your mind to close the store."

He stuffed the receipts into an envelope and finally looked up. "I'm tired."

I blinked at him in disbelief. "Have a nap before dinner."

"Not that kind of tired."

"What kind of tired, then?"

Harry looked around the store at the old shelves, the same old merchandise, the same dirty view out the front window. "Tired of doing this," he said, "day after day."

This was not the Harry I knew—stalwart, reliable, even optimistic, in his peculiarly sceptical way—and I could only attribute this sudden turn to a symptom of some other problem, depression, perhaps, or the early stages of senile dementia. "Take a vacation. Take the whole summer off. Rent a cabin somewhere up north, then you can go fishing every day."

"That's not really the point," he said.

"What *is* the point? I don't understand what you're getting at."

"It's not about fishing. It's about the store…my life, this city…I don't know."

"You don't know," I said, flatly.

"Believe it or not, Mavis, I don't always have all the answers."

"That's the first thing you've said that makes sense. Jesus, Harry, you're talking about turning our lives upside down, and you can't even say why."

"I told you, I'm tired."

"That's not a good enough reason. This is crazy. Are you sick? Maybe you should take a couple of Advil."

"I'm not the one who's sick." He was referring, of course, to me and my deadly disease.

"You look a little pale. Do you have a fever?"

"I'm not three years old. Don't talk to me like I am."

"I just think you should get some rest. You're talking nonsense."

"I haven't made a decision, yet."

"Are you doing this because I'm dying?"

This was a subject Harry stubbornly refused to engage in. "I told you, I haven't made my decision."

"You can hire someone after I'm gone. Someone better." I had no illusions about my value as an employee. "Get a new sign for the front, one of those back-lit ones. Spruce the place up a bit. Put an ad in the Yellow Pages."

Harry just glared.

I tried to adopt a more serious tone. "Look, Harry, this place is your life. You were born in that room upstairs. That's your name hanging over the door. You don't just throw it all away because you're tired. When was the last time you took a vacation?" We both knew the answer, but I wanted him to say it.

"Never."

"Exactly. It's no wonder you're tired. Rent a cottage and spend the summer listening to the crickets mating. I can look after things here while you're gone."

Harry barked.

"I'll hire some college student for the summer. A business major."

"I have to start dinner," he said. The discussion was over. He locked the till and shuffled upstairs, leaving me with my broom and a cold sweat.

But whether or not he was serious about throwing in the towel, giving up the family business and the only life he had ever known, is now moot. Unless there is a surprise awaiting me in Harry's Last Will and Testament, Templeton Hardware, with all its accoutrements, will be mine. Quite a windfall. It's not every day one inherits a crumbling and draughty live-over, stuffed with second-rate merchandise, located in a neighbourhood renowned for employing the greatest number of break-in artists of any district in the city. Did I mention there is no free parking for Templeton Hardware customers?

An alert observer might also note that the recipient of this bequest is himself standing in the lobby of the Great White Tower, awaiting (patiently!) the Ultimate Otis, which will elevate him to the Penthouse of Eternity.

It seems my destiny does not have room for entrepreneurship. Having had three years to get "things" in order, I have left behind a will, too. I am leaving everything I own to Harry.

7

After driving three tense hours, I steered the Pinto off the highway and pulled into a Mobil gas station. The car needed fuel and I required cigarettes. And apart from refuelling, I also faced an unpleasant task that I could no longer ignore.

I pumped gasoline into the Pinto's hindquarters and extracted Harry's credit card from his rear pocket, and then clumped into the convenience station. The interior was blazing with fluorescent ambiance, while the air conditioning worked hard to convince visitors that Indian summer wasn't over. I gripped my arms and scanned the shelves—a dizzying array of shrill colours, bold exclamations, a fortification of potato chips, candy bars, salted peanuts, Hollywood magazines, road maps and other merchandise, each vying for my attention. After a day taking in the monotonous North Dakota countryside, my eyes swam in this unlikely deluge of marketing bravado.

And underlying this was the buzzing anxiety of leaving the old duffer too long in plain sight. It would take only one car to pull into the other side of the pumps, a friendly motorist spotting the green Pinto and its sole occupant. "Don't see many of these old girls on the road nowadays," he'd holler to Harry, who would respond by slowly leaning away from the friendly conversation. At that moment the stranger would surely detect the occupant's waxy complexion, the unmoving chest, the vacant stare. Or maybe not. As a rule, humanity is blind to the more unpleasant aspects of life—the most unpleasant aspect being death—but I couldn't be certain. My point of view was tainted by the conviction that, once you know someone is dead, there is no way to fool yourself into believing otherwise. How someone else might see things is unknowable.

Moving with as much haste as I could muster, I took a large mineral water from the refrigerator, gave in to the allure of the salted peanuts, and began my search for moist towelettes. But after moving up and down the aisles for several minutes, I was finally forced to admit defeat and ask the teenage girl behind the counter for help locating the item.

Bored wasn't a sufficiently strong word to describe the devastating lack of interest the young cashier had in her surroundings. In colour she resembled Harry: bloodless and waxy. If it weren't for the refrigerant air, she might have begun to decay. Her eyes, set well back in her skull and spaced too far apart to be attractive, were fixed on an unseen horizon, miles from this backwater county. She must have spent every minute of her work shift dreaming of plucking off her paper hat and hitching a ride with the next mud-spattered Bronco that pulled into the station. She couldn't be bothered to make eye contact with her customers, preferring instead to inspect the backs of her hands, as if etched in their surface she might discover the meaning of this pointless life. "Over there, on the bottom shelf, if we have any left, in with the diapers and other baby stuff." She snapped her gum and aimed a pale, skeletal finger towards the far corner.

I was suddenly brimming with sympathy for this sad girl, and I wanted to offer her a token act of kindness, give her a small morsel of hope for a future that was unlikely, from what I could see, to improve. "Thank you so much, young lady," I said.

It worked. My gracious tone reached into the deep well of her ennui and pulled her to the surface. We needed only a sound effect—a *whoosh!*—to make the moment complete, as her reluctant eyes located my face, the face of a kind stranger, the most hideous face imaginable outside mythology. The poor girl visibly recoiled, clamping her eyes shut and taking a step back. When she reopened her eyes and noticed the ogre was still standing on the other side of the counter, she adjusted to this new reality with youthful aplomb.

"You're welcome," she said, without smile.

"By the way," I said, now that I had her attention, "is there a men's room?"

I drove the Pinto around the side of the building and parked close to the door. The engine continued to sputter pathetically after I shut off the ignition; this road trip was testing the car's mettle. I lit a cigarette and lifted the hatchback. From inside Harry's cardboard suitcase I removed a neatly folded pair of grey wool trousers and a white Arrow shirt. I was about to close the hatch when I remembered having seen a salsa stain streaked down Harry's blue tie. I removed a clean tie, also blue, and brought these items into the restroom.

The rich smell was the first thing to strike me, an odour unique to service station washrooms, a pungent blend of the chemical and the organic. If nothing else, it was a change from the ripe air inside the car. The room contained a toilet and sink, but the space looked like a bunker on the losing side of a battle. The faucet dribbled water into rust-stained porcelain. The mirror was pocked with years of accumulated splatters, bits of brown paper, anonymous hand prints. In the toilet bowl bobbed an empty plastic Coke bottle, a post-modern turd. The paper-towel dispenser, which had once hung on the wall next to the sink, lay on the floor in the opposite corner, crumpled, the victim of a random act of vandalism. Next to the sink sat a trash can that looked unused. It was the only clean item in the room. Beneath the strewn litter, the tiled floor (once white, but now the colour of ten thousand brands of shoes, urine, vomit, other bodily expectorations) sloped inward, towards a central drain. A naked light bulb illuminated the scene with ghoulish effect. I decided it would do.

It was time to get on with the task, before I lost my nerve.

After kicking aside the litter, I returned to the car and unbuckled Harry's seatbelt. As I leaned in, a waft of excrement enveloped me, left a dry, powdery taste in my mouth, seeped into my sinuses, making them throb. When I gripped the old duffer's shoulders, I discovered they were hard as wood. *Rigor mortis* had begun to set in. Had I not been turning to stone myself—albeit at a significantly slower rate—I might have felt squeamish about handling a stiffening corpse, but, to my insensitive touch, Harry's limbs felt not so different than my own. Now all I had to do was extricate him from the car.

To gain some manoeuvring room, I pulled the lever and pushed Harry's seat back as far as it would go. Harry did not recline along with the seat; he would be locked in this upright posture until the effects of *rigor mortis* receded. His hands were folded neatly in his lap—as I had placed them, hours earlier—and he seemed almost serene, apart from the ghastly expression of terror on his face.

With one knee locked in place and the other as stiff as an old gate, I was forced to jack-knife at the waist; not the preferred method for lifting a heavy object. I tilted Harry towards me and attempted to lift him by the armpits, after which my plan was to sling him over my shoulder, fireman-style, and transport him in that fashion to the restroom. My forty-three-year-old back objected to this plan with a searing bolt of pain. Regrettably, Harry was floating somewhere in the space between the seat and my shoulder when the pain struck, and the resulting spasm forced me to let go of him. He hit the pavement with a graceless thud.

Even more regrettably, while I spat a few choice oaths into the wind and regarded Harry's semi-foetal form on the ground at my feet, the door to the ladies' restroom swung open and a woman stepped out. She wore the familiar red-and-white tunic worn by Mobil Service Center employees. Around her willowed the pungent vapour of marijuana, the effects of which could be seen in the glassy sheen of her eyes. The open car door partially blocked her view of the scene, but that there was an old man lying on the ground at my feet was unequivocal. Older than her sepulchral compatriot and already resigned to a dull life at an interstate gas bar, this woman's adolescent fantasies of escape must have been abandoned long ago. She might have thought I was some hooligan who had pushed an old man down, and was now preparing to relieve him of his wallet. Not that it meant anything to her, and not that she was prepared to do anything about it. Perhaps she was only dismayed that a crime on her shift was an unwelcome inconvenience. For all I knew, she merely wanted her cut of the take. Her vacuous stare was inscrutable.

To deflect any accusation, I tipped an imaginary flask to my lips and shook my head sadly. The young woman, wavering slightly in the breeze, seemed grateful for this uncomplicated explanation, and ambled back to her duties in front, leaving me alone with my (apparently) drunken charge.

Once the woman had gone, I dragged Harry by the wrists, up the curb and into the restroom. I reasoned there would be no harm done, except to a pair of pants that were already soiled beyond salvation, and were due for the trash bin. Harry himself would suffer only the passing indignation of having been accused of drunkenness, and being handled like a sack of grain. It was a sufferance I was willing to have him bear. After pulling Harry's legs across the threshold, I shut the door and pressed the lock button. I was not looking forward to the next phase of this task.

Never in my life had I changed a diaper, and I dare suggest, without a point of reference, that it is not the same undertaking when the subject is an old man of recent demise. Admittedly, I had selfish reasons for doing it now, unappealing as it was. Even with the Pinto's windows lowered, with the crisp country air circulating through the cabin, the smell of shit emanated from Harry vigorously, a constant and putrid reminder of his condition. More significantly, it was unlikely such a powerful stench would escape the notice of the cagey customs official who awaited us at the border.

I tore open the package of moist towelettes and set it on the rim of the sink in preparation. For some reason, the antiseptic perfume triggered my gag reflex, forcing me to breathe through my mouth. Harry was lying on his side, his back to me, looking more than ever like a drunken wastrel curled up in a shop doorway. The air of indigence about him was exaggerated by the dark stain seeping through the seat of his pants. Had he been alive, this scene would surely have mortified him straight into an embarrassed coma. He was a man whose bodily functions were a matter of utmost privacy. In all the years we lived together, he never failed to lock himself securely in the bathroom, as if I might barge in and discover he evacuated waste like everyone else. If he was having a difficult time, he would run the tap, in order to cover the disagreeable sounds, and would afterward bomb the tiny bathroom with a noxious cloud of air freshener, a further and final denial on his part of the workings of nature.

But Harry was now above earthly mortification. I suspect if he had been looking down on this scene, he might actually have been amused by *my* discomfiture. He might have said to Sara Glynn, who would no doubt be floating next to him in the heavenly ether, *It's about time he showed a little gumption.*

My desire to procrastinate was conflicting with the desperate awareness that some other bloated motorist might at any moment come pounding on the door. "Go pee in the field," I'd shout, wondering how long the lock will hold out. "I don't have to pee, that's the problem," the intruder would return. And I'd have no choice: "I had Mexican for lunch, buddy. You might as well shit in a bag!" With any luck the desperado would give up and invade the women's bathroom. If I'd been thinking clearly, I would have fashioned a crude OUT OF ORDER sign.

I rolled Harry onto his back. He looked like road kill—like an unlucky raccoon that wasn't able to amble across the highway quickly enough. His knees were in the air, the soles of his shoes pointing north, arms bowed outward as if to make room for a deep breath that would never come. I unbuckled his belt, unbuttoned his trousers and shirt, and reflected on how much easier this task would be if my legs were more flexible. Now that my back had been strained, it was especially painful to lean over. Using the walls for support, I tried to push Harry's legs flat, but they remained resistant to my feeble leverage. I had two hundred pounds to offer, but it was an engineering conundrum, trying to find a way to use all that weight. I swung my left leg over Harry's torso, so that I was standing over him like a gloating victor, one foot on either side of his rigid form. I leaned forward, as if to touch his face, and slowly let my weight shift backward, using gravity to gain momentum, until I fell onto Harry's legs. But it was only a partial success. His legs—obeying the obstinate and inextricable laws of physics, a subject to which I had paid scant attention during the significant years of school—began to give under my weight, and then sensed it would be easier if they simply spread apart, permitting my buttocks to continue unimpeded to the hard tile floor. The residual inertia drove the back of my head into the wall. I gripped my throbbing skull and slid sideways until my temple met the chipped porcelain corner of the sink. I cried out, more in frustration than pain, and when I touched my temple, my fingers came away bloodied. Undeterred, I was determined to get this nasty bit of work done and get back on the road.

As I sat on the cold floor, fingering my temple and bolstering my resolve, there was a knock on the door. I was sore and bleeding and cross. "Out of order!" I shouted. There was a moment of silence outside, and then I heard shoes scuffing away. Some people can take a hint. Slowly regaining my feet, I saw that Harry now resembled an aging porn star: mouth open, pants open, knees open, an open invitation for anyone desperate enough to take up his offer. It was an appalling sight. I pushed his mouth shut, and tried to force the thought from my head.

In the end, I got the laws of physics to work for me. I stood Harry on his bowed legs, tipped him forward over the sink until his forehead touched the dirty mirror, and stripped him with relative ease down to his undershirt. When I saw the scope of the mess down below, I considered returning to the over-lit aisles out front to acquire rubber gloves. I will say it again: one's first attempt to change a poopy diaper is best conducted on a child under two years of age; add seventy calendars and all charm is lost. I had not previously thought myself queasy by nature, but this was nearly more than I could bear. It was all I could do to contain my Mexican Fiesta. By the time I was done, I had used all thirty wet wipes—the last five to scrub my own hands with Lady Macbeth fervour. *Out, damned spot!* I muttered to Harry's backside. *Who would have thought the old man to have had so much shit in him?* It was a rhetorical question.

Harry was once more clean and fragrant, once more a tolerable travel companion. After stuffing the soiled clothes in the waste bin, I turned him out in the clean trousers and shirt, careful to fold his blue tie into a neat Windsor knot, as he would have done himself. I stood behind him, at last, checking his reflection in the mirror. I thought he looked pretty good for a dead man. His coiffure was more or less intact, and his stubble was sufficient to lend him a worldly suaveness that had escaped him in life. Looking beyond Harry at my own reflection, I saw a man of middle age in rumpled clothing, face slick with blood and sweat, the remaining strands of his hair seemingly caught in the act of fleeing. I looked hung-over, even though I have been a steadfast teetotaller. I looked like the survivor of a recent calamity. I looked like hell and back. I looked away.

- - -

Freshly changed and back on the road, Harry seemed happier, his overall aspect little less dreadful. He and I both were adjusting nicely to his recent death. I felt I could really begin to like him in his current state, silent as he was, an agreeable companion. Still, I was aware his time above ground was finite. The decaying process will have already begun beneath that new suit, beneath that old skin, and a pallet of fragrant wet wipes would do nothing to fend off the stench that was to come. I knew that our time together was running out.

Bob Dylan mewed at us through the tin speakers under the Pinto's dashboard, an emission of mid-range frequencies that made the poet even more incomprehensible than usual. *Admit it, Harry, you were wrong about him. He's no more subversive than vanilla ice cream.* Harry's lack of denial said it all. I turned up the volume. *Nothing but gibberish, Harry, baby talk.* I think I had him convinced.

We were making good time. I could feel another decision coming on, and I made it with rare confidence, turning west off I-29, onto a narrow secondary road. *Let's take the scenic route.*

There wasn't much that was truly scenic. Still, my city eyes appreciated the quiet uniformity of the landscape. This being mid-October, the fields had already been stripped of their crops, the soil turned in preparation for next season, or left to the scrub, something for the livestock to mooch over. These quadrate parcels, separated by ranks of elm that protected the soil from the brisk prairie winds, seemed to me of such tangible value, simple and complete in their purpose, I felt physically and spiritually rejuvenated by the sight of them. I began to choke up. Or maybe it was the melodious masterpiece by Seals & Crofts, *Summer Breeze,* that brought a tear to my eye.

I turned north at the first opportunity, so that we were running more or less parallel with the interstate. Gravel pinged off the Pinto's fenders, and the dust raised by the tires wafted through the open window. We met no other cars on this road, and I was grateful for the solitude as I steeled myself for the border crossing.

- - -

I wish Harry were here, next to me in this cornfield. I wish he had waited for me, so that we could depart together. I wish we could have lain together, side by side, on this hard bit of ground—on our backs, of course—and had one last pointless argument. There is something unfair about this scene. To be separated by a short plot of ground, a shallow ditch, a hydro pole, a thin pane of glass, it doesn't feel right, somehow. Harry is confined to the Pinto, my cigarettes within easy reach, but he never took up the habit, and it's too late now. Meanwhile, I am stranded out here, exposed to the elements, which are pleasant enough for now, but could easily change without notice. It would not surprise me to see a funnel-shaped cloud drop from the moderate North Dakota sky, touch the horizon, do the coochie-coo across the prairie, pick me up along the way, and deposit me in some fantastical county, two dimensions east.

We left Kansas a long time ago, Harry.

My heart is giving me trouble. The autopsy will be less a medical exercise than it will be an adventure in spelunking. I suppose they will investigate the narrow stone caverns of my atrophied chest with a snake lens, or perhaps with miniature robots. Amazing! I am leaving behind a world of wonders. And what will they learn from this post-mortem exploration, what will they discover that I couldn't have told them myself, while I was still alive? That sometimes the answers, the explanations, are of no ultimate value. We want to know, but the knowing doesn't help, doesn't make it any easier for the rest of us to go on living. They can study the ancient hieroglyphs scratched into the walls of my failed heart, but the message they will find will be a mundane one, a story without either climax or moral. *Gone fishing, no forwarding address.*

There is not much pain, I have so little feeling left. And because I continue to live, at least for the moment, I can only conclude that the heart attack that dropped me in this tricky spot was a tremor, a hint of bigger things to come.

Speaking of tremors, Mount St. Helens is preparing to erupt for the second time in recent history. That looming event, which had been reported to us on the all-news radio station this morning, is being carefully monitored by scientists and nearby residents of that bucolic, if volatile, corner of Washington state. During its most recent eruption, back in 1980, an old curmudgeon named Harry Truman was buried inside his Spirit Lake lodge beneath a hundred and fifty feet of rock and ash. Like my Harry, this one was also a life-long skinflint. Along with a number of firearms, with which he had famously protected his plot of land in the shadow of the mountain, he was reportedly buried with a small fortune, stashed in the lodge's safe, proving once and for all that you can take it with you.

Old Truman had every reason to believe the mountain was about to come down on his head, and he made the decision to remain where he was, in his home at the foot of a volcano. Whether he was noble or crazy, that old man, I can't say. I will say

I'm monitoring my tremors with more than scientific interest. The needles are *scratching-scratching*, the signs are there, the big one is coming!

God damn you, Harry, for leaving me alone like this.

I seem to be losing my faith.

- - -

The greatest test of my faith came when I was handed my death sentence by Dr. Podink. *To put it in the simplest terms, you're turning to stone. And that's bad. Three to five years. Of life. Remaining. There is no known cure.* What do you do after a diagnosis like that? Gorge on junk food? Rack up a long tab at the nearest tavern? Visit Swiss spas? Fall on your knees and pray like hell? All of the above? I was never much for prayer, even though there is a chance someone else's prayers penetrated the walls of my incubator and guided me safely into the world of the living. I hadn't the taste for liquor, or the means to visits exotic health resorts, and, thanks to Harry's influence, junk food held little fascination for me.

After receiving the devastating news of my deadly disease, I spent the next twenty-four hours in bed. I told Harry it was the flu. The truth was, I couldn't talk to him about it until I had spent some time alone with my own feelings.

There was nothing I could do to alter the course of this disease. I was defective merchandise. *No returns, no exchanges. All sales final.* The doctor explained there would be medication to help me cope. She then asked me if I was a man of faith. I told her it was a work in progress, my faith.

And what was the nature of my conversation with myself during my daylong sequestration? Here is an excerpt:

"Well, Mavis, now that we're under the sheets together, what do you want to do?"

Take a nap. I'm beat. Bad news always makes me sleepy.

"You sure that's a good idea?"

We're playing hooky, just like the old days, eh? Remember those days?

"I remember, sure. But what I mean to say is, time's running out. What did the doctor say? Three to five years? An eternity to a kid who wants to bunk off a day of school, but it might as well be the day after tomorrow to a man of your age."

I'm not so old. I don't feel old.

"You're walking like an old man, I've noticed."
True.
"From this moment on, every minute is precious."
Every minute before now was precious.
"Very philosophical of you."
People die every day, sometimes for no reason, sometimes unexpectedly. One minute you're crossing the street to mail a letter, the next you're hugging the grill of some drunk's Monte Carlo. Gone, just like that, with two kids at home, waiting for you to get back and make them lunch. A stack of unpaid bills, upcoming vacation that you've bought and paid for, doctor's appointment next Thursday, two video rentals that need to be returned. So much unfinished business. Including all the things you haven't said to your loved ones, all the good-byes that won't ever happen, now that you're dead. If I'd been born in another time, I might have been sent away to die in some foreign war.
"God and country."
Life is always a risk. Stray bullets, leukemia, grizzly bears, hurricanes and serial killers. War. Famine. Rare and incurable diseases. Nobody asks you if you want to be born. They just pull you out and drop you into the arena, the whistle blows and the game begins.
"You win some, you lose some."
Thanks for the cliché, but if losing means death, everyone's a loser.
"I see what you mean. Maybe you get extra points for making it to your seventies."
That makes Harry a winner.
"Okay, then, let's say eighties."
Now you're talking.
"But tell me how you're really feeling. Any regrets?"
No.
"None?"
Well…
"Go on, let it all out. It'll do you good."
I don't want to die.
"There it is. The truth sets you free."
The truth is, I don't want to die.
"Feel better?"
No. I don't want to die.

"I hear you."

Please, god, don't make me die.

"Now you're starting to sound pathetic."

I don't care. Did I mention that I don't want to die?

"You'll finally meet your mother."

There is that.

"She won't recognize you. You're all grown up."

Maybe she'll be disappointed.

"No."

How can you be sure?

"Mothers never are."

Unlike fathers.

"Fathers need their sons to be like them. Mothers just want their sons to *be*."

I think Harry will be disappointed in me for dying. He'll say it's my fault.

"That will be Harry's problem."

He needs help in the store.

"He'll manage."

He'll miss me when I'm gone.

"So will I."

I'll miss you, too.

"Maybe a nap isn't such a bad idea, after all."

Playing hooky.

"Like being a kid again."

8

The middle of three children, Sara Glynn Valentine had been held in special regard by a mother who was noted for an overbearing sense of decorum and a conservative streak to span the Great Lakes. Irene Valentine was a woman capable of waxing dramatic on the need for, and benefits of, superior breeding and education (in that order), and also railing against the various and seemingly endless ways the world and its inhabitants offended her. Until her tragic death, Sara Glynn represented, in Irene's view, a flawless example of what a first-class upbringing could achieve. As for the man responsible for her daughter's downfall, she reserved a vigorous contempt that she would take to her grave.

Like any sensible patriarch, Joseph Valentine nodded agreeably at his wife's ostentatious opinions, and bowed to her will in all matters of family. He knew when to keep his mouth shut.

The Valentines had received Harry Templeton as a potential suitor for Sara Glynn with no small reluctance. In another time, the parents might have bundled up their smitten, naïve daughter and whisked her off to a spinster aunt in Europe, separating her from the foolish distraction of unwelcome love, and thus giving them a chance to find a good and proper match for the girl. As it was, things remained reasonably polite only because Irene Valentine, upon hearing about the proposed match, fled the room before she could unleash the full load of her wrath. And while it may have been a laudable and heroic act of restraint, it was to be the only time Irene ever attempted to confine her true feelings.

Sara Glynn, who was as single-minded and determined as her mother (although perhaps slightly more temperate), encouraged her family to remember Harry was the proprietor of a "successful business."

But success can be measured in many ways, and one business is not the same as the next; not in Irene Valentine's book. "Maybe if he were the CEO of a *chain* of hardware stores, maybe *then* he might be acceptable," she said. But the look on her face indicated it was a *big* maybe. And while she could find little with which to fault the young Harry Templeton personally—he was neatly, if modestly, dressed and excruciatingly polite—she was unable to entertain him as a potential son-in-law, and referred to him afterward, and forever more, as "that broomstick vendor."

In the end, even the formidable Irene Valentine could not defeat Sara Glynn's enthusiasm for the marriage, and, in these modern times, there was little she could do to prevent it.

For his part, Harry could not wholly justify Sara Glynn's designation as a "proprietor of a successful business." Templeton Hardware's success could be gauged more accurately by its longevity than its pecuniary rewards. And he would never be able to live down Irene Valentine's label, at least in the eyes of his future in-laws. No matter what one thought of such things, there was no denying he sold his share of "broomsticks."

Whatever it was Sara Glynn saw in Harry (and here I don't wish to speculate), she alone saw it, and, god bless her, loved him for it. And it was her capacity to love deeply and completely that got them through the perilous landscape of courtship, saw them safely to the altar, heedless of the jeers from the peanut gallery.

The wedding-day photograph that has stood faithfully at Harry's bedside for these many decades bears monochromatic testament to the disparity between the young couple, at least in the physical sense, and casts some lingering doubts, in my mind, on my late mother's judgment. (Conceivably, I came by my great weakness honestly, after all.)

Sara Glynn was light without being pale, with an open face and soft features that hinted of the Silver Screen ingénues of Hollywood's golden age. To look at her face, which enjoyed a mutually advantageous relationship with the camera lens, one could easily imagine her swooning into the lumberjack arms of Clark Gable, peering up at that rugged face with absolute trust and adoration. Yet she was no wallflower, no trembling ingénue, no pushover. "Stubborn," as Irene Valentine would put it, during moments of grief-stricken weakness, throwing the word down as the singular flaw in her daughter's makeup, and the one that eventually brought her down.

Harry was more Elmer Fudd than Clark Gable. His posture, standing in the light of Sara Glynn, was that of a short man who aspired to tallness, shoulders warped like the corners of an old rug, chin retreating under weak lips, chest sloping downward to meet a trifling paunch. His black-rimmed spectacles were too wide for a face with eyes positioned so close together—the effect giving him the appearance of being slightly cross-eyed. A set of small ears stuck out at right angles from the side of his head, and from the lens's perspective might have been attached to the stems of his glasses. This somewhat comical illusion made his nose seem likewise fake. Whenever I looked at that photograph, I always imagined the seconds after the shutter *clicked*, when he would remove the glasses in order to rub the flash from his eyes, and off would come those ears and that nose, like a joke-shop prop, leaving Harry looking like an incomplete Mr. Potato Head.

"She loved dogs, your mother," Harry once told me.

He had caught me gazing into the grey tones of that bedside photo—which I occasionally did during my lonesome and brooding adolescence, attempting to imagine, without much semblance of reality, what it might have been like to grow up having a mother, someone to dole out affection, kiss my boo-boos, turn down my collar, smooth out my uncooperative hair. I dreamt of a house filled with the rich smells of vanilla and freshly baked pies, longed to hear the soft timbre of a woman's voice ring through the rooms, a tinkle of laughter like Christmas bells, a feminine touch to the décor.

Harry peered through the window of that picture frame as if he might once again hear the photographer's gentle commands ("Look this way, please…fine, lovely…), as if he could hear Sara Glynn's blithe responses ("Hurry, please, before these shoes completely cripple me."). Was that a dog barking somewhere in the near distance, outside the range of the camera's view?

"She always had a dog when she was growing up," Harry said, finally. "But they're jealous animals, territorial. Your mother didn't want to bring a dog into the house until after you were born. That was the plan. Wait until you were born and then get a dog."

I held my tongue, even though I might have asked him why he didn't follow through with the plan, why I never got my dog. I would have had at least one friend. But I understood. It was her plan, not his, and after Sara Glynn died, her plans died too.

"They never forgave me for your mother's death," he said, meaning the Valentines.

Whatever the medical evidence to the contrary, it was Irene Valentine's (and therefore every Valentine's) view that Sara Glynn's death was nothing short of Divine reproof for a marriage that was, by any standards, unsuitable. Had she selected a good Methodist heart surgeon instead of "that broomstick vendor," she would surely be alive today, a happy mother and wife, comfortably ensconced in a manicured community, serving iced tea to the "ladies" under the shade of well-placed imported elms that, in the height of the season, would only partially block the view of the country club fairways. But all that was an alternate reality that would never come to pass.

And how did I become so familiar with my grandmother's intimate feelings on the subject of Harry and Sara Glynn? She told me, of course, believing that the truth (*her* truth) could only benefit me, in the end. I don't wish to portray the Valentines in an overly critical light. Their only real crime, as far as I was concerned, was an enduring and unshakable elitism.

The Valentines were an "old money" family, with roots that burrowed deep, reaching back to the days when Toronto's streets were muddy tracks, rutted by wagon wheels and sullied by horse patties. Two ancestors had been capable and popular mayors during their respective eras, a third having made such a significant contribution to what is now the suburb of North York that a street bears the family name. The Valentines were Upper Canada royalty, moving among a small core of powerful and resourceful families that brought organization and industry to a territory that had only recently risen out of a barbaric and war-torn wilderness. These families of wealth and education—and, in some cases, peerage— created jobs, encouraged political stability, wrote legislation, tamed the wilder elements on the fringes, paved the roads (eventually) and erected spectacular buildings, some of which still stand today as testament to their vision of a New World, and their wherewithal to construct it. How could Harry compete with that?

After Sara Glynn turned blue in the delivery room, the only tangible part of her that remained was packed into little old me. The onion. The Valentines must have wondered, as did I, eventually, how such a beautiful woman could have produced this bruised and wrinkled fruit. They must have waited with grim patience for me to outgrow my "ugly baby" phase, transmute into the latent features that had made my mother such a captivating vision. And they must have quietly begun to panic when, by the age of nine, I still looked like something the cat dragged in.

"How did you meet?" This was not the first time I had asked Harry this question, but he had deflected all my previous queries indelicately, and without apology. Now, for the first time, he seemed in a mood to open up. But he looked haunted by the spectre starting back at him from that photograph. Memory is a tricky and unreliable thing, fallible, prone to defensive acts of metamorphosis. Had she really existed? Had she really loved him? Looking at the old man sitting on the bed beside me, it seemed improbable—must have seemed improbable to him, in spite of the photographic evidence, and in spite of my presence beside him—which was physical (incontestable?) proof of the unlikely union. If my vegetal physiognomy was any indication, Harry might be accused of repressing the very real memory of having had relations with a turnip.

"She came into the shop one day," he said. "She was canvassing for a charity, something about animal rights. I don't remember. I wasn't busy, so we just started talking. That's about it."

Surely, that wasn't about it; still, it was something. I wanted him to say more, tell me how her beauty had affected him, how she had turned heads wherever she went, how proud that had made him feel; how her hand felt in his, her breath felt on his neck, how her gaze made him... It wasn't the dirty details I was after. I just wanted a few scraps to hold on to, a few brush strokes to fill out an incomplete picture in my mind. But these scraps were denied me. I don't think Harry had access to them himself. I struggled to declare my own feelings to Harry, to give him something as a means of opening a dialogue, but the words were waylaid somewhere between my brain and mouth. There was a barrier between the two, an invisible membrane, which permitted only the most insignificant words to pass through. Anything meaningful was turned back. Border guards of the soul.

Had I been able to articulate my own heady feelings on the subject of my absent mother, I'm not sure Harry would have understood. The hole in my heart was in a different spot than the one in his. My longing was an intangible one, like that of a man born without sight, who can only imagine light and colour in the most abstract way. Harry is the man whose eyes were plucked from his skull during the prime of his life, after having gazed upon one of god's brilliant angels. In this respect, perhaps I was the lucky one. I didn't really know what I'd been missing.

While Harry was reluctant to mine the emotional core of his doomed love, he did eventually dole out a few unembellished facts. This much I knew: when Sara Glynn Valentine tinkled the bell over the door of Templeton Hardware for the first time, Harry was the sole owner and operator of that enterprise, a young man with manners, tidy, utterly confident inside his dusty environment. He had been orphaned at the age of twenty-five, after the senior Templetons departed simultaneous for the next world, the unwitting victims of a corroded gas line that seeped death from behind the stove and poisoned the air in the upstairs apartment.

Young Harry had been working late, sharpening a lawn mower blade in the basement workshop, while his parents prepared to retire to their beds, as always, by half past eight. By nine o'clock, Harry finished his task and felt he had earned a reward, so he locked the store and made the fifteen minute walk to Ginny's Tavern, a relatively clean establishment that catered to the working men of the east end. Harry was a second-tier regular at Ginny's, two or three times a week taking a stool at the far corner of the bar, exchanging polite nods with Ginny himself, and also with the top-tier regulars, mostly older men who gummed the rim of their ales, waved four-digit hands under each other's noses to emphasize a drunken point, and challenged each other to games of pool—straight pool/shirts-and-skins/snooker. Harry would not rise above his second-tier status at Ginny's because he never drank more than one beer during any given visit. Alcoholism would never be his demon. As for his parents, the senior Templetons did not drink, were passive supporters of prohibition, were devout secularist, suspicious of religion, but nevertheless forever on the lookout for sin and sinners. They would certainly have had something to say to their son, had they known he frequented taverns while they lay snug in their beds. But they never found out.

Harry slowly finished his single beer, then nodded to Ginny and the regulars, and made his way contentedly back home. When he opened the door, he detected the distinctive odour of natural gas and sensibly refrained from switching on the light. Instead, he ran to the payphone across the street. But the emergency crews could not save the senior Templetons from their toxic fate. Neighbours were evacuated from the vicinity while the building was ventilated, and the two bodies were eventually wheeled out the front door, stuffed in the back of an ambulance and driven away, never to return.

The incident was deemed an accident, even though Harry knew that his mother had been complaining for weeks about the faint smell of gas in the kitchen. The senior Templeton had registered the complaint, and filed it in the 'to do' bin in the back of his mind. And Harry, who had also noted the complaint, had learned over the years that it was unwise to take initiative under his father's austere nose.

As a result of the tragedy, Templeton Hardware lost two days of business, the first being the day after the gas leak—the time necessary to properly air out the building—and the second being the day of the funeral. Harry's work ethic was unimpeachable. (He similarly closed shop on the day I was born, and again on the day he put Sara Glynn underground.)

Incidentally, my mother never worked in the store. The "Mom and Pop" chapter of the Templeton Hardware history was closed with the passing of my grandparents. During the short period she was married, Sara Glynn continued to toil for the benefit of this planet's helpless animal population, or so Harry told me. She had no interest in the business of hardware beyond the lifestyle it afforded her—which was not much of a lifestyle when compared to her well-heeled upbringing. But, if Harry is to be believed, she seemed to either not notice this lowered circumstance or not care. At any rate, she never gave Harry a reason to believe she was dissatisfied. How's that for true love?

- - -

It should have surprised no one that the Valentines disapproved of Sara Glynn's marriage to Harry Templeton. Irene was a notorious snob, even amongst her peers. If Harry had had money, had made a real—or at least a financial—success of Templeton Hardware, earned enough to make a rich girl comfortable for the rest of her life, he would have remained, in Irene Valentine's eyes, coarse, poorly (publicly!) educated and unsophisticated. Well, even Harry would admit you can't please everyone.

Long afterwards, when it was ancient history and he could almost laugh about it (or, at least, see it with some objectivity), Harry described to me his first visit to the Valentine family home.

"I thought the place looked like a hotel. A big old, fancy hotel."

"When were you ever in a hotel?" I said.

"Don't be a smart-aleck."

"Well, it *is* a hotel," I told him. "A big old hotel for rich lunatics." I knew what I was talking about.

Harry gave me the evil eye, so I shut up, let him get on with his story.

"When I knocked on that door, I can tell you I was pretty scared. I didn't know what to expect. They were polite at first, but I could tell they didn't like me. They looked at me behind those polite smiles like I was a homeless wino, begging for spare change. But your mother, Sara Glynn, she just pretended everything was fine. She held my hand and wouldn't let go for anything, rattling on about the store, and how successful it was…"

I held back a sneeze.

"I thought Irene was going to have a stroke, right there and then. She was rubbing a vein in her neck, like it was hurting her. She kept calling me *Mister* Templeton, like I didn't really deserve to be called mister. And the retarded boy—"

"Robyn," I said.

"—the retarded boy sat in the corner, muttering to himself. Then he would suddenly shout, 'Where's your broom?', and then he would sing a made-up song about hammers and nails and cross-cut saws. Of course it wasn't his fault, being retarded and all—"

"Maybe that's not the right word, Harry."

"Pick your own word, I don't care. Do you want to hear this or not?"

"Sure, sure. Go ahead."

Harry sniffed the air for any hint of further interruptions, and then resumed. "Anyway, I'm sure he got those ideas by listening to

Irene and the rest of them. Old Joseph, he was a nice enough fellow, or at least he seemed not to really care one way or the other about us, about the wedding. He always looked like he had more important things on his mind. He didn't say much. Still, your mother and me, we decided to elope after that. It seemed best to do it that way, so we went down to City Hall. Sara Glynn brought a couple of friends as witnesses. None of the Valentines came."

"A blessing," I said.

"Your mother was devastated. She wanted a big wedding. Girls all want a big wedding, the big cake, the reception. She wanted her family to be there."

"How about you?"

"Maybe it wasn't a big, fancy wedding, but I thought it was nice, just the same. To tell the truth, I can't say I ever grew especially fond of her family."

Nor did I, but nobody says you have to like your family. And nobody says your family has to be nice.

9

True to his generation of men, Harry knew from the day of my birth, from the day of my mother's death, that he was out of his element as a single parent. He was unequipped to nurture. Throughout his wife's pregnancy, Harry had concerned himself mainly with the operation of the hardware store, because what more can a man do for his family than *provide* for them? He frankly hadn't given much thought to the actual and specific maintenance his child would require, the putting of food inside the child, and then the removal of the waste that came out; the wiping of bottoms and noses and tears; the simultaneous pacing and jouncing that somehow puts the child into a much-desired state of calm. The doctors' appointments, babysitters, school registration, skating lessons, birthday parties, all cramming the calendar, demanding…always demanding. Harry had counted on having Sara Glynn around to take care of those details, as they arose. The parental duties, as far as he was concerned, were fairly well delineated. What he hadn't counted on was her death; for that he had no contingency.

Had Harry been less bewitched by the lingering spirit of his recently departed wife, had he possessed a clear and untroubled head, he might have chosen, after a suitable period of mourning, to remarry, might have selected one of the many compassionate spinsters—fleshy and bespectacled maidens, knitting away long, lonely afternoons with fancies of romance and sugar cookies—who populated the cosmopolis, and who would have eagerly given themselves to the role of mother to a motherless child and wife to a wife-less man; and, let's face it, Harry was no great catch in the looks department, and I don't need to mention his award-winning personality, but he was a modest bread winner, and, thanks to the formidable influence of the women in his life (his late mother and his late wife), he treated the better sex with a deference that was rare for men of his generation. Many a snaggletooth and hair-lipped bachelorette would have been grateful to receive his attentions, if only he had been inclined to give them. Even for the sake of his newborn son, he was unwilling to lift his chin and look opportunity in the eye.

Harry's grief over the loss of Sara Glynn was of the blinding and deafening variety, lowering him into a well of depression in which he could see only the stone walls of his grief and hear the reverberations of his own sobs. And it was inside this pit of despair that he made the monumental decision to give me up.

To be fair, I don't know if the proposal originated with Harry or with the Valentines, but it wouldn't have happened without Harry's nod. I was not party to the negotiations, was out of the loop. All I knew was, I dozed off in my second-hand crib above the store on Gerrard and woke up surrounded by the oppressive gloom of century-old mahogany. In my peaceful slumber I had been bundled up and transported, unawares, to Russell Hill Road, to the house my mother grew up in, the grand old Valentine mansion.

It was an antediluvian Tudor monstrosity, its old ribs heavy with the meat and blood of great, stubborn age. The hardwood floors and softwood panelling wore a tired sheen of listless years. The plumbing creaked in despair as the house settled uncomfortably in its seat, trying to release the aches of old age from its joints. Leaded glass deflected all but the most feeble rays of sunlight, leaving the high-ceilinged rooms in dreary shadow. The medieval oil furnace, the heart and voice of the old manse, thumped and gurgled, sending up from its bowels an old man's smell that reached every corner of the house.

There was history there, but it was a history no one outside the core family would be interested in, a history coloured by idle remonstrations of a "boorish" proletariat, of a government that didn't do enough to preserve the old ways, of the low-brow speculators who bought their way into the once-exclusive neighbourhood and made their swinish noises around backyard pools, disrupting two hundred years of affluent tranquility. Into this bitter-tasting history I wrote my own short page: call me Heathcliff.

I was the tatty ragamuffin, brought into the parlour under (in this case) the matriarch's greatcoat, settled comfortably next to the crackling hearth and informed I was, in no uncertain terms, a member of the Valentine family. Since half the blood in my veins was Valentine blood, the information was redundant; but over the subsequent decade, I was never again made to feel entirely welcome under that roof, blood or no blood, was thereafter looked upon as little more than a stray urchin, a glorified family pet, falling in the pecking order below the family's beloved Scotch Terrier, but (fortunately) above the neglected throng of goldfish, who too frequently met an unpleasant end in the great porcelain vortex. Had there still been stables on the grounds, I might have spent my youth brushing a gleam into the buff flanks of my master's prized Hanoverian, scraping away its muck. As it was, I took advantage of the available shadows and lurked there, reading the books snuck from the household library (which was, to my mind, the only impressive thing about the house), and avoiding the Terrier, who knew my position on the totem.

Don't get me wrong. This is no Dickensian sob story about the poor boy fallen into the clutches of treachery; there are in my tale no Mr. Limbkinses, no Faginses, although my situation brought me to the very frontiers of orphan-hood. I certainly felt like an orphan, having lost first my mother to the distress of childbirth, and then my father, temporarily, to a weakness of will (or was there more to it than that?); and I wondered, more than once over that ten-long-years stretch, whether I might have been happier living in a genuine orphanage, rather than in the Russell Hill Penitentiary, as I had come to think of it.

And who were the players in this childish tragedy? (Melo-drama?…Comedy?) Unassuming types, by the look of them, tidy and well-groomed, educated, well-mannered, slice them open and the blood will run blue.

Sitting at the head of the table was the titular head-of-household, Joseph Valentine, a man of erect posture and upstanding principles, soft-spoken, tweed-garbed, an impassive and gentle soul who nodded serenely at dinnertime conversations, but seemed always to have his mind occupied elsewhere. A man of breeding and culture, as they say, and not some small intellect,

Joseph was responsible for the vast private library at my (discreet) disposal. To say he loved books would have understated his obsession by a wide margin, and it was a genuine love, of both the physical manifestation of a book and the varied effects of the language inside. Yes, he had a preference for eighteenth and nineteenth century first editions, no matter the topic, whose value was adjusted with each appearance on Sotheby's podium; but it was more than an investment to him. Several times a year, the Valentine library was visited by wide-eyed scholars from around the world, who came to lay their hands on the real thing, read the passages within the delicate bindings, in the original—a sort of academic pilgrimage for these lovers of literature.

Each weekday morning, Joseph Valentine read The Globe and Mail over a poached egg, and then departed for his office. Since the family business was the maintenance of the Valentine fortune, amassed by Joseph's ambitious and adept ancestors, and since this fortune was ostensibly supervised and nurtured by a crack team of Bay Street professionals, an outside observer might wonder what Joseph Valentine's daily business might have been in that Spadina Avenue office. But I knew, as did the rest of the family: in that space, which occupied the entire third floor of the Chandler Building, was housed the truly priceless half of Joseph's book collection. He spent his workday sitting behind a Gregorian desk, turning the delicate pages of Daniel Defoe's *Memoirs of a Cavalier*, calling his full-time secretary, Wilma, to duty when he needed her to locate the etymological dictionary or bring him a sandwich.

The other Valentines were indifferent to Joseph's occupation, allowing the old man his eccentricities. Only I showed any interest in the objects of his private passion, but I was never invited to his office, never saw the other half of that magnificent library, the most significant private collection in the country. My existence registered only on the far edges of Joseph Valentine's peripheral sightline. After all, wasn't I just another family pet?

As for the true monarch of the Valentine clan, I will save her for last.

In the meantime, here are two supporting players in this *dramatis personae*: Robyn Valentine, the eldest of the Valentine children, the only son, and unlikely heir apparent; and Mercedes Valentine, born two years after Sara Glynn, my Auntie Benz.

(There will be a third character making an entrance, by and by—a *bit* player, if one measures these things with a yardstick—who will ultimately be responsible for my eviction from Russell Hill Road.)

If I was fictional Heathcliff, Robyn Valentine was historical Claudius—the stuttering patsy who was elevated to the purple, against all common sense. There is no kinder way to say it: Robyn was *simple*, possessing a vocabulary more befitting a six-year-old who is just beginning to explore the nuances of syntax and grammar. During dinner, he might announce, apropos of nothing and interrupting some other conversation, "That dog down the street bited some kid, today. I seen the whole thing from my window." And while he imparted this bulletin, bits of partially masticated rice or spinach would drop from his mouth onto the table at his elbows.

"Really?" someone would say, more from politeness than interest. "You don't say?"

And Robyn, thus encouraged, would press on. "The black one. I seen it before. That family that has the bad roof."

He would be making reference to one of the more modest houses that bunched up further down the hill, the unfortunate result of some larger property having been severed and parcelled out during hard times. The house in question had been purchased by a young couple who, according to Irene Valentine, were out of their depths, having insufficient resources, it would seem, to replace the chipped and discoloured roof shingles—deplorable negligence, and an ongoing eyesore for those who lived uphill. Irene never failed to comment on it when the opportunity arose. "If one can't afford the upkeep," she'd say, "one can't afford the house."

Her son, having few original thoughts, was a parrot for all the things he'd read or overheard, reciting them in his childlike way, often without seeming to understand them. His opinion of the "bad roof" and the people who lived under it, with their antisocial pooch, would have originated with his mother.

"That black dog poops on the sidewalk," he'd say, flakes of pastry erupting from his mouth to emphasize his *P*'s.

"Not a subject for the dinner table, Robyn," Irene would say, averting her eyes from her son's crumbly discharge.

Even as a youngster, I understood this to be a conspicuous breach of dining room etiquette, but no one ever discouraged Robyn Valentine's habit of speaking with a mouthful of food. Or perhaps the nuances of good manners dictated this no-see/no-hear/no-say policy. Either way, it was my misfortune to be situated at the table directly across from the heir, from which position I could not avoid witnessing the bits of foodstuffs leaping like paratroopers from his gaping mouth to the linen tablecloth below—*Jeronimo!*—or clinging bravely to the outcroppings of his lower lip and chin. The bits that his fork managed to manoeuvre into his mouth were smacked around noisily by his clumsy lips and tongue, until the combined sight and sound put me off my own food.

As for his childlike aspect, out of place as it was in a thirty-something man and impossible to conceal, it seemed it, too, was possible to ignore. To my knowledge, the subject of Robyn Valentine's mental development never arose, either openly or in hushed whispers under the cover of the mansion's pervading gloom. The family acted as if it were perfectly normal for a grown man to write letters to the editor of The Globe and Mail, as Robyn did with compulsive regularity—on such regurgitated topics as land transfer taxation and the government's arguably unfocused foreign policy in Southeast Asia—in crayon. And Santa Claus, too, received an annual list from Robyn Valentine, who always requested the same thing: a hover-car fuelled by love. Each year he seemed a little disappointed when Santa brought him a new cardigan and some Old Spice.

But over the years Robyn was openly kinder to me than were the other Valentines, displaying his affection by rumpling my hair or patting my shoulder, making gentle cooing sounds. "Good boy," he'd say, making it sound like "Goo bow." He gave a similar benediction to the evil Scotch Terrier, Prickles; and Prickles, who saw himself above his station, would become offended and attempt to remove one or two digits from Robyn's affectionate hand—nearly succeeding on one occasion, which required a trip to the emergency ward.

Taller, darker and more laconic than her sister, Mercedes Valentine was a black hole to my mother's supernova brilliance. She consumed light, as well as food and knowledge and love, and by way of some complicated mechanics of super-physics, gave up nothing in return. Auntie Benz was a one-way street, all things flowing in and nothing coming out. By the time I awoke for the first time in my new room in the converted linen closet at

Valentine House, Mercedes was preparing to abandon her recent university enrolment and vacate the premises, having somehow promised herself to a sociable graduate student named Phil. I was one of three hundred guests who attended the wedding, although I have no specific recollection of the event.

Six months later, she gave birth to my only cousin.

Eschewing the automotive theme that had been such a burden throughout her life (a trauma I would grow to appreciate, in my time), Auntie Benz christened her first and only child, mundanely, David. I had my own private names for him: Bugsy, Ratface, Judas—for he was a thuggish, rodent-like creature whose motives and fealty were forever in question, at least as far as I was concerned. When David was one and I was two, mother and son moved back into the family home, leaving Phil to his anger management seminars and his Filipino masseuse.

David and I never hit it off. That's the way it goes. We both should have been grateful for the companionship, should we not? Almost like brothers. In the end, a little too much like the Original brothers. David, of all the members of that household, was the least willing to see me as a peer or equal. In spite of my year's advantage over him, I was just another plaything, in his eyes. For example: when David was five and I was six, we marched up and down Russell Hill Road, my cousin gripping the handle of the dog's leash that was fastened around my neck. "Heel!" he'd shout, every few steps, and I'd stop tugging the leash, earning myself a cracker. And if one of my paws strayed off the sidewalk onto a neighbour's lawn, a rolled-up newspaper would meet the back of my head. "Bad boy!" David's idea, this was. Yes, I had agreed to it, in part because I thought it was one sort of a game when it was really another, and also because I wanted David to like me—a labour that did not come to fruition, and one that I eventually abandoned.

After her crushing defeat by marital life, my aunt, the black hole, swirled with ever greater force through the hallowed halls of Valentine House. She sucked in all available sympathy, down to the last, lonely, sub-atomic morsel. When she attempted speech, it was like trying to decipher a recording, played backwards underwater. Even without comprehension, the tone of the message was depressing enough to launch a sorry whale on to the nearest beach. But I gleaned, over the years, that the experience of her brief and unhappy marriage had transformed her into a stubborn man-hater. Only young David was able to successfully interpret her whale music, reciting his mother's wisdom for the rest of us: "Mommy says all men are evil." Even I knew that was probably the wrong message to be sending one's son.

"Men *are* evil," said Robyn, spewing creamed corn.

Every second Sunday, in the years immediately following Auntie Benz's return, Phil came to the house on Russell Hill Road to dine with the Valentines and spend a few quality hours with his son. I was too young to understand the awkward dynamics of these visits, but the tension was palpable, even to me. Phil had come from another old-money family; though, for reasons that were never openly discussed, he had access to little of it himself. But, even with a pedigree, and with at least the prospect of family money, he lost favour with his in-laws. Irene Valentine could not abide a man unable to hold his temper or conduct his affairs with discretion. When David was three and I was four, Phil took a job and moved to Germany. Postcards arrived for a time, and then they, too, stopped coming. And even though David and I were now both fatherless creatures, it was not a situation that brought us together, as one might think. David was a mama's boy, which was a role I couldn't identify with, and that difference, I think, drove a wedge between us, prevented us from becoming closer than we were.

But the predominant force in the Valentine house was my grandmother, Irene Valentine.

She was—to further the cosmic analogy—a force of galactic proportions. Her gravitational pull reached into the furthest reaches of the Russell Hill universe. She not only administrated Valentine House but was active in the neighbourhood Residents Association, a unified front against insurrection by haughty upstarts (new money), development (no milk marts to bring down the tone of the area), and in general anything that could be described as *progress* (a profanity in the Valentine house). She carried the banner at a series of civic meetings, leading the charge against a real estate developer who proposed, obscenely, to clear four lots, which the developer already owned, backing onto the ravine, on which he planned to erect a row of million-dollar duplexes.

"I don't care if you sell them for *ten* million dollars, give them gold-plated window casings and park a Jaguar in front of each one, they will never be anything other than *duplexes*." She rehearsed her public speeches at the dinner table. "It's that dreadful Victorian influence we can't seem to shake in this city. Those Victorians, who were too stingy to pay the taxes on a respectable property, and so stuck two houses together with nothing but a sheet of wallpaper between them. Well! That may be fine in Parkdale, but around here it does nothing but lower the value of the *real* properties, and invites all manner of riff-raff to think they can move in. My God, if we're not careful, we'll be living next door to the Beverly Hillbillies." At this thought she nearly swooned. "Many of the families in this neighbourhood have been here for generations. We need to protect our way of life. We need to take action against this invasion. The wolves are at our doorstep, and they are bent on our destruction."

Yes, Irene Valentine was a snob. She felt herself sullied by the proximity of the common man. She had once suggested to the neighbourhood association that they erect a wall, from St. Clair south to Davenport, enclose their community in stone, install uniformed guards at the gates—but the other members assumed she was joking, and laughed off the comment, leaving Irene flushed and disappointed.

Still, I want to say that Irene was a grab-bag of conflicting traits, because while she enjoyed her "elite" status, she was also capable of great generosity, donating her time and boundless energy, and many sizeable cheques, to a variety of worthwhile charities. She was a crusader for local efforts to help teenaged girls get off the streets of Toronto. It was an issue that she felt strongly about, believing that the only thing preventing these wayward young ladies from abandoning the raw life of a vagrant and attaining a job on the floor of Holt Renfrew was a good haircut and a new silk skirt. "Girls need to feel pretty. After that, they can do anything."

And it was through her indomitable (and charitable) will that I was "saved" from a life of ignorance and penury under the charge of that "broomstick vendor." Even though I was a half-breed, to her way of thinking, I was deserving of a better fate than Harry could provide. And I was, after all, her grandson; blood was blood, even if it was watered down. I absorbed the subtleties of this theory and was grateful to Irene for what she had done. I had no reason to doubt a great favour had been bestowed on me. From my childish vantage, on the "have" side of the street, I could see no advantage to existing on the "have not" side, on which Harry lived.

I barely knew Harry during those first ten years. He came round only at Christmastime, usually on the afternoon of Christmas Eve. He would arrive at the Valentine residence in his old Nash (the Pinto still a spermatozoid in the design culture at Ford Motor Company), the sight and sound of which never failed to enrage Irene Valentine. Harry compounded the offence by parking his dilapidated car at the very end of the driveway, closest to the street, making his disadvantaged presence even more apparent to the other residents of Russell Hill.

Looking back, I can see how he must have been intimidated in those ostentatious surroundings, outnumbered and out-gunned in every way; but, at the time, I saw only a strange little man who didn't have much to say, and who was clearly uncomfortable in the presence of his only begotten son. See Harry: on the eve of my sixth Yuletide, sitting on the edge of his seat cushion as if he were preparing to leave, even when he had only just arrived, ignoring the teacup at his elbow, answering polite, insipid questions about his welfare with maximum economy, all the while, nervously twisting his wedding band until the skin beneath must have been raw. See Mavis: the reticent child, shoved from behind by a hand of encouragement, compelled to approach the old duffer, my father-in-theory, but an in-the-flesh-stranger, thrust onto the stage of this comic opera. Harry's eyes, magnified by convex glass to terrifying proportions, blinked.

"Hello, Mavis," he said, his thin voice as unfamiliar as his white pressed shirt and odd smell.

Irene Valentine cleared her throat, a signal to me. I was still preternaturally shy, and, like all children, had been instructed to avoid strangers; yet, here I was, faced by the strangest stranger of them all. Even without the traditional scar slashing his cheek, without the gaping trench coat, without the cute puppy with which to lure me to some inexpressible horror, Harry made me uncomfortable. I didn't need an adult to tell me this was a man I should steer clear of. So why was Irene Valentine pressing her fingertips into my spine, propelling me towards the very doom I had been warned of? What had changed in the universe to bring about this contradiction?

"Hello, Mavis," repeated the stranger named Harry.

"Hi," said I, searching his face for signs of a scar.

"Do you remember me?"

There was no memory available to retrieve, only the echo of Irene's voice in my head: "He is your *father*." Spoken in her usual inflection reserved for things undesirable.

"No," I said.

Harry blinked, as if I had said something incomprehensible. After an awkward pause, he said, "I have something for you." His hand found a gift-wrapped package that had been concealed on the seat cushion behind him.

When he held out the gift, I looked to Irene for approval. She gave a quick nod and wiggled her index finger impatiently.

"Go ahead and open it," said Harry.

Another signal from Irene sanctioned this contravention in Valentine protocol (presents were ordinarily not opened until Christmas morning). I accepted the parcel from Harry, careful not to let his hands touch mine, and sat down on the rug at Joseph's feet—a safe distance. Aware that the spotlight was still upon me but grateful to be across the room, I tore the wrapping with a child-like lack of decorum.

And what sort of gift did the boy receive from the father-stranger, the strange father? What does a father give a son who already has everything—at least, everything the father is unable to provide? More important: what does a boy of five need from his father? And what does the father get in return? The questions swirl like bats around the ceiling of this memory, swooping and retreating, refusing to alight long enough to meet answers. But the theme is clear: everyone has needs; and it is those needs that motivate us to action—or inaction, as the case may be. Harry must have needed something from me; otherwise he would not have put himself through the agony of those visits to Russell Hill Road, which, to a poor hardware man from the east end, might as well be the inhospitable surface of Mars. And the Valentines must have had their own reasons for permitting this annual incursion by the "broomstick vendor," needs that went beyond the legal and moral rights of visitation granted any father (speculation: they were keeping their options open—a sensible precaution that paid off in a few short years). Even little Mavis needed something, and I dare say there is no visible end to the list of things a five-year-old needs. But there must have been one thing, an overriding need, the mother-of-all-needs that lurked just beneath the obvious childish demands for food/security/attention/sugary treats. What did I need? Love. Not aunt-and-uncle love, not best-friend love, certainly not the sort of love one might express towards a favourite food or stuffed toy. But the One Love that should have its own word, something to separate it and raise it above the mundane loves that fill our daily lives; I am talking about the resolute, unconditional love a parent gives a child. Mother-love. Father-love. Is that too much to ask?

Back to the moment: a present is about to be uncovered. The suspense circles like a hungry shark…

Lurking beneath the wrapping paper, encased in a thin cardboard box with a clear gel window, sat a Wilson *NFL Official Bronze Leather* football. Demonstrating for everyone present that this man, this "broomstick vendor," did not know his son at all. A football? *Sports* was a subject that did not often arise in the Valentine house, the prevailing attitude being that such activities were the domain of the working class (notwithstanding polo). I was mystified by what I might do with such a thing. As I removed the specimen from the box and rolled it over in my tiny hands, the tip of someone's shoe jabbed my lower spine. "Thank you," I said.

"You're welcome, Mavis."

I took the football into the far corner of the room and fumbled with it incompetently.

Following this grave ritual, there was stale, laboured conversation among the adults, mention of recent weather patterns, the state of business at both ends of the represented spectrum, general reflection on the quickening passage of time (in reference, I took it, to my own growth), and other trivia. And at the earliest convenient moment, Harry rose from his chair and announced his leave-taking.

With exaggerated solemnity, we stood at the front door and shook hands, he and I.

"Good-bye, Mavis," said Harry.

"Bye."

I didn't miss him after he was gone. I was too young to know what I needed.

The only other occasion during which I was reminded of Harry's existence was my birthday, when a card would arrive in the mail, festooned with rabbits and balloons and professionally wrought curlicue wishes. But these birthdays of mine, the first nine, anyway, were not particularly festive occasions for me. That one day of the year, the eleventh of June, was always met by dour faces, tear-streaked cheeks, averted eyes, quiet prayers—because the day of my birth was also the anniversary of a beloved daughter/sister/mother's death, because *he* lived while *she* died, and what is the meaning of that? For everyone else, the day of my birth was less celebrated than endured.

I did not mourn the loss of Sara Glynn, not on that day—the only day of the year I didn't grieve, in one way or another, for my dead mother, didn't lament the hole she left in me. Selfishly, I wanted to *celebrate* my birthday. I was, after all, a child, with the egocentric view of the universe that all children have. On that one significant day of the year, I thought a little attention to the living might have been in order. Yes, motions were made: the presentation of a too-sweet cake—chocolate, because that's what boys prefer—gift-wrapped tokens piled on the table before me, faces turned my way, showing mouths with upturned corners that contradicted the down-turned, joyless eyes. I didn't understand what it meant, these contradictions, not until later. But I knew it wasn't right, that I was somehow being blamed for something. I now know: I was simply being blamed for being alive.

Only the cook, Mrs. Tattu, a broad, dark woman whose capacity for cheerfulness was a singular, if rare, incongruity in Valentine House, made me feel special on that day, luring me into her kitchen with a crooked finger, where she would present me with a frosted cupcake, impaled by a single small candle.

"You're gon be a big ol boy," she'd say, watching me devour her homespun goods. "Um hmm."

The rest of the year, Mrs. Tattu kept her good cheer mostly to herself, and was perfectly willing to swat at David and me as we skidded through the kitchen, threatening the order of her domain. "Lord, take it outdoors, 'fore I tan two hides!" And her vast arm would windmill in our direction.

"Stupid fat jig," David would say, breathless, after we reached our destination behind the garden shed, where we would set bugs alight with stolen matches.

"Yeah," I'd wheeze. For years I thought "jig" was a term used to describe cooks.

David's day was not complete until he had brought Mrs. Tattu to the very brink of a stroke. It was under his direction that we ran the kitchen gauntlet, with my cousin, as always, taking the lead. Those were the conditions of our relationship, one of leader and follower, and they were clearly defined and unvarying roles. I was as natural a follower as David was staunch in his resolve to play the perfect villain. I never once detected in him a trace of remorse. The boy was missing parts upstairs, the most significant being a conscience. This shortcoming was demonstrated to me vividly, one day, when David was eight and I was nine.

We had spent an active Sunday afternoon playing in the ravine—the one now contaminated by the presence of those million-dollar, gold-plated duplexes (the profanity of *progress* being, at the tail end of the twentieth century, an unstoppable juggernaut, even in the face of Irene Valentine's objections). And let me be clear: David was not my friend. For nine years I was imprisoned with the pint-sized rogue, and for most of that time I successfully avoided him. Yes, I had initially tried to make him like me, as I did the rest of the Valentine clan, but as he grew, and as his character became clearer to me, I abandoned the effort, preferring the solitude of Joseph's library to the many perils of aligning myself with my cousin.

Unlike me, David had plenty of chums from school, or right there on Russell Hill Road, who were amenable to following his impish lead. But there were times when those friends—accomplices!—were unavailable to him; that's when he would enlist me, using bribes or threats, to accompany him on whatever nefarious enterprise he had in mind.

On that warm Sunday afternoon, I reluctantly followed my cousin into the ravine, where we prowled the grounds in search of sticks the right length and thickness to wield as provisional swords. And, like any young boy, I soon forgot I was there under duress, and got into the spirit of things. Having acquired two suitable specimens, we went on the hunt for prey. In my mind, this was the sort of imaginative play boys gravitate towards, for are we not genetically inclined to warfare? Do we not hide behind fallen tree trunks and *rat-a-tat-a-tat* krauts/japs/aliens who lurk, unseen, just over yonder, say, behind that rustling bush? *It's them or us! We're the last hope for the entire world! Shoot now, ask later! Get 'em boys!* Kid stuff, I say. Yet, I believe there was no distinction in

David's mind between fantasy and reality, that his idea of creative play had nothing to do with *pretending*, that one either did something or didn't do something, but to only imagine doing a thing was a waste of a good plan.

"We need to find a dragon to slay," he said, arcing his makeshift sword through the air, enjoying the low musical note it played.

"Two dragons," I suggested, knowing he would take all the credit for a single kill.

"Ten fucking dragons!" And his sword sang a dirge for those doomed beasts.

Alas, there was a shortage of fire-breathing creatures in our ravine. There was, however, a boy and his dog.

"Over there," shouted my cousin. "The dragon keeper and his beast!"

I had already spotted the pair, ambling along the dirt path in our direction, and had dismissed them as fair game. The dog was an undersized mutt with tense white curls, a drooling black grin and a Looney Tunes bearing. Led by its shiny black nose, the dog twitched nervously at the boundaries of its leash, sniffing every broken twig, blade of grass, empty soda bottle, as if some primeval canine legacy could be detected but no longer interpreted by this soft, domesticated creature. I recognized the boy from the neighbourhood, but knew only his first name: Trevor.

"That's no dragon," I said, speaking of the dog. "It looks like one of Nana's wigs."

David giggled, no doubt conjuring some future lark involving our grandmother's splendid collection of falsies, a plot to be stored away for the future. As for this so-called dragon, David was determined. "It's a baby dragon. If we go after it, we can flush out the mother."

On the surface, and still within the boundaries of my imaginative terrain, the plan should have seemed sound, but I had a bad feeling about it—an internal and unspecific warning system that kicked in whenever I was engaged with my cousin. I was about to suggest we search for more suitable quarry when David unleashed a savage cry and dashed forward, led by the tip of his sword, charging the unsuspecting pair. "*Get em!*"

Hearing the battle cry, Trevor looked up from his daydream and froze on the path. He seemed to recognize the hunter leading the charge and, no doubt aware of David's reputation in the neighbourhood, turned to flee. But his pooch, whose raw instincts bravely reasserted themselves, had a mind to stay and fight, barking with a madness that echoed back through ages. The pair were at odds in their purpose. Trevor, turning to flee, yanked the leash, pulling the mutt out of his defensive stance. Off balance, the pair struggled momentarily, until the boy was able to convince his companion it was not a fight worth having.

By this time, David had gained some ground. I, on the other hand, had chosen the coward's path, lagging behind, stepping forward at a pace steady enough only to keep the event in sight. I dropped my own sword on the ground and became merely a witness.

And what did I witness? A pursuit, one-against-two, and not a fair fight, given my cousin's zeal. Boy and dog—the mutt now leading the retreat, stretching the leash in the direction of escape— left the path and made for the embankment that rose to meet St. Clair Avenue. All the while, I could hear David's sword singing its victorious ballad, could see it dancing in the air above his head. The embankment slowed them all down, giving the impression that the scene, like in the movies, had switched to *slo-mo*. I had fallen so far behind, the three subjects were mere scrabbling specks. And just above these specks was the roil and grumble of city traffic. Streetcars ground noisily east-west, flameless dragons of impressive proportions, and surrounding those monstrosities were the doodlebug cars/motorcycles/panel-vans/taxis that filled in the available spaces.

I saw Trevor stumble on the hillside, and the pooch, now disconnected from his master, made a quick getaway up the slope, disappearing over the crest. So much for primeval canine legacies. I heard Trevor call the dog's name: *Spencer!* And I heard, as well, David's savage yelps as he closed the gap.

From above, the familiar clang of the streetcar bell sounded... ten/twelve times...and the momentum on St. Clair came to a stop. When Trevor mounted the crest and disappeared from sight (last seen moving towards the halted streetcar, beneath which lay the doomed dragon, Spencer), David called off his pursuit and came running back to meet me.

"What happened to you, sprain an ankle, or what?"

I forged a minor limp and let the story stand.

David was stoned to the gills on adrenaline, his eyes frantic, exalted. "Little fuckers got away, did you see?"

"Yeah," said I.

"Lucky bastards."

I hobbled along beside David. "Yeah, lucky."

10

That same year, shortly before my tenth birthday, there was a robbery at the Valentine house.

It was early May, and several days of unrelenting rain had left the air damp and the ground sodden. The drizzly morning had started badly for me. One of the regular schoolyard hooligans, an eighth-grader named Cameron Faminow, chose this day to add me to his roster. Having worked through his usual band of daily victims ahead of schedule—before the sounding of the first bell—Cameron hadn't quite depleted his store of pent up aggression.

I had peripherally noted the *castrato* arias the weaklings sang as their share of the bully's rage was doled out, but it was, to my ears, simply the normal sounds of another day at Frontenac Middle School. I was hunched down against the back wall of the school, Jules Verne's *Round the Moon* nestled in my lap, unaware I had caught Cameron's attention until the paperback disappeared from my hands.

"Whatcha reading, butt face?" Cameron loomed over me, turning the book over in his hands as if he had never seen one before. "Makeup tips for ugly assholes? Do-it-yourself plastic surgery?"

I stood up calmly, refused to be drawn into his anger. Living under the same roof with Bugsy-David had hardened me to this brand of tyranny. Cameron Faminow had three years and thirty pounds on me, and he was capable of delivering a sound punishment, but he didn't scare me. If a drubbing was in the cards, I would bear it with a stoicism that would have impressed even Harry.

Cameron's father was a retired professional hockey player, toothless and brutish and crass, and rich enough to afford to upset the civilized tone of Irene Valentine's beloved neighbourhood. Gord Faminow was the worst of the local upstarts because his crowd was a motley crew of steroid-fuelled troglodytes, whose boorish grunts penetrated the leaded panes with threatening ease. Like father like son.

"Give it back," I said, confident my appeal would be denied.

He looked at me with feigned innocence, and then pitched the book over my head, where it landed on the low school roof. "Give what back?" He held his hands out, palms up.

There was no reasonable way to retrieve the book, and besides, it was probably lying in a mucky rooftop puddle, absorbing three days of constant rain. I would have to explain the loss to the librarian and hope she would understand. If she was unsympathetic and insisted I pay to have the book replaced, I would have to face Irene's displeasure over the cost—something I did not look forward to. What I had learned over the years about the rich was that they loved to spend money only when it was their idea, a way of demonstrating their limitless generosity. If not of their own volition, they spent always with utmost grudge.

It was all very tiring, this bully business. I just wanted to be left alone. "You're a dick," I said, walking away.

Cameron followed closely behind. "You're the one looks like a pig's balls." Bullies must always have the last word, and I was happy to let him have it, but he wasn't ready to let it go. "You look like a fugging coconut with lips."

A handful of nearby witnesses giggled, which only encouraged him. And anyway, it was true. I continued with a purposeful stride towards the entrance, estimating that the bell was about to ring. We were not permitted to enter the school until first bell.

"You look like a piece of cheese that's been in the fridge too long," he said. "You look like a steaming pile of dog turds." He was running out of good material. "Your father must have porked a fugging goat!"

By this time, I wasn't listening, or at least not closely enough to be offended. But then something hard suddenly struck my right ear: Cameron's fist. Now that the words had failed him, he used what he had left. Everything turned black-and-white for a moment, and there was a loud ringing inside my head. I stumbled, dropped my satchel on the muddy ground. As I reached for it, Cameron's foot connected with my back. My hands and knees scraped the tarmac. I could feel the wetness of the rain-soaked ground come through my pants.

An adult voice yelled, "All right, there!" Soon, an arm was pulling me roughly to my feet.

The adult was Mrs. Wainstock, the vice principal. Built like a starving mime and nearly as pale, she held onto my elbow with unexpected strength. As I shook off the attack, I saw she had Cameron by the collar. He was as afraid of Mrs. Wainstock as everyone else, for good reason. She was a ruthless coadjutant, the perfect counterpart to the principal, Mr. Fellows—a corpulent and benign coward.

"Shame on you boys," she said.

Her use of the plural struck me like a slap. Even the most subjective witness would have seen that I was a victim. I suppose the shame was mine for being weak, submissive, for presenting such an easy target. And was my ugliness not the greatest and most shameful sin of all? Did my appearance not invite scorn and ridicule? Did my very presence in the schoolyard not pose a threat to peaceful conduct among the student population? Well, that speculation came later. All I knew at the moment was that I was being unfairly accused of being a trouble-maker.

Mrs. Wainstock was an active combatant in God's mighty army. Her only divergence from accepted form was that there were, in her opinion, too few "deadly sins" on the official list, and one had only to spend a brief time in the company of school-age boys to agree. "You know better than this. What sort of example are you setting for the younger children? Shame, shame!" First bell rang, punctuating her reproach.

"It was just a game, Missus Wainstock," Cameron whined. "We weren't doing anything."

Mrs. Wainstock looked down on him with righteous pity. "I know exactly what you were doing, Mister Faminow. Your games are well known to me. And you do not help yourself by lying."

Cameron shifted, as if he were about to break free—but when faced with genuine strength, bullies are cowards. "I'm not lying," he said, looking to me for support. "Tell her what we were doing, Mac."

I lowered my head and said nothing. He might have been more persuasive if he had at least known my name.

Mrs. Wainstock adjusted her hold on my arm. "Let's go, boys. Inside."

Held firmly in the grip of one of the Lord's fervent warriors, Cameron Faminow and I were marched into the school—which now thronged with an ogling student body—to the dreaded confines of the vice principal's office. Once incarcerated, we were positioned against the wall, just inside the door, "shamed" into submission at last.

"The wicked will always meet justice in the end," intoned the vice principal, evangelically. She was turned away from us, fitting a key into the top drawer of a filing cabinet. "Unless they are made to see the light, bad boys will grow up to be bad men." She was full of useful aphorisms.

I considered informing Mrs. Wainstock that I was not wicked, but merely a victim of wickedness, at least in this instance, but I knew that attempting to put the burden of guilt on my thuggish companion would only get me unwanted attention from him later, when there would be no adult around to save me. I also reasonably suspected the vice principal would be disinclined to hear my testimony with an objective ear.

Mrs. Wainstock turned from the filing cabinet holding a strip of black leather, two inches wide, sixteen long, a half-inch thick: The Strap. Cameron Faminow made a mouse-like sound. He appeared to have met the fellow before.

"Crime is the disease," said Mrs. Wainstock, "and punishment is the cure." She tapped the business end of the Strap in her open palm.

Cameron made his final pitch for mercy. "We were just fooling around. We weren't really fighting, were we?" He looked to me for corroboration one final time.

But any advantage I might have gained by agreeing with him, supporting his fiction that we were merely "fooling around," was eclipsed by the indignation I felt towards being accosted in the first place. I had no friends at Frontenac, and no matter the outcome of this day, Cameron Faminow would never become one. And Mrs. Wainstock was too caught up in her own moral passions to become either friend or ally to this lonely and misunderstood child. In answer to Cameron's plea, I faced Mrs. Wainstock and presented my palms.

Minutes later, after receiving a punishment I didn't earn, and after a dire, if largely incomprehensible sermon, I was standing in the corridor outside the office, rubbing my sore hands on my hips. Cameron Faminow stood beside me, his menacing presence only slightly diminished by this experience. His fate would surely live up to Mrs. Wainstock's worst fears. He had some parting words for me: "I'm gonna get you, you fugging dog-faced weasel."

I gave him a thin smile and turned away. But rather than hustling to my classroom, as Mrs. Wainstock had instructed, I headed towards the nearest exit. I'd had enough lessons for one day. Hitching my satchel over my shoulder, I pushed through the door and trotted across the empty soccer field, left the school property. I was a bad boy, all right, and it remained to be seen what sort of man I would grow up to be.

- - -

During those early years on Russell Hill, the ravine was my steadfast sanctuary, a refuge from the loneliness that stuck to me like an unwanted shadow, a place to which I could escape the oppressive air inside the Valentine mansion. Cutting like a green blade through the uptown neighbourhood, the ravine was a natural playground for children and other small critters, featuring open culverts to explore and hills to conquer and ancient, majestic maples to lure the adventurous ones skyward; and it was relatively free of tramps and muggers, who seemed to prefer the downtown parks, where garbage and spare change were more plentiful. Hunchback widows, weighed down by glossy fur coats and diamond rings and faded memories of old lovers, roamed the paths, trailing their fashionably trimmed shih tzus, serene and unafraid, while random youngsters ran wild and teenagers lingered indolently, smoking cigarettes and grinning at their secrets.

On this miserable day, the park was deserted, save the black squirrels and me. The sky was low and heavy, as if only the treetops kept it aloft. Feeling listless and demoralized, I was in a mood to walk, without plan or destination.

After days of constant rain, the ground was soft underfoot, brown water pooling in the low points on the undulating path. I made a game of dodging the puddles, a boy's version of hopscotch. The brutal sounds of traffic seemed far away, muted.

By lunchtime I was thoroughly damp and beginning to chill. I climbed the embankment—the same one Trevor and his unlucky pooch had scrambled up, trying to escape the dragon hunters—crossed St. Clair, and ate my lunch in the Westgate Mall. As soon as I settled on the wooden bench outside the pharmacy, I began to regret the loss of my book, the one now rotting on the school roof. There was nothing for me to do except watch the elderly shoppers shamble delicately to their errands and wonder, idly, if they were afraid of dying. I suppose this bleak subject occupied my mind because the adults closest to me, Irene and Joseph Valentine, were, from my youthful perspective, old beyond redemption (although they were then only in their fifties). Did these doddering crones feel the Black Rider stalking them, know their days were numbered, that at any moment an artery might blow, the skull filling with blood, cardiac failure, lungs forgetting what to do next? As they muttered their quiet prayers, was anyone listening? Did they even know their lives were pointless? Did they cling to their faith in desperation, lie in bed and pray for a painless end? Did they dwell on regret? I scanned the passing faces and tried to determine if they were happy or sad about their lives. Most, I thought, were of the latter group. Pulled down by the gravity of a lifetime of disappointments. Skin eroded by the stinging winds of guilt. Wondering if their hips will get them safely to the bus stop. Trying to remember if they had taken their medication before they came out to the mall. Some of the old ladies wore plastic bonnets because of the rain. The shrivelled up old prunes wanted their hair to look good, wanted their husbands to think they were still pretty.

I knew about pretty. Even these old folks, who had lived for centuries, survived wars and famine and domestic tyrants, had seen the worst of the worst, they always gave me a second look, the double take. They couldn't believe how ugly I was, but were silently grateful that I wasn't their problem, were relieved to know I wasn't calling them Grandma & Grandpa. *Take a good look while you can*, my mind shouted at them. *Before that blood vessel bursts, before the hip packs it in.*

It seemed fitting that my afternoon should be spent in such a dark occupation. After a morning of bleak injustice, under a sky that was not so much grey as simply nonexistent, it was no wonder my mood was black. And I didn't know it yet, but the gods of injustice were not through with me.

- - -

When the large, ornate clock in the mall's courtyard showed three-fifteen, it was time to venture back in to the drizzle and make my way home. Having never cut class before, and seeing myself chiefly as invisible to the school authorities (notwithstanding my recent encounter with Mrs. Wainstock), I had no reason to believe my absence would be noted. It came as a surprise, then, when I stepped through the rear vestibule of the mansion, the "mud room," and was met by a Valentine contingent. Absent from this ominous delegation were Robyn Valentine (who was no doubt in his room, composing another crayon polemic on import levies) and cousin David, who, I knew, was in his bed with a fever. The rest, including the evil Scotch terrier Prickles, stood rank and file in the kitchen, looking grim. Mrs. Tattu stood in the background next to her great stove, waving a wooden spoon, as if to ward off a hex.

I was confused and a little overwhelmed by the reception. This grim family assembly could only mean bad news. But what? Had someone died? Had David unexpectedly succumbed to the flu? Robyn hadn't been sick, so far as I knew, but he had his share of problems. A neighbour? Business associate? Maybe it wasn't a death at all. Maybe it was something worse than death; maybe those Bay Street Wonderboys had lost the family fortune. That would account for the look of wretchedness on Irene Valentine's equine face. The prospect of having to sell the house and move in to some narrow Victorian duplex, with its paper-thin walls and absence of "grounds," would surely pinch her face in such a manner.

I dropped my damp satchel on the floor next to the door and prepared myself for the worst possible tidings, whatever they might be.

"Is there something wrong?"

While the others shifted uncomfortably on their heels, Irene Valentine stiffened and hoisted an artificial eyebrow. Her lips, reproduced by Revlon in brilliant scarlet, puckered into a wrinkled knot, like an exit wound on a gunshot victim. She spoke in a quietly menacing tone. "Step this way, Mavis." With that command, she turned and left the kitchen.

I followed her to the living room while the others shuffled in after us. Irene took her usual throne in the Queen Anne chair next to the fireplace—which had been stoked for the rainy day. I lowered uneasily into the blue armchair, the one that wasn't nearly as comfortable as it looked, and the spot Harry always occupied during his annual visits. Mercedes, Joseph and Prickles arranged themselves on the sofa. Mrs. Tattu stayed behind in the kitchen, to tend to her steaming pots.

"What's the matter?" I directed the question to the room at large, but I should have known that Irene Valentine was going to chair this meeting.

"I'll get right to the point, Mavis. It's about my pendant."

It took my brain a moment to make the unexpected shift, confirm that I hadn't misheard. "Pendant?" I couldn't see what a pendant had to do with someone dying, or the loss of the Valentine fortune, and I certainly failed to comprehend what it might have had to do with me.

"My antique circus elephant, the one you were admiring only just a few days ago. You may remember *that* pendant."

I remembered. A gold elephant with diamond-encrusted ears and ruby eyes; the elephant was balanced ridiculously atop a platinum ball (also speckled with diamonds), while cupping a white pearl on the end of its trunk. The previous weekend, Irene had been soaking a few pieces from her reportedly priceless jewellery collection in a cleansing solution at the dining room table, and I indeed became fascinated by that particular item, thinking mainly that if only all jewellery were crafted into exotic creatures like this one, I might take a keener interest in such otherwise pointless accessories. I also had to note that David had been with me on that afternoon, and it was he who had pointed out the elephant pendant to me in the first place.

It was a piece David had seen before. He lifted the precious pachyderm from the soaking bowl and dangled it before my dazzled eyes. "Pretty cool, eh?"

I had never seen anything like it before. "Yeah," I said.

"*Yes*," said Irene Valentine, pedantically.

"Yes," I repeated.

My grandmother had reserved just enough patience for this brief interruption in her task, but she was ready to have us move on to other mischief. "Put that back, now, David. It's not a toy for little boys to play with."

"We're not playing with it, Nana. We're just looking." He let it hang between us in a hypnotic fashion.

But Irene Valentine was not to be challenged. With a swift but gentle motion, she removed the pendant from my cousin's grip and replaced it in the bowl. "Run along outside," she said.

We obeyed, careening at top speed out of the dining room, through Mrs. Tattu's territory, prompting the usual protests from the cook, and fell, laughing, on the soaked grass out back. The rain had taken a brief pause, although the heavy sky promised more to come. I quickly regained my feet, brushing at the wet spots on my pants, but David, who was less aware of such things, rolled onto his stomach, heedless of the wet grass, and stared into the distant hedgerow.

It was a rare day that we were spending together, and my cousin had so far been relatively subdued, less willful than usual, his energy stemmed, unknown to us at the time, by the flu that was just beginning to take hold of him. When he was like this, when he was not plotting some preposterous or dangerous prank, I almost liked him. I could begin to imagine a day, perhaps in the near future, when he will have outgrown this naughty phase and become something more like a friend, even a brother, or at least someone who didn't make the hairs on my neck bristle.

"When I grow up," he said, "I'm going to have a statue just like that elephant, only it's going to be full size."

I stood by the old stone birdbath, stirring the stagnant water with a finger, which released a faint odour like rotting flowers. "What for?"

"To put in the front garden. I'll have water shooting out his trunk into a fish pond."

I was perhaps too young, then, to assess the aesthetic merits of such an ostentatious plan, but I understood the practical issues. "That's dumb. First of all, it'll be too expensive. There probably isn't enough gold left in the world to make a whole elephant. And even if there was, you'd have every robber in town trying to steal it. It wouldn't last a single day."

David was undeterred. "I'd have guard dogs chained to it. And maybe remote-controlled machine guns that'd shoot anyone who came too close."

"The machine guns would shoot the dogs."

"No they wouldn't."

"Whatever." It was his stupid fantasy, not mine. He could pretend all he wanted.

Now, in the Valentine living room, Irene was eyeing me in a way I didn't like at all. "The pendant is missing, Mavis. It appears to have been stolen."

"Who stole it?" The question came out as a reflex. I didn't expect an answer.

Irene crossed her arms. "That's the hundred-dollar question, isn't it?"

Joseph Valentine said, "The window in the den was open, so it's possible someone could have got inside the house that way. But there's no actual evidence of an intruder."

"Whoever it was," said Irene, "they took *only* the pendant. No other valuables were taken, thank God."

Joseph continued. "There was family in the house when the crime took place."

"I was here," said my aunt, so quietly I wasn't sure she'd spoken at all.

Irene said, "David was in his bed, and Robyn was right here in the living room with me until lunchtime. Nobody heard or saw anything out of the ordinary." She looked around the room, as if she expected culprits to spring out from behind the draperies. And then her eyes settled again on me. "You understand what we're saying, Mavis?"

I shrugged, which I knew was a gesture my grandmother disapproved of. But I couldn't stop myself.

"We're suggesting whoever did this was not a stranger. We believe he moved around the house as if he belonged here, which is why no one noticed anything unusual."

"And," said Joseph, "he may have opened the den window to make us *think* a stranger had come inside. Now do you understand?"

I nodded. But it all sounded like the farfetched plot to a book. I made a mental list of potential suspects: any number of David's closest friends, a few neighbourhood teenagers known to be troublemakers, couriers (a shifty lot), the mailman (whose ruddy and pockmarked complexion convicted him, in my mind, of many unspecified crimes), Joseph's brother's ex-wife's nephew, who was in fact a convicted felon, but who had never set foot in the Valentine house, and whose unfamiliar face would surely not pass the halls of Valentine House unnoticed. But none of these suspects stood out, and I concluded this train of thought was a dead end. It had to be an outsider. My life was not so sheltered that I was unaware there were individuals of a criminal mind who targeted wealthy homes, and who were willing to enter those homes even while the residents were present. To do such a thing required bravado I couldn't fathom, but I knew it existed in some men. No, I thought, if they wanted to get to the bottom of things, they should be looking for a professional thief. That was my opinion, but the air in the living room was charged with such a thick current of tension, I was afraid to voice it.

Irene shifted in her throne. "Do you have anything to say about this, Mavis?"

At the very least, I understood the missing pendant must have meant a great deal to her, and I could sympathize with anyone who was, like me, having a bad day. "I'm sorry," I said.

"Are you?"

"Sure…I mean, yes." Irene Valentine had raised me to be precise with my language.

There was a long, uncomfortable pause, and I got the sinking feeling I was supposed to say more. I wasn't sophisticated enough to grasp the implication that I was being accused of this crime, that the only thing expected of me was a full confession. It didn't help that I was innocent; it merely made me appear unrepentant.

"You have nothing more to say?" asked Irene.

Something occurred to me. "Have you called the police?" I thought I was being helpful, but looking back, I could imagine how that query might have been received, given the presumption of my guilt.

"No," said Irene. "Not yet, at any rate. We are still confident the guilty party will find the strength of character to return the item and atone for this unfortunate and ill-considered deed. Of course, if that doesn't happen, we may have no alternative but to involve the authorities."

There was another uneasy silence in the room that was broken when Robyn Valentine shuffled in, looking glum. As always, he was dressed as a college TA: brown slacks, pale blue short-sleeved shirt, argyle vest, bunny slippers. He held an envelope in his paw.

"The stamps are broke," he announced, to no one in particular. "I been licking them and they don't stick. They're broke." He dropped the envelope on the floor, and from his other fist released a crumpled strip of postage stamps that fluttered to the carpet next to the letter. He then turned heel and exited, his bunny feet shushing up the stairs. A moment later, his bedroom door slammed.

Joseph retrieved the items from the floor, inspecting the crinkled and damp stamps. "He just needed to peel off the wax paper."

"Well," said Irene, exasperated, "put the stamp on for him. And be sure to tell him, so he'll know for next time."

He did as he was told, and set the envelope gently on the coffee table. Now that the distraction was over, all eyes fell once again upon me—all except Auntie Benz, who continued to stare morosely at her knees.

Irene fixed me with a steady glare. "You were not in school, today, Mavis." This was not a question.

At this sudden disclosure, my face must have registered a trace of guilt, or what seemed to the others like guilt; but I was merely surprised that anyone at the school had noticed my absence, and had gone to the trouble of ratting me out. I felt no real guilt over my truancy, given the injustice I had suffered at the hands of Cameron Faminow and, more significantly, Mrs. Wainstock, whose blind devotion to her own god-given authority left no room for fairness or truth. Too late, I felt I needed to defend myself. "I was punished for something I didn't—"

"I am aware of the facts, Mavis. I spoke at length with the vice principal. She told me all about your behaviour, this morning."

"But I didn't—"

"I know that boys will be boys, and no doubt your partner in this shameful display encouraged you, but that's no excuse."

"He's not my partner," I said. "He's just some bully."

"Associating with bullies will not help you grow into a useful member of society. Perhaps we should be taking a greater interest in the children you play with."

"We weren't playing. He was hitting me. And then Missus Wainstock took us both to—"

Irene put up her hand to silence me. "Your excuses don't interest me, right now. It's a discussion we can have later. What I'd like to know is where you went *after* you left the school."

I told her how I had spent my day, first in the ravine, and then at the mall. When I finished, she looked out the window, as if a better truth could be found there. At length, she returned her gaze to me. "Did you come back to this house at some point during the day?"

"No. I told you, I was in the ravine, and then—"

"I know what you told me. I was hoping you might have suddenly remembered your activities more clearly, now that we are all sitting here, talking about it."

I shook my head. "I haven't forgotten anything."

It seemed that wasn't the correct answer. Irene sighed. "I'm sorry to hear you say that, young man. I suggest you go to your room now, and think about your actions today. An evening of solitude and quiet reflection might jog your memory."

I wasted no time escaping to my bedroom. I closed the door and lay on my bed, leaving the light off. As Irene instructed, I thought things over, but the only conclusion I reached was that I seemed to be marked for persecution, for some unaccountable reason.

- - -

The creak of the doorknob jolted me out of a light doze. The sun had nearly set, the room was a collage of shadows in varying depths and textures. A vertical wedge of light grew, and a small shadow stepped into the room. The shadow coughed. I heard a soft rubbing sound, and then a hand found the light switch.

"Hi," said David.

I propped myself up on my elbows. "I don't think you're supposed to be in here. I'm supposed to be alone. I'm in trouble."

He shut the door quietly and looked around the room, as if casually looking for something. "I know. You stole Nana's elephant."

The accusation launched me off the bed. "I didn't steal anything. You better not say that again."

He shrugged. "I don't care, dummy. You think I care? Go ahead and steal all her stupid jewellery, see if I care."

I was several inches taller than my cousin, and I leaned over him to help make my point. "I didn't steal it. I wasn't even here."

David received my denial with calm scepticism. He backed away from me and began slowly pacing the room, opening and closing drawers, looking in the shoe boxes where I stored my Lego pieces and toy soldiers, and as he conducted this dispassionate exploration, he said, "I thought I heard something this afternoon, when I was in bed."

"You heard the thief?"

"Well, I heard something...someone. I thought it was you."

"It wasn't me. I told you, I wasn't here."

David opened my wardrobe and stuck his head into the darkness. "It *sounded* like you."

"That's stupid. How can you say it sounded like me? What do I sound like?"

He removed his head from the wardrobe. "I don't know. You just sound like *you*. I can always tell who's coming down the hall. Everyone has their own sound. Like Uncle Robyn, see, he's got this sort of weird shuffling sound, like he's dragging his feet. And Nana always makes a clicking sound, and she walks real fast. My mom's the only one that doesn't make any sound. She can sneak up on me every time."

"Well, you're wrong about today. You didn't hear me. I was at the mall."

"That's what *you* say."

"That *is* what I say, and it's the truth."

He coughed again, sat down on the end of my bed. "You don't have to lie. I won't tell them. I steal stuff all the time."

"What do you steal?"

"Just stuff. Whatever I want."

"Like what?"

"Like chocolate bars from the Milk Mart. That old chink is blind, or maybe just stupid, I don't know. He sits behind the counter all day, watching TV. So what I do is, I buy something, you know, like gum or something, but I got three Milky Ways in my pocket that he doesn't know about. It's easy."

"You'll get caught."

He just smiled. " I won't ever get caught. *You* got caught, but that's because you're stupid."

"I didn't get caught, I got blamed. It's not the same thing."

"It's all the same to them." He jabbed a thumb over his shoulder. He meant the rest of the Valentines. "It doesn't matter if you really did it, so long as they think you did. You should just tell them you did it."

"Why would I say I did it when I didn't?"

"They'll be easier on you, that's why. Say you're sorry, then they'll love you again."

I doubted it. They didn't appear to love me before they thought I was a thief. "I'm not going to say sorry for something I didn't do."

David stood up. "Suit yourself. Don't make any difference to me." He snapped off the light and quietly retreated back to his own room.

I stood in the darkness of my room, too discouraged, too indignant at having been falsely accused, to consider what the real consequences might be. I lay down on my bed again, glad for the growing darkness. I wanted to disappear. And I would, by and by.

11

I was left alone for the night to reflect on my alleged crime. After David slunk out of my room, there were no further intrusions. There was also no dinner for the young thief. The hunger sat in my gut like a cramp. My stomach was a knot of clay, firing in the heat of my lonely insecurity. Before long, the sun vanished and the room fell into complete darkness, and the drizzle outside turned into a pounding torrent that made me think, inaptly, of an extended round of applause, an ovation. I felt the person most deserving of an ovation was whoever took Irene's valuable pendant and shifted the blame to me. A dirty trick, maybe, but there was no denying it was a success.

Over the next several hours, I heard each member of the family mount the creaky staircase and make for their respective beds, and I realized, with demoralizing comprehension, that I was able to identify each one by the sound of his footsteps, as David had earlier claimed to do. So who had David heard from his sick bed that afternoon? There were many more hours of sleepless solitude in which to ponder that question, but the answer wouldn't come until morning.

The rain stopped sometime during the night, the torrent dissipating so gradually I didn't notice until it had ceased. Lying on my side, atop the bed sheets, I finally drifted into a near-sleep state, not deep enough to dream, and shallow enough that I remained aware of the room, a tilted view, under-exposed, an image frozen in time. After a time that was either long or short, the room began to lighten, faint shadows appearing in the corners. The room had originally been intended for utility rather than human occupancy, so the window, which looked down on the driveway, was small and high up the wall. Even on the brightest day, it was impossible to judge either the weather or the time of day without standing on a chair and looking out beyond the shade of the eaves.

It was Saturday morning, and the household slowly began to rise. Robyn Valentine's doorknob jarred me awake, clattering like a tin can full of pennies as the heir emerged from his room, which was directly across from mine. I listened to him shuffle past my door, muttering quietly to himself, and descend the stairs. Soon afterward, I heard Joseph follow Irene down to the dining room. And then I heard David's door open, his feet pattering along the hall to his mother's room; a few minutes later Auntie Benz and David hurried down to join the others. Prickles, the evil Scotch terrier, spent a long minute sniffing at the crack under my door before trotting off to see what was for breakfast.

I rose from bed and knuckled the grit from my eyes. Mounting the chair beneath the small window, I could see that the sun was well up, but languished above the same grey sky that had lingered over the city for a week. Another dismal day. Abandoning the narrow view, I brought the chair to my desk—a valuable satinwood escritoire that dated back to a previous century, a more civilized time, so claimed Irene—where I counted the days on my calendar until my birthday. Fifteen. Not that anyone else was looking forward to it.

I still wore the previous day's trousers and pullover; they smelled of rain and the mossy ravine. I used my fingers to ruffle my hair into its usual disorderly shape, and thought, somewhat hazily, that a bath might be in order this morning. I felt the gritty rings of dirt encircling my ankles after a day of puddle jumping in the ravine. Yes, a long, hot bath might just be the thing to salve my bruised spirit. But my resolve quickly deserted me when I heard Irene's heels clipping up the stairs.

She entered without knocking, looking flushed and troubled. "Well!" she said, as if she had just caught me in another act of thievery.

I had no response to her exclamation. Her anger frightened me a little, although I tried not to show it. Over the years, I had quietly pitied those who met the wrong side of Irene Valentine's wrath, and now, it seemed, I was on the business end of that famous spleen.

She surveyed the small room, as if she expected to see plunder stacked in every corner. Without another word, she stepped across the room to the old steamer trunk that served as my toy box, and on top of which sat two shoeboxes, one filled with Lego pieces and the other with my collection of green plastic soldiers. Showing an uncharacteristic lack of decorum, she peeled the lid off the first box and upended the contents. A troop of infantrymen from the Second World War clattered across the surface of the trunk, a few good men skidding over the edge to their doom. Collateral damage.

I was baffled. "What are you doing?" My query went unanswered.

Meanwhile, the rest of the Valentine clan were arriving, one by one, peering expectantly through the open door. Irene, possessed by the fervour of her undisclosed task and no doubt grateful, as always, for an audience, picked up the second shoebox and dumped the contents on the steamer trunk, burying the surviving soldiers in an avalanche of primary-coloured Lego blocks. Had she come in here just to mess up my room? When I glanced towards the crowded doorway, I caught my cousin's gaze. David looked at me with a familiar smirk on his small face. He appeared uninterested in what Irene was doing, and I realized at that moment why: he *knew* what she was doing. He winked at me and crossed his arms in a satisfied manner. I suddenly felt very hot.

Irene furiously raked her fingers through the heap of moulded plastic until something in the scattered mess glittered. Irene picked it up, turned to face her audience, and triumphantly presented the priceless elephant pendant for all to see.

Auntie Benz moaned softly, as if to say this was merely further proof (as if any were needed) that life was a cruel and inhospitable province, populated by villainous and untrustworthy *men*. For once, I agreed with her outlook. Prickles barked once and scampered away, electing not to stay for the denouement. Robyn, positioned at the rear, stood on his tiptoes, trying to see better and muttering, "What's the thing? What's the thing?" There was a blue ink stain in the corner of his mouth. Joseph Valentine shook his head, as if he regretted this outcome but wasn't really surprised by it. Predictably, David-Judas said, "Told ya."

Irene swivelled towards me, pinching the pendant between her thumb and forefinger. "Still have nothing to say, young man?"

I said plenty. The sight of that glittering heirloom—the smoking gun that would prove to be my downfall—released a torrent of words. I pleaded my innocence with a passion I hadn't known before, testified truthfully that I most certainly did not take the thing, did not hide it—so conspicuously!—in the shoebox, would never have committed such a crime, especially against my own family. I uttered the name of someone who *was* inclined to acts of mischief and thievery, a resident who had recently confessed that he routinely shoplifted for the thrill of it. I was certain that David had surreptitiously dropped the pendant in my shoebox during his puzzling visit, the evening before. It was well within his nature to take pleasure in my persecution. I was just another bug under the hot beam of his magnifying glass. So, yes, I accused him. But without the evidence to back it up, the accusation merely cast me as a liar as well as a thief. I might as well have been talking to the old gurgling furnace. My defence was dismissed as easily as the perished goldfish were flushed. The verdict came in the form of Irene's parting words:

"Sooner or later, bad blood will rise to the surface."

With that inexplicable statement ringing in my ears, I was left for another lonely afternoon of quiet reflection, while the rest of the family convened downstairs, to determine my fate.

- - -

This was not the first time Irene Valentine had made allusions to my *blood*, but it was the first time she had used it as an open condemnation of my character, and I could only wonder if she might be right. But her charge of "bad blood" said as much about not only Harry but also Sara Glynn, my mother. I knew my grandmother held no good opinions of the "broomstick vendor," but her criticism had painted him more fool than villain. And surely she didn't intend to indict her own daughter, who appeared to have been nothing if not gentle and kind (Sara Glynn must have been generous to a fault if she married Harry). I began to wonder if there wasn't a morsel of truth in Irene's conviction that I was somehow polluted by corrupted genes. How would I know for sure if I was being controlled by inner forces, misguided by metabolic thugs invisible to the naked eye and largely undetectable by the lens of science? Were there worse things lurking in my sanguineous cocktail, awaiting the right moment to ambush me? Was I predestined to be a thief? Or worse?

If only for my own sanity, I had to believe not. Besides, in matters of a criminal nature, I was too much the coward. Growing up under the unforgiving rein of Irene Valentine, I was instilled with a deep and abiding fear of authority that extended to include anyone in a uniform (policemen, security guards, bus drivers, hotel doormen, the postman), and my teachers at school. My fear of being caught surpassed any impulse I might have had to steal something.

Was I a liar? I concede that lying was a convenience I occasionally employed, but the lies themselves were kid stuff, and most often involved withholding a truth rather than giving a falsehood. Yet, in the case of the missing pendant, I had been utterly forthcoming about my movements and motivations during my day of truancy, the day of the robbery; I had told the truth and been punished anyway, a lesson that I would not soon forget.

In the solitude of my oversized linen closet, I lay on the bed and listened to the heart beating in my chest, the pulse in my neck and temples, all that allegedly dubious blood. If it was in some way contaminated, it might explain why I was too weak or too stupid to protect myself from a pint-sized thug. And I couldn't ignore the fact that my cousin was, like me, filled only halfway with high-octane Valentine blood. The sad symmetry of our two lives continued, because David was also a victim of forces outside his own biological tides: abandoned by a selfish father, warped by a black-hole mother, bullied by an overbearing grandmother. It didn't require a degree in psychology to see that David's anti-social behaviour was a cry for attention, a plea for a little love and guidance.

It took time—years, really—but eventually I forgave my cousin, not only for stealing my grandmother's precious jewellery and pinning it, so to speak, on me, but also for all the other schemes and devilry he perpetrated over the years. *Dear David, wherever you are, I forgive you.*

- - -

Excreting a noxious haze and pitiful squeaks, Harry's old Nash turned in to the Valentine driveway early that evening. From the confines of my room, I heard his arrival, recognized the *blatt* of his car. I saw from my window that he had once again parked at the end of the drive, exposing the Valentines to the ridicule of the other neighbourhood snobs. But if Irene Valentine was offended by this predictable impudence, she must have taken comfort in knowing that this would be the last time Harry and his old clunker would pollute her environment.

The door chimed, and there were indistinguishable words spoken in the foyer. Sitting on the edge of the bed, I expected to hear footsteps mounting the stairs, was waiting for more lectures, this time from the stranger; my *father*, doling out lofty strictures, or some form of punishment—grounded for a month, perhaps. My palms tingled, ghostly traces of a sting, a corporeal memory of the "strapping" I'd received from Mrs. Wainstock. But the footsteps retreated instead to the living room, and for the next hour Irene's voice rose and fell. I imagined Joseph Valentine's head, nodding and nodding in agreement. I could see Harry Templeton sitting awkwardly on the edge of his seat, staring vacantly at the mosaic patterns in the carpet at his feet, overwhelmed and powerless. Now and then I heard Prickles bark his two-cents' worth.

After Irene Valentine had finally said everything that needed to be said, there was a soft knock on my door. Since it seemed to me my right to privacy and common courtesy had been revoked, I didn't bother to answer. The door opened and Harry stepped in, alone.

"Hello, Mavis."

I rose from the bed, stood an arm's length away, curiously glad to see him. I suppose I was simply relieved it wasn't Irene Valentine.

He shuffled his feet clumsily, surveyed the cramped room. "How are you?"

Believing the question was largely rhetorical, I merely shrugged.

Harry looked towards my small, high window and seemed to find some conclusion there. "It's getting dark. Let's get your things packed up, before it gets too late."

"Packed?"

"Your things."

"Why are we packing my things?"

Harry looked down at me with a mixed look of confusion and pity. "Don't you have some things you want to take with you? Your clothes? A few toys?"

"Where am I going?"

His face changed, as he suddenly understood. "They haven't told you anything, have they?"

I shook my head.

He stepped towards me and put a hand on my shoulder. "I'm taking you home."

"Home?"

"My home."

Was this my punishment? Send me away for a few days with this old fool, until I've learned my lesson? A grounding was bad enough, but *this*… "How long am I going for?"

His eyebrows went up. "What do you mean?"

"How long do I have to stay at your house?" I tried to keep the whine from my voice, make it seem a simple enquiry.

Harry looked at the ceiling and scratched his chin. "Um, forever."

12

The evening was cool, and there was no evidence the car's heater functioned. My few belongings were stuffed pell-mell in two cardboard boxes, which were jammed in the space behind my seat, but I was too agitated to locate a sweater. I accepted the chill as just another aspect of my unjust punishment. The radio was on, tuned to a news broadcast. Outside, under the glow of street lights and illuminated storefronts, pedestrians strolled the sidewalks, dog leashes and shopping bags gripped loosely, as if there weren't a worry in the world. They had no idea the world was coming to an end.

Harry cleared his throat. "Your grandmother told me what happened."

"I didn't do it," I said to the side window. My voice cracked. I was close to tears, but determined to hold them off. It was calming to have something to concentrate on.

"She says she found the watch in your room."

"It wasn't a watch, it was a pendant, and David put it there. I didn't see him do it, but he took the stupid thing, and then he blamed it on me."

Harry pondered that for a moment. "Why would he do that?"

"He's always trying to get me in trouble," I said. I passed a glance at Harry; he stared ahead, concentrating on his driving. "I don't think he likes me very much."

He nodded at this.

We drove on, leaving behind the tony mansions, the long driveways occupied by cobalt blue Jaguars, the professionally manicured grounds. Soon, office towers rose up and drifted by; banks slept on corner lots, dull and lifeless; English-style pubs inveigled the over-nineteen crowd with promises of dark beer and authentic Britannic ambience. And then we crossed the Bloor Street viaduct, traversing the Don Valley and entering the unfamiliar territory known as the East End.

"Almost there," Harry said.

Strange, angular letters stood over narrow shop fronts along Danforth Avenue. We were passing through Greek Town, where a seemingly disproportionate number of restaurants operated, and apparently thrived.

"What's *souvlaki?*"

"I don't know," Harry admitted.

I would later learn that Harry was the only east ender who didn't know what souvlaki was. He had never set foot in any of the local restaurants.

The exotic bustle of Greek Town soon petered out, fading in to a stretch of drab low-rise buildings and tired businesses. We rolled past a boarded-up theatre, the marquee now showing the facility was for sale at a reduced price. We turned south on Woodbine, headed towards lower ground, passing beneath the railroad tracks that divided East York in to "north of" and "south of" halves.

When we stopped at a red light, Harry said, "Here we are."

I scanned the intersection. Apart from a brightly lit convenience store on the north corner, it was dark and undistinguished. Two-storey brick storefronts crowded the corner, looking old and unloved, the colour of clotted blood, the flat roofs a haven for pigeons, the street-level façades attractive to retail entrepreneurs because of the low rent. Looking east/west, I saw that these businesses quickly gave way to residential properties, many of which were duplexes—Irene Valentine's bane.

Harry noted my swivelling head and assisted me by pointing a stubby finger at the significant address on the southwest corner. And there it was: Templeton Hardware. In the display window—lit only by the ambient street lights—I saw an array of items: toaster, skill saw, stainless steel pots, vacuum cleaner, other things I couldn't make out. The place looked old, frayed at the edges, a little seedy. Silhouetted against the brick façade, a pair of stout pigeons marched like incompetent sentries across the narrow ledge over the painted wooden sign.

"That's it?"

"That's it."

"You *live* here?" The concept of living where one worked was alien to me.

"In the apartment above."

I looked at the two narrow second-floor windows. The entire unit appeared to be marginally smaller than the dining room at the Valentine mansion. But I was about to learn that any comparison between Harry's existence and the Valentines' swish lifestyle was meaningless. One might as well pit the old Nash against a Lamborghini.

With the green light, Harry passed through the intersection and turned in to the alley. He manoeuvred the car into a cramped space behind the shop and switched off the ignition. "Mavis," he said, staring in to the darkness of the unlit alley. "I want you to know that I believe you."

"What?"

"I believe you. About the pendant."

He was trying too hard, even I could see that, but his sympathy felt genuine, and that surprised me. Having been unexpectedly summoned by the Valentines and instructed to repossess his ten-year-old son, he must have been as anxious as I was. We were both suffering the discombobulating effects of having been blind-sided.

"Welcome home," he said.

The alley smelled of damp earth and garbage. I heard the car's engine *tick* with heat as I followed close behind Harry towards the plain, unmarked rear door. Something alive shifted nearby, one of the city's scavenging wildlife, but I forced myself not to panic.

Harry rattled his key-ring in the darkness. "The light's burnt out," he said—not an auspicious omen for a hardware empire. After several attempts, he finally got the door open. "Come on in, this way."

Directly ahead, a narrow staircase led to the second floor. Another door to the right led, I guessed, to the shop. Harry moved aside and waved his arm towards the stairs. I crossed the threshold and looked up. The wooden steps sagged with age and use, worn to the bare wood after generations of footfalls. At the upper landing, a low-wattage bulb stuck out from the wall, casting a faintly yellow light over the space and attracting a small swarm of moths that orbited the hot casing. A plain door at the top marked the entry to the apartment. I felt vaguely ill, but whether from fear or hunger I couldn't say.

"Go on up," said Harry.

I hesitated a moment, wishing I had another option, but the invitation, casual and encouraging as it seemed, was a command. Where else would I go? Each step groaned under my sneakers, and, as I ascended, the moths fluttered with increasing urgency, as if my unexpected arrival meant something to them. The yellow lightbulb buzzed. My mind was busy with the notion that this was my punishment for telling the truth, for trying to keep the bad blood at bay. This was my penalty for being ugly as sin.

At the top landing, Harry struggled again with the keys until the door swung inward. "Here we are," he said. "Take off your shoes over here." He indicated a rubber matt, just inside the door.

While Harry returned to the car to collect my belongings, I heeled off my sneakers and ventured into the living room—four strides across one way, six strides the other. The Valentine living room (which was not to be entered by children without permission) was a relative square, fourteen strides across. This room was further confined by a ceiling that hung low, almost within my reach, it seemed. But it was the smell that made the greatest impression. The air in the living room on Russell Hill carried the remnants of old fabric and a wood fire; Mrs. Tattu's kitchen smelled like something comforting, coriander or fennel or cocoa, depending on what she was cooking; Sylvester's Bakery was redolent of all things sweet; Daniel Fromm's house, where David and I sometimes played, always smelled like dryer exhaust, because his mother was obsessed with clean linen; the classroom at my former school wore the slightly piquant odour of damp socks, which wasn't entirely unpleasant. Harry's apartment had an atmosphere all its own. There was nothing sweet in the mixture, nor could I identify any single component, but it wasn't entirely unfamiliar: it was the smell that always came off Harry himself, during his Christmas visits to Russell Hill. I took it in and released it, in and out, trying to decide if it was unpleasant.

"You might be used to something a bit more fancy," Harry said, standing at the doorway, holding one of my boxes. "But it's not so bad, is it?"

I shook my head, breathed through my mouth. "Is there a bathroom?"

The bathroom was a shocking medley of green, from the pale green porcelain sink to the deeper green wallpaper to the oval bath mat that resembled a patch of well-trod grass. But the room was tidy, and seemed to somehow resist the thick air that infused the rest of the flat. I lingered a few extra moments over the cool draught rising from the toilet, then splashed water on my face at the sink. When I emerged into the narrow corridor, Harry was waiting for me.

"Your room's down here," he said, leading me to my first pleasant surprise. My bedroom was larger than the closet I had occupied in the Valentine house. A double-size bed was situated along the wall to the left, a tallboy against the opposite wall, and an old rocking chair sat in a corner. Most impressive was a window that I could look out of without standing on a chair. Granted, the view was of a brick wall, but still I was impressed.

"This is nice," I said, and I meant it.

Harry looked pleased. "My bedroom is right next door, if you need anything." He left me alone.

I didn't sleep at all that first night. I lay awake listening to all the new sounds, including the grinding of the streetcars that passed every twenty minutes, and the strange silences that fell in between. My mind refused to stop turning over the events of the past two days. I couldn't quite believe that my life could have changed so significantly, so quickly. I wondered if this was all part of some bigger plan, but no answer came. I stared at the ceiling and listened to Harry snore until the sun came up.

Home at last.

13

History is everywhere, and it is not always on an epic Valentine scale. Templeton Hardware had its own history, and Harry was its steward. And since it was my history as much as his, he made some modest effort to impart it to me. But I'm sorry to admit I was a reluctant student, both in business and history. Tales of dead ancestors, struggling in the New World against poverty and sickness and mounting competition in an expanding marketplace, only weighed down my weary eyelids. And the minutiae of the retail industry were, to me, only marginally less soporific than algebra. It didn't help that Harry's delivery was tedious as a yogi's mantra, and his narratives had none of the dramatic highs and lows of the fiction I devoured in my lonely room above the store. He was no competition for Melville or Golding.

Still, I must have absorbed some of it over the years, storing it away quietly until my middle age, when it finally began to mean something to me. Eventually, we learn that history is an old man's sport.

History:

Early in the twentieth century, a ship departed the misty docks of Liverpool and, after chugging steadily westward for some weeks, glided into Halifax harbour. Among the passengers on that steamer were my five-month-old grandfather, his father (a serious young man with an inclination to brood behind his impressive moustaches, and remembered best for his dismal inability to rise to his sweeping, unrealistic ambitions) and his plain, stoical mother, who cradled the infant boy in her arms in such a way that he had an unobstructed view of his new homeland. And before they lost their sea legs, the young family mounted a locomotive that huffed-and-puffed an inconceivable distance westward, until it ran out of steam on the north shore of Lake Ontario.

Carrying on their backs everything they owned, the Templetons arranged passage on a vegetable cart to the nearby town of East York, selecting the destination in part because that was where their ride, the produce merchant, was going, and also because York was a name both familiar and pronounceable. Once they were deposited on the muddy sidewalk of that village, they never left.

Despite the seemingly limitless opportunities for a man with "gumption" in the newly conquered colonies, success eluded my great-grandfather. All that concentrated brooding fostered plenty of ideas for amassing fortune and influence, but if a few of these ideas didn't require a substantial and unattainable investment of capital, they all required a sensible, detailed business plan, which was something he was unequipped to provide. Over the next two decades, he did, however, manage to meet and enter into partnership with nearly every crackpot and grafter in Upper Canada, before he finally succumbed to defeat and settled into the comforting arms of liquor. By then his po-faced wife had withdrawn her support of his erratic and invariably doomed business ventures, retreated into her own silent world, weaving lace for pennies and nicking hits of medicinal brandy.

Three decades after the vegetable trolley delivered the Templetons to their adoptive town, as the first global depression was beginning to recede, my grandfather (no longer a babe-in-arms) got the notion that the hardware business was calling him. A young man now of modest education and passable intelligence, and also in possession of his father's passion for success, he left his parents to their miserable solace in drink, found himself a like-minded wife, took a small loan and opened shop at the intersection of Woodbine and Gerrard. The timing couldn't have been worse. With so many of our country's men away, fighting for freedom and democracy in the Old World, there was suddenly little demand for tools of trade—the principal trade now being the killing of German boys and men. Along with a shortage of customers was a dearth of, among other things, iron and rubber, two elements on which the hardware industry depended. Faced with ruin, and burdened by the haunting image of his father's extravagant failure, my grandfather had an epiphany. He expanded his inventory to include bolts of fabric, kitchen appurtenances, rolls of wallpaper, and, perhaps his most ingenious idea: stationery. With so many fathers and brothers and sons overseas, the business of correspondence was in a boom. So, positioning his willing and capable wife in a place of prominence in the shop, grandfather set out to bring in the neighbourhood women who, previously, would never have considered entering a hardware store.

The strategy worked, at least well enough to see the shop survive the war, and a mighty partnership was born in my grandparents. From then on, my grandmother was never anything less than an equal partner in the business, involved in all aspects of its operation. This was a time in history when a large contingent of the female population had entered the workforce, but where many of these women took up jobs in factories and offices out of personal and national necessity, my grandmother's ascension in the business world happened voluntarily, and with the full cooperation and encouragement of her husband. She was no "Rosie the Riveter."

If you were wondering why my young and seemingly healthy grandfather was not shipped overseas with all the other young men to fight the Nazi hordes, the explanation is this: his left leg was two full inches shorter than the right, a handicap that excluded him from service. Because of this congenital defect, he grew up to be a fairly competent amateur cobbler, fashioning for himself the elevated soles needed to compensate for this shortcoming.

Once the war ended and the fighting men returned home, the hardware business flourished. The nation entered a period of zealous reconstruction and renewal—even though the bullets and bombs had fallen elsewhere. It was a post-war mindset: out with the old, in with the new. Expansion was everywhere, including the census. With so many babies being born, homes were being renovated and expanded at an unprecedented rate, which meant, of course, that building supplies and tools were in great demand.

It was during this optimistic era that Harry came of age and began his apprenticeship in the family trade. He was twelve when the war ended, and he was sorry it was all over before he had a chance to shoot some "Jerries."

Too late, kid. History.

- - -

My grandfather didn't live long enough to witness his beloved town of East York devoured by the greater metropolis of Toronto, a union he would surely have condemned, a fulfilment of the erroneous notion that bigger is somehow better. Harry, who in so many other ways was his father's son, was modern enough to accept this new relationship as something that could at least be endured, provided trash removal services improved. And he suffered less so than his father the ascetic symptoms of agoraphobia. He wooed young Sara Glynn Valentine with Sunday drives through the bucolic lanes of Saint Jacob and Collingwood and East Gwillembury, easing her into love from within the poky confines of the old Nash Metropolitan.

History:

After Sara Glynn went underground, the appeal of the Sunday drive became less urgent to Harry—until he liberated me from Russell Hill, installed me in the apartment above the hardware store, and then tried to work out what to do with me.

Harry had no natural instincts as a parent. He had to assemble his paternal role from scraps, without the benefit of instructions or manuals, using the traditional system of trial and error. I'm sure he believed these weekend outings, being confined together in the close quarters of a puny car for interminable hours, would offer a chance for the two men to become reacquainted, develop the sort of relationship a father should have with his son. But Harry was stricken mute for long stretches, having not a clue what to say to me; and for my part I was prone to motion sickness, unaccustomed as I was to the somewhat hostile relationship the Nash had with the irregular rural roads. And while he attempted to raise topics of conversation he felt would appeal to a boy of ten—cars (a subject of some fascination for him, but not for me), sports (a field he was uninterested and misinformed in), space exploration (much in the news, back then, with the moon landing fresh in the world's mind), and other banalities—what Harry eventually learned from these excursions was that his son (turning a pale shade of oatmeal in the passenger seat, as the car wended bumpily through the foothills) had his own opinion of things.

"The Flyers are in Philadelphia, not Boston. And who cares, anyway?"

Or:

"They can't colonize the moon until they find a better way to get people there. Those rockets are big, expensive bombs. And even if they get them there, nobody wants to get dropped into the middle of the Indian Ocean when they get back, and then spend three weeks in quarantine."

You have to admit, I had a point. And you can thank Joseph Valentine's subscription to Science Digest for cultivating my opinions on the matter.

My blossoming articulation and overall literacy carved a wide gully between us, and marked a break from the great Templeton tradition of eschewing books. My paternal grandfather held the nineteenth century view that within books, and literature in particular, were harboured the inevitable seeds of evil. Harry was more pragmatic, supporting the position that reading was simply a frivolous waste of time. "Books are for those who can't do," he'd say, confusing the axiom as it was routinely applied to teachers. But I was hooked at an early age, and, as I've said, had a significant private library at hand during my formative years. It was a love—the only love of my life—that I never outgrew. I was thrilled to discover the Public Library within walking distance of my new home.

It wasn't long before Harry took my interest in reading as a sign of potential trouble. Remember: this was not long after that infamous business outside the small town of Woodstock, N.Y., the supposed high point of an era noted chiefly for producing a mob of "long-haired freaks" who marched insolently out of Ashbury Park and corrupted an entire generation of susceptible youths with the seditious notion of free speech; and also introduced those youths to the liberating effects of LSD. This was, to Harry and his peers, nothing short of a revolution against decency and morality, and so he was vigilant, lest I be drafted into the revolt.

Harry worried needlessly; I was well out of the sphere of that nefarious influence. He watched me carefully for signs of a rebellion that I can safely say never came to pass. Still, when he caught me with a copy of *Lost Horizon*, he thought he could see the crystal-ball reflection of my imminent downfall. Harry knew nothing of the book's contents. He read the title and formed an opinion based on the multitude of possibilities it suggested, none of which seemed positive. Had my mother been alive, or had there been a wise uncle or friend available to support Harry through this crisis, he might have been "talked down" from his panic, but Harry's isolation was nearly as complete as mine. He had his regular customers, with whom he exchanged pleasantries, commenting on the weather or the threat of another postal strike, but these were "first name" acquaintances, nothing more than friendly strangers, in whom Harry could not confide. He had no real friends, and no family, other than the son who was the source of his growing anxiety. His conversations with his own conscience could not have calmed him much, there being no objective voice of reason in the mix. In an effort to deflect me from any potentially perilous course, Harry made some hard decisions.

As a pre-emptive measure, he banned "rock 'n' roll" from the house. This was not a serious deprivation for me. I was ambivalent towards music in general, and my sketchy forays into the popular music of the day were merely half-hearted attempts to fit in with my peers. My alienation at school, and in the playground, was somewhat moderated if I kept up with CHUM's Top Forty. If I could hum a few bars of *Hey Lawdy Mama*, I might not feel entirely like an outcast. But I was just as happy to keep my transistor radio tuned to the classical station, at least while I was home, especially if it got Harry off my back.

In order to expose me to good, wholesome values, Harry bought a television set. Those were the days when the medium was gaining popularity in Canadian households, but there were plenty of intelligent citizens who believed television was a passing fad, a foolish and expensive gamble for the unwary consumer. To Harry it was an investment in my future, or in *his* hopes for my future, doled out in thirty- and sixty-minute parcels by such innovative and forward-thinking men as the brothers Warner and Messrs. Hanna and Barbera. Harry was immediately captivated by the televised newscasts, the important issues of the day reported by men of distinction and integrity. I appreciated the apparatus for its entertainment value, looking forward to weekly offerings from Walt Disney and the Smothers Brothers and Rowan and Martin, but I continued to wear down my library card to a crinkled stub— this in spite of Harry's most devastating measure: he demanded approval of every book I read. I surrendered to this outrageous edict, and then spent the next year reading, as far as Harry could tell, *Charlotte's Web*—an obsession he deemed odd, but hardly subversive. The other books, the ones I was really reading, were kept from Harry's prying eyes.

Our tedious Sunday drives continued for several years. During that time, the Nash was traded in for a brand new Ford Pinto. But soon after that proud acquisition, Harry had finally had enough of my complaints, my slouching resentment, and my growing sophistication.

"Llamas do *not* have pouches," I'd mumble, after Harry imparted some erroneous fact regarding the local wildlife.

"What?"

"You're thinking of kangaroos. There are no kangaroos in Canada. They come from Australia."

"Don't be a smart-aleck, Mavis." This was Harry's standard reply whenever I was right. "Look," he'd say, blocking my view with his stiff arm as he pointed out the window. "Cows." And there would be the cows, disinterested voyeurs of our weekend travels.

"Huh," I would mutter, bored and a little nauseated.

Until our cross-continent adventure began, I had travelled only as far as Harry's puny Nash—and subsequently his green Pinto—carried me. A handful of voyages into the wilderness north of highway 401, bumping along two-lane blacktops that weaved like the chain of a delicate necklace through the Ontario heartland, past apple orchards, sod farms, jumpy goat herds, the monotony broken at intervals by whistle-stop villages, those pearls of antique bargains and chip wagons.

For any young boy, the Sunday drive is a mild form of punishment, a penalty for some unnamed transgression, a deprivation of valuable weekend time that would be better spent reading a book or watching the new television. But it's also a virus—this travelling—that burrows under the skin and lays dormant, patiently passing the years until the boy becomes a man, and then it unleashes in that man a powerful feeling, an idea, what might be called a *faith,* that there is a larger world out there, and it is worth exploring. When this virus eventually struck me, I shrugged it off with a vitamin and a sniff. I possessed a rare immunity to its effects, wondering briefly if I might like to see other cities, distant provinces, tropical islands, exotic new cultures. I took a pass and wondered no more.

In recent years, I had become more amenable to the Sunday drive, having even gone so far as to suggest one myself, the first such drive after a hiatus of some years. I think Harry was so taken by surprise, he immediately agreed to the idea. It was a largely pleasant excursion, the day a little cold for the season, but clear and bright. Perhaps because the idea for the drive had been mine, I complained less than usual, restricting my comments, if I recall, to the subject of Harry's aggravating inclination to stab his foot at the gas pedal. It was his habit to accelerate nearly to the speed limit, and then relax his leg, letting the car drift until the trailing cars gathered inches off the rear bumper, and then his toe would reach for the pedal again, during which my head would nod and nod, until my neck began to ache.

"Jesus, Harry, I'm getting whiplash."

"What?"

"Can't you keep your foot on the gas pedal?"

"What are you talking about?"

"You're stabbing the gas pedal with your foot."

"I'm doing no such thing."

"You've got the seat back too far. You should move it forward, so you can reach the pedals. It's not safe, driving like that."

Harry was sensitive about his shortness in a way that I never was about my ugliness.

"Well," he said, after giving my suggestion its due consideration, "I've only been driving for half a century, so it's only fair I should take advice from someone who's driven two or three times in his entire life."

"Whose fault is that?" I said. "You won't let me drive your precious car."

"You ride the brake."

"I do not. You just don't want anyone else to touch your baby."

"Don't be foolish."

"I'm getting a sore neck. You're stabbing the gas pedal. I don't need to be an expert to see that you need to move your seat forward. That's all I'm saying."

A sedan passed us on the left, horn blaring. The driver was making signals with his hand, but I missed his message.

Harry was unmoved by my rebuke. "Maybe you should save your money and buy your own car. Then we can go for a drive in the country in *your* car, and we'll see who gets whiplash."

It was a way to pass the time. Since I lived with Harry, and worked with Harry, since I spent nearly every waking minute with Harry, or so it seemed, it was no surprise we had run out of small talk years ago. The only thing left between us was this trivial squabbling. I was right, though: he did stab the accelerator.

14

The neighbourhood I returned to just before my tenth birthday was distinguished by no particular ethnic stripe. There were a handful of Greeks who had migrated east from the city's Grecian epicentre at Pape and Danforth, and a tight knot of Italians who lived around the corner, smoking hand-rolled cigarettes on front porches that overlooked well-cropped lawns. The rest of us were marked by our collective (and, for me, extraordinary) impoverishment. I admit I was unprepared for the recurring, and eventually predictable, deprivation I suffered in Harry's care. Under Valentine rule, the lacking had been of an emotional nature; gifts were often lavish, but for my maternal clan, the spending of money was a convenient substitute for what they could not afford to give, which was love.

Harry had no access to that sort of economic liberty. He was aware of every penny earned, and every one spent. Until I moved back, I had never heard the phrase, "We can't afford it." The first hundred times I heard it from Harry, the statement baffled me. But in time I adjusted to this new reality, and gradually came to understand that, in the ongoing struggle to make ends meet, in this hand-to-mouth existence, I had joined the majority, and thereafter didn't miss the silver spoon that had been plucked from my mouth. And I saw no evidence that the Valentines were happier for having all that money.

The most recent decade has seen the aging baby boomers move into my neighbourhood and renovate the modest Edwardian houses, bringing to the area a new aspect: a division of classes. So far, Harry and I have benefited little from the influence of this middle class influx, but I see the change as a good thing, in general, and do not mourn the loss of the old neighbourhood.

History:

During those first years after my return, I was terrorized by a fearsome old curd who lived two doors down from the hardware store.

The Lucky Hair beauty salon was run by a tacky beautician named Glory, a South Korean refugee who brutalized the English language and winked lasciviously at the men who strolled past her front glass. In her early middle age, Glory was in possession of the sort of figure that went out of fashion with the passing of Marilyn Monroe, but one that still managed to catch the eye of the less discerning local gents—those who pined for the olden days, when a well-fed woman was still considered attractive. Despite giving the impression of a prostitute going to seed, Glory was a harmless and sociable presence in the neighbourhood, a friendly soul who chatted effusively with Harry, even though he openly disapproved of her, and tended to respond to her in monosyllables. Glory's only real flaw, as far as I could see, was that she was a poor judge of character. She let the upstairs apartment to a suspicious character named Shemp. And it was old Shemp who became my nemesis.

Shemp was a widower, a category Harry had been a longstanding member of, and one to which he, Harry, was naturally sensitive. I was forbidden to speak ill of Shemp in Harry's presence. Because his wife had died, Shemp was to be afforded all due respect. That was Harry's opinion.

Local rumour had it Shemp had tightened a homemade garrotte around Mrs. Shemp's thin neck, cut off her air supply, cut off her head and arms and legs, and pitched the disassembled wife down the well of their rural farmhouse, just outside the town of Windsor. He then vanished into the seedy underbelly of Toronto, blending in easily with the poor folk, who tended to ask few questions, or at least seemed to accept pat answers. This is the sort of dark rumour that circulates through every neighbourhood, in one form or another, propagated through the playground grapevine, the details improved and embellished over time, until it becomes worthy of official lore. I don't remember where I first heard the rumour about Shemp, but I believed it. One look at the man and it was easy to believe just about anything.

Apart from his diabolical reputation among the neighbourhood kids, I remember old Shemp, among the many tormentors of my youth, because he was my first exposure to the seamy guild of border guards. Before (killing his wife and) moving to my street, he had defended Canadian interests at the Detroit-Windsor border for forty years, sniffing out drugs and aliens, thwarting draft dodgers and cigarette smugglers. He was perfectly suited to the work, having limited cranial capacity and a passionate love of rules. And retirement hadn't slowed him much. From sunrise until the dinner hour, he occupied the screenless second-floor window of his apartment and guarded the sidewalk below with professional vigilance. His introduction to me, soon after I returned to Harry's corner, was an inauspicious beginning of a relationship that did not improve over the years.

"Helt!" The voice rattled like an empty dump truck above my head. In that single word was the hint of some foreign accent, or a speech impediment, or some combination of the two. *Helt?*

I had been on my way to the library when this command came down out of a clear blue sky. My *faith* momentarily shaken, I looked up and saw, hanging over the window sill above the Lucky Hair salon, a monumental elbow, stained with fading tattoos and the creeping, hair-rimmed spots of age. And this bovine extremity hovered in the sky in what could only be described as a threatening fashion. Although my inner voice suggested I make a run for it, I was gripped by an unaccountable fear of this monstrous appendage, and the absolute authority of its voice.

"Whet's your business?" demanded the limb.

"What?"

And a face suddenly appeared above the elbow—one even more hideous than my own, which redeemed old Shemp by a small degree, at least in my eyes. Skin like a blackened banana, mottled, bruised, rotting from the inside, a pair of grey eyes punching through, judging the world with the dispassion of a surveillance lens, tumorous nose, mouth like a knife wound, scalp overrun by hinterland scrub. "Don't *whet* me, you guttersnoop."

"What?" I was slow on the uptake.

"Are you diff, or just stupid?"

"Um…"

"State your business, son, or I kin't let you pass."

This was news to me. I had committed to memory Harry's ten commandments, his list of rules required to survive in and around the city streets, and under his roof. *Look both ways before crossing; Don't accept anything from strangers; Stay out of the park at night; Eat everything on your plate; Don't talk back to your elders; Don't give coins to street people; Don't litter; Stay away from the railway tracks; Don't pet strange dogs; Don't chew gum.* Apart from chewing gum (a treat I never acquired the taste for), I had breached most of his edicts at one time or another, sometimes wittingly, sometimes not. And Harry was occasionally forgiving, in his churlish way, of my youthful errors in judgment. "Don't make the same mistake twice," he'd advise me.

Now there was a new sheriff in town, and I feared there was going to be trouble. I decided to play it safe, until I could assess this new authority.

"State your business, or I kin't let you pass."

"Hardware," I said. And having made the admission, I had to wonder if I might be accused of lying, since my initiation into the family business had not yet officially begun.

The arm disappeared into the apartment and the head leaned farther out. I could smell the stale tobacco coming off its breath. (As well as contributing to my irrational fear of authority, I blame Shemp for my nicotine habit; it was one of his discarded stubs, which I had picked up off the sidewalk below his window, that provided my first taste of the foul weed. Within Harry's manifesto was no mention of retrieving cigarette butts from the gutter.)

"My name is Shemp," said the head. "Say the name for me."

"Shemp," said I.

"Very gud, son. Now, tell me your name."

"Mavis," said I.

His throat made a disparaging sound. "Well, Meevis, I'm gun be watching you."

It was Harry who told me Shemp had been a border guard, and explained what such a person did.

"He stops people from coming into Canada?"

"Only the wrong kind of people."

"And he stops people from leaving Canada, too?"

"No. The Americans do that."

It was baffling to me why this should be necessary. I couldn't imagine who the "wrong kind of people" were, and Harry was not specific. The intrigue of international relations was too abstract to hold my interest for long.

"All you need to know is, Mr. Shemp has served this country faithfully for forty years. Show him some respect."

(Incidentally, old Shemp lived to a respectable age of ninety and, not surprisingly, was never formally charged with his wife's suspicious demise.)

Harry had never crossed an international border, not until just a few days ago, when we entered the United States together. I can report that the guard who leaned in our car window and questioned us about our intentions on American soil was as nice as can be. He was young and tall, tricked out in a smart grey uniform that fit him very well, and he posed this question: "What's your business?" Before I could inform him we were in the hardware business, Harry said, "Just passing through, sir." I had never heard Harry call anyone "sir" before, and it made me smile.

"Very good," said the border guard. He was an American, of course. He was protecting the interests of his country, and appeared to be proud to do so. Right before we drove on, he suggested we have a nice day.

Over time I learned to avoid Shemp's mean gaze and confounding abuse, skirting his bovine limb and his foul stench. I never saw him out of the context of his second floor window, had no idea if he was tall or short, or perhaps confined to a wheelchair. If he ventured to ground level, it must have been after my bedtime or during school hours. Eventually, I fell out of his crosshairs as he shifted his sights to fresher targets, younger and more vulnerable. I outgrew him. By that time, my body was striving mightily for greater heights, my voice was beginning to shift to a lower register, and I was already a slave to tobacco. Somewhere in there, Harry brought home the green Pinto like a proud Papa. I continued to devour the library, one book at a time. And I remained an outsider to my peers.

- - -

Notwithstanding the football Harry gave me for Christmas when I was five, I never took to athletics the way a good Canadian boy should. In order to escape Harry's dull presence, I sometimes watched the neighbourhood lads transform Beaton Street into Maple Leaf Gardens, re-enacting historic World Cup hockey matches with adolescent bluster. *He shoots, he scores!*

Haaaaaaah… goes the crowd, which consisted of me, perched on the low brick wall that bordered the nearby park, and a shifty colony of black squirrels who will cheer anyone for nuts.

The Italian boys in particular took up this activity with menacing enthusiasm, casually denouncing their fathers' game of bocce in favour of this new and exotic hinterland tradition. They knew how to fit in. I was never invited to play, and would have declined anyway, having neither a hockey stick of my own nor the dexterity to use one. I was not a weakling, but I accepted even then that I lacked physical coordination, was a cup short of finesse, and these were shortcomings that could only have been overcome by possession of a handsome face. Alas…

Harry was in full support of my lack of interest in thuggish sports, those activities involving physical contact or teamwork— the two elements that make such sports appealing to the common man. I attribute this rare like-mindedness to our both having grown up without siblings (I refuse to put Bugsy-David into that role).

History:

In my fifteenth year, I began my junior year at Lord Beaverbrook High School. Even with over eight hundred peers jostling me in the crowded corridors, I remained at best a ghost, invisible and anonymous to the others—to the ones who mattered—and at worst an easy target for the usual derision of my girly name and my ground-pork face. I floated in the periphery with the other ghosts, the rejects, the defectives, the deviants, and was not surprised when I wasn't recruited by any of the cliques. Shunned by the jocks, the brains, the drama geeks, the motorheads, even the "Bishops of Beaverbrook" (the chess club), they all avoided making eye contact with me. And if I had plenty of company out there on the margins, there was no camaraderie, no safety in numbers, as we were picked off, one by one, by the predators. But I wasn't looking for membership in any faction. I just wanted to be left alone with Fowles and Vonnegut. Or so I thought, until my first sighting of Trevor White.

During my first week at school, I heard his name spoken with such wonder and awe, intoned with such mythological reverence, even by the jocks, that I assumed he either wasn't real or couldn't possibly live up to the legend. Yes, there was legend attached to his name. Trevor White had been in jail (untrue), outrun the cops (true) on a stolen motorcycle (untrue; it belonged to his cousin), impregnated (true) a city counsellor's daughter (untrue; it was the counsellor's niece), was asked to tour (untrue) with Steppenwolf as a back-up singer (he contributed vocals to two tracks on their *Hour of the Wolf* album), was a devil worshipper (unknown). It seemed that no one knew Trevor personally, but nearly everybody knew someone who did, which lent support to my theory that he didn't exist.

Proof to the contrary arrived at the schoolyard on the Monday morning of my second week at Beaverbrook. There was a hum in the far corner of the yard, beyond the baseball diamond, where a crowd had begun to gather. I thought at first it was just another fight; the jocks, I'd noticed, felt they had something to prove, on a fairly routine basis. But soon that mythological name was floating on the light morning breeze like a mantra, growing steadily until it was a chant: *Trevor's here...Trevor's here...*

The gravitational pull of legend was palpable. Kids were running, openly eager to get a glimpse of Trevor White, or at least sauntering in a seemingly casual manner, as if it didn't really matter, as if they might as well get a little closer, see what was up. But it did matter! Even I found myself moving in the direction of the hubbub. Why not? There were still five minutes remaining until the first bell, and my corner of the schoolyard was now deserted. As I drew near the assembling crowd, there was a carnival buzz in the air. We were here for the show, and the show was about to begin. I hadn't spotted Trevor White yet, but I knew where he was by following the direction in which every head was turned. And then one head rose from the sea of bodies, as if by magic. The legend, I quickly realized, had just stepped onto the retaining wall. He was now looking down on his audience, his arms coming up in an evangelical gesture of benediction.

"Greetings, Beavers!" he shouted. The crowd responded with a roar.

I stood at the rear, twenty yards away, and looked for obvious signs of divinity in the figure standing on the low wall. What I saw was a boy-version of the late Jim Morrison—that dark, intense and charismatic singer/poet, whose premature death was still fresh in my generation's mind. Shrouded in a draping tangle of black tresses, Trevor White, at seventeen, was unassumingly short (I had already achieved my full stature, which was just another thing to be self-conscious about), thin but looking fit and agile, with deep-set eyes that lurked in the shadow of a prominent brow and looked out at the world with a knowing, slightly cynical gaze, as if he'd seen things we couldn't imagine, as if there were truths behind those eyes that a mortal would be unable to endure. They were intelligent eyes (rumour had it his IQ surpassed 160), but his grades, according to legend and school records, reflected a lack of focus on things academic. Arriving a week late for the school year gave credibility to that theory. He wore a brilliant white shirt, unbuttoned to the sternum, and a pair of jeans that looked as though they'd seen their share of adventure. But his most prominent feature, the thing that drew the eye and demanded attention, was a wide and active mouth that turned slightly upward in the corners, a mouth with a built-in grin, a mouth that wanted to smile, that heeled obediently but impatiently, like a pup waiting for a stick to be thrown. This mouth wanted to spread out and say, *Look at me, listen to me!* And we did, we did.

The mouth now said this: "Hey, sorry I'm late, guys."

The crowd laughed.

The mouth said, "Lost track of the time, I guess." The mouth was clever, full of ingenuousness—of the most subtle and counterfeit kind.

Yeah, roared the crowd, as if they knew what he meant, as if they, too, lost entire weeks out of their lives without noticing.

The mouth said, "But I'm here now." And the crowd cheered.

On cue, the bell rang, and the crowd began moving slowly towards the concrete steps of the old school building, taking with them the demigod, Trevor White. Hands clapped his shoulders and arms and back, as he was manipulated towards the school. Everyone wanted a piece of him, to be close to him, to touch him if they could. Get a word from him, a personal word, or a moment of eye contact. Anything.

I never got close, not that morning. But I admit I wanted to. I was drawn in, just as everyone else was. There was something about him, a strange and inexplicable force that affected those around him. And if I envied him for his popularity, his good looks, his unusual power, it was a good envy, not the sort of envy that might have caused me to dislike or resent him. On the contrary, my envy made me like him more. Like everyone else who knew him, or knew of him, or knew someone who knew him, I wanted to be counted among his intimate circle of close friends—whoever they were! Surely those closest to him knew the truth from the fiction, and I wanted some of that truth. For any teenager, intelligence—which is to say, information regarded as secret or specialized—is power, and power keeps the bullies at bay. If only I could get close to Trevor, I might, among the many benefits of such a glamorous friendship, also profit from his protection.

These were the lofty and hopeful thoughts that occupied me while I took up the rear and dissolved into the mass of students in the school corridors. And as I marvelled at my first exposure to Trevor White's dazzling charisma, I had to wonder if my mother, the late Sara Glynn, had also possessed a similar influence, a force that drew others in, attracting the weak and the downtrodden, the simple-minded and the ambitious. Gravity.

As the weeks progressed, and as I grew more acclimatised to my new school and my ghostly role within it, I had many more sightings, fleeting and distant, of Trevor White. He was always surrounded by an ever-changing clutch of acolytes, circling like electrons orbiting a nucleus, the female electrons outnumbering the male, two-to-one. But I couldn't get close enough to become part of that atomic mass.

In early October, Trevor's band, The Jaunty Heretics, played to a standing-room-only crowd in the school gymnasium during lunch break. The sweat-drenched writhing, the sleepy-baritone ululations, the microphone clutched as a drowning man clings to a buoy: these things only embellished Trevor White's likeness to The Doors' former front man. None of the boys in the audience could get within forty feet of the stage, not with the mob of girls taking up the frontline positions, gyrating hysterically and tearing their hair. As always, I lurked on the fringes, avoiding the mosh, tapping Morse Code on my thigh in loose accord with the music. Whatever may or may not have been true about Trevor White, he was this: a rock star.

It happened by accident, my first close encounter with Trevor White. The lunchtime concert was over, and I had stepped outside to have a cigarette before afternoon classes began. I used the side exit, which led to the teachers' parking lot, because it was, for the most part, unused by students. It was a quiet place where I could smoke in peace. I leaned against the low concrete parapet at the top of the steps, in disregard of the school regulation that required smokers to perform their foul habit not closer than forty feet from the school's walls. I was often joined by smoking teachers who, with a nod and vague smile, would then ignore me. So it was somewhat unexpected when the heavy door opened with a crash and the Heretics' bass player backed out, carrying his guitar case in one hand and his amplifier in the other. He was a tall, hairless, ectomorphic creature, on the down side to thirty, I guessed, clad in denim pants and vest that didn't quite conform to the sharp angles of his meatless bones. Spread improbably across his thin arm was a tattoo of an eagle. I knew, from Trevor's onstage introductions, that the bass player's name was Pauly. Pauly was now struggling under the weight of his gear, so I reached out and held the door open for him.

"Thanks, mate," he said, speaking with a foreign accent I couldn't identify. He gave me a friendly nod and began the laborious descent to the parking lot, where the band's van was parked.

I let go of the door. But when it struck something hard— prompting an angry expletive from the other side—I grabbed the handle and yanked it open again. This time it was Fletch, the lead guitar player, hauling an almost identical burden: guitar and amp. Fletch was shaped like a gourd, a pock-marked and unshaven gourd. Black hair leapt from his scalp like a wad of much-used steel wool. He wheezed audibly and stank of sweat. It wasn't clear if Fletch was his first or last name, but whichever the case, he answered to it.

"Ay, Fletch," shouted Pauly, who had reached the van. "Hurry up with the keys, will ya?" The van evidently belonged to Fletch.

"Fuck you and your horse," said Fletch, breathlessly. "This shit's heavy." He took each step as if it might be his last.

Before releasing the door again, I peered inside, making sure it wouldn't close on another over-burdened musician. The heavy old door clanked safely shut. I had just leaned back against the ledge when I realized someone was standing in front of me.

"Hey," said Trevor White. He had appeared as if by magic. "Got an extra smoke?"

With my heart pounding a furious beat, I tossed him the pack and scrounged desperately for something cool to say, or something clever, or at least something that wasn't foolish…but came up with nothing.

138

Trevor lit one of my cigarettes and returned the pack. "What's your name?"

A lump the size of a peach suddenly lodged in my throat. It was my name that was stuck there, wedged behind my tongue just long enough to make the silence uncomfortable—for me, anyway. And then it released, dropped from my mouth like the last words of a condemned man. "Mavis," I croaked. I wasn't sure what to expect—a peel of wild laughter, a roll of the eyes, scorn, pity, fake sympathy.

"Good to meet you, man."

Man?

"Trevor," he said, his right hand hovering between us.

"I know." I tentatively offered my own hand, and when they came together, Trevor pumped vigorously, shaking loose some of my nervousness. "Good show," I managed to say, wishing I'd said "*great.*"

"Thanks." He ran his fingers unselfconsciously through his wild hair. He was in possession of a vanity that was both genuine and merited. "We're breaking in a new drummer, so we need the workout. We got a gig Friday, over at Winston's. You know that place?"

I nodded, hoped the lie wasn't transparent.

"Yeah, you should try and come. We're opening for April Wine."

"Sounds great," I said, imagining myself trying to explain to Harry that I was going to a downtown club, where, as a minor, I wasn't legally permitted to enter, in order to watch The Jaunty Heretics and April Wine rock out… At that point, my imagination failed me.

Trevor was watching me carefully, looking me over. He didn't seem to notice I was an ogre. "What are you, grade nine?"

"Yeah."

"Missus Rufus for math?"

"Yeah." I dropped my spent cigarette over the ledge.

"She's a maverick," he said.

I nodded, having no idea what he meant by that.

"If you can, sit by the window," Trevor said. "She's sensitive to light. Sit by the window and she won't see you too good. If you're asleep, or something, all she'll see is a silhouette."

"Thanks, sure."

Trevor flicked his smoke towards the parking lot.

The door swung open again, this time accompanied by the crash of muted cymbals, and Denny, the new drummer, stumbled out, bearing the oversized hatboxes that contained his toms, a stack of Zildjians pressed under one of his arms. "Out of the way," he muttered impatiently, as if he didn't recognize his own celestial lead singer.

We gave him room to wield his load—the first of several, it would turn out.

"That's why I'm no longer a drummer," Trevor said to me, as we watched Denny struggle with his instrument. "Too much shit to lug around."

I thought it was a small price to pay, to play in a popular rock band, but I didn't say that to Trevor.

"Hey," said Trevor, "thanks for the smoke."

I nodded as nonchalantly as I could. "No problem."

He favoured me with a dazzling grin before making motions to rejoin his band mates. At the bottom of the stairs, he turned back. "Hey, listen, man. Why don't you come over to the house, later? After school, I mean."

"Um—" This offer was so unexpected, I was rendered speechless. What did he mean by "the house?" Whose house? Did someone like Trevor White have parents, or did he live in one of those communal flats, with artists and musicians all living together, sharing mattresses on the floor, burning incense, growing pot on the kitchen window sill, reading poetry to each other with a backdrop of Pink Floyd and The Dead? Apple crates and lava lamps. Quadraphonic sound. Dreaming of absinthe afternoons in Paris, hanging out with models and prostitutes.

And how would I fit into that scene? With my sand shoes, my knapsack stuffed with paperbacks, my utter lack of sideburns? Harry had cautioned me tirelessly about associating with hippies. "They're weak and lazy, each and every one, Mavis. They'll never amount to anything. And they're more than happy to drag you down with them." But Harry was never clear about his definition of what a "hippie" was. Long hair? Anti-war sentiments? Facial hair? Or did he mean any boy between the ages of sixteen and twenty-five, regardless of sociopathic leanings? Whatever Trevor White's intentions, Harry surely would have taken one look and disapproved, which was enough reason for me to say, "Sure. I'll come."

He gave me the address—which, surprisingly, was only a few blocks from the school—and disappeared into the van.

The afternoon bell rang and I went inside, merged with the other students, feeling a little light-headed after my encounter with Trevor White. Who had invited me to his house. As if I were his great friend. Me. Mavis Templeton. The ugly ghost. If only I'd had a friend to share my good fortune with.

The hours lay before me the way I imagined the vast, shimmering dunes of the Sinai had lain before T.E. Lawrence as he set out on his impossible Arabian mission. Time no longer existed as the inexorable, forward-marching juggernaut, but now sat like a granite monolith, black and dense and immoveable. I admit my concentration, during my three remaining classes of the day, was somewhat below par, as the most probable fantasies played out in my mind: We, Trevor and I, sitting knee-to-knee in his basement studio, hugging our respective guitars, hashing out a clever bridge for a rock anthem that would instantly climb the Billboard charts and secure its position—and our fame—in the annals of musical history. "Chemistry," I'd tell Rolling Stone magazine. "Connection, man. That's all. Same as with the Beatles. Pure chemistry." Despite his ownership of the band's van, Fletch would be out. Mavis Templeton, appropriately (if unofficially) rechristened Richard Keith, playing the part of the introspective and enigmatic soul of the band, would be in, the new lead guitarist for The Jaunty Heretics.

One happy footnote: in the world of rock, it's all right to be ugly.

Did I mention my relative indifference to popular music? Not to mention I neither played nor owned a guitar, or any other musical instrument? (In grade one, I had been banished from the recorder group because of my tin ear and unpredictable meter.) Never mind. This was a fantasy, fed by the elixir of legend. Spending an afternoon with Trevor White, what should I expect, except something extraordinary?

When the three-fifteen bell rang, I made for the exit without stopping at my locker to deposit my books. With an over-laden knapsack slung over one shoulder, I geared up to an Olympic-style walk, headed for Wembly Avenue. In only a few minutes, I was standing before a modest, two-storey house, settled in the shade of a well-treed street. It looked pretty much like all the other houses surrounding it, with a small, neat lawn, an orange tabby dozing on the porch railing, a white Datsun parked in the driveway. For several confused minutes I stood on the sidewalk, unsure of what to do next. Had I written down the wrong address? Was Trevor pulling a prank, sending me to some random house? One thing about teenagers: they possess a morbid fear of anything that might embarrass them; I was no exception. I was reluctant to knock on an unknown front door until I knew for sure.

"Something I can help you with?" said a voice. An old woman with a towering grey bouffant stood on the next-door porch. Her tone was more suspicious than helpful. I suppose she thought I was casing the joint for a late-night burglary.

"Does Trevor White live here?"

The way she seemed to momentarily lose control of her left hand, and the way she rolled her eyes, before disappearing through her front door, seemed the best confirmation I was going to get. Hoisting my bag more securely on my shoulder, I mounted the steps and rang the doorbell.

"Hey!" said Trevor, beaming from the semi-darkness of the foyer. "Cool jacket."

I looked down at the jacket, as if I hadn't seen it before. Harry had bought it for me, second-hand, at Goodwill—not because it was "cool" but because it had cost only seven dollars. "Thanks," I said to Trevor.

"Come on in, man." He stepped back and I entered.

A stained-glass window gave the foyer a slightly eerie cast of mottled colour. To the left, through closed French doors, was a small, tasteful living room, a television set flickering in the corner with no one watching it. A carpeted staircase to the right led to the second floor. Ahead, at the end of the corridor, I could see a slice of the kitchen, where, my nose told me, someone was baking muffins.

But where were the poets, the prostitutes, the water pipe, the "Tommy" poster? Had French doors replaced beaded curtains as the latest fad? Would a rock star really drive a Datsun? Bake muffins?

"Do you live here alone?"

142

Trevor laughed. "Good one," he said, turning to move down the corridor. "Come on."

As we approached the kitchen, I saw a woman—Mrs. White, I presumed—standing over the stove, one hand mitted, a lean, attractive woman in her forties, dressed as if she had just got home from the office. She fussed with something I couldn't see, but which must have been the fragrant muffins. Beside her, talking animatedly but apparently not helping with the baking, was a college-aged girl, severely blonde and quite possibly the most beautiful girl I'd ever seen. I nearly collided with Trevor's back as I my gaze lingered on this stunning girl. But my glimpse was fleeting. Before we reached the kitchen, Trevor turned through a narrow door to the right: passage to the basement. Where the recording studio no doubt sprawled in a tangle of wires and metal racks and black boxes with glowing red lights, guitars standing rank-and-file along the wall, drum kit spilling out of the corner. I reset my priorities, left the girl behind, and pursued Trevor down the stairs.

Nothing could have prepared me for scene that faced me when I arrived in Trevor White's basement: a rec room, panelled in light oak; navy blue shag carpeting; faux-medieval-torch wall sconces; a sequence of illustrated dogs, wearing knickers and polo shirts, and wielding golf clubs, framed and hanging along the side wall. At the far end of the room sat a vast billiards table, glowing green under a bank of brilliant light. And in the foreground, facing another television, was a well-worn flower print sofa, upon which sat a plump, sad-looking boy, perhaps a year or two younger than me.

"This is Oliver," said Trevor.

"Hi, Oliver," I said, hoping the kid would scram once the jam session began.

Oliver's eyes flicked over us, then returned to the screen.

"Say hi to Mavis, Oliver."

"Hi," said the boy, weakly.

Trevor looked at me sympathetically. "Sorry, man. He doesn't get out much."

I shrugged the kid off, gave the room another quick scan. There were no guitars, no drums, no wires tangled across the floor, no microphones hanging from the ceiling. There was no indication a rock band had ever passed through this space. It was as generic and suburban as every other rec room in the neighbourhood. What was going on?

I turned to Trevor. "What are we going to do?"

He shifted on his feet, and, for the first time, seemed uncomfortable. "Right. Well, I gotta split for a while. Band practice. But why don't you and Oliver hang out? Watch the tube for a while."

If he had asked me to iron his shirts and fold his socks, I wouldn't have been more staggered. If he had suddenly realized I was just a dumb kid, a talentless and useless nobody, and ordered me out, I would have accepted that as a realistic end to my fantasy. If he had asked me to polish the chrome on his motorcycle or do his homework for him, I would have gladly done it. I was under his spell, his to command. But this? Had he invited me over to his house so that I could babysit? Was I to expect the going rate of fifty cents an hour? Help myself to anything in the fridge? Should be home before midnight? Call if there's an emergency, number's on the fridge door? What the hell was going on?

Before I could ask, Trevor had gone, leaving me behind with this strange and morose kid. Oliver. The little brother. There was no family resemblance. Was Oliver adopted?

"Tricked you, didn't he?" said Oliver.

"What?"

"He does that. Brings kids home for me."

"Trevor?"

"He thinks it's weird that I don't have any friends, so sometimes he brings me one."

"Um..."

"You don't have to stay. Don't feel like you have to."

"Well..."

"Batman's on," said Oliver, whose eyes hadn't left the screen. "I like it, but Cat Woman's weird."

"Weird?"

"She's too old, or something. She reminds me of my French teacher, Missus Lambermont."

"Uh huh," I said, without much enthusiasm. I was trying to decide if I should leave. After all, I *had* been tricked, hadn't I? I had read Homer, so I knew that the gods were always toying with mortals, playing little games with them, as much for their own amusement as for any practical or beneficial purpose. So what was

Trevor's motive? Was he truly interested in finding a friend for his lonely brother—which could be seen as noble—or was this just a practical joke? Was he now riding shotgun in Fletch's van, having a big laugh over this prank? Complicating my thoughts was the possibility that, if I were to leave now, I might not get another glimpse of that beautiful girl upstairs. Who was she? The sister? What was her name? My feet felt glued to the carpet.

"You like Smarties?" Oliver jiggled the glass bowl resting in his lap, rattling the candies. "I've got lots."

It wasn't the enticing rattle of Smarties that made up my mind to stay; it was the feeling that, after this unexpected betrayal by Trevor, after being setup and then left behind, if I simply walked away, I would have left with nothing. By staying, I had something, if only the brief company of a strange kid, and the possibility of another sighting of the goddess upstairs. *Better than nothing.* I dropped my knapsack on the floor and settled on the sofa, next to my new friend.

Oliver suffered the twin disabilities of corpulence and an indissoluble sullenness. It was no surprise to me he had no friends. He was a sad, plump boy who, between fists full of candy, chewed his fingertips until they were red and raw. He smelled faintly of urine.

We stared at the screen for a while. Batman and Robin were in a tussle with some of the Penguin's henchmen. *Blam! Ker-Zow!*

"What grade are you in?" I asked, during a commercial break.

"Seven. I was held back last year. I should be in eight."

"How come?"

He shrugged. "I missed a month of school. Broke my ankle on my bike. Want to see the scar?" Without waiting for an answer, he parked his right leg across his left and peeled a dirty white sock off. "See there? My front tire went through a sewer grate and got stuck. I went flying over the handlebars, nearly got creamed by a car, missed my head by an inch."

"Too bad," I said, meaning the accident, and realizing too late how the comment might be taken. But Oliver didn't seem offended.

The show came back on, so the discussion of his broken ankle petered out.

"I wish they were dead," he said, when Batman was over.

Batman and Robin? The Penguin's henchmen? "Who were dead?"

He jabbed a thumb towards the ceiling. "Ken and Barbie."

"Who?"

"My brother and sister."

I thought about Trevor, his legendary fame and his indisputable talent, his good looks and charisma, and I easily brought to mind the image of the sister, whose intense beauty had shaken me. "They seem okay," I said, understating my opinion by a significant margin.

"They're not okay."

"What's wrong with them?"

"There's nothing wrong with them. That's the problem. They're perfect, both of them. Absolutely perfect."

As an only child, I had no reference point for understanding sibling rivalry. "You don't really want them dead," I said.

"If I had a gun, I'd shoot them."

"That's dumb."

With surprising agility, Oliver sprang to his feet. "Let's play pool."

I was equally surprised by the turns his mind made. "I've never played before."

"That's okay. It's not hard." Oliver had a plan.

"Um," I said, after he summed up the main thrust of his plan, "I don't think billiards is an Olympic sport. I'm pretty sure about that."

Oliver just shrugged. "I'll go pro, then. That's where the money is. You and me, we can become the best pool players in the world. All we gotta do is practice."

The point, I gleaned, was for Oliver to finally out-perform his perfect sister and perfect brother in something. Anything. He was tired of being the fat one, the stupid one, the one who can't do anything right. Not tall enough, thin enough, old enough, cool enough, smart enough. Too lazy, spastic, useless. Billiards was a way to finally get noticed.

"I just have to get real good at it," he said. "I'll break."

Ten minutes later, it was clear to me that we would never be billiardsmen of Olympic caliber. Oliver's game was impeded by a formidable girth and, I discovered, rather poor eyesight. As for me, I poked the balls futilely, duffing them here and there, until I managed at last to drop one in a side pocket. It was an act of sheer luck, as I had been aiming for the corner. Still, I cheered my lucky success until Oliver informed me that I had failed to "call the shot."

I looked incredulous.

"It has to come back out," he said, plucking the ball from the pocket and placing it on the marker.

I accused him of making up these ridiculous rules to serve his own advantage, to which he took offence, labelling me with a string of derogatory grade-seven-level nouns. Shortly thereafter I called him a fat loser and he called me a retarded orangutan, and I left his house, scuppering my prospects with the perfect sister.

Also left behind was my fantasy partnership with Trevor White, my career as a songwriter sunk before it had begun. I never exchanged another word with Trevor White after that day. Shortly after the Christmas break, his family moved to Thunder Bay, and he disappeared forever into legend.

In any case, Harry refused to allow my assertion that luck played even a small part in the game of billiards. "Skill and science, kid, skill and science. Luck is for poker."

I never felt especially endowed with skill or luck.

- - -

The orange and magenta is draining from the sky. I can feel the darkness descending like a cool blanket as I lie in this cornfield and await Eternal Sleep. But perhaps I am being overly pessimistic, perhaps I lack *gumption*, as Harry so frequently asserted, for I have just pulled off a miracle, the second of my life, a feat of defiance against an increasingly cynical world, the second in a set of extraordinary bookends to bracket my blessed life. Only moments ago, without a single soul present as witness, I mustered the strength to roll onto my back. Praise god! Where is the media when you need them?

I can hardly describe the relief I feel. There is something sharp now driving into one of my kidneys and I embrace the pain, wallow in it. The North Dakota sky is vast and unclouded, beginning to light up with stars. *Look at that, Harry. Heaven.* The infinite galaxy wavers behind my tears.

15

All is blue.

The moment of my death must have come and gone without my noticing. For this I suppose I should be grateful. Quick and painless is the preferred method. But I am a little disappointed, would have liked an opportunity to say something profound, a few parting words for posterity, even though there was no one to receive them except a pair of nosy crows. Harry expired on the heels of a rather mundane *Auck!*, which should make me feel better about my own stony silence, but doesn't. I feel nothing except fearless exultation and a rush of air that tussles my bangs and whistles past my ears. I am flying through an infinite sea of blue, en route, presumably, to cloud nine, or wherever trustees of the minor faiths are assigned for their Everlasting Peace. Only there are no clouds in sight, not even a small, puffy one, off in a corner. There is only blue.

But wait! There is something entering my peripheral vision, a crack in the otherwise seamless cerulean fabric. *Lo, Harry, look yonder.* I know he's around here somewhere. *Heaven is invaded by UFOs.*

- - -

Harry was always a detractor of all things unknown or unknowable. With predictable scorn, he derided the industry of fortune telling, with its *hocus-pocus* and its gullible adherents. Clairvoyants and palm readers were charlatans, while mediums, with their promise of contact with the dead, bordered on the criminal.

"I'm sure," said Harry, "these people can find things to do, other than swindling poor widows."

Big Foot hunters, conspiracy theorists, alien abductees, exorcists, ghost busters, all fell squarely in the absurd. The notion that our planet was regularly visited by little green men from coordinates beyond Ursa Minor was, to Harry, simply preposterous. When he caught me with a dog-eared copy of Von Daniken's seminal work, *Chariots of the Gods*, he launched into one of his well-worn harangues about the perils of literature.

I had just returned from another dreary day of high school, and when I dropped my satchel on the floor next to the till, where Harry was pricing down some of the older stock, the offending paperback shook loose and dropped to the floor. The old duffer's eyesight was better than I had thought.

"What's this?" He picked up the book.

"A book," I said, with a resigned sigh.

Harry gave me a hard look. "I know it's a book, Mavis. Don't be a smart-aleck." He inspected the front cover. "I've heard about this one."

I nodded, tried to inject my voice with a casual tone. "It's a popular book. You should read it." I knew he wouldn't. Harry hadn't read a book since his own school days.

"It's one of those books about Martians." He dropped it on the counter.

"Well," I said, "it doesn't mention Martians *specifically*."

"Fairy tales and gibberish. I thought we'd talked about this before. Did you forget that conversation?"

"It's not fair, Harry." I was never able to bring myself to call him Dad. "Just because you don't believe it, doesn't mean I can't."

"Yes, it does."

"It's not fair." I continued to throw that timeworn phrase at the old duffer, even though I was perfectly aware that nothing about life was fair.

He picked up a Stanley cross-cut saw (which was now marked down to less than wholesale) and wobbled it ominously in the air between us. "You see this?" His sharp tone attracted the wary attention of our only customer, who was milling by the paint brushes.

"Yes."

"What is it?"

"A saw."

"A saw, that's right." He pressed the business edge of the saw against the corner of the wooden counter. "Tell me what will happen if I move this saw back and forth."

From the corner of my eye, I thought I detected a nugget of interest from the customer, who must have been wondering if there was a seminar on proper hewing techniques taking place at the front of the store.

Harry was impatient for my answer. "What will happen?"

"Um, it will cut the wood?" I'm not sure why I made this a question. I certainly knew what a saw did.

"Correct." He lowered the saw, placed it back on the display. "Now, show me a UFO."

I glanced around the store, in case we had one in stock. "I can't," I admitted.

"Show me a Martian."

"I can't. But that's not—"

"Show me evidence, no matter how small, that Martians exist. If you can do that, I'll give you a ten dollar bill. Any piece of evidence and I'll buy you a new bicycle...no, I'll send you to Disneyland. Just show me the evidence."

"Of course I can't. You're not—"

But he refused to hear my argument. He stalked away to attend our lone and perplexed customer. And I was afterward more careful about stuffing my books to the very bottom of my satchel.

- - -

Now that I have my evidence, Harry is not to be found. Where is the old duffer when I need him? *I want my bicycle, Harry. I want Disneyland.*

Too late, too late.

My unidentified flying object, my ticket to the Magic Kingdom, draws further into my line of sight, and I swoop down in order to meet it halfway. But it must be farther away than I first thought, because no matter how much speed I gain, it remains little more than a gleaming speck. It leaves in its wake a cottony tail of white smoke, not unlike today's modern...um...jetliners.

I feel like a fool.

An honest mistake. I was bamboozled by this flawless firmament, an illusion of infinite blue, intensified by the squirrelly effects of my withdrawal from nicotine, and bolstered by the belief—no, the absolute certainty!—that I would not survive the night in this cornfield. I was hoodwinked by a clear prairie sky, by a northerly wind that never seems to let up in this flattened and exposed piece of the world, by the numbness that is slowly overtaking my body as my transmogrification into a living fossil progresses.

He's alive! cries Doctor Frankenstein. *He's alive!* Before I've had time to think about it, I have sat up. Miracle Mavis strikes again!

I knuckle away the grit that has accumulated in the corners of my eyes and glance yonder. The car sits where I parked it the day before, ten yards away, at the shoulder of some unidentified and isolated road. The low morning sun illuminates Harry's tilted face, giving him a peaceful aspect and an angelic glow. A trick of the morning light causes his wings to flutter. I already know this will be a day filled with miracles. And here comes another one: see the monster, cobbled together with used parts and unwanted leftovers, face twisted into a revolting grimace, reeking of earth and moist towelettes, quivering from the effects of rebirth, see him rise from the ground and stand erect in a remote cornfield, take in all the degrees of the horizon, shuffling his bearish feet tentatively as he turns (his neck having a limited swivel arc), see him brush the dust from his elbows and attempt perambulation, swagger towards the singular anachronism in this panoramic scene of bucolic charm, the green Pinto. *See Spot run.*

After what seems like an eternity, I am once again sitting in the car. *Hello, Harry. Did you miss me?* The engine starts with an eager growl, as if the Pinto, too, has been blessed with a new lease on life. While waiting for the engine to warm, I light a Rothman's and fill the compartment with glorious fumes. O, how I had missed the bouquet of that sacred agricultural conflagration!

I don't realize how cold I am until the heat begins to trickle out of the vents, setting my bones to thaw. By the time I drop the spent butt out the window, the convulsions begin to subside, and some of the feeling returns to my limbs. The radio plays the opening bars to Johnny Nash's classic, *I Can See Clearly Now.* I pass a last glance over my shoulder, towards the cornfield that nearly became my final resting place. It seems harmless now. I spin the wheels, throw some gravel, steer the car on to the road. The journey has resumed, a little behind schedule, but back on track. *Tally ho!*

I locate the Interstate without much trouble and the Pinto rolls nicely into the flow. I draw up behind a twenty-five-foot Prowler, settling in to ride the trailer's slipstream up to the border.

Harry is a little grey around the cheeks, but otherwise looks good, seems to be enjoying the ride. *Look, Harry, cows!* But I think he has finally exhausted his enthusiasm for the species, lost his taste for the majestic rural scenery altogether. I admit the countryside has lost some of its previous lustre for me, too; I suppose a lingering symptom of having spent the night prone in a field.

The truth is, I am beginning to miss the Palaeolithic grinding of the Toronto streetcars, the sweeping, indecipherable *gangsta* tags that bespatter every available surface, the collective hum of two-point-three-million air conditioners, the rattling carcasses we like to call taxis. I miss the unexpected zephyrs, redolent of sausage-dogs and garbage, that embrace me as I walked my city streets; I miss the artful pose of the warped blue bicycle frame, stripped of its useful components, chained to the light standard in front of the store; I even miss the mournful bray of the bloated, scavenging raccoons that rummage the trash bins in the alley outside my bedroom window.

If only Harry hadn't gone and died, I could have declared this road trip an *adventure,* something positive we could have reminisced about for years to come. We had travelled farther than either of us had ever been before, seen new skylines rising over the horizon, witnessed stunning foreign sunsets, driven alongside awesome, turbulent rivers. On the road, we were able to bond in a way that wasn't possible back home, living amidst all that past history, with the dreary family business hanging between us like a dead weight we were trying to balance. Our journey into the strange—or at least the unknown—had forced us to pull together, to work as a team to navigate this new landscape. Sure, we picked at each other's scabs, bickered as we always had, but it was a token effort for both of us. We were changing in subtle ways; though I can't say whether Harry was loosening up in his old age, or whether I was becoming more like him. Either way, it was a positive step for us.

But now, with all this time on my own to think, I can't help wondering if Harry gave up a little too easily, as if he wanted to get there—the Eternal Palace—ahead of me. Maybe he felt it was the natural order of things, the father going before the son. And perhaps he was a little put out that for the past three years, since the diagnosis of my fatal disease, it had all been about *me*, all about my impending death.

I shouldn't have such thoughts about the old dead duffer. I know that I should be grieving, sorry for my loss. In death, Harry should have shed the superficial remnants of all those little things that, in life, had made him irritating or narrow-minded or frustratingly tight-lipped. I should be eulogising him as the most generous of men, honest, gracious, a noble spirit, a rare, sensitive soul. It's more than a mere defence mechanism that causes us to forget the unlikable qualities of the deceased. We really do seem to love them more after they're dead, or at least dislike them less. We are able to love them in a way, and with a freedom, that we were not permitted while they lived. The predictable steps through the grieving process are a means of packaging the deceased, wrapping the memories of them in a comfortable lace shawl and placing them in a cosy corner of the mind, where they can be visited with relative fondness.

But for the moment I am shielded from grief by the impenetrable armour of my mission to get Harry across the border, back to his native soil. I will do this for Harry, if it's the last thing I do. And it may well be.

At least this expedition has not been boring. All these years, I believed I was no thrill-seeker, that my family history resounded with dullness, that my name, Templeton, loosely translated, meant *humdrum*. After all, the recent Templetons have uniformly lacked spirit, have shed their faith, like a snake giving up its skin, because faith calls for commitment, and commitment leads almost certainly to action, and action, as we all know, is accompanied by a degree of risk. And how much risk is too much? One can't live in the world without encountering random dangers—a falling tree, roaming wolves, pollen—but how to keep it to a minimum? Simple enough: don't put yourself in the way of risk. Advice to live by. Not for my recent ancestors, these unnecessary risks.

Did this make them cowards? Did their inaction, their stillness, suggest a lack of integrity or moral fibre? Who am I to say? I'm one of them. All I know is, they donned camouflage garb, ducked their heads below the trench and plugged index fingers into ears.

To dig a little deeper, go back a little further and trace my lineage to its thirteenth century roots in Ayrshire (which I recently did, with the aid of the Public Library), one finds an abundance of heroes. They called themselves "Crusaders," but they were also rectors, landlords, community leaders, keepers of the lands and of the faith. They were nothing short of heroes at a time, and in a world, fraught with risk. How could I fail to be impressed with such blood coursing through my veins? Just look at the Templeton coat of arms: the silver church below a white lamb waving a red banner of victory. Let the Valentine clan chew on that! In any case, I'll have some stories to tell when I return. If I am lucky, there will be a kindly nurse at Traxco-Meriwether Industries who might lend a sympathetic ear to my unbelievable tales. A nurse named John, if I have any luck at all.

Yes, once I deliver us safely back to Canadian turf, I will continue on to our destination, as planned. I've reached this decision without assistance or counsel, and I am certain it is the right one. They will surely know what to do with Harry. And to avert suspicion, I will inform them Harry was well and alive when we pulled into their vast multi-level parkade, that he was overcome by the extortionate fee they demand from visitors who merely wish to park their car. The old duffer was always sensitive about parting with his precious rupees.

A sign has just informed me the border approaches: 14 miles. Once I do a rough conversion to kilometres, nerves begin to settle in. Stuck as I am behind the trailer's ample posterior, my view ahead is peripheral, but I detect nothing out there in the wings to evince this approaching change.

On my map, the borders are delineated by razor-sharp lines. Over the past few days I have crossed a number of these lines and, apart from the Bluewater bridge—which was an awe-inspiring piece of engineering, and a fitting marker of international friendship—they have been uniformly disappointing. A sign reading, "You are leaving here," another sign reading "You are entering there." Nothing topographical to distinguish Here from There. Only once, as we rolled out of Illinois and into Wisconsin, was there an indication that something had changed: inches past the "You are leaving Illinois" signpost, the smooth and black asphalt abruptly ended, became a mottled and bumpy patchwork that was unworthy of its "highway" designation. It was clear to me whose tax dollars were being put to practical use. *I'll miss you, Illinois!*

Time to get my story straight:

State your citizenship.
"Canadian, sir."
What about him? Is he all right?
"Oh, that's Harry. He's been a little under the weather. I warned him not to order the shrimp."
His citizenship?
"He's Canadian, too. We're both Canadian. Would you like to see our passports? I have them right here."
What was your business in the United States?
"Just passing through, sir, on our way to Edmonton, Alberta. It's a shortcut, believe it or not."
How long have you been in the United States?
"Since Monday afternoon, sir. So that's, what, four days?"
Are you bringing any goods purchased in the United States?
"No, sir. Harry doesn't like to shop. A bit of a skinflint, to tell the truth."
Any firearms, weapons of any kind, alcohol, drugs, wildlife, agricultural products?
"There are my blood pills, sir. I have a doctor's prescription."
Have you visited a farm during the past four days?
"No, sir." (An egregious and convincing lie. Damn you, cornfield!)
Don't see many of these on the road, nowadays.
"Thirty years of faithful service. All original, even the paint. Leaf green, that's what they called it in the brochure. Yes, sir, she's a classic."
Move along, gentlemen. Have a nice day, and welcome back to Canada.

The rehearsal is a success.

I am trusting that our border guard, whoever he is—and assuming he is not cut from the same bolt as old Shemp, B.G. (Ret.) (and wife-killer)—will act true to good Canadian form, nod politely and go out of his way not to offend. On top of everything else that has happened to me during this eventful voyage, I don't wish to be disillusioned about my national identity.

I give Harry a final inspection, and regret not having a hat for him to wear, something to cast a bit of shade over his pale features. A pair of sunglasses, too, I think; but then reconsider, I'm wrong about the sunglasses. They would only arouse suspicion. *Onward!* I bellow at Harry's hatless head.

16

A distance of fourteen miles is equivalent to approximately twenty-two-and-a-half kilometres. The green Pinto, which was assembled some years before my homeland converted to the more sensible metric system, was outfitted with a speedometer that conformed to the old imperial standards, those still used by the United States of America. I am cruising at fifty miles per hour, which, by modern Canadian measure, is approximately eighty kilometres. My travel time to the border is roughly seventeen minutes. But who's counting?

I ride the slipstream generated by the Prowler and tap my thumbs on the rim of the steering wheel. *Layla* ekes out of the radio. My memory cells fill in the holes lost to a poor signal and inadequate speakers. *A love story, Harry. Love is in the air.*

Nine miles.

Before the second refrain, we drive into a wall of water. It takes a harrowing moment for me to remember where the wiper switch is located, and then two imperfect triangles open up before me. Raindrops the size of pennies slam against the hood of the car, against the windshield, against the road, exploding on impact into individual bursts of blinding mist. Eric Clapton disappears beneath the roar of the downpour. I let up on the gas pedal, but that causes a set of brilliant lights to grow ominously in my rearview mirror. A transport truck, judging by the height of the lights, an impatient driver hovering over the vast wheel, cursing the puny insecurity that blocks his way. I gently toe the accelerator back up to cruising speed.

Five miles.

I want more than anything to smoke, but I don't dare remove my hands, even one of my hands, from the steering wheel. A kernel of tension appears between my shoulder blades, spreads outward to grip my shoulders, arms, chest. My stomach chooses this moment to rebel against its contents, the former Mexican Fiesta. The party is over. But there is no stopping, not even if a Mobil station appears in my peripheral sightline, which it doesn't. Under no circumstance am I going to encourage a rear end collision in this Pinto. Through the air vent comes the smell of mashed worms.

Three miles.

But who's counting?

Two red rectangles of light hover in the mist in front of me. The Prowler's tail lights. Now and then, they flash brighter for an instant. Someone up ahead is riding the brake. A Nervous Nelly. Flashes of lightning fill the cockpit with dazzling brilliance. As spots float across my retina, I realize it is the truck behind, shooting its high beams into my mirrors. *Where does he expect me to go?* I ask Harry. I had heard that long-haul truckers routinely pump themselves with drugs, caffeine pills, amphetamines, cocaine, anything to keep them awake. They molest hitchhikers, haul mobile casinos and brothels, dabble in serial murder to break the tedium of the job. One can't get through life without hearing such things, rumours, myths, partial truths. Sometimes, like this moment, for instance, it's better not to know.

And while I try to forget everything I had ever heard, the odometer slowly rolls over, and the white needle of the speedometer subtly moves in a counter-clockwise direction as I maintain my distance from the leading trailer, which is slowing. I think I can hear, beneath the pounding rain, a weather report peeping out of the radio. As if it would help me get through this. The forecast calls for pain, as the song goes.

One hundred and fifty yards.

The sudden appearance of a guardrail, just off the right shoulder, catches my eye. What does this guardrail mean? I envy the trucker his elevated status. Is the rain easing off, or am I just getting used to it? Pintos and their exploding rear ends: fact or fiction? Is the tail-gating trucker on drugs? Is he asleep up there? How many adults will a twenty-five-foot Prowler sleep comfortably? Is the weatherman aware it's raining over here?

The impact is not as intense as I might have imagined. Unlike the modern automobile, with its crumple zones and impact beams and safety cages, a trailer is not engineered to bear up in a collision so much as give way to it. Still, this Prowler's rear end is effectively defended by a steel bumper, situated at a height that invites the nose of the Pinto to wedge cosily underneath.

Every adult knows it's not safe to ride in a trailer as it is being towed from one campground to the next. There is the risk of a hitch failure, or a propane tank failure, or, most likely of all, a collision with some inattentive motorist. It happens all the time, so I've heard. Pay attention, children, there's a reason for all these rules.

As my nose is so rudely sniffing the trailer's behind like a curious canine, I make note of the brilliant white light that is bleaching the cockpit of the Pinto, and I think: Is this the light of god shining down on me? *Look out, Harry, here I come!*

The second impact is better described as a nudge. The transport truck, decelerating to a speed of approximately five-miles-per-hour and pregnant with inertia, embraces me from behind, kisses my ass, to put a somewhat crude spin on it, with just enough force to ensure my connection to the trailer is secure.

And then everything stops.

Including the rain, which is migrating south. Including the Pinto's mangled engine.

But not everything stops, because there is the crackle of sporting news issuing from beneath the Pinto's dashboard, and there is the Peterbilt's powerful engine purring over my shoulder, and there is shouting from several directions, footsteps approaching. Everything is getting uniformly further away as my thumping heartbeat fills my skull with its irregular rhythm.

I feel myself falling, nothing to do but wait for sudden contact with the ground.

- - -

Another irrational fear I carry from childhood is of high places, what a psychologist would call *acrophobia*. Many people have this fear and I dare suggest it's not so irrational when you think about it. Any smart-aleck will tell you it's not the height you should be afraid of, it's not the fall from that height that ought to put the fear of Pete in you, 'cause it's the landing that's gonna kill you. *Har har*. Vertigo, a word used to describe the dizzying effects one feels when standing in a high place, is often a symptom of acrophobia. Someone once made a movie about that effect.

I am still falling—or more like floating in a downward direction. But where is the impact?

Everything takes too long, these days. No matter how quickly we progress—instant communication, supersonic travel, accelerated education—it's never fast enough to satisfy. My generation was the first to articulate and act upon this universal injustice, as it applies to the young, the original shaggy rebels with our rallies and marches and unfurled banners decrying the slowness of the changes we required. We were the first to say, *We don't want it now, we want it yesterday!* I blame television, although Harry would have disagreed. If I had done my duty as a human male and propagated my species, my children would be complaining to me about waiting forty-five seconds for a music download. *Forty-five seconds, Dad!* What are you going to do?

There is a tugging in my chest, the needles are *scratching-scratching*. I had predicted the big one, but I sense this may be just another warning tremor. I keep my eyes clamped shut and remain still, as if I can somehow avert the heart attack by sheer will. *Come on, little fella, don't give up on me, yet.*

During the seven-tenths of a second preceding my initial contact with the Prowler, I had turned the steering wheel hard right, too little and too late to avoid the collision, but enough to put the Pinto at a slight angle. And because I was a little off-square when the transport rig nudged my hindquarters, the pressure forced the driver's side door outward, breaking the metal seal and leaving it slightly ajar. Whether dumb luck or act of god, I am withholding judgment for now; either way, it saved my life, because I am not falling so much as flying, supported in my Superman pose by a masculine presence, yanked from the tin wreckage—with relative ease, thanks to the driver's-side door malfunction—by means of manly arms. So, when I open my eyes, what I see is the asphalt passing below me, some all-weather hiking boots trampling the paved landscape.

My anonymous saviour sets me down on the opposite side of the road, leans me gently against the cold metal guardrail. With my legs stretched out in front of me, I feel the cold, wet gravel through my pants, feel a biting Canadian cold front filling the space the rain left behind. Before I can begin to shiver, a rugged face lowers itself into view.

"You okay, buddy?" asks the man. He wears the uniform of a Boy Scout leader. He is a walking collage of badges and pins. He wears a neckerchief, secured by a brilliant gold clip. He looks prepared for anything.

I move my head noncommittally. The Boy Scout leader lays a bearish hand on my shoulder, but I do not feel it.

"Hang in there," he says, and then his face lifts out of the scene.

Now I am looking at the green Pinto, wedged between trailer and truck. It doesn't look so bad from where I sit. Maybe not a total write-off. A little insurance money to pound out the dents and give her a fresh coat of paint, maybe red, with a white racing stripe up the hood and over the roof, maybe a twenty-first century sound system, one of those gas pedals shaped like a foot. *Times, they are changing, you old duffer.*

And I see Harry, his familiar profile, head tilted forward, looking down at his knees, his glasses gone, ejected from his nose during the impact, the rest of him safely restrained by the seatbelt. He looks incomplete without the glasses, looks dead, as if his spectacles could conceal his lack of soul.

And here we are again, Harry trapped in the car, ten yards away, and me, helpless on the ground, exposed to the whims of nature, immobilized by fate. The urge to get up off the wet ground is stronger than my feeble bones can manage. My left leg, the one long-locked in place, is now bent at an unnatural angle, the lower half pointing thirty degrees north. I am now a casualty, a statistic. There is pain down there, but it is far away, which is both the curse and the blessing of my greater ailment; the further it progresses, the less I feel.

And I see something move in the corner of my eye, a hand waving, just to my left. A child, a girl about eight, observing me from the parted curtains in the Prowler. Had she been in there the whole time? I shudder at the thought. She waves a small hand at me and ducks back into the darkness of the trailer. I know the type: she is shy, but she wants to be noticed all the same. *I see you, little girl.*

And there is more movement on the far side of the Pinto. The Boy Scout leader is there, pulling on the passenger-side door, trying to get it open, get Harry out. There is urgency to his action; he doesn't know the old duffer is dead, has been that way since yesterday and no amount of CPR will bring him back. *Take your time, good buddy. No hurry*, I want to shout, but all that comes out is a vague "Uh—", a sound open to interpretation.

And I see the witnesses gathering on the sidelines, other motorists and passengers looking on, a few pressing buttons on their cell phones, summoning the authorities, calling CNN, letting their agent know they'll be late for the audition due to traffic. But the authorities are already on the scene: men and women in grey uniforms, others in spiffy blue ones, all with spit-polish shoes and stiff collars, the men sporting bristling moustaches. Trained not to smile. Experienced at sniffing out drugs and aliens and liars. They arrive on foot. When I look to my left, I see their booths, Canadian and American, their respective clubhouses on the sidelines where they drink their coffee and smoke their cigarettes and interrogate the liars, punch data into computers, kennel the sniffing dogs.

And I notice for the first time the white painted line, emerging from beneath my damp buttocks and continuing across the blacktop, where it disappears underneath the Pinto. On the south side of the line is stencilled U.S.A., and on the north side is this word: CANADA. I am divided, halfway home, neither here nor there.

And I look at Harry, who waits with grave patience for his rescue. *Sorry, Harry. Another few inches and we'd have been home free.*

And there is a burst of shouting from somewhere south, a fit of agitation from the bystanders who have gathered there. Before I can take my eyes away from Harry, he disappears. In fact, the Pinto disappears. A second transport truck, barrelling towards the Canadian frontier, has emerged from the north edge of the storm at highway speed, unaware of the situation ahead, and, having applied the brakes much too late, met the rear end of the Peterbilt. The force of that connection shifts the Peterbilt forward until its purring grill presses against the rear wall of the Prowler. The Pinto lies like road kill beneath the mighty cab.

And then there are flares burning red on the road to the south.

And I see a worried father walking the little girl away from the trailer. Her forehead is bleeding, but she looks more scared than hurt.

And ambulances begin to arrive.

And state troopers.

And I look for the Boy Scout leader who carried me to safety, but I can't find him, never see him again. He had been standing on the other side of the Pinto, attempting to reach Harry, when the second truck struck the first and the Pinto vanished.

And all this I witness with increasing passivity. The noise, the numbing cold, the dull ache in my too-bent leg, all of it is filtered through a thick layer of submission to some larger force that is lifting me slowly out of the scene. The way the northern trapper, stranded in the whorl of the blizzard, finally surrenders to the drooping eyelids and yawning mouth, and lies down to a peaceful slumber. But as the scene begins to glow like a reflection in a rippling bowl of milk, I grasp the handles of my frail faith and tip myself over, stretch my back across the pebbly roadside, lace my fingers piously across my chest and lock my gaze towards the roiling heaven above.

Just in case.

17

I awoke in an ambulance.

A pretty woman, in a white martial-style shirt festooned with medical insignia, sat on the bench next to where I lay. She gazed out the square windows in rear, seemingly distracted by some faraway thought—something pleasant, or at least mundane, because her face looked untroubled. I imagined she was deciding whether to prepare chicken or fish for dinner, wondering which her boyfriend would prefer.

"Have the chicken," I said.

She turned her pretty eyes to me. "Just relax," she said, no doubt accustomed to the delirious mutterings of her clients. "You'll be fine."

Her smile melted my heart, and I found myself wanting to believe everything she said, including the unlikely assertion that I would be fine; but this fair paramedic didn't have all the information at her fingertips.

"I've never fathered a child," I said.

She patted my hand. "Some men would consider that a blessing."

I was fairly certain she was making reference to her boyfriend, who must have had issues with commitment.

"I'm the last Templeton, you know."

Her eyes wondered if I might have recently escaped from a cult. She was trying to decide how to handle me.

"After I'm gone," I said, "that's the end of the line."

"I'm sure you've got a few good years left. Why don't you just take it easy and enjoy the ride? We'll be there soon."

"Actually, I've pretty much run out of good years. Did I mention that I'm dying?" There was no pity in my voice. In fact, I felt strangely content, as if my troubles were now in someone else's hands, as if all the decisions were now, and forever more, removed from my plate. I was free, and I was unafraid.

She asked me what my Christian name was.

Christian? Did I qualify? I decided to take the risk. "Mavis," I said, without experiencing the usual cringe. "Mavis Templeton."

Her face registered nothing at the revelation of my girly name. "Well, Mavis, you have a broken leg, but you probably won't die from it. You might end up with a bit of a limp, though."

"It's my heart that's broken." Among other things.

She said nothing to this, but though she didn't move away from me physically, her face grew distant. She thought I was flirting with her, and as a scrupulously professional woman, she had a duty to deter my advances.

I wouldn't presume.

"It wasn't the accident that did this to me," I said, touching my chin. "I was born with this monster's face."

"You're not a monster, Mavis. You're just in shock." Her eye contact was now sporadic. I had crossed some invisible line, made the jump from patient to potential nutcase, thanks to a few careless remarks. Well, I've been called worse. In an effort to shut me up, she fiddled with the IV bag that hung between us, increasing the flow of drugs into my system. "The hospital is two minutes away. Just relax."

"Are we in Edmonton already?"

"Edmonton?"

"I thought the drive would be longer."

"Where is Edmonton?"

"It's the gateway to the Great White North," I said, beginning to feel the effects of the intensified IV drip.

"We're not in Edmonton, we're in Grand Forks. We'll be at Altwell Health soon."

I tried to digest this information. "So I'm not in Canada?"

She shook her head, as if the very idea were preposterous, as if Canada were no more real than Lilliput. "Of course not. Here we are." A moment later, the ambulance jolted to a stop, and there was a flurry of activity as my stretcher was bumped out the rear doors of the van. New faces appeared, and the attractive paramedic's face began to retreat. I hadn't even had a chance to ask her name.

"Good-bye!" I shouted, as the gurney rolled towards the glass doors.

The pretty paramedic and her male partner, the driver, remained behind. I was someone else's problem now. She returned a faint smile and lit a cigarette. Her partner whispered something in her ear and she laughed, gave him a little shove. The glass doors whisked closed and we turned a corner.

In the emergency room, I was shifted from the gurney to a large examination platform. I was numb to all but the faintest physical sensations, as if I were separated from my wrecked body by thick padding, and I concluded this was the effect of whatever miraculous fluid was being fed into my veins through the IV. It was a thicker and more pleasant feeling than the dullness caused by my Scleroderma. The emergency room doctor in charge of my case was a tall, gaunt man with an enormous wedge of nose that supported tiny rimless spectacles, and a deeply corrugated brow, rippled by a lifetime of squinting through his myopia and the strain of holding up that colossal beak. He inspected my broken leg with the air of a man who had seen worse. He called out orders to his subordinates and began to cut away the remains of my trousers.

"I don't suppose," I said, to the room at large, "that anyone has a cigarette?" Even during an emergency, needs must be met.

"Those things'll kill you," said a nurse who was close to my ear.

"It's a risk I'm willing to take."

But the discussion of my nicotine habit was a low priority with this group. Someone asked me if I was allergic to anything, especially medications or antibiotics. I responded that I was mildly allergic to New Democrats, but that just earned me a few blank stares. This was a humourless bunch who clearly weren't keeping up with the Canadian political scene. Well, I couldn't blame them, really, given the soporific nature of my country's affairs of state, with its mélange of tedious and gnarly old men in grey suits whose idea of scandal rarely involved former models. Someone else leaned in to my ear and inquired if I might have health insurance, to which I responded by losing consciousness.

- - -

I noticed the sheriff's deputy right away. He was effectively blocking the exit to my private hospital room with his gladiatorial physique. There was some primitive grunting, and I was surprised to discover it was coming from me—a symptom, apparently, of my rise from a pharmacological haze.

"Do you know where you are?" he said, and I marvelled at his ability to speak without moving his lips. But after a few confused moments, I spotted the other gentleman standing at the foot of my bed. This second visitor was more human in proportion, being merely a large man in a plain white dress shirt and grey slacks. He might have been dressed by Harry, except the blue tie had been forgone.

"Who are you?" I asked the second man.

"Special Agent Compton. North Dakota Bureau of Investigation." He held up his identification, as if this were a Hollywood movie. "Do you know what year this is?"

I had just surfaced from a festival of strange, vivid dreams, and hadn't quite shaken off the mist of those subconscious images. My tongue felt as if it were upholstered in suede. "Will it make a difference?"

"Do you know your name, sir?"

"Do *you* know my name?"

Agent Compton's face set, and the goliath at the door shifted menacingly in his creaking boots. "Are you saying you don't know your name, or are you being a smart-aleck?"

I had a sudden vision of Harry, the old duffer, sitting across from me in the kitchen, looking over the rim of his newspaper with a disappointed expression. No one had a lower tolerance for smart-alecks than Harry. And then other memories flooded in: the fatal lunch at Uncle Jim's Mexican Fiesta, Harry's last gasp in the desolate parking lot, a long night face-down in a cornfield, a fender-bender at the border. A phantom whiff of moist towelettes filled my nostrils, caused my gag reflex to shudder.

"I'm not sure what I remember," I said, swallowing bile.

With precise movements, Agent Compton lowered himself into a hard chair near the head of my bed. He smoothed the creases in his slacks with his palms. "Let's start with your name."

"Mavis Templeton." I could give a straight answer, when it suited me.

He nodded, made a brief entry on a small pad, then looked unflinchingly at my repulsive face. "You were involved in an accident on Interstate twenty-nine. Do you remember that?"

I said that I did.

"You were travelling in a green Ford."

"The Pinto. A classic automobile."

"At the time of the accident, who was driving the car?"

"I was."

"There was another man in the car with you."

"Harry, the old duffer."

"What is his relationship to you?"

"Was."

"I beg your pardon?"

"Was. He's dead. You should use the past tense."

"How do you know he's dead?"

"He wasn't a bad father, you know. All in all."

"You haven't answered the question."

"There are no real answers in life, Agent Compton. That's what my faith has taught me."

"There are answers, plenty of them. Let me repeat the question. How do you know your father is dead?"

"How do you know anyone is dead?"

"That's not an answer."

"He stops breathing."

"I think you're being a smart-aleck."

"First he starts sweating, then he gets this look of terror on his face, and with his last breath he says something profound."

"Answer the question, sir."

"It's the greatest and most terrifying question in life: What's on the other side? We fear the unknown, and there is nothing more unknown than what happens to us when we die. You're looking for answers, Agent Compton, and you will get an answer to the biggest question of all, sooner or later. But by then the question won't matter."

He was jotting more notes on his pad, deliberately ignoring my oration.

"Are you a man of faith, Agent Compton?"

He looked up from his pad, but said nothing.

"Too many people wait until the last minute, but that's a risky business, if you ask me. For all we know, 'seniority rules' apply Up

There, just as they do down here. Why take a chance? Grab a faith, any faith, and get some years under your belt before the bell rings. That's my advice to you."

From what I could tell, Agent Compton had plenty of time. I doubted he had reached forty, yet. Of course, I was forty when my legs first started aching. At forty-three, I am a living fossil, a stone monument to a life hardly lived.

"How do you know your father is dead?" This young fellow was tenacious.

"Because he is not here. He has always been there for me, except for those first ten years, or so."

"When the truck collided with your car, your father sustained serious injuries."

I had a brief flashback to that scene. I had been looking at the Pinto, and the old dead duffer strapped in the passenger seat, when it…they…all of it simply vanished, replaced by a juddering black leviathan.

"There was another man there, a boy scout leader. He was trying to get Harry out of the car. One minute he was there, the next minute he and Harry and the car were gone."

Agent Compton tilted his head slightly to the left and tapped his chin with the dull end of his pen. "Jack Horner," he said.

"Jack Horner. Little Jack Horner."

"He died at the scene."

"He was trying to save Harry."

"That might be true."

"He was too late."

"What do you mean?"

"He saved my life, though. He rescued me from the car and then went back for Harry."

It seems to me this accident was an example—a *tragic* example—of how wrong things can go when poor decision-making runs rampant.

See Mavis: driving in disagreeable road conditions, with his stiff legs and slow reflexes, with the rain pelting down and limited visibility. See the trucker: hovering inches off the Pinto's rear end, forty tons of crushing steel bearing down on the tin bug, a stopping distance off the edge of the graph. See the young girl: with a bleeding forehead because she was permitted to ride in the Prowler, even though every sensible adult knows the dangers. See the Boy Scout leader: playing the hero, saving my life and then risking his own to go back for Harry. Fools, all of us. Damned fools! Take one bad decision away from the scenario and reduce the tragedy exponentially. Put one sensible person into the mix and see how things might have turned out. A happy ending, or at least a non-event.

Is it my fault a hero is dead and a little girl hurt, possibly scarred for life? God knows, and He isn't talking. I began to cry, right there in front of Agent Compton and his gladiator. Huge tears launched from my eyes as I wept like a ten-year-old boy who didn't know where he belonged. I sobbed like a man faced with the great terror of the Big Question. And the strange part is, I didn't know exactly why I was crying. Was it Harry? The Boy Scout leader, Jack Horner? My own looming death? Not everything in life has a simple explanation.

Agent Compton waited patiently for this squall of grief to dissipate, and then offered me a clean handkerchief from his pocket. I wiped my eyes and blew my nose, aware that crying did not improve my aspect, and returned the snotty handkerchief.

"Where is Harry now?"

The agent replaced the handkerchief in his pocket. "He's in our custody."

"You've arrested a corpse?"

"In the morgue."

"Round the clock security, I suppose. They get away, now and then, do they?"

"Is everything a joke to you?" He wasn't angry. His question seemed sincere.

"Harry always took everything too seriously. That was his problem. You're in danger of falling into the same trap."

"Life is a serious business, Mister Templeton."

"Life can be a joke, depending on your point of view."

"Your father's death is no joke."

"No."

"The medical examiner performed an autopsy on your father, this morning," he said. "It's a matter of course in a situation like this."

"The Pinto didn't explode."

"I beg your pardon?"

"Don't you find that interesting? It's too bad Harry didn't live long enough to see that old rumour put to rest. He'd be pleased as punch."

"What rumour is that?"

"I'm worried the insurance company won't cover the cost of fixing it. I think it's going to need a new paint job."

"Your car?"

"Of course my car. What are we talking about here?"

"I'd like to know that myself."

"Are you married, Agent Compton?"

He nodded. "Seven years."

"Kids?"

"Two boys."

"Good for you. Your job here is complete."

"Not quite. You're not answering my questions."

"Not *here* here. I mean here, in this life. We were put on this earth to breed, you and I. Nothing more. Shoot our seed into the wind and hope for the best. You must be very proud of your boys."

"Yes."

"I haven't gotten around to it yet, myself. Haven't found the right woman. Still playing the field, as they say."

"There's plenty of time."

"Alas."

"Is there something you'd like to tell me?"

"I'm terminal."

He stopped taking notes and raised an eyebrow. "Cancer?"

"Scleroderma." I gave him a moment to let that sink in.

"Dandruff?"

I laughed for the first time in days, a sudden detonation that caused the gladiator to palm his holster. I can only blame the drugs.

Agent Compton waved a hand over his shoulder. "The doctor didn't mention this…*condition*. He said you had a mild heart attack, and you have a broken leg. And you may be suffering from shock."

"My leg was bent thirty-five degrees north. Seeing as how that leg hasn't bent in any direction for more than a year, I suppose I ought to be grateful. And the only shock was discovering I wasn't in Canada. Come to think of it, maybe you can answer a question for me. Why am I not in Canada?"

"This was the closest hospital."

But he answered a little too quickly. He wasn't telling me everything. I made a face that let him know I was on to him.

"Look, Mister Templeton," he said, flatly. He had recovered his G-man grit. All he needed now was a trench coat and fedora. "Why don't you ask me why my bureau is investigating a simple traffic accident, out in the middle of nowhere?"

"All right."

He waited a moment for me to ask, realized I already had, and went on. "Are you aware that there is a proper procedure for transporting deceased persons across an international border?"

"No."

"It's not an overly complicated procedure. A bit of paperwork, a rubber stamp or two. The applicant requires a death certificate."

"I see, yes."

"Do you?"

"Yes."

"Is there anything you want to tell me?"

"You don't look like a secret agent."

"I'm not a secret agent."

"Where is your trench coat and fedora?"

"I'm a man of finite patience, Mister Templeton."

"If I had to guess, I'd have said you were in advertising. You'd only have to wear more black."

"My brother is an art director at Saatchi & Saatchi. He wears nothing but black."

"Aha!"

"We don't speak."

"I'd give anything to have a brother, even an estranged one. Being an only child is a lonely business."

We ruminated silently on the subject of siblings, or lack thereof.

"I'll tell you what, Mister Templeton," he said, finally. "I'm going to assume, for your sake, that your lack of cooperation in this interview is the result of your recent ordeal. Maybe you are suffering from shock. In any case, it's clear that you are not prepared to answer any of my questions directly, so, instead, I'm going to give you a few answers that I already know. If you feel up to it, you can corroborate my answers. Otherwise, I'll take your silence as affirmation. Is this clear enough?"

"I'm all ears, Agent Compton."

"Okay. First, the medical examiner determined that your father, at the time of the accident, had already been deceased for approximately twenty-four hours. You should know that this is a fairly exact science, these days." He paused to interpret my silence. "All the major injuries to the body appeared to have occurred post-mortem. But since there was so much damage, we can't determine the exact cause of death. Do you know what that means?"

I felt a drowsy haze descending between my guest and me. I'm afraid I yawned at that moment, no disrespect meant to Agent Compton, who was doing a fine job of interrogating me.

"It means we can't rule out foul play."

I wasn't offended by the implication. This former jewel thief can't be so easily hurt. Bad blood will always rise to the surface, sooner or later. Isn't that right?

"And because you attempted to leave the state with a deceased person, that puts it in my jurisdiction."

"You think I killed Harry?"

"I didn't say that. But if you'd like to make a statement, I'd be glad to take it."

"Thank you, no."

"I'm going to be honest with you." With that face, he could have sold me any number of products or services I didn't need, and at that moment I was convinced advertising was his calling. "I know your father died the day before the accident. It's my job now to figure out the manner of death. Frankly, I think he had a heart attack or stroke, something like that. With all due respect, he was not a young man. What I don't understand is why *you*, sir, refuse to cooperate. It's the sort of thing that only brings suspicion down on you. If your father died a natural death, you have nothing to lose by answering my questions in an honest and straightforward way."

Well, there was the crux. What did I have to lose by telling the truth? Everything. Ask Mrs. Wainstock, the righteous vice principal. Ask the warden of Russell Hill Penitentiary, Irene Valentine. And here is a truth that can be taken, coming from me, with a modest grain of salt: people are generally disinclined to accept the word of a man who is as ugly as sin. Handsome is good, ugly is bad. Handsome is truth, ugly is a lie. My cousin David was a sinner of biblical proportions, and yet he never failed to talk his way out of trouble because he was as cute as a button.

Again: what did I have to lose? The small morsel of my remaining dignity. Yes, my number is nearly up. *Ba-dum-pah! Thank you, thank you very much.* My lowercase faith may not get me a beachside penthouse in the Eternal Estates, but it just may get me in the neighbourhood. Here on the home stretch, I thought I was in the clear. I had done my adult best to walk the good path in Harry's moral wake, the safe and decent road. Keep that bad blood in check. And now this. Another page in the file folder awaiting me Upstairs. "What have We here, Mavis? Code seven-dash-four: parricide!" *But I am innocent of the charge.* "O! how many times in a day We hear that line, son? Give Us a break. The truth is written all over your face." *Ask Harry yourself. He must be up here somewhere. Check your files again. I'm innocent, I tell you.* "We'll be the judge of that."

Telling the truth has not always worked for me. The man sitting next to me, demanding the truth, wearing his idealism like a badge of honour, undoubtedly wants justice for all, including me, but he is ultimately destined to be let down by a system that has a different agenda. Real world justice is not about honesty and fairness; it's about answers, an explanation, the convenient disposal of a problem. Who did it? He did. No more questions, Your Honour.

Agent Compton's face set into a hard look. "There are plenty of case files on my desk at the moment that require my attention, Mister Templeton. I don't enjoy wasting my time."

"I find that it's sometimes hard to tell if time has been wasted until afterward, and, of course, by then it's too late. You can't get that time back."

He appeared to not hear what I had said. "Did you have anything to do with your father's death? Yes or no?"

"It's my fault."

At last I had pleased him. "Your fault? How?"

"I forced us to stop for lunch. It was a grave mistake, I should have known better. Harry wasn't ready for anything that exotic. We should have kept driving until we found a better place, one that could make him a grilled cheese sandwich."

"When was this?"

"Wednesday."

"The day prior to the accident?" He scribbled in his note pad. "Do you recall the name of the restaurant?"

"No."

"Do you remember where it was?"

"No."

I was no stool pigeon. Let Michelin and the feds figure it out for themselves.

"Okay, what happened at this restaurant? Did you have a fight?"

"Certainly not. We had lunch, a rather pleasant lunch, although I can't recommend the chili. And my Coke was flat. Apart from that, it was perfectly civilized."

"I don't understand what this has to do with your father's death."

"We were two thousand miles from the ocean."

Agent Compton looked blank, waited for me to explain.

"The bread man never showed up, honey. Don't you see?"

He tapped his chin with his pen, and then jammed it in his shirt pocket. "Tell you what," he said. "I'm going to end this interview right now and let you get some rest. I want to believe you're not jerking me around on purpose. But I'm going to come back tomorrow, and we're going to finish this. How does that sound to you, Mister Templeton?"

"Agent Compton, I like your gumption."

18

The next morning, I saw Agent Compton, but he didn't see me. I had just stepped out of the hospital's gift shop, a fresh pack of Dunhills pressing through my shirt pocket, when I spotted the agent standing in front of the elevator doors across the lobby, this time without his bodyguard. He wore the same grey slacks and white shirt as the day before— his G-man uniform. As he waited for the lift to arrive, he was reading his notes, preparing to finish his interview with me. An interview that would never happen.

I had awakened early with a throbbing leg. The male duty nurse, Randall, had suggested that, rather than increase my morphine drip, I might try getting out of bed and taking a little stroll through the corridors, get my blood circulating.

"You're going to have to get used to those crutches, sooner or later."

Nurse Randall was young and fit, looking as if he'd never had a sick day in his life. He was full of broad smiles and hearty advice, especially as it pertained to diet and exercise, and on those subjects he carried a distinctly pedagogic air that belied his youth. And while I've never been completely comfortable around jocks, I found Randall's cheery confidence contagious.

"The sooner you get moving, the better you'll feel."

I believed him. After so many days, drugged and confined to bed, I was ready to move again. But I had a problem.

Randall smiled his confident smile, knowing that this problem, the first problem of the long day ahead of him, was easily solved. "Get yourself upright, and I'll be right back."

He made it sound easy: *Get yourself upright*. Neither of my legs wanted to bend, one because it was encased in plaster from above the knee to the ankle, the other due to an overdose of collagen—the poison that my body was generating with obscene gusto. My back was sore from inactivity, and my arms, though still somewhat mobile, were weak. My head felt heavy and my heart raced. Even my eyes stung, as if I'd just emerged from a burning building. I was a wreck. But after a few minutes of unrefined flailing, and after generating a few well chosen expletives, I achieved a semblance of uprightness. At first, I sat like a child in a high chair, with my stiff legs cantilevered over the edge of the bed like a pair of fallen trees; but gravity soon took hold, pulling them slowly downward until my heels touched the floor and I was more-or-less in a leaning position. The pain, especially beneath the plastered leg, was exquisitely refreshing, and caused me to forget about my burning eyeballs.

"Good," said Randall, returning just as I gained this precarious position. "Very good, Mister Templeton. Here, take these." He handed me a neatly folded solution to my small problem.

I inspected the clean pants. My own jeans had been cut to ribbons by the emergency room doctor, moments after my arrival at Altwell Health, and the rest of my belongings had been crushed inside the Pinto. I had been left, literally, with only the shirt on my back. "They're quite *blue*," I said, holding them up between us. They were identical to the pants Randall was wearing.

"I always keep a spare in my locker."

"Maybe you could help me get them on," I said, smiling hopefully.

But Randall just glared with good-natured brutality, his active eyebrows insinuating I was acting like a princess. "We'll have to slit the leg part way, to fit the cast through. I'll go get the scissors. You figure out how you're going to get them on." And he trotted off, shoes squeaking healthily. He was right, of course. I no longer had Harry to help me. I was on my own. I needed to figure out a few things for myself. Like, for instance, how to dress myself. I didn't panic. I didn't even swear. Not much. If I had learned anything during the progression of my illness, it was that I could no longer take simple things for granted. After only the briefest struggle, I concluded that getting socks on my feet was a pipe dream; I would go sock-less. The pants were another issue. I could not forgo pants without attracting the wrong kind of attention. I had to find a way to get them on, if for no other reason than to spare myself the humiliation of facing Randall with this failure.

To an observer, it might have seemed as if I were wrestling a ghost, limbs wheeling, head joggling, straining against some unseen force. Suffice to say I broke a sweat, which raised me in Randall's esteem when he returned with the scissors. I had the blue pants as far as my knees, and could get them no farther without the slit.

Randall hooted. "Good work!" He gave my shoulder a hearty slap, which I didn't feel.

Moments later, I was dressed and mobile.

Randall brushed some invisible dirt from my shoulder and adjusted my collar. "Just up and down the hall, now."

"Sure, sure," I said, setting off on my new crutches, a little unsteadily.

He proudly watched me go, offering a coach's encouragement. "That's it. Check your balance. Watch out for that cart. Don't forget to stay on the third floor."

The problem was this: Altwell Health was, for better or worse, a smoke-free environment. Addiction has no respect for rules. The third floor would not do.

On the elevator ride down, I struck up a conversation with a shrivelled geezer named Berle. Berle told me, with no small relief, that he was about to die, at long last. I could see why: emphysema. The oxygen tank was a giveaway. With every laboured breath, it seemed Berle's entire body was expanding and contracting, attempting to extract every molecule of oxygen it could, before the end. "Don't get me wrong," he said. "I don't *want* to die. I'm just tired of living like this." He waved a weary hand at his oxygen supply. "Takes all the fun out of living when you can't breathe."

I let Berle know that I, myself, was in the process of dying from Scleroderma, which I felt put us on common ground. But the old codger seemed genuinely distressed by my news. "Terrible!" he wheezed.

"We all have to go sometime," I said, philosophically.

Berle shook his head. With his failing lungs, the words did not come easily. "Too young, too young," he wheezed. I tried to make calming noises, tell him it was all right, reassure him that I was ready for it, and so on, but he put up a knobbly finger and collected a deep breath. "I'm eighty-six," he said, at last. "No matter what they say, what I'm going to die from is *old age*. You are too young to go. That's the difference."

I agreed out of politeness.

The elevator dinged and the door opened to the lobby. I bobbed forward on my crutches and Berle shuffled behind in his slippers, pulling his mobile oxygen tank along like a dog on a leash. I bade him well for his remaining time and he wished me likewise, and I made for the gift shop near the exit, feeling surprisingly good about life.

Soon after that, I saw Agent Compton across the lobby, looking thoughtful and earnest. He was in the wrong business, and I felt sorry for him as I made for the front doors. He deserved a better life with his wife and sons. I quietly prayed that he would reconcile with his estranged brother, the art director.

My first draw on a Dunhill made my head swim and my lungs burn in a satisfying way. It had been days since my last cigarette. The morning air carried a hint of winter, causing me to shiver as I stood under the portico and surveyed the surrounding neighbourhood—which consisted of wide thoroughfares, funnelling traffic swiftly past clusters of blocky, uniformly monotonous Factory Outlets, discernible only by their Las Vegas-scale signage. At five storeys, Altwell Health was the tallest building I could see from where I stood, but its designers had clearly put little thought into aesthetics, unless they had intended the plain concrete box to blend in seamlessly with the nearby Sight&Sound Superstore and Sofa-Rama. Well, nobody said a hospital had to be beautiful. So much for the view.

Still too early for visitors at the hospital, most of the people coming and going were staff, glowing in Altwell blue. It seemed to me those going in were happier than those coming out; maybe just coincidence. After tossing the third cigarette butt into the gutter, I watched a red-and-yellow taxi pull up. A well-dressed woman emerged from the back seat, tugging a leather briefcase. Not a nurse, I thought, and not a doctor; perhaps a senior administrator or a member of the board of directors—one of the few who decided who was entitled to help from Altwell Health, a difficult fiduciary decision. She disappeared briskly through the glass doors.

I turned my attention back to the taxi, which idled just a few yards away. The driver appeared to be concentrating on something in his lap. Consulting a map? Counting his money? Picking a ketchup stain off his slacks? I had never been inside a taxi. Harry had steadfastly refused to authorise such an extravagant expenditure. And because the old duffer was repeatedly offended by the Toronto cab drivers' lack of roadway skill and manners, he balked at the idea of employing them, preferring, when the rare need arose, to suffer the crowded tedium of public transit. But I was intrigued. To be honest, I couldn't help thinking this might be my last chance to have a hack experience. So I pushed away from the pillar I'd been leaning against and swung forward on my crutches.

When I tapped a knuckle on the glass, the driver looked up from his magazine and lowered the passenger-side window. I leaned down as far as I was able and said, "Is there a bus station in this town?"

I angled awkwardly across the rear bench, hardly burdened at all with my few remaining belongings: wallet (passport enclosed), crutches, Cherokee shirt (red), blue pants (one leg slit with surgical precision), brown loafers, seventeen Dunhill cigarettes, Bic lighter (purple). All of which were jostled mercilessly. The taxi appeared to no longer have a functioning suspension. Coming from someone who crossed half the continent in a Pinto, to call this a rough ride was significant.

"What kind of car is this?" I asked, trying to make it seem like a friendly enquiry.

The driver caught me in the mirror with a lethal glare. "Is Chayvee!"

"Ah," I said, as if I had understood. If I had owned dentures, I'd have been searching for them on the floor by now.

"Amriken!" he shouted over the roar of the engine.

We suddenly bottomed out on an insignificant flaw in the pavement.

"I beg your pardon?"

"Amriken Chayvee!" He pounded the steering wheel, to emphasize his point.

"Ah," I repeated. The conversation petered out after that, the driver concentrating on a sequence of near-misses, while I attempted to not slide to the floor. But Grand Forks is a small city, and an objective onlooker would note that the drive took only a few minutes, and not the several terrifying hours it had seemed to me. We rattled to a stop near the entrance to a building that must have looked, when it was built back in the Fifties, like a sneak peek into the "Future." A plaque beneath an abstract chrome sculpture informed me the building's original function was as the city's new opera house. Twenty years later, around the time Harry traded in the old Nash for Ford's revolutionary Pinto, a committee finally acknowledged that the structure was better suited, stylistically and acoustically, to housing busses. Mozart was shifted to a better facility across town.

When I stepped inside the bus station, I understood how any self-respecting tenor would be offended. The din was a living thing, hovering over us like a noisy, irritating drizzle as we travellers followed the signs that directed us to the ticket counters and embarkation gates. I purchased a one-way ticket and waited briefly at platform D, enjoying the hubbub around me. It felt good to be a part of the moving world again. A short time later, I was settled in the rear seat of a Greyhound coach, bound for the border, and points north. Final stop: Winnipeg.

I was sorry to have missed Agent Compton. I had enjoyed our time together. I hadn't meant to skip town when I left the third floor and descended to the lobby; my unofficial discharge from the hospital was not premeditated. But at this stage in my life, it's hard to let opportunities pass. One of the gods had brought me that taxi—a gift I could not refuse. Well, I can't deny I'd had the foresight to bring my wallet and passport as I tipped away on my new crutches. Anyway, I'm sure Agent Compton would have gained little by asking me more questions. The best thing was to file the paperwork and close the case. Agent Compton would be home in time to have dinner with his family, spend a little quality time with his growing boys. The secret to a successful life, I've learned, is in setting priorities. My own priority, I realized, was to get home, and then to formulate a plan to get Harry back.

Seated next to me on the bus was a grandmother named Earlene, soft and plump and smelling of cookie dough. Earlene was returning home, to the town of Brandon, after spending a week with her grown daughter, who had married an American and now lived in a nice neighbourhood in a Grand Forks suburb. While I nodded politely and made agreeable noises, Earlene showed me pictures of her grandchildren. I let her know that, while I approved of children in principle, I had none of my own. I chose not to let on that I was dying.

After squeezing her plump backside into the adjoining chair, she acknowledged me with a kind smile and noticed my blue pants. She introduced herself and then asked if I was a nurse. I replied no, but I was considering a change of career, and was trying on the uniform to see how it felt. It was a harmless joke on my part.

"And how does it feel?" she asked, in all seriousness.

"You know," I said, "I think it feels pretty good."

"My youngest sister, Del, she's been a nurse for forty years. Heavens! The varicose veins on that woman. But she loves the work. Myself, I had a sit-down job, just part-time, you understand, answering the phones. My husband, rest his soul, he needed me at home. I guess we're old fashioned that way. Anyways, at least I wasn't on my feet all day, like poor Del."

"I have a little trouble standing for long periods, myself," I said.

Earlene laughed, a sound like someone walking softly on gravel. "I imagine you would," she said, rapping her knuckles lightly on the plaster cast that encased my broken leg. It made a hard, slightly hollow sound. She could have rapped on my thigh, six inches above the cast, and got almost the same effect. I was as hollow as a chocolate Easter bunny.

And I remembered Harry, during one of his rare attempts at levity, trying (for some reason I could not recall) to make me smile. He opened his mouth as wide as it would get, and then rapped his knuckles on the top of his skull. It made the very same hard, slightly hollow sound that my cast made when Earlene knocked on it. "Nothing inside," Harry had said. "Empty as a coconut." He knocked a few more times and grinned like an idiot. I must have smiled after that, if only for seeing Harry try so hard to be amusing. But the smart-aleck in me couldn't resist reminding him, "Coconuts aren't empty. They're filled with a fibrous pulp and about a pint of water." That took the wind out of his sails, as I remember it. My god, I was a terrible smart-aleck.

I confess I did not pay strict attention as Earlene prattled on about her family history. Other people's children and grandchildren are ultimately not very interesting. She was like a television set left on, even when no one was actually watching it, a soothing wash of sound.

Earlene eventually ran out of stories and went quiet, and I noticed she was fiddling nervously with the strap on her purse. Her calm and cheerful disposition seemed to have gone. "I hate this part of the trip," she said, when she saw me watching her.

"What part is that?"

She pointed a finger at a passing road sign that announced our imminent arrival at the border. "Customs." She pulled a wad of Kleenex from her purse, didn't seem to know what to do with it, and stuffed it back in the purse. "They just make me so nervous. I don't know why. It's their manner, I guess. No matter how many times I cross the border, I never seem to get used to them."

I gazed out the window, looking for…I don't know…something familiar. The last time I had been here, there hadn't been much in the way of landmarks, apart from the metal guardrail; the overriding feature, as I recall, had been a pounding rain that had obliterated everything else, at least in my mind. So, what did I expect to see out the window? Fading skid marks? A bent hubcap lying in the gutter? Blood stain? As the bus slowed down, I did see something, but it was not familiar; it had been placed there recently. Just off the east shoulder, within view of the Customs barracks, which were now visible just ahead, was a small white cross that was planted in the grass and adorned with a fresh wreath. I didn't need a closer look to know what it was: a marker for a fallen hero, a Boy Scout leader who had been prepared for anything, who came to my rescue, heedless of his own safety, and gave his life in the line of duty.

The scene disappeared in a rippling blur as I was suddenly unmanned.

"Everything all right, Mavis?"

I was turned away from Earlene, so she couldn't see me cry. "I'm allergic to wheat," I said, passing my sleeve across my eyes.

"Poor thing. Two of my grandchildren have asthma, and the other one can't eat strawberries. I don't know what it is, these days. So many of the kids have these things. It's terrible."

With a nod and a sniff, I agreed. The bus hissed to a stop, and I noted we were straddling a white painted line.

- - -

Not long after I was ejected from Russell Hill Road and returned to Harry, I endured a brief and unhappy enlistment with the scouting organization.

During those early months, Harry was anxious to see that my needs as a developing child were met, by way of local activities and clubs. There were interminable weeks of swimming lessons, until I faked a near-drowning that convinced the duffer that maybe swimming wasn't for everyone. Piano lessons were investigated and abandoned after the teacher told Harry the lessons would not come to much if I didn't have a piano at home. As luck would have it, the teacher's family owned a piano shop. But Harry was dubious.

"Why would I pay all that money for a piano, when you can't even play it?" he asked me.

"I think the point is, I'm supposed to practice between lessons."

"They should lend us a piano until we know you can play. What if you're no good?"

"That's a distinct possibility," I admitted.

"How can they expect families to simply go out and buy pianos without knowing? We're not all rich, like your grandparents."

"Well," I said, "they don't have a piano, either. I think Auntie Benz has a violin, but I never heard her play it."

Then Harry got his most inspired idea: Cub Scouts.

"It's perfect. You go camping and hiking with other boys your age, and you learn all kinds of valuable things, like how to light a campfire."

For a change, one of Harry's ideas didn't make me wince, sounded as if it might actually be fun. But I wasn't taking chances. I had to remain sceptical until I learned more. "I know how to light a campfire."

"Without using matches," he said.

"Why would anyone go camping without matches?" It seemed a sensible question, but Harry accused me, naturally, of being a - smart-aleck. "I guess they might forget to bring some," I said. "Or maybe they thought the other person had brought them. Or maybe they lost them somewhere in the woods. I suppose if it rained, the matches could get wet, and then they wouldn't work—"

"For crying out loud, Mavis. It's just an example. You don't have to take everything so literal. There are lots of other things you learn in Cubs."

"Like what?"

"I don't know. You have to go and find out for yourself."

I was calmly resigned to the prospect until Harry brought home the required uniform: grey wool shirt, green shorts, matching green skull cap with gold piping and a miniature visor—a bastardized baseball cap for a drooling toddler. "I'm not wearing that. And what's *that* thing?" I said, pointing to a red piece of cloth.

"A neckerchief."

"A what?"

"It's like a tie."

"You didn't tell me I had to wear a tie."

"All the other boys will be wearing them."

That didn't reassure me. "All the other boys could be wearing skirts and lipstick. That wouldn't mean I'd do it, too."

Harry made a disparaging sound. "You're just being foolish. Look, it's a uniform. Thousands of boys all over the world wear this uniform. They all wear the tie. You don't have to wear the tie all the time. Like when you're camping. I'm sure you get to just wear regular clothes when you go camping."

"Maybe I could use the tie to help get my campfire going," I said, "if my matches aren't all wet, or lost."

"Don't be a smart-aleck. Anyway, they give you badges."

"Badges?"

"For doing things."

"What things?"

"Things like being able to light a campfire," he said, trying to drive home his point. "Or building a birdhouse. I think there's one for stamp collecting. Don't you have a stamp collection?"

"I don't think collecting stamps is exactly a life-saving skill."

"Maybe not, but you still get a badge for it. You sew the badges onto your uniform." The old duffer had clearly done his homework.

"I don't know how to sew."

"That's one of the badges. Sewing. You should get that one first. Learn how to sew, get your sewing badge, and then you can sew on all your other ones, as you get them."

"Sewing is for girls."

Harry looked offended. "Really? Who do you think put the hem on your pants? The tooth fairy?"

I shrugged. I hadn't really noticed the hem before.

"For your information, I did."

"You know how to sew?"

"You may have noticed, Mavis, that there are no women around here to do the sewing. Just like there are no women to do the cooking and the cleaning. Who do you think does those things in this house? Secret elves?"

"That would be sort of cool." I didn't want to give Harry his due, which was unfair; but I was just a kid, after all. In time, I would realize that Harry was never much of a cook, and his competence with a needle and thread would only just barely earn him a Cub Scout's sewing badge. Still, in the end, I have to give him credit for doing those thankless and mundane tasks.

As for Cub Scouts, I agreed to attend the first meeting, to see what it was about. The club met on Wednesday evenings in the school gymnasium. As we sat in a large circle on the floor, I recognized two boys from my class, both of whom went on to ignore me. The Scoutmaster was our gym teacher, Mr. Cunningham—not a good sign, given his reputation for cruelty. He was teeming with fervour for his pack, spittle collecting in the corners of his mouth as he paced the floor in his white sneakers and preached the gospel according to Scouts. Key words rang out like a sniper's potshots. *Cooperation! Respect! Honesty! Health and Fitness! Courage! Responsibility!* And so on. I ducked, angry with Harry for getting me involved in this organization. It was a brand of zealotry that I couldn't abide. The deciding moment came when Mr. Cunningham led the pack chant:

Akela, I'll do my best,
To do my duty to God and the Queen,
To help other people, and
To obey the law of the Pack.

It didn't sound right, to me. And nobody explained who Akela was, and why we were making promises to him. Sitting cross-legged in the circle, I mouthed an approximation of the words, and crossed my fingers to nullify the pledge. Later, when I described for Harry what had gone on at the meeting, he was torn between his own aversion to cults and the practical loss of the money he'd spent on the uniform. In the end, he relented. I never went back.

"I probably won't be lighting too many campfires, anyway," I said.

Harry grunted. He'd never lit a campfire in his life, either. "The sewing badge would have been nice."

Despite my personal aversion to the pack mentality, I've no doubt the scouting organisation delivers on its promises for many happy boys around the country. Look at Jack Horner, the Cub Scout who became a Boy Scout who became an Eagle Scout who became a Scoutmaster, and who knew what the meaning of courage was. He made the pledge to the mysterious entity, Akela, and followed through, saving my life and giving up his own in an effort to save Harry. God bless you, Jack Horner.

- - -

The bus exhaled and two representatives of the Canada Border Services Agency boarded, one male and one female. I began to sweat. When I glanced at Earlene, I noted she was roseate with nerves, her plump fingers fidgeting with her passport and her customs declaration card. I had to wonder if maybe she wasn't holding a bit of smack, after all. She had once again removed the Kleenex from her purse, but still didn't know what to do with it. I clutched my own documents with a firm grip, and with my free hand attempted to smooth down the remains of my hair, as if good grooming might help. I prayed my broken leg would gain me some sympathy, something to offset the natural prejudice these officials would have for a man who was criminally ugly.

Come on, Mavis, what's the worst they could do? They could arrest me; though for what, I couldn't say, unless my quiet escape from the hospital was an unlawful act. I suppose these frontier guardians might merely *suspect* me of something—smuggling drugs or rare birds, maybe—remove me from the bus and interrogate me in the confines of the barracks, a furry canine sniffing at my cuffs, a tepid coffee languishing on the table in front of me. The same five questions answered repeatedly. *No, I haven't visited a farm recently. No, I've no exotic wildlife hidden on my person. No, I don't approve of drugs or drug-takers. No, I've never been convicted of a felony. No, I am not now, nor have I ever been, a member of the Communist Party.* They'll never take me alive.

The officers were making their way from the front of the bus to the rear with cheerless efficiency, giving each passport a nominal glance and each declaration card a marginally deeper perusal, because duty quotas must be met. Although their demeanour was one of professional detachment, their movements and underlying air was somewhat offhand. They didn't expect trouble.

Two rows up, the female officer's eyes passed over me, and then returned for a second look, an exercise I was accustomed to. The second look puts them into one of two camps: those who immediately dislike me because I am ugly, and those who want to have little to do with me, but are nonetheless sympathetic to my plight. I sensed this woman fell into the second group, which was bound to make our impending transaction easier. When a third glance made note of my broken leg, I knew I would have no problem. She had just returned the documents to the man sitting in front of me, and was turning my way, when her male confrère took a large, awkward step, angling between us and nearly tripping over my extended leg. To regain his balance, the male officer shifted his considerable weight and grabbed the nearest headrest. His uniform creaked ominously.

"Sorry, Owen," said the female officer, as if it had been her fault. I could see she was one of those selfless women who always took the blame, if only to keep the peace. She was in the wrong business.

Ignoring his partner's apology, Officer Owen gave me a look that implied it was my fault, that I had intentionally attempted to trip him. An enormous hand spread open before me. "Passport."

Silently, I placed the passport and declaration card on his open palm.

Officer Owen looked at his hand as if I had just shat on it. "I said *passport*. When I want your declaration card, I'll ask for it. Do you understand?"

I quickly removed the offending paper from his palm.

Now that I had publicly offended him twice, he took greater interest in me, his last supplicant. He thumbed slowly through the passport, looking for customs stamps from destinations that might give a clue to my troublesome nature. Of course, there were no stamps. I had never been anywhere until now. As he worked his way from the back page to the front, he stopped on the information page, where my name and photograph and personal data were laid out. His eyes flicked from the page to my face, and back again.

"Are you travelling alone?"

"Yes, sir."

His glare lingered on me longer than was comfortable. "You're not with anyone?"

"Um," I said, "I've been having a nice chat with this kind woman next to me, but we've only just met on this bus."

Earlene shifted uncomfortably in her seat. I should have left her out of it.

"Well, Mister..." He searched the page. "...Templeton. Even for a simple guy like me, it's hard to believe you were born in 1932. And I can tell, even when you're sitting down, that you are closer to six feet than five-foot-seven, as it indicates here. And the photo clearly shows a blue-eyed man who actually looks seventy-two."

"Um," I managed to say.

"I suppose there's a simple explanation."

"I gave you the wrong passport."

Officer Owen nodded, as if that were the explanation he expected. "How many passports do you possess?"

"Just the two," I said, offering him the second one, my own. "That one belongs to my father."

As he inspected the second passport, he asked, "Where is your father?"

"He died, sir. Fairly recently."

His eyes lifted from the page, searched my face for a lie, returned to the page. "Why are you carrying his passport?"

"To be honest, sir, it's the only photograph I have of him, such as it is."

The officer nodded; it was too preposterous to be untrue. "Give me your own passport, and your declaration card."

I handed over the documents. After a token glance, Officer Owen kept the card and returned both passports. "I'm sorry for your loss. Welcome back to Canada." He and his partner briskly exited, and we were soon rolling into the Canadian prairies.

Home, at last.

19

It was Earlene who noticed the throng awaiting our arrival at the Winnipeg terminus.

I had been dozing, exhausted after an overdose of Earlene's extensive family history. I never missed Harry's surly reticence as much as when the third wad of photos, this one at least four inches thick, emerged from her carry-all. She was working backwards in history, so this last collection had proved to be rendered in sepia tones. I felt awash in fatigue, yawning deeply and searching in vain for any distraction out the window, before sinking into a light sleep.

Earlene had remained alert, and was among the first to notice the peculiar crowd loitering on the sidewalk. "Look at all those cameras," she said, nudging me with her soft-tipped elbows. "D'you think there's a movie star on the bus?"

I moved my shoulders sleepily, in something vaguely like a shrug.

She prattled on, excitedly. "I saw Shirley Maclaine once, you know. Drove right past me in a white limousine. The window in back was rolled down, and there she was, looking right at me. Well, I remember thinking, that's not something you see every day. And what do you suppose I did?" She didn't wait for my answer. "I waved to her, of course. And she waved right back, just like we were old friends. Isn't that nice? I think a lot of those Hollywood stars would have just looked the other way."

"Uh huh," I said.

"Anyways, you never know where you'll see one. A few years back, my friend Joanna sat down at the dollar slots in the Flamingo Hotel. That's in Las Vegas, you know. And who was sitting at the very next machine? Don Rickles! He told her he was killing time before his second set. Well, Joanna couldn't believe this famous man was just sitting there like a normal person, talking to her and all. She got him to autograph a napkin, just to prove to everybody back home, you know."

"Right."

"I always keep an eye out, now. You never know who you're going to see. I didn't recognize anyone when we boarded, but it's hard to tell sometimes. When they're not wearing makeup, those movie stars look just like anyone else."

She held up her copy of People Magazine, and there was a photograph of Annette Benning, out for a day of grocery shopping in downtown Malibu, decked out in baggy sweats, her Hollywood hair collected in a plain scarf. She could have been any mom at the local market—except I had to quietly acknowledge that the paparazzi still got the shot, despite the disguise.

Earlene's head swivelled as she scanned the bus for the apparent celebrity. "This is so exciting."

I knuckled the sleep from my eyes and looked out the window. There indeed seemed to be a shifty crew lurking at the arrivals platform, many of whom were armed with professional-gauge lenses, and all of whom looked as if they had just emerged from a dank tavern, where they had been marking the hours in front of stale pints, waiting for the "target" to show up. I was not interested in celebrities, but for Earlene's sake I put on a wan smile.

The bus made a final turn into its assigned stall and hissed to a stop. There was the usual murmur from the passengers as they stood and stretched their limbs, pulled down tote bags from the overhead stowage. Yawns floated through the bus, joints creaked. When the door opened, the atmosphere changed, releasing the filtered Greyhound air and inviting in the diesel-infused draughts of the terminal. A sort of congenial chaos ensued as the more impatient passengers gently pushed forward, encouraging the slowpokes. I remained in my seat at the rear, as patient as Job, with my broken leg extended up the aisle. I had no luggage to retrieve. The only things I had with me were the clothes I was wearing, including the blue pants that Randall had given me.

As the passengers began to disembark, I could see the press corps was on the ready, lenses poised. There was no doubt they expected someone important to get off our bus. I could only assume they had been misled, and were destined to be disappointed. Now that she had stowed her People magazine and photographs, Earlene, too, was ready to leave. I leaned a little left, permitting her to squeeze into the aisle.

"I have to catch another bus to Portage," she said, wearily. "Good luck with the nursing, Mavis."

I made farewell sounds and watched her cookie-dough backside waddle towards the front of the bus. When she disappeared down the stairwell, the driver, who had been helping his passengers step down safely, mounted the stairs and surveyed the interior of the bus. I was the only one left.

"Need some help, sir?" He was a trim man in his middle years, with a thoughtful, slightly wry face, though I sensed his concern was genuine.

I balanced on the crutches and slowly made my way forward. "I'm doing fine," I said, cheerily, "all by myself." I'm certain that, in the low light of the bus, the driver was unable to detect the tears that were gathering for a jump from the rims of my eyes.

After the accident, after Harry and I were finally and truly separated, chinks began to appear in my defences. Without warning or provocation, I was now prone to increasingly intense moments of grief. I had been able to cope with Harry's death so long as I still had him with me, beside me in the car, where I could talk to him, where he could still offer up a silent reproach, if the need arose. But I was unprepared for what remained of my life without him. And worse still, I had somehow managed to return to Canada having left him behind. That wasn't part of my carefully conceived plan. *Where are you, Harry?*

"Beg your pardon?" asked the driver.

I blinked back the tears and cracked a hideous smile. "I said it's starting to snow." A few large flakes floated past the window.

"Welcome to Winnipeg," he said, drolly.

As the tips of my crutches touched the pavement outside the bus, there was a sudden surge around me. The paparazzi were closing in, and the barrage of flashbulbs and shouts caused me to flinch. The driver's hand found the center of my back, steadied me. "You the movie star?" he asked. He must have known I was no Hollywood hunk. This was just his sense of humour.

I turned to look at him. "What do they want?"

With a shrug, he admitted he had no idea. He then offered to escort me to the taxi stand at the far end of the terminus. I declined his kind offer; he had done enough, already. It was time for me to take care of myself. Better late than never.

Like a swarm of agitated bees released from Uncle Jim's lopsided hive, the rabble of press dogged me as I hobbled into the bustling station. Microphones and foot-long lenses orbited like so much space junk, while voices barked, hoping to get me to turn this way or that. How did they know my name? What did they want with me?

Two uniformed policemen soon arrived. Not liking what they saw, they positioned themselves at the vanguard of this strange parade and beat a path for me, with shouts of "Step aside!" and "Move!" The mob parted like wake, but refused to disperse, closing in at the sides, taking up the rear, taunting me with incomprehensible questions.

And then one clear voice emerged from the cacophony. An athletic man in an expensive grey suit had elbowed his way to the space just to my left. He had perfect television hair and two rows of uniform teeth that were an unnatural shade of white. As he stuck his microphone indiscreetly under my chin, I saw a jewel-encrusted gold watch hanging heavily from his wrist. He wore tortoise-shell glasses that had lenses of plain glass. I had stared into Harry's magnified peepers for decades, so I knew how prescription lenses distorted the eyes from an observer's point of view. This fellow wore glasses for reasons of fashion, or perhaps in order to appear smarter. Surely a human male specimen this perfect wouldn't be nearsighted.

He repeated his question, clear as day. "How does it feel to be a fugitive, Mavis?"

I stopped hobbling. The mob also halted, reduced their gabbling to a murmur. They were about to get a sound bite.

"I beg your pardon?"

"How does it feel to be a fugitive?"

I scanned the faces around me. The policemen looked appalled. They were waiting for an excuse to make good use of their truncheons.

"How do you know my name?" I said.

The mob snickered at this foolish question. They were the experts when it came to questions. The reporter gave me a consoling grin. "Are you innocent of the charges?"

Fugitive? Charges? I was accustomed to generally not knowing what was going on, but this was a new level of ignorance, even for me. It was clear something had happened between the time I had boarded the Greyhound bus in Grand Forks and arrived in Winnipeg, something big—or at least something big enough to nudge the press out of the tavern. As for offering a statement that might satisfy this cynical crew, I was at a loss. It seemed I was in need of answers more urgently than they were.

"I'm sorry," I said. "I have a plane to catch." To the great relief of my police escort, I began moving again.

The flashy reporter matched my pace, kept a firm hold on his slot at my side. He leaned in closer. "Brent Gilmore, Channel Three NewsFirst." He presented his right hand, realized both my hands were occupied with the awkward task of operating my crutches, and withdrew it. "Listen, Mavis…mind if I call you Mavis?...super. Listen, Mavis, NewsFirst wants an exclusive."

I was barely listening. The reporter's teeth were fascinating for their manufactured perfection.

"I have a car waiting outside. We can be at the studio in minutes. You give us ten in the chair, answer a few easy questions, and I'll personally bring you to the airport. Don't worry about your flight. The station will make all the arrangements. What do you say?"

"Thank you, no. I'll make my own arrangements, Mister Gilmore."

He was not so easily deflected. "Hey, I know, guy. You're looking at all the offers. But NewsFirst is the big boy in this town. We're the highest rated newscast west of the Canadian Shield. We've got the coverage you need to get your story out there." His gold watch jangled musically. "And remember this: there's going to be a crowd three times this size waiting for you in Toronto. If you give us the interview, I'm sure I can convince my producer to put you up in a hotel overnight, get you on a flight in the morning, and keep it all quiet so those hacks back home won't even know you're coming. You won't get a better offer from Channel Six." He winked at me. "And I have one more thing to offer—unofficially, of course. My brother-in-law is a senior acquisitions editor at

Random House. We can get you a six-figure book deal before you've unpacked your suitcase."

"I don't have a suitcase, Mister Gilmore," I said. "As you can see."

"Just an expression, Jack."

"My suitcase was lost in a terrible and tragic accident, along with my father, my car and a very brave Boy Scout leader."

"Whoa! Save it for the studio. Let me call my producer. We'll get you out of this place in two seconds."

"Thank you, no."

His perfect teeth disappeared behind a frown. "Whatever you do," he said, quietly, "don't give it up for Channel Six. They're a bunch of penny-pinching clowns, they have no viewership, and they'll renege on all their promises. And I ought to know. I used to work for them."

He fell back into the mob, disappeared with his gold watch and toothy grin. The others, having got their b-roll footage for the evening news, or candid snap for the front page, filtered away. If Brent Gilmore couldn't get the story, I gathered, they knew they were wasting their time. Soon, it was just me and my police escort making for the exit. They looked glum, as if I had somehow disappointed them, denied them an opportunity to show their stuff.

"No comment," said one of the cops, fingering the highly polished knob of his nightstick.

"What?" I wasn't sure if he was talking to me.

"Next time, just say, 'No comment.'"

"Oh, right."

"See you in court," said his partner, and they vanished into the crowd, on the hunt for a new disturbance.

The flight from Winnipeg to Toronto was short and uneventful. Everyone aboard seemed unaware of my newsworthy status. And because I was lame, the airline staff was attentive to my needs, going so far as to upgrade me to business class, where my leg would have more room to extend.

I did my best to appreciate and enjoy my first airplane flight. The window seat to my right was unoccupied, so I raised the armrest between the seats and angled towards the porthole. I wished Harry could have seen the world from thirty-thousand feet. The miniature towns, lakes, rivers, patchwork farmlands, and eventually the sprawling metropolis that spread along the north shore of Lake Ontario like breeding cancer cells: Toronto. Surely this vista, this perspective on the world, would have changed the old duffer forever. He might have rediscovered his own long-lost faith. I know that mine was never so strong as during that flight. And the flight attendant brought me champagne. New headline: *Mavis Templeton—Teetotaller no more!*

20

The air in Terminal 2 at Pearson Airport was filtered, artificial, devoid of smell and taste. I felt as if I had landed on the moon, where the atmosphere would be generated from stainless steel canisters. I fell in step with the other moon men, moving through narrow glass corridors, down escalators, along blank and seemingly endless passageways, following a sequence of signs that directed us towards the luggage carousels and exits. Hampered by the crutches, I quickly fell to the rear, until my fellow passengers left me behind and vanished around a bend. But I wasn't alone.

Sylvia was in her late twenties, nearly a match for me in height, hair pulled back in a complicated braid, wearing a deep blue uniform that nicely accentuated the fundamental differences in shape between men and women. She was towing a compact travel case with built-in wheels and an extendable handgrip. Sylvia was a stewardess.

"Actually," she told me, "we're not called stewardesses anymore. We're called flight attendants."

"Why is that?"

She gave a little shrug. "I guess for the same reason they call garbage men *sanitation engineers*. It sounds better. It's supposed to make us feel better about ourselves."

"I like the word *stewardess*," I said. "It's more personable."

"To be honest, I think the word got a bit of a reputation back in the Seventies and Eighties. All those young, pretty women travelling the globe in search of adventure. Some of the old-timers tell me it was quite a time. A lot of action, if you know what I mean."

Not really. But I nodded anyway.

"Of course, that was before my time."

She seemed to regret having missed those good old days, and I didn't blame her. It's natural, I think, to believe one has somehow missed the better times by a hair's breadth. There is always some geezer telling us how great things used to be, before we came along and messed things up.

"Still," I said, "it must be exciting, what you do. All those exotic destinations, new faces every day..."

"It's a living," she said, mysteriously.

"Where are you from? Originally, I mean."

"Edmonton."

My heart of stone fluttered, and I nearly tripped over my crutches.

Sylvia put a hand on my arm. "Are you okay?"

"The crutches. I'm not used to them."

"I had crutches when I was eleven. I was jumping on a water bed and I lost my balance. Went over the side and broke my leg."

"I'm sorry."

"Actually, it was sort of exciting. I got a lot of attention, and I managed to get around pretty good on the sticks. It must have hurt, but I don't remember the pain at all. Isn't that funny?"

I said that it was.

"I guess children don't feel pain the way grownups do," she said.

I wanted to say, *No, children feel a different kind of pain, an internal pain that isn't caused by falling off a bicycle or a water bed. They bleed slowly, hemorrhage from internal injuries whose origins are better sought by therapists.* But I reigned in those melancholic reflections. I was enjoying this conversation with an attractive woman, and decided it would be impolite to lower the tone to such depths.

"I was on my way to Edmonton, before the accident," I said, bringing us back to the topic. "I didn't quite get there."

"Lucky you," said Sylvia.

"You're not fond of your hometown?"

"If you ask around, you'll find quite a few flight attendants hail from Edmonton. The girls can't get away from the place fast enough."

"It can't be as bad as all that. I grew up here in Toronto, and it certainly has its seedy aspects, thieves and pimps and smog alerts, and so on, but it also has its charms."

"I had lots of girlfriends that had babies before they were old enough to vote. And don't think for a minute that there was a wedding ring to go with it. There isn't enough for a good, wholesome teenage girl to do in that town. Everyone is just *hanging around.*"

"Hanging around?"

"You know, waiting for something to happen, waiting for life to begin. Somehow they seem to get knocked up while they wait, and then it's over before it's even started. Nothing much ever happens there. That's the problem."

"There are a few people out there who are trying to save my life," I told her. "That's something, to me, anyway."

Sylvia didn't appear to hear what I said, momentarily lost in her memories of all those hometown girlfriends whose prospects were lost to a moment of weakness—victims of a poor decision—in the back of some boy's van.

We had finally caught up to the other passengers. The luggage carousels were spinning slowly in the middle distance, and the automated doors beyond would soon part us. I would be sorry to see her go. I got the feeling her friendliness towards me was genuine, even if I was just another customer. It didn't seem to matter to her that I was unspeakably ugly—and lame to boot. The decrepit ogre. Frankenstein's fantastic experiment coming apart at the seams.

I asked her, "How long are you in town?" It wasn't a line, in the traditional male sense. Polite conversation had never been my strong suit, so I was armed with only the most obvious small talk.

Sylvia gave me a long sideways look. "Just overnight. I'm off to Montreal, first thing."

"Um," I said. I had now officially exhausted my conversational repertoire.

Fortunately, Sylvia was better equipped. "Do you want to get a drink?" When she saw me hesitate, she added, "After a flight, I need a little wind-down time, otherwise I can't sleep. One thing about this job, it plays buggers with your sleep patterns."

"I don't really drink," I said. The champagne she had served me during the flight had given me a headache.

"I'm sure we could rustle up a ginger ale."

Of course I agreed. I may be a virgin, but I'm not a complete fool.

- - -

Harry had enjoyed beer with the same dedication I reserved for tobacco; but he demonstrated a quaint self-discipline in his vice that I seemed to lack in mine, a restraint that might be described as fanatical. Until the last day of his life, I never saw him drink more than one beer.

"One a day," he'd say, tipping the glass so that he had a perfect, one-inch head. "Everything in moderation," he'd intone, squinting suggestively at me through the yellow swirl of my billowing cigarette cloud.

By my seventeenth year, I had begun to feel the insidious effects of peer pressure. O, how the praises were sung, all across the school yard, for the one ingredient guaranteed to turn any gathering into a party: alcohol! With dramatic exuberance, my boastful peers described weekend binges, gave lurid accounts of "wild" parties in anonymous basements, from which they staggered, lost and blind-drunk, through darkened alleyways in a futile search for home, puking into privets or passing out in back seats—and these thrilling adventures were complemented by admiring (and intoxicated) females, rock music, occasional bonfires, petty mischief and not-infrequent fisticuffs. I saw that my brothers at Lord Beaverbrook High took seriously their duty to explore the nuances of soft drugs and alcohol consumption. Naturally, I eventually grew curious.

Even at that age, I could see my future laid out before me: a continuation of my apprenticeship in the store, standing alongside the old duffer, ringing up sales, watching the traffic speed by, the coming and going of the seasons marking a rotation of stock from snow shovels to garden hoes to barbeques to fanned rakes, the years turning over on these quarterly servings, each turn desaturating me a little more, until, like Harry, I blended perfectly into the dreary background of Templeton Hardware. I knew there would be no alternative for me, no college or university, no career. Like any *dauphin*, my course was set on the day of my birth. Somehow, I would have to cope.

One Friday after classes had ended, I loitered in the schoolyard, shuffling in the periphery of a group of boys from my eleventh-grade class. I felt indolent, forcing down the daily pressure to hurry home, help Harry through the last hours of business before he closed shop. For a change, I wanted these two hours to myself, to do with as I pleased. So I lingered beneath the basketball hoop, as if I belonged to the group. They were not jocks and not geeks, but something in between and popular enough for it. I was on speaking terms with most of the boys, although there was nothing there that could be considered friendship. But they at least had shown restraint, during our three-year acquaintance, in the persecution of the ugly kid with the girly name, tolerating my presence in their school with casual indifference. They neither included me nor actively rejected me from their congress.

"I could do it," Colin Peters was saying. He was a dark and sullen boy with thin black hair that hung over his forehead like melted candle wax.

"No, you couldn't," one of the others said.

I had wandered into the middle of a conversation. I inspected my Adidas and gave every appearance of listening.

"The trick is to have no emotions. You get up in the morning and you go to work, but you leave your emotions at home."

Tony DiFrancesco made a scoffing sound. "My dad has a cousin in Sicily who's a hitman, and he's just fucking crazy. That's what you gotta be. Fucking *crazy*."

Colin was shaking his head. "As long as the guy deserves it, it's easy. You're doing everyone a favour by knocking the guy off. That's how I look at it. Stay calm, put the guy in the sights, then *blam*. Another asshole bites the dust."

"You're afraid of Mrs. Houlihan's chihuahua, you dope," said Tray Keeler. The others laughed.

Red blotches grew on Colin's cheeks. "Yeah, well, that little bastard's bit me a bunch of times."

"Maybe you should *take it out*," said one of the others, prompting more snickers.

Someone else said, "It'd be like training. Start with tiny dogs, and work your way up to humans."

"Go ahead and laugh, but I'm totally serious. I'm gonna to do it, you just watch."

"I got a neighbour that plays that Indian music real loud," said John Bowles, a kid with simian features and the worst teeth I'd ever seen. "Can you do something about him?"

"Shoot his stereo to death," said one of the boys.

"Assassinate the bastard's speakers!" shouted another.

A chorus of pleas rose, appeals to rub out strict parents and rich uncles and a fair number of fellow students who had caused offence for one reason or another.

James Braddock, the unofficial leader of this group, turned the conversation to suit himself. "When I grow up, I'm going to be a professional alcoholic."

"Alcoholism can't really be considered a profession," I said, quietly. "You might call it a *vocation*, though."

They all turned to look at me, shocked not so much because I was there but because I was suddenly participating.

"A what?" said Tony DiFrancesco. Most of these boys, I knew, were barely literate.

"A vocation. It's sort of a *calling*, you know, like someone who becomes a priest." I was merely attempting to be clever. I knew perfectly well that alcoholism was an addiction; as an incorrigible smoker, I knew a thing or two about addiction.

There was an uncomfortable silence as the boys absorbed my cleverness. And then James began to nod. "Yeah, man, that's it. A calling. I'm going to be the fucking Pope of alcoholism."

Laughter erupted from the group, and suddenly I was in.

"I got a twenty-sixer of Jack Daniels in my knapsack," said James. "Let's go behind the tennis courts and pray!"

Amid laughter and genial shoves, we trooped across the soccer field to a small grove on the far side of the fenced tennis courts. Under an old maple tree was a wooden bench—in imminent danger of collapsing from neglect and vandalism—and several boys competed roughly for a place on it, until four emerged the winners. They rocked victoriously on the flimsy structure, jostling for elbow room.

As presumed leader, James Braddock played the role of someone who was above such juvenile sport, standing apart, watching with amused forbearance. He had intelligent and active eyes, and he was among the lucky few who got top grades without having to work for them. This gift stimulated in him a breezy confidence that bordered on arrogance, and made him believe that everything in life was easy. In this way he reminded me of my cousin, David, and I didn't envy him for it. James was no thug, but I suspected that both he and David would one day meet a world that was considerably less munificent, one that would no longer hand out accolades free of charge. *Quid pro quo, boys, QPQ.*

Once the bustle subsided, James pulled the bottle of whiskey from his satchel, twisted off the cap and tipped it to his mouth, taking in three long pulls. Somehow he managed not to choke, but his watery eyes betrayed him. He hadn't quite been prepared for the burning effect of the whiskey. After a moment of paralyzed silence, he recovered his facility for breathing, and held up the bottle. "Who's next?"

Each boy sampled the drink in turn, one or two barely wetting their lips, perhaps afraid of smelling of alcohol when they got home. John Bowles, the monkey-faced boy with the noisy neighbour, overestimated his tolerance, gulping ostentatiously before shooting two streams of liquor out his nose in a golden spray that spread across the front of his jacket. As he fell to the ground in an exaggerated fit of coughing, we all knocked about in hysterical laughter.

Then the bottle came into my hands. I hesitated, eliciting a round of jeers from my companions. Bracing myself, I took a mouthful, holding it for a moment, feeling the slight burn in my cheeks, my sinuses contracting from the pungent bouquet. And then I swallowed. Several years of hard-core smoking, I discovered, had desensitized my throat to this new and harsh insurgence; it went down without a hitch and settled hotly in my midsection. I was impressive.

"Good one, man," said Colin, the future hitman.

I received nods of approval all around. Tray Keeler said, "Hey, James, you got some competition for that job as Pope." Everyone laughed, including James; though there was a fierce edge to his look that said he'd rather have the job to himself.

So, without declaration or ceremony, it became an unofficial contest between James and me. As the natural and rightful leader, he needed to save face; as the rookie, I needed to prove myself. Of course, such analysis is flimsy when you consider we were simply two hormonal teenaged boys in possession of a nearly full bottle of liquor. It went quickly, as I remember it, but I was hardly in a position to gauge the passage of time. I have no recollection of my departure from the schoolyard, no memory of the brief—and presumably non-linear—walk home. In my mind remain still-frame images of the toilet bowl, polluted by the toxic contents of my stomach, of Harry's slippered feet on the bathroom floor beside my face, of his short, thick fingers on my shoulder. There is a snapshot of the kitchen table, set for dinner, two plates of steaming ham and mashed potatoes and canned peas, another snap of my untidy bedroom and the unmade bed, which had never before looked, it seemed to me, quite so inviting.

Later, when I opened my eyes, the room was dark and blessedly motionless. I could hear the television faintly; the music told me the late news was ending. The clock at my bedside confirmed it was eleven-thirty. Soon, Harry was shuffling around the living room, switching off lights. He came down the hall, stopping in the bathroom. When I heard the water running, I realized I was tremendously thirsty, but I did not want to move from my bed; I was unsure if I *could* move. A minute later, Harry was standing in the doorway, a slightly rumpled silhouette. He was watching me in the dim light from the hallway, no doubt searching for signs of life.

"I'm awake," I croaked.

He stepped to my bedside and held out his hand. It took me a moment to see the glass of water. "Thought you might want this."

With some groaning effort, I propped myself up and took the glass from him. "Thanks."

"Feeling a little better?"

"Uh huh," I said, gulping down the ice-cold water.

He took the empty glass from me. "If you're hungry, I can warm up your dinner."

The thought of food caused my intestines to contract. "I don't think so."

He looked at me in silence for another moment. "Well," he said, at last, "see you in the morning."

To his credit, Harry never mentioned the incident. In the morning, we had a mostly silent breakfast. There were two Aspirin on the mat next to my plate of dry toast. The rattling newspaper did my pounding head no favours, but I was grateful to have been spared the lecture. The old duffer knew when a lesson had been learned. Without Harry's overt help, I easily made the decision to abstain.

- - -

"This way."

Sylvia led me past the carousel, where the other passengers waited for the conveyor belt to tumble out their battered luggage. We went through a service door intended for airline personnel, and an escalator took us to the departure level. Our destination was a bar that lurked gloomily in a far corner of the retail area. The interior was aglow with a tacky collection of neon beer logos that brushed us all in a sickly palette of hues. We settled on stools around a tall, round table that overlooked a blank stretch of tarmac. I lit two cigarettes and gave one to Sylvia.

"Thanks," she said. "How did you know?"

"Lucky guess."

"These things'll kill you, you know." She inhaled deeply.

"Not likely."

I told her my story, the abridged version. It was easy to tell. They were mere details.

"My God," she said, when I had finished. But it was a polite exclamation, as if the story had pertained to a mutual acquaintance, one neither of us had seen for years.

"Touch my arm," I said, offering the limb across the table.

She put her hand on my forearm, just above the wrist, pressed the tips of her fingers into my petrifying flesh, as if to feel the freshness of a bread loaf. I had a sudden urge to open my mouth wide and rap my knuckles on my skull, but I resisted. And when I lowered my arm to the table, her hand remained. Innocent contact between two friendly strangers. It was a touch that stirred in me all the old and unrealized longings I'd held for my mythical mother, the inherent need I had for simple marks of affection. This harmless physical contact with a woman who, only one hour earlier, had been merely another anonymous member of the service industry, meant everything to me.

"I'm staying across the street," she said. She was chewing the ice from her empty glass. "At the Sheraton."

"That's convenient." I was aware my response was ambiguous.

Seduction was a new arena for me, and I wasn't sure I was ready for it...at my age. Technically, I knew what to do—the "ins and outs" of sexuality being a staple of modern literature—but reading about it and doing it were two different things. If my life had followed the standard script, I would have spent my teenage years, like every other boy, groping for the proper techniques and protocols of this primal act. At that age, one is accustomed to making a fool of oneself. At forty-three, the revelation of my ignorance could be catastrophic.

But was it my own precious ego I was protecting? I felt I could survive the humiliation, knowing I would soon be dead. Was it for Sylvia's benefit, then, that I was demurring? Bad enough she had to pick up the ugliest man on the flight as a means of reliving a past that belonged to another generation; she would then face a long, bleak future burdened with the ineradicable memory of my incompetence, my inexperience, my *virginity*—the consequence of poor decision-making. I didn't think this memory would serve her future sense of nostalgia for the "good old days." And surely this pretty, young woman could do better than this!

"I really ought to be getting home," I said.

Sylvia swallowed her ice chips. "Oh. All right."

It must have seemed a cruel fate to be rejected by this ogre. But how to explain? *You're not my type. Maybe if you had bolts screwed into your neck, perhaps if your forehead had more of a Neanderthallic shape. Anyway, it's not you, it's me. I'm the one with the problem. Too much baggage. I've exceeded the two-bag limit. Har har. You're a nice girl, and you deserve better than me. I may be turning to stone, but some things remain soft...*

I didn't say any of that, of course. What I did say was just as wrong: "Maybe some other time."

"Sure, Mavis, no problem. I have an early call." Sylvia was a trooper.

With the brisk manner of the professional traveller, she shouldered her purse and took up the handle on her small suitcase.

"I'm going to stay and finish this," I said, indicating my ginger ale, which was now flat and warm.

She leaned in and kissed my cheek. "It's been interesting talking to you. Good luck with your father and...well...with everything."

I watched her emerge from the beery gloom of the bar into the brilliant and unflattering light of the terminal, her small wheeled box trailing like an obedient pooch. As she vanished into the crowd, I felt just a twinge of regret. My last chance to make a man of myself just walked away from me, and this loss was the result of my cowardice—not, as I might have liked to believe, some noble act of chivalry. A small voice in my head urged me to go after her, but it was interrupted by another voice:

"Good grief. There you are!"

I was confronted by another woman, and this one didn't seem all that happy to see me.

21

The woman blocking my view of the retreating stewardess glared at me with open hostility. I estimated she was closer to fifty than I was, but in possession of a brisk youthfulness that some rare individuals retain, no matter their age. Trim but not bony, short but in no way dwarfish, she could have easily passed for thirty from only a modest distance, a combination of fashion and self-possession. Her shoulder-length hair was arranged in a contemporary style, a colour that was neither blonde nor auburn nor flaxen, but some unaccountable blend of the three, depending on the available light. The pale blouse and fawn skirt encouraged the eye to admire her shape, the small waist, the smallish breasts aggressively positioned, the legs of a girl who once aspired to the ballet. All together, the effect was alluring, and a little daunting.

The woman shifted so that her hip jutted in an angry fashion. "Jesus God, Mavis. Have you been in here all this time?"

"I was having a drink with a friend," I said, in a neutral tone. "I'm sorry, but have we met?"

She took the stool that Sylvia had recently vacated. "Of course we haven't met. That's the point, isn't it? You've caused me a lot of grief in the last forty-five minutes."

"I see," I said, not seeing at all.

She was furiously adjusting herself on the stool, as if it weren't meant for a human derriere. All this activity made me jumpy, and prevented me from inquiring further into her identity, at least for the moment.

"Well," she said, finally satisfied with her position across from me, "at least the press gave up. They think you snuck in on an

208

earlier flight." She stopped fidgeting and looked me directly in the eye. "You can thank me for laying that groundwork."

"Thank you," I said.

She took a few deep, restorative breaths. As she did so, five more years disappeared from her face. Eventually she smiled, but it was more cunning than friendly. She was about to speak when the bartender appeared.

He was a swarthy and morose eastern European whose career options now appeared to be at their lowest ebb—perhaps a former university dean who had lived the Bucharest high life, now reduced to wiping sticky tables in a lifeless colonial beer stall, his former intellect swirling down the drain along with the backwash, Eminescu's *A Dacian's Prayer* never far from his lips. In any case, the arrival of new clients, I had noted, seemed to put him out.

"White wine," said my new companion, without looking at the bartender. She had no time for bit players in the drama of her life, it seemed.

He grunted and turned to leave.

"Wait!" Now she turned her gaze on him, drilled him with a suspicious look. "Is it a local brand?"

On his journey to rock bottom, the man had clearly faced tougher foes than this chic firecracker. He wiped his bearish paws on the rag tucked in his waistband. "Goot vine, okay," he said, with his thick Romanian consonants, pretending not to understand.

"I don't want a local wine."

"Is goot, ya?"

"Does it have a cork?"

"Eh?"

"Bring the bottle here, so I can look at it." But she could see by his blank stare that this was not worth the trouble. She was not going to get a decent Châteauneuf-du-Pape in this joint. "Never mind. Bring me a vodka rocks." The bartender grunted, then vanished into the darkness of his Moldavian funk.

I thought this might be the moment to inquire again. "I'm sorry, but do I know you?"

Almost before I had finished speaking, she stuck her hand across the table. "Evelyn Wharton, Fielding-Meyer & Associates. I'm your lawyer."

"My lawyer?"

She scrutinized me. "For now."

I bore the scrutiny like a pro. "Why do I have a lawyer, Ms.—
"

"Wharton."

"—Ms. Wharton?" I put a fresh cigarette between my lips.

"You're not going to smoke, are you?"

My Zippo opened with a familiar metallic *chink* and the flint rasped. "We all have our vice," I said, exhaling.

"My mother died from lung cancer three years ago," she said.

"I'm sorry." A blue vapour hung suspended between us. "I know what it is to lose a parent."

"She never smoked a day in her life. It was my father's smoke that killed her. My father, who is still alive, and still smokes two packs a day, and who will probably live to be a hundred." She didn't seem pleased by the prospect.

"Who knows how long any of us has left?" I said, lamely. But I should have known she was not the philosophical type.

"He can't forgive my mother for leaving him alone to fend for himself."

This woman had issues, I thought. She ought to try therapy, but I was not the one to tell her.

The bartender emerged from the gloom and placed a glass of red wine at Ms. Wharton's elbow. When she saw the mistake, her face set for a conflict, and then let it go. And then set again. It was clearly not in her nature to give up a fight—a trait that would serve any lawyer well—but there was another force, tiredness, maybe, that was asserting itself within her. By the time this internal struggle was won, she'd gained back those five years, and the former dean had retreated to his poetry behind the bar.

"It's late, Mavis," she said, fingering the stem of the unwanted wine glass. "Let's get down to business."

"You're the boss."

"I'm *not* the boss. I work for you." Her lack of humour could be seen in the neat press of her blouse and the calculating slant of her mouth. "Nevertheless, it will be my work that solves your current problems, so I recommend you take what I say seriously."

"As you wish."

She paused, assessing my lack of seriousness. "As you know," she resumed, "we have two separate but connected issues to deal with. First, there is the investigation by the U.S. authorities into the death of your father. Now, I feel this is nothing more than a bureaucratic mix up, too many agencies involved. The FBI have interviewed you, and they—"

"—The NDBI," I interjected.

"What?"

"It was the North Dakota Bureau of Investigation."

She drew several irritated breaths to get her wind back. "Right. Either way, they have the coroner's report, so I'm not sure what more they need. Someone hasn't filed his paperwork, is my guess."

"Agent Compton was very nice,' I said. "But he's in the wrong field. He should be in advertising."

Evelyn Wharton was unaccustomed to being interrupted. I had broken her stride again, but she ploughed forward. "We don't want this accusation hanging over your head, so we'll get on the Bureau's back, to get them to sort themselves out."

"What difference does it make? What can they do to me?"

"That'll depend. For now, all they're asking for is your cooperation. But there's always the chance they could bring the matter to a grand jury, and that could mean extradition for you." She must have seen something like shock cross my face. "Don't worry about it, Mavis. It's a worst case scenario, and unlikely to happen. Assuming, of course, you're innocent. Then again, if it does come to that, we'll be in a fairly weak position to prevent it. We might stall for time, but in the end you'd probably have to go." She bravely puckered up and tried the red wine. The look on her face confirmed the dubious vintage. "The other issue is your attempt to cross the border with a cadaver. That one's a bit more tricky. Both sides of the border have an interest, and there seems to be evidence against you, although I haven't seen the paperwork. I've had word that the RCMP is launching an investigation. At this point there's no way to know if it will lead to charges."

"Strictly speaking, I suppose I *am* guilty of that one," I said.

She *shushed* me. "Don't say that, Mavis! Don't ever say that again, not to me or anyone else. Do you understand?"

"No."

"It doesn't matter. It only matters that you obey me. You are innocent, totally and completely innocent of all charges. That's the only thing you need to understand."

Ms. Wharton was so vehement, I could only agree.

"I want you to promise me that you won't ever admit guilt again, unless I tell you to."

"Okay."

"No, I need you to *promise* me."

"I promise."

The tension in her neck released. She made a move to take up her wine glass, then reconsidered. "Good," she said. "So, the first thing we do is get the Americans off your back. If we don't deal with this carefully, they won't let you back into the United States. You'll be *persona non grata*."

"That's nothing new," I said. "Anyway, I have no plans to go back there."

"Unless they extradite you."

"That won't happen, either."

"Don't underestimate the Americans. They usually get what they want."

"They won't get me because I'm innocent," I said. "Besides, I'll be dead before they can say Kalamazoo."

"Good, good. Keep telling everyone you're innocent." The red wine wasn't *up to scratch*, as Harry might have said. Ms. Wharton shifted the glass to the side, leaving more room for her animated hands.

"But I *am* innocent. It's not like I'm just saying it."

"Listen, guilty people try to put the blame on others, shift the focus away from them. But innocent people are outraged that they are being blamed for something they didn't do. Understand? That's how it works. Or at least that's how the public sees it, and that's how a judge and jury will see it."

"I don't care how they perceive me. I just want to get Harry back."

Ms. Wharton became very still, examining me as she might assess a debatable work of art. Her eyes narrowed, as if she were filtering the scene through the mesh of her eyelashes. At last she said, "Can you add a hitch to that?"

"I beg your pardon?"

"Your voice. Say the line again, only this time add a little hitch, like you're about to cry."

I experienced the most powerful déjà vu. "What line is that?"

"'I just want to get Harry back.'" Her hands began to wave, shooing away invisible flies. "Wait. Use the word *father*. It's more powerful. Okay, try it once more, this time with the hitch."

I repeated the line—I'm sorry to say without much feeling. I don't pretend to be an actor.

And Evelyn Wharton, who was, from a judicial perspective, an experienced director, was disappointed by my feeble effort. But like any good director, she knew that the best way to draw a performance from her client was to be positive and supportive. "We'll work on it, Mavis. Don't worry."

"I'm not worried."

"Good, that's good. Just promise me you'll work on the hitch. It'll make all the difference."

I managed to avoid making the promise.

"I know this is all strange and overwhelming. That's why you need to trust me. We'll get your father back, but it's complicated, and it's only going to get worse."

"What do you mean?"

"I mean, it's already becoming a political hot potato. In case you hadn't noticed, our relations with the Americans have been somewhat strained, lately."

"That doesn't have anything to do with me."

"It has everything to do with you. You and your father are shaping up to be the prize in a power struggle. It's a conflict that needed to happen, and you came along at just the right moment. Both sides need to make their point, but they also need to save face. And for that to happen, everyone has to follow the script."

"There's a script?"

"Don't play naïve, Mavis. You're a smart guy, you know what I'm saying."

"I've never really followed politics." That was a partial truth. Thanks to Harry's influence, I had maintained a passive interest in the political landscape, but I had never actually voted. I always accompanied Harry to the polling station, made the motions of an earnest and informed voter. But once I stepped behind the privacy barrier, alone with the inevitably questionable selection of candidates, I suffered a sort of stage fright, a paralyzing fear that my decision might have an impact on my country's future. I was unwilling to take the blame. All I could do was fold the unmarked ballot and drop it quickly into the box, and then let Harry praise me for the successful commission of my duty to Queen and country. He never knew.

Harry was a dedicated (but unregistered) supporter of the Progressive Conservative Party. He was drawn to them chiefly because they called themselves conservatives, and his loyalty never wavered, even after the party dropped the "progressive" element and adopted a strikingly fundamental stance. I had no political allegiance. I felt that any of the major parties would do a bang-up job of running the country into the toilet, and then sending us the bill for that disastrous plumbing job, with interest.

Ms. Wharton was undeterred by my political apathy. "You'd better brush up. You're in the game now. It could be weeks before the Crown decides whether to charge you with anything, but it's in our best interests to expect the worst. That means I'm going to need all the details from you, in order to prepare a defence. Should we need one," she added. She talked energetically for another twenty minutes about developing strategies and collecting affidavits and reading the political climate. I stopped listening fairly early on.

When she finally ran out of steam, Evelyn insisted on paying the bar tab. Just as well. Harry's credit card had taken a beating over the past few days. I followed her down the escalator and through the automated doors that released us into the fusty air of the Greater Metropolis of Toronto.

"This way." Her heels clipped towards the parking garage.

"Harry never could abide parking fees," I said, doing my best to keep up on my crutches. A hotel shuttle bus thundered past, inches from my backside, as we crossed the roadway. We entered a tunnel that ramped upward, leading into the multi-level parking bunker. On the third level, we approached a navy blue convertible BMW, angled arrogantly across two parking slots. Above the rear bumper was a personalized license plate: SHARK. A shadowy figure lurked beyond the hood.

Evelyn Wharton had spotted the lurking figure, too. "What are you doing there?" she demanded. "Get away from my car!"

The garage exploded in light.

- - -

After the flash of light, there was a pause, and when I opened my eyes, Evelyn Wharton was hovering over me. She was wearing a tailored chartreuse silk business suit. As my eyes adjusted to this bit of magic, I noted we were no longer in the airport parkade, and Ms. Wharton was able to hover over me because I was lying in bed.

"What happened?" I asked, my voice barely audible above my pulse.

A hurricane swept across Evelyn Wharton's face. "Fucking press!" she said, with characteristic vehemence. "We were ambushed."

"Ambushed," I said, liking the word. Or maybe I had inherited Harry's irritating habit of repeating everything. Echolalia, I think they call it. As far as I know, Scleroderma doesn't cause psychosis. It must be the bad blood, catching up with me. A thief, a malingerer, and now an echolalist.

"The doctor said you had a minor heart attack."

Another tremor. I had to wonder if any heart attack could be considered "minor."

"I can't get a restraining order against the press," said Ms. Wharton, slightly defeated, "but I've let it be known that their hounding has driven you to the brink of death. By six o'clock, the media will be tearing each other to shreds trying to distance themselves from the creeps who lurk in shadowy parking lots. It won't make a difference in the long run, but in the short term they may back off and give you a bit of breathing room."

Breathing room. Echolalia.

Ms. Wharton glanced around the room, spotted the hard plastic chair—designed to encourage visitors to keep their stay short—and decided to stand, after all. "Listen, Mavis, I spoke to a friend at the American embassy this morning. It may not be as bad as we first thought."

Thought.

"Officially, they're sticking to their story. You're a person of interest, and they'll pursue the investigation into your father's death until they are satisfied. But quietly, they want this whole thing off their plate. My friend couldn't give me specific details, but it has something to do with water."

Water.

"The northern states are negotiating with the provinces to get access to our water. Now that the media has put your story on the front burner, there's a lot of pressure on our government to intercede on your behalf. There are rumours they'll walk out of the water talks unless the Yanks leave you alone and send your father home." She was pacing the room, which was not an unpleasant sight. "Marion Burns is going to give a speech in the House of

Commons this afternoon, try to bring the Liberals to the field, get them to take up the fight properly. Your fight, that is. It remains to be seen if they'll do it. Politics is a dirty business. Everyone has an agenda. But you can bet there will be a few telephones ringing in Washington tonight."

Washington.

"In the meantime, I'd like to get a full statement from you. I think I mentioned this before. I want you to tell me everything that happened, everything you can remember, from the time you entered the United States with your father until I met you at the airport. Every detail matters, no matter how small. I want to know the route you took, the hotels you stayed at, the restaurants you ate in, the people you met, the gas stations you stopped at, the malls you shopped at—"

"We didn't go to any malls," I said. "Harry didn't like to shop."

"You must have slept somewhere. I want to know about it."

"I spent the night in a cornfield."

"Wait a minute," she said. "I'm not ready." From her briefcase she removed a steno pad, dropped it on top of a metallic cabinet—an arrangement of electronics that monitored my cardiac performance and reported my scores to the nurses' station—and began to take furious notes on the page. When she was concentrating, Evelyn Wharton looked her true age.

"I'm not sure I can afford to pay you," I said. This was a thought that had occurred to me the night before, as we were sitting in the airport bar. But I didn't get the opportunity to mention it, and then we were ambushed...

She looked up from her tablet and frowned. "Don't worry about the bill."

"You're doing all this for free?"

Ms. Wharton made a barking sound. "Do I look like someone who does anything for free?"

"Um, no."

"Like I said, don't worry about it. Someone else is picking up the tab."

This caught me off guard. "Really? Who?"

"I can't tell you."

"Why not?"

"Because they asked me not to."

"Why would they do that?"

"Listen, you're supposed to be telling me about your trip. Where was this cornfield, and why were you sleeping in it?"

"I had to urinate."

"What?"

"There was a canola field, but I decided to keep going."

"I'm not sure what you're getting at."

"I was in a hurry."

"Was it a cornfield or a canola field?"

"There was no corn, though. Someone had taken it away."

Evelyn Wharton clicked her pen and looked out the window. "I need a coffee."

Coffee.

22

The cardiac ward in Saint Michael's Hospital is my new home for an indefinite period. I am plugged in, which means the doctors and nurses can easily monitor my decline remotely. Since my faulty heart is the result of an incurable malady, there is not much they can do. We are at the mercy of time and nature.

Like the first time I was in a hospital, forty-three years ago, the media is hot for the story, and, like the first time, they will get the story with or without my consent. No fluff piece this time. I'm big news. Ask anyone. I am, to put it modestly, the central figure in an international "situation." My fate has been hitched like a sidecar to the roaring beast of politics, and my very liberty hangs in the balance. Not that I'm worried. They can't hurt me, and by "they" I mean anyone, foreign or domestic, government or individual. This close to the end, I'm already answering to a higher authority. There's not much left down here that can scare me. For all I know, a glitzy trial would be an entertaining way to kill time before I move on to more eternal matters. That's my opinion.

I admit I'm surprised that there is a *public* opinion regarding my welfare. I am a casualty of merciless bureaucrats and government interference; that's the view from *our* side. From *their* side, the American side, I am, variously, a smuggler, a fugitive, a "person of interest," possibly something worse. Reports in the media vary in tone, depending on which side of the border they originate, but the bare facts are the same: "Two Canadian men were stopped at the U.S. border on October 23rd. One man was injured and the other was pronounced dead at the scene. A third man, unrelated to the pair, was killed in a collision involving the Canadians' vehicle. No criminal charges have yet been laid. The investigation continues." In my opinion, I am a victim of poor decision-making, and my lowercase faith assures me that is no crime. On the positive side, thanks to the miracle of Photoshop, I don't look so bad on the front page of the National Post.

- - -

Testing, testing. One...two.

Is this thing on?

The wheels turn slowly inside a small plastic window, spinning arrogantly, as if I am expected to put all my remaining faith in this technology. But I don't have the faith to spare. It is a hand-held recording device, about the size and thickness of a package of cigarettes, manufactured by the Sanyo Corporation. It fits neatly in my hand, and I can operate it—which is to say, turn it on and off—with only the smallest movement of my thumb.

I have my lawyer to thank for this miraculous device, my angry lawyer who doesn't want to visit me because I make her cross. Evelyn Wharton, of Fielding-Meyer & Associates, wants a record of my side of the story. That's what she asked for: *my side.* I tried to tell her there was only one side to the story, which was mine. "It's a one-sided story, Ms. Wharton," I said, the last time she came to visit me.

"There's no such thing as a one-sided story, Mavis. That's why I'm asking these questions. That's why I'm asking for your side."

"Who else would have a side to my story?" I wasn't intentionally provoking her. It was an honest question. At least, that's my side of it.

"You don't seem to understand that I'm trying to help you. As far as I'm concerned, you can dick the cops around all you want, but you're not doing yourself any favours by evading my questions. You have to decide," she said, exasperated, "if you really want my help."

I smiled serenely and looked her straight in the eye. We were on a topic I knew something about. "Life," I said, "is a long succession of decisions, Ms. Wharton, some easy, some not so easy." I attempted to exude an air of profundity. "Should I do something or not do it? Turn left or right? Go out or stay in? How do I choose between ten candidates, one-hundred-and-thirty channels, twenty-three thousand books, three billion potential soul mates? When to tell the truth, and when to tell a lie? And given the interconnectedness of all these decisions and the multitude of people involved in them, who is to blame when something goes wrong?"

When she is getting particularly upset with me, Evelyn Wharton's eyes flicker from my left shoulder to my right, then look briefly heavenward before settling back on my own eyes. After my little speech, her eyes do this. Left, right, up, down. Like an exercise, or a mantra performed by rote. I don't think she is aware of this ocular reflex.

"I'm doing my best for you, Mavis, but your cooperation is crucial. If you want to make the right decision, I suggest you help me, so that I can help you."

What she said makes sense to me. Really, it does. And she has the uncanny ability to say my Christian name with a straight face. Evelyn Wharton is an impressive woman, and a credit to the Bar.

After my disappointing performance during our last meeting, after I failed to help her in her efforts to help me, she concluded that she could best serve my needs by limiting our personal contact. Now she calls me from her cell phone. That way, if I begin to upset her, if I give her the wrong answers to her vital questions, or, as is frequently the accusation, don't give her an answer at all, she can pretend she is driving into a tunnel, where the cellular signal will be lost. *Hello? You're breaking up...* I think Ms. Wharton is sly, and I mean that in the most complimentary way. Any self-respecting lawyer would be proud to be called sly, and Evelyn Wharton is no exception. When Ms. Wharton thinks she is being sly, a crease appears to the left of her mouth, a crease that looks like a parenthetic bracket. I imagine Ms. Wharton right now, driving her BMW through a long tunnel, fiddling with the backlit keyboard on her cell phone, a sly bracket creasing one side of her face.

Visiting hours are over. The corridors of Saint Michael's Hospital have fallen quiet, except for the soft pad of an occasional passing nurse. My dinner tray was removed by a mute orderly who will not return until morning, at breakfast time. The duty nurse is scheduled to check up on me at eleven o'clock, and she is prompt, which leaves me with three hours of solitude. The growl of traffic outside my window is fading to a low and sporadic hum that rises and falls like an ebbing tide. I am alone, and I have a story to tell.

But despite the smooth mechanics of the tape recorder's on-switch, my thumb refuses to co-operate, does not like the feel of moulded plastic, rejects the empty promises of technology. At heart, at my core, I am an old fashioned boy. I will tell my story, "my side" of the story, and I will tell it to the only person who really matters. And I know that she has no use for modern electronics; has, in fact, no thumbs with which to operate such a thing; so, instead of relying on gizmos, I will do things the traditional way: I will talk. And she will listen.

Dear Mother...

23

My nurse has just left in a huff. I'm not having much luck with women. Something about me seems to aggravate them. I am stymied. The nurse's name is Maureen and she works the night shift here at Saint Michael's Hospital. When I politely inquired about her exotic accent, she informed me she had arrived in Canada from Anguilla, back in 1979, a young, single woman in search of opportunities beyond the scope of a Caribbean island with thirty-five square miles of sun baked territory.

"Like livin on a slave ship," she said of her microscopic homeland. "No room for a woman ta move. Knew everyone by name, and they all either a brother or cousin, not one worth the shirt on is back. Doan wan be wife to none of those rumbums. Got meself out just in time." So she came north and earned herself a nurse's uniform, elected to marry her job instead of some "rumbum," and has no regrets and no desire to return to her native country. "Doan like ta feel the sand between me toes. Give me snow every day of the week an I be happy."

She prefers working nights, she told me, because she likes "peace and order." As the lead nurse on the nocturnal shift in the cardiac ward at Saint Michael's, she pursues those two nouns with vigour, which accounted for her untimely interruption of my narrative. Forever on the prowl for visitors who have overstayed their welcome, Nurse Maureen heard "voices" emanating from within my private room, and strode in with a mind to evict the interloper. What she found was just little old me.

"Who you talkin to?" she demanded, blocking the exit with her impressive circumference.

"No one," said I.

"I heard talkin, no mistake."

"Um, yes. I was talking," I told her, a little embarrassed. "To myself."

She gave me a look that implied she will not tolerate monkey business on her watch. "You got sometin wrong more than your heart, mon."

Although I wasn't sure if she was joking, I smiled and nodded. I was anxious to get back to my story, now that I was on a roll. "My dear nurse," I said, "you would not believe all the things that are wrong with me." I hoped that would put an end to the speculation.

She looked me over in sturdy silence, making her own assessment. "Peace and order," she said, and then she was gone. I listened to the squeak of her sneakers retreating down the corridor.

The sand is running through the glass as if there is no tomorrow.

Had I more time left, I might have committed my life more appropriately to the page. Yes, a memoir of Irish scope in its shocking depravity, dripping with violence and pathos. Perhaps a series, beginning, naturally, at the beginning. The first instalment, *The Miracle of Mavis Templeton: The Early Years*. The foetus unceremoniously disgorged into a cruel world before its time, fawned over by masked heroes and lorded over by devoted church ladies, only to be abandoned by an ill-equipped father who became, for a decade, less than a figure-father, more a ghost, pursued by his own spook, and whose spook also haunted the son, leaving man-and-boy with hole-riddled hearts, damaged goods, no need for allegations of child-beatings, no potato-crop-failings or pub-brawls to raise the dramatic timbre, only mention the simple act of rejection, introduce the posh penitentiary with its heartless guardians, an advantaged disadvantage under the care of upper crust ogres...no, not ogres but oafs at least, oafishly bending-twisting a young mind out of shape, into something less useful, pricking holes until all potential has leaked out, sucked into black holes and cold-air returns, leaving a withering shell that eventually hardens, begins to crack, turns to stone...

And part two, *Mavis Returns: The Middle Ages*. Not bad, not bad at all. The title sells it, for after the beginning, after the glitzy entrance, the rest is a series of departures and returns, and so the boy, our hero, after serving ten years, is released for good behaviour, or wait…because there were rumours of scandal circulating through the usual channels, a theft, they say, an unsolved crime, but the truth will be recorded, not an admission, not a confession, just the plain facts, and his departure from Valentine House leads, in the natural, cyclical rhythm of the universe, to his return to his father's home, a rinkdinky existence on the wrong side of the proverbial and literal tracks, departed general population of Russell Hill Road and returned home, only to find himself in solitary confinement, spends the next three-plus decades tapping coded messages on the walls, gets no response from the other side, no answers at all…

The third and final instalment, the last panel for the literary triptych depicting my life, *Mavis in the Field of Dreams*. A joke, this title, a little levity to offset the tragic ending, which I suppose will be written not by me but a third party, maybe Nurse Maureen, who, seeing that no story is complete without the ending, will take pity and tie up the loose ends, fashion a touching epilogue, close the final chapter, leave to posterity the poignant tale of the Last Templeton…

But I am wasting precious time.

- - -

Early morning.

After a long night of spiritual dictation, interspersed with intervals of fitful sleep, I lie in my bed with sepulchral stillness. Nurse Maureen has gone off-duty, presumably retired to her lonely, contented bed. Swaddled in the brawny care of Saint Michael (archangel and patron saint of ambulance drivers, radiologists and haberdashers), I shift on my bedsores in search of relief. There is a large window to my right, but only dregs of sunlight filter through the soot-covered glass.

The mute orderly, the same one who silently removed my dinner last night, and who never seems to leave the hospital, has brought my breakfast: scrambled eggs, dry brown toast, diced melon and strawberries. Only the toast has any flavour at all, and it is not a pleasing one. I shudder to think of the process these courses went through before they found their way under my chin. The man who put them there is a tall, hairless creature, whose voiceless labour and calm reserve brings to mind the eunuchs of old, those servants of the Egyptian Court, notorious for their quiet grace and silent treachery, slipping hemlock powders into the soup tureen with a magician's dexterity. I see my eunuch as a self-appointed Angel of Mercy, bringing down judgment on those patients at Saint Michael's whose lives he deems no longer meaningful. And maybe he's right. I am in no position to disrupt his good work. If I have made his list, I am resigned. In any event, I am hungry, so the tasteless eggs and the limp fruit and the dry toast are going down the hatch.

Hanging from an impressive tubular framework in the far corner of my room is an antique colour television set, which I can operate with a remote control. Because I am my father's son, the set is tuned to the morning newscast. I am the lead story. Some of the b-roll footage of my arrival at Winnipeg has made its way here. A woman's voice is saying much the same thing Evelyn Wharton has said: to the U.S. government I am a suspect; to Canadians I am an unlikely symbol of tragic injustice.

"The Deputy Minister of Justice, Jonathan Wilkes," says the voice-over, "will meet later today with Senator Mary Walsh, the former high school teacher who turned to Democratic politics ten years ago, after her only son was wrongly convicted, and eventually executed in a Texas prison, for the rape and murder of eight-year-old Jessica Nettles. Sources close to the Senator say she is very interested in getting to the truth of this matter."

Truth. Echolalia strikes again.

The scene changes to show a plain, well-dressed woman standing on the front lawn of the Parliament buildings in Ottawa. A stiff tailwind ruffles her feathers. "While the outcome of these talks does not guarantee a happy ending to this story, they will no doubt shift the bureaucrats on both sides of the border into high gear towards a resolution. I spoke last night with family members, to get their reaction to what they see as 'trumped-up' charges by U.S. law enforcement."

Family members.

Cut to a man in his forties, smooth pate ringed by a tidy blonde hedge, eyes a fierce blue, cunning, small frame wrapped in Harris Tweed, mouth wide and hungry. It takes a long moment for me to recognize my dear cousin, David, long enough to miss his first words.

"… reprehensible that they would persecute a family that has suffered so much, already. We grieve for Uncle Harry, and pray for his timely return…"

Uncle Harry.

"…This is just another example of American bullyism. First Afghanistan, and then Iraq, and now they've trampled a defenceless Canadian family."

Cut to the corner of Gerrard and Woodbine, a sad, tired storefront with a peeling sign: Templeton Hardware. The 'CLOSED' sign hanging in the door. Unlit merchandise sulking behind smudged glass. Spent cigarette butts dotting the sidewalk. Litter tumbleweeding past the door. I notice that some vandal has finally removed the old bicycle frame from the light post, depriving the façade of its only artistic value.

I hadn't seen the store since the morning Harry and I departed on our cross-continent mission. It seems like only yesterday we were filling the hatchback with our second-rate luggage; and at the same time, it seems I haven't been there in months, years even. And now everything will be measured in terms of before-Harry's-death and after-Harry's-death. The shop will never be the same again. I will have to consider taking up Harry's plan and selling, since I've demonstrated time and again that I am not up to scratch in the business of hardware. Not to mention, once again, that I'm dying. Best to get things settled before I go. With whatever pittance the sale of the shop brings (the real estate itself must be worth something), maybe I'll move north and take up fishing, a gesture of respect to the old duffer. We'll have something to talk about for Eternity. *It's not so bad, Harry, except I'm not fond of touching the worms.*

Cut to the windblown reporter, standing now at the balustrade at Niagara Falls, the Rainbow bridge looming in the background.

"Canada-U.S. relations have been tested on a number of issues in recent years. Now, with a change of guard in Ottawa, political analysts expect an easing of the tension that grew out of the terrorist attacks of nine-eleven. The visit to the capitol, last month, by President Bush seems to signal a renewal of the long-standing fellowship between our two nations. But this incident can only slow the healing process on both sides. As for the fate of the late Harry Templeton, we'll have to wait a little longer.

"Reporting from Niagara Falls, this is…"

I switch off the television and push away the eggs. My legs have begun to throb. I feel light-headed. All that bad blood is having trouble moving through my atrophying veins.

- - -

When I was forty-three and my cousin David was forty-two, we were reunited in the parkland setting of the Metropolitan United Church, which occupies a vast plot of land adjacent to Saint Michael's Hospital. The grounds are shaded by ancient elm trees and furnished with convenient wooden benches. The church itself is a monolithic testament to mankind's devotion to the spiritual realm.

I failed to locate David in the telephone directory; his surname, Howald, belonged to his absconded father. It was my irritable lawyer, Ms. Wharton, who tracked down his unlisted number.

"I've been expecting you," he said, into the telephone. He sounded to me like any respectable man of middle years, far removed from the thug I knew as a child. We all grow up, eventually. "I would have come to the hospital sooner, but things have been a bit hectic around here." *Here*, he explained, was the Valentine mansion.

He agreed to make time in his busy schedule to meet me this afternoon, so I have arrived at the chosen spot, under one of the great elm trees, in a self-propelled wheelchair. My doctor insisted on the wheelchair, even though I will be discharged from the hospital tomorrow morning, now that my dodgy heart has settled into a comfortable routine. Golden leaves crunch under the wheels of my transport. The resident squirrels are busy doing some last-minute winter gathering. The sky is a solid mass of cloud, a hint of the coming season, washing everything below in a flat, hazy light. I feel a slight chill, pull up the collar of my jacket, enjoy the sensation of coldness—as I do every sensation, these days. Any feeling is better than no feeling.

David arrives by taxi, emerging from the backseat wearing a London Fog that collects his small frame nicely. Through a pair of oval spectacles he scans the park and locates me, puts a hand up as hello, makes his way towards me.

"Mavis," he says, shaking my hand vigorously. "Good to see you."

"Hello, David." I am a model of graciousness and decorum. For both of us, a Valentine upbringing shines through.

He glances around and spies a nearby bench, occupied by a dozing vagrant. "Over here," he says, moving towards the bench.

I follow, enjoying the modest strain of rolling the wheelchair across the short grass.

David nudges the vagrant's shin with the toe of his spotless Italian leather. "Wake up, Dad. Wake up!" The old man rouses slowly from his stupor, regards the intruder with something less than interest, and makes a sound that might be either a threat or a cough. David drops a fiver in the old man's lap. "Go ride the subway for an hour." The vagrant, taking this to be a splendid idea, snatches the bill and shuffles away before his good fortune once again turns south. My cousin takes his five-dollar seat and I roll up close, until our knees nearly touch. I am torn between my unsavoury history with David and my quiet but growing need for family—any family, now that Harry is gone. David wears the uniform of respectability, but I see that not far beneath the rich nap of his Saville Row wardrobe is the same gangster who filled my sneakers with Robyn Valentine's shaving cream, the same would-be dragon hunter who chased a harmless pooch under the wheels of a streetcar, the same thief who...

"Been a long time," he says, smoothing a crease in his overcoat.

"You're still in the house on Russell Hill."

"Grandpa died two years ago. I suppose you didn't know that."

"No."

"Someone had to take care of Nana. She's going to be ninety this spring."

"Ninety."

"Still a fucking virago, the old broad, but the bones are starting to crumble. Mom thought it would be best if I moved back in. It's not as if Robyn is any help."

"Goo bow."

"What?"

"I said it's good of you."

"Yeah. I sold my place in Yorkville for a nice little profit, so it wasn't too much of a hardship, moving back. Besides, Mom never really got over my leaving home in the first place."

"She was devoted to you, I remember."

"She refused to come to my first wedding, you know. She didn't talk to me for six months."

"You're married."

"Twice divorced. She told me I was making a mistake, that first time, but I went through with it anyway. Of course, she was right. Diane turned out to be a nutcase. But, you know what they say about love being blind."

"Sure, sure."

"The second time around we eloped. I didn't want to hear all the same old speeches."

I try to imagine my Auntie Benz giving a speech.

"Lasted six years with Renee before she ran off with some two-bit actor and half my money."

"I'm sorry to hear that."

"Next time I'm just going to find a woman I hate and buy her a house—save me the trouble of marrying her."

I smile.

"I heard that joke somewhere," he says.

"Sounds like you've had your share of trouble with women."

He nods, looks me over. "Speaking of trouble, this is some shit you're in."

"Bad blood."

He laughs. "The old broad was really hung up on that, eh? If it makes you feel any better, you're not the only one who got the 'bad blood' speech."

"It doesn't help to be ugly as sin."

David's face contracts into a frown as he tries to determine whether I meant him or me. If I had long ago accepted my role as Frankenstein's monster, my cousin clearly has issues with his own retreating hairline and spreading crow's feet. His vanity is not surprising to me. I can only imagine how insufferable he would have been twenty years ago, at the zenith of his youthful beauty and charm. For all I know, he might have gotten away with murder. In any event, I can see he is not comfortable with the topic, so I deftly change it.

"I saw you on television."

"Irene nearly had a coronary when she heard about..."

He hasn't got a measure of my grief, so he is treading carefully. A considerate boy, after all. But there is nothing he can say that will bring the hurt closer to the surface. My grief does not bend to the wind of mere words, but ebbs and flows as a tide, moved by forces as immeasurable and unknowable as any divinity.

"Surely she wouldn't have been too broken up about Harry's death. To say that she never liked him would be understating it."

"It's the publicity that upsets her. The telephone is ringing. There are reporters knocking on the door. She's mortified by the attention."

"I know how she feels."

"She's afraid they'll dig up all that ancient history. The daughter who married down, and then died giving birth to—" He stops himself from saying more, and I can see it is still difficult, unnatural, for him to be kind. But he's trying, that's the important thing. "Look, I don't mean to say anything bad about your mother or Harry. I didn't know either one. I'm sure they were good people."

"I'm sure they were, too."

"Sara Glynn was always Irene's favourite. She made that clear enough, over the years. Imagine how my mother felt. She could never live up to the sacred idol your mother became in Irene's eyes. It was only natural that Irene didn't like Harry. He was the original jewel thief, when he walked off with your mother." A small grin appears on his face. When I fail to respond to his casual allusion to the long-ago event that led to my deportation from the Valentine house, he says, "That was a long time ago. We were just kids. I had no idea they would send you away. It was supposed to be a joke."

"Never mind. It was for the best."

Now that I have said it, I truly mean it. My life—my real life—was with Harry, living in the drab apartment, with its faded carpets and threadbare furnishings, with the lingering smell of linseed and fried sausages, rattled by the passing trolleys, infused with the stale air of unrelenting poverty. Minding a store that was unprofitable, unappealing, uncompetitive, two generations behind the times, little more than a twelve-hundred-square-foot life jacket, keeping two pitiful heads bobbing just above the waterline. I never belonged to the Russell Hill crowd. And, in the end, I couldn't live up to the Heathcliff role, lacked the ambition required to take control of the Valentine estate and make it mine.

"It was good of you to speak up for Harry. He'd be glad to know you did."

"It was Irene's idea. She blames herself for not preventing the wedding."

"It was a love match."

David hoots, and there is a trace of the old mischievousness in there. I quietly promise myself I will not let him bully me, if it comes to it.

"It's not so far-fetched to believe they were in love. It happens more often than you think."

David looks at me with something like pity. "Harry didn't talk much, did he?"

I admit the old duffer was inclined to reticence. "He told me enough to know that Sara Glynn was devoted to him."

"There's more to the story than you think," he says. And suddenly there is the face I remember so well: the pint-size bully who could wield a secret as effectively as any practical weapon. *I know something you don't know...*

Before I can address this taunting mystery, our attention is drawn to a nearby disturbance. A bag lady, wrapped in layers of dirty sweaters, shod in pink flip-flops and crowned with an unravelling turban, has accidentally overturned the shopping cart she'd been pushing through the park, spilling the contents of her itinerant existence across the grass. There is nothing of any value there, except to the bag lady, who is now slowly, calmly, painstakingly replacing her belongings in the cart. I admire her fortitude, if not her circumstances. When I look at David, I see he is revolted by this woman's very existence. He wonders if another fiver will make this one disappear, too. But it's no surprise to me that Irene Valentine's snobbery has woven itself into my cousin's fabric. He didn't stand a chance against her fierce influence. I got away in time, it seems, to be spared that unseemly trait, and I have my companion to thank for it.

Watching as the bag lady reassembles her life, David says, "You should talk to Nana. She'll tell you the truth about your parents."

The way he says this, I'm not sure I want the truth.

- - -

Harry taught me a thing or two about truth.

As far as teenagers go, I was neither the best nor the worst of the breed. Passing through the usual phases one expects of adolescent boys, my hormone-induced traumas were comparatively minor. I was by turn sullen or quarrelsome, challenging Harry when I felt stung by the injustice of his house rules, or withdrawing from his strict conservatism—which was to me, at the time, an ideological crime of the worst order. And it was during this period that I established a pattern of behaviour that would set the tone for the subsequent three decades: whatever Harry said, whether true or not, I made it my duty to disagree with him. The result was that every conversation between us, sooner or later, degenerated into an argument.

Of course, by the end, this constant bickering had a charm all its own, an innocuous way of passing the time, a means of satisfying that need for human contact. There was no enmity, really, but those early patterns are the hardest to shed. By the ripening age of sixteen, I was well established in this stroppy routine, mercilessly picking away at Harry's half-baked opinions, and his patience.

History:

"Trudeau had every right to roll out the tanks," Harry said.

We were discussing the October Crisis, an event that, in 1970, had gripped the nation in fear and divided it in opinion. The Front de libération du Québec—an arguably organized league of Francophone separatists—perpetrated a pair of political abductions, one of which resulted in murder. In an effort to hunt down these "terrorists," our feisty Prime Minister invoked the War Measures Act, mobilized the Canadian Armed Forces and suspended our civil liberties. Many people, myself among them, believed this was a gross overreaction to what was, as far as we could tell, a routine police matter. Harry had, for once, set aside his conservative leanings and supported Trudeau's radical decision. I couldn't resist challenging the old duffer.

"He was trying to catch mice with hand grenades," I said. "He was giving his minions free reign to break down a door in Kamloops and arrest the occupants without warrant or charge, all because the FLQ snatched a few politicos three thousand miles away. Every cop with a grudge could take revenge with impunity. We had the army roaming the streets in battle gear."

"What's wrong with that?" said Harry. "I felt safer knowing those fine young men were out there, protecting my life and property."

"Those 'fine young men,' as you call them, were a bunch of pimply-faced kids, not much older than I am. How would you feel about me walking around our streets, seething with hormones and armed to the teeth? Would you really sleep better tonight knowing that I could shoot first and ask questions later, all in the name of national security?"

"These things are more complicated than you think, Mavis. You don't have all the facts. The truth is, there was a clear danger to the public, which means Trudeau had no choice."

"How can you say that? It's nothing but propaganda. It's what they want you to think."

Harry made a sound of exasperation. "What do you know about it? Truth is never black and white."

"I know the truth when I hear it," I said. Admittedly, a weak argument.

"You think so? Let's see."

He removed from his pocket an antique pocket watch—a bauble, manufactured on the cheap in India, that had come down from his late father. He suspended it between us. Long ago separated from its gold-plated chain, the old watch kept poor time and looked the worse for wear. As heirlooms go, it was without any but sentimental value.

"Pretend you don't know what this is," he said, pinching the watch between a thumb and forefinger, the backside facing me.

I huffed in exasperation, but then relented with a shrug. I confess I was curious.

"Tell me what you see. Describe it for me."

I was willing to play his game. "A gold metal disc, about two inches in diameter."

He nodded. "Anything else?"

"There's some sort of knob on top, and a loop, possibly to attach the metal disc to something else. And there's a scratch, about an inch long, more or less in the center."

He seemed satisfied with my answer. "All right. Now I'm going to describe this object to you, from *my* point of view. It's a disc, like you said, but it has a glass front. Behind the glass are little marks, twelve of them, and three sticks, each one a different length and thickness, that rotate around the little marks at different speeds."

I take in this data. "So what?"

"Who's telling the truth?"

I'm ashamed to admit I hadn't caught on to his game yet. It's so obvious now, but back then I still had a lot to learn, even from a simple mind like Harry's. "We both are," I said.

"But what if I were to call you a liar for saying my watch had a scratch on it? What would you say to that?"

"I can see the scratch," I said. I pointed to it. "It's right there."

Harry shook his head. "There is no scratch. I don't see the scratch. I think you're a liar, Mavis."

"This is a stupid game."

But Harry wasn't giving up on me. "What about you?"

"What about me?"

"You could accuse me of lying about the glass face and the rotating sticks and the twelve little marks. Here we are, both looking at the same object, but from different angles. We're looking at the same thing, but seeing something different."

"I get it, sure." I thought there wasn't much of a climax to this game.

"This watch," he said, "is *truth*. We see things from our own point of view, and everyone's point of view is a little different. You see? Pierre Trudeau was looking at the detailed side of the watch when he ordered the army into the streets. We were looking at the blank side. All we saw was the scratch. He was the one who knew it had the little marks and sticks and glass. And both points of view are the truth, as we see it."

Okay, so the old duffer had his moments. I'll give him his due credit, posthumously.

- - -

After dropping in my lap the prospect of Irene Valentine's "truth" about my parents, David shook my hand. "I have a meeting," he said. "Listen, don't be a stranger. Keep in touch." He adjusted the collar of his coat, waved down a taxi, and soon vanished into the uptown traffic.

I remained a while in the park, enjoying the sharpness of the late autumn air, watching the homeless population set up camp under the protection of the church grounds. I thought about Irene Valentine. When did she ever lack the truth in any matter? But I had learned from an early age to take my grandmother's truths with reservation. If she had something new to tell me about Harry's relationship with Sara Glynn, I'm not sure I would believe her.

I might listen, just the same.

24

Nurse Maureen has just marched into my room. Her arrival informs me of the shift change at the hospital. I am glad to see her. To be honest, I have less affection for the day nurses, who, as a group, are wont to complain a bit too freely about the difficult conditions they are made to work under, and who glance at their wristwatches as if that will make their coffee breaks arrive sooner. Whether or not they are justified in their complaints, they would benefit from a little discretion.

In spite of her natural capacity to instill fearful respect, I have grown fond of my nightshift overlord...or perhaps "fond" is the wrong word to describe the comfort I get from Nurse Maureen's thoroughness, and her patent need for peace and order. I respect and admire her devotion to an intense and sometimes brutal profession—a commitment, in her case, no less whole than a nun's fidelity to her God.

"What you bin doin, mon?" she says, circling my bed in search of disorder. "All the blood gone from your face."

Had she chosen a more domestic path in life, Nurse Maureen would have been a formidable mother. No needle-scratching gizmo can match her talent for lie detection; she can spot a partial truth from a hundred yards, and she has a policy of zero tolerance for circumlocution. With hardly a glance my way, she can tell my day has been eventful.

"I met my cousin today, in the park next door."

"Uh huh." This is her code for *you're not telling me everything.*

"He's the only cousin I've got, and I haven't spoken to him in thirty-three years." I let the power of that statement hang between us, sure I have satisfied her enquiry.

Nurse Maureen busily tucks in the sheets at the foot of my bed, even though I have explained to her that I don't like the sheets tucked in. My layman's diagnosis is claustrophobia.

"Uh huh," she says.

Under the threat of those two meaningful syllables, I must reveal all. "The cops were here this afternoon."

"*Ha!*" Now that I have come clean, she straightens up, cocks her hip and props a big fist on it. "What dem boys want?"

Answers.

- - -

Flush from my outing to the church grounds, I wheeled into my room on the fourth floor of Saint Michael's, and the toe of my left shoe—the prow of my rolling ship—collided with a pair of strange knees.

"Mavis Templeton," said the policeman, stepping aside.

"A coincidence. We have the same name."

"Sergeant Iverson," he said, clarifying his identity. "I'm with the RCMP."

His navy blue uniform surpassed the Metropolitan Police in overall splendour, but fell somewhat short of the awe-inspiring red livery of the traditional Mountie. In these modern times, I noted, things rarely change for the better.

"Where did you park your moose?"

Iverson pulled his head down into his shoulders. There was a glint in his eyes that told me this man had a sense of humour, but reserved its use for his off-duty hours. "I get that all the time," he said, dryly, "and it always makes me split a gut."

As I struggled to remove my jacket in the confining seat of the wheelchair, I assessed the unexpected visitor. I put him well into his fifties, old for a policeman. After years of running down felons and launching over fences in pursuit of justice, now probably a desk pilot. His proportions brought to mind a comic book hero gone to seed: the pigeon chest thrusting outward, casting a shadow over a spreading waistline; thighs of fallen oak, whittled down to pencil sticks at the ankles; arms resembling good Easter hams, where the meat falls sharply away to bare bone; head the shape of a carved pumpkin collapsing on itself weeks after Halloween.

Topping it all was a scrub of red thistle that was beginning to lose its colour. To my eye, he was nothing short of Captain Magnificent, a caped crusader, endowed with the diminishing powers and fading glory of superhero days gone by.

"Look here, Mavis...mind if I call you Mavis?" His tone hinted the question was rhetorical. He was looking over the room with the eye of an experienced investigator. I had no doubt he had already checked it over carefully, before I returned. Professional curiosity, he would have called it, had he been caught rummaging the cupboard. He would have found no contraband, no weapons, no drugs except those supplied legally by the hospital. I was not a threat.

By this time I had removed my right shoe, but the left was beyond my reach. I leaned forward and extended my arms helplessly, demonstrating my problem to the policeman. "Do you mind?"

With clicking knees and a middle-aged grunt, Sergeant Iverson knelt down and obliged me, untying my shoe and placing the pair neatly at the foot of my bed.

"I have the same problem, some days," he said, rising, not without some effort. "And these boots are murder on the arches."

"I suppose I should have left my shoes on, if you've come to arrest me."

"That's not why I'm here," he said.

"Just a friendly visit, then."

"Something like that."

"I'm popular these days, if I do say so myself."

"Right." He crossed the room and leaned his backside against the window sill. Even from that distance he could see that popularity could never have been much of a burden to me. Not with my face.

"To be honest, most of my life I've been invisible."

Iverson didn't know what to make of that.

"When you're as ugly as sin, people tend to act as if you're not there, which isn't a bad way to get through life, I admit."

"Some people are like that," he said. Insensitive, he meant. He was a man who'd been around, seen more things than most. He knew about people.

"If they can't ignore you, they're cruel, as if you were just another animal at the zoo, as if you don't have ears or can't understand what they're saying. They can't believe something this hideous can walk around, free as a bird. In the animal kingdom, I would have been killed by the herd, or at least abandoned. In Caesar's day I would have been sunk in the Tiber and quickly forgotten."

"Well, now…I don't think that's—"

"Now that I'm a person of interest, they can't get enough of me. They want to put me on television. They want to ask me questions, learn everything there is to know about me, the schools I've attended, the books I've read, the places I've been. Favourite food. Favourite colour. What brand of toothpaste I use. Where I get my shirts laundered. Where was I on the night of suchandsuch. They send interns into dank basements to root through the mouldy records of my life, and then print all that personal history in the newspapers, for the consumption of an interested public. I'm a movie star, Sergeant. Did you know I've been linked romantically to several supermodels in some of the most reputable tabloids? The rumours aren't true, of course. I had a brief fling with a stewardess, but it wasn't serious. There are no wedding plans in my immediate future, just to clear that up."

"Sensible," he said, a cynic.

I noticed he took no notes. Where Agent Compton of the NDBI had been meticulous in his interrogative methods, Sergeant Iverson was less formal, distracted, maybe a little slipshod. This man, despite his Marvell physique, wore the self-conscious and vaguely dejected air of a circus bear in a tuxedo. He had outlived his enthusiasm for the job, was pacing himself as he counted down to a well earned retirement.

"Was there something you wanted to ask me?"

He pushed off the window sill. As he turned, I saw there was a dusty smudge on the tail of his jacket. "Not exactly," he began. "It's more of a warning."

Warning.

Damn you, echolalia.

"Some of my superiors think you should be charged."

Charged.

"Attempting to unlawfully convey a deceased person into the country, interfering with a cadaver—they haven't figured it out, yet."

"Once you let one dead person in, there's a stampede at the gates. You have to keep these things in check, nip the problem in the bud."

Sergeant Iverson kept a straight face. He was unflappable. "It's a crime. I'm sure your lawyer told you that."

"We don't really speak the same language."

"I know what you mean. Anyway, my superiors are getting pressure from powerful offices."

Superiors.

"It's a waste of time, if you ask me. The whole thing."

"Where would we be without law and order, Sergeant? There would be bedlam in the streets. Anarchy."

The irony was not lost on him. "Off the record, most of us are on your side. I want you to know that."

"Nevertheless, you might still come for me."

"I don't make the decisions, I just follow orders. But I wanted you to know that there's a decision coming. I can't say when, and I can't say what the decision will be. There's some out there that think it's in everyone's best interests to give you up to the Americans."

"Everyone's best interests except mine."

"Exactly right. Not yours. International relations, and all that. Keep the peace. The needs of the many…"

"The lamb."

"Sorry?"

"I'm the lamb, being led to the altar." Does my lowercase faith have room for spiritual martyrs, I wondered? Saint Mavis.

"Something like that."

"They'd better hurry."

"What's that?"

"I was wondering, Sergeant…I was just wondering what happened to the bright red tunic and the Stetson?"

He looked himself over and seemed ambivalent. "It's a new look. What do you think?" He still hadn't noticed the dusty smudge on the tail of his jacket.

"It makes me proud to be Canadian."

"Listen," he said, adjusting his holster, "I better be going."

"Your moose double parked?"

"I'm splitting a gut, Mavis." As he reached to door, he turned back. "By the way, this conversation never happened." He touched the side of his nose and squeezed out the door.

- - -

The orderly—the silent eunuch, the angel of mercy—has just wheeled in my dinner: sliced ham with mashed potatoes and soft medallions of boiled carrots. Before he could escape, I asked him how well he had slept last night. But he is a crafty one, this orderly. He won't be caught out so easily. He merely smirked in his sly way and pushed his trolley into the corridor. Yesterday, when I asked Nurse Maureen about the mute orderly, she made the sign of the evil eye and scooched away to some imaginary emergency. As a practitioner of the voodoo arts, she is governed by ritual and superstition.

As with every meal served at Saint Michael's, the one before me bears the aroma of something inorganic, like the tin-can air of a moon colony. This cuisine has not been prepared so much as processed, sterilized, perhaps irradiated. I have to wonder if continued exposure to these dishes will cause my pecker to shrivel up and fall off; but then I think: what would it matter? Unlike so many other men, I have not been led through life by that fruitless appendage. As I bring the fork towards my mouth, I catch the faint smell of almonds coming off the ham. The meat hovers over my tongue; there is a decision to be made, and with every decision, as I well know, comes a certain degree of risk. I consult the essence of my faith, my lowercase faith, and find I cannot so easily surrender to the whimsy of some other apostle, no matter how passionate his devotion. I must follow my own banner.

I set down the fork and push the tray aside. *In my own time, dear angel.*

And it is now, after an unsettling meeting with my cousin and a peculiar conversation with the police, that I realize I have not smoked a single cigarette since my admission to the hospital. Will this be the last miracle of my life? Not only do I have no idea where my cigarettes are, I am pleased to discover that I don't really care. If the brave and hardworking doctors at Saint Michael's can do nothing about my faltering heart, they have at least cured my incorrigibility. I am smoke-free for the first time in three decades.

- - -

My discharge from Saint Michael's is imminent. At eight o'clock this morning, only thirty minutes from now, I will be emancipated, cut free of the tubes and wires that connect me to the hospital's eyes and ears, severed from the medical umbilicus and released back in to the wild, to fend for myself. Alone. Or mostly so. Evelyn Wharton is scheduled to make a rare personal appearance, ostensibly to see that I arrive home safely.

The telephone had roused me from a troubled sleep shortly before seven. It was Ms. Wharton, calling from the plush depths of her BMW.

"Good news, Mavis," she said. "There's been a drive-by shooting in Scarborough. Happened early this morning. A pregnant woman caught in the crossfire. Bullet through the head." She sounded breathless from excitement, but it might have been the cellular static.

"Um," I said, "maybe I'm not quite awake yet, but was that the *good* news you were mentioning?"

"The press was camped in front of your place overnight. They were tipped off that you were coming home this morning. Now they have this, and it's big. We couldn't have asked for better timing. They'll be all over this one for days."

"It's as if we planned it," I said, ironically.

"We got lucky."

Some people aren't so lucky, I thought. I had to ask: "Out of curiosity, Ms. Wharton, where were you early this morning?"

But she wasn't listening. "This traffic is murder. Jesus God, where are all these people going, so early?"

As if to answer her question, the blatt of car horns came through the earpiece, and the sound from her end of the line suddenly faded, as if her phone were submerged in the shallow end of a noisy pool. There was a scuffing sound; I could only assume she had dropped her phone face-down in her lap. Through the scuffing came the muted hint of a brewing row. I could hear nothing coherent of the exchange, but the enraged tone spoke clearly enough. Evelyn Wharton fired a series of verbal salvos in the direction of the other motorist—the "accused," as she might say, the presumption of guilt dripping off her lips. Someone, I feared, was about to learn that, in future, he should pick on someone his own size.

And because I was raised a polite boy, I held the receiver patiently against my ear, waiting for this temporary distraction to pass. It didn't occur to me to hang up and go back to sleep, which would have been a sensible thing for a sick man to do. I felt no pangs of concern for my lawyer, who had demonstrated in so many ways that she was capable of holding her own in a scrape. I waited, trying less and less, as the long seconds passed, to attempt to decipher the details. Just as my mind began to drift lazily across a glassy lake, north of the Haliburton Highlands—the tip of my fishing pole dipping almost imperceptibly from the tension of the trailing line, a fat perch nosing in on the gleam of the lure—the cell phone resurfaced with a crackling *rush.*

"Sorry," she said quickly. "Listen, I'm twenty minutes away. I'll see you then." And she rang off without even confirming that I was still on the line.

I had only just replaced the receiver when it rang again.

"I forgot to tell you," said Evelyn Wharton. "They're sending your father home." There was the unmistakable squeal of rubber tires, and the line went dead.

Welcome home, Harry.

- - -

Ten days have passed since Harry blew a vital gasket and slumped over the steering wheel of the green Pinto, died in the arms, so to speak, of his second great love. Eight days he's been locked in a freezer in the Grand Forks coroner's office, tagged as evidence and guarded against escape.

But who's counting?

Words rise and retreat in my mind, tinted with accusation. "…your father…sustained bodily injuries that he couldn't possibly have survived." "…unable to determine the cause of death." "…can't rule out foul play." My fault, all mine. My decision to lunch at Uncle Jim's Mexican Fiesta. My fault. When that proved a fatal mistake, it was my decision to prop him up and drive on, pretend it never happened. My god, I was talking to a corpse! What was I thinking? Why didn't I call the police, have him pronounced dead, acquire the straightforward documents required to bring him home for a decent, private burial? Didn't he deserve that? Yes, of course he did. Then again, he deserved a better son.

Failure: measured by degrees. I'm no longer sure it matters how many notches the needle passes. If one wins a race, does it matter by how much? A win is a win, just as a loss is a loss. From the very beginning I have disappointed everyone with a consistency that could only be credited to an inbred weakness. Bad blood. Among the Valentines, I didn't stand a chance. My fussy grandmother, Irene Valentine, was forever vigilant against these sanguineous contaminants, for which she had a nose, and of which, I suspect, she was mortally afraid. I had polluted the family gene pool, and was eventually—but not entirely—flushed from the system. And Harry, although he possessed no class prejudices and was uninterested in the genetic sciences, felt constantly betrayed by my apparent and intractable shortcomings. If I were to take a more poetical attitude, I might claim to be merely, and eternally, misunderstood. The artist's prerogative. But I am no poet, and so I am left with a sketchy track record and poor prospects. When I finally catch up with Harry in the Great Hereafter, how will I answer his accusing stare? There is only one thing I can say: *Even though I failed and failed, I did my best.*

At least I can honestly say I've never intentionally caused anyone harm; small consolation when I consider the harm I've imposed unwittingly. Maybe it's no coincidence my show is being cancelled halfway through the third act. The forces of justice will have their way in the end. Nature strives for balance, weeding out weakness, in all its various forms, and my lowercase faith accepts this as a sensible means of sustaining order in the universe. The occasional appearance of chaos does not represent a lack of order so much as an equalizing operation, a restoration of balance. And my compensation for having the plug pulled ahead of schedule, for having been short-changed from the very beginning, for having kept the faith, such as it is, is an eternity in the rolling green pastures of the Afterlife.

Could be worse.

25

Evelyn Wharton dropped me off moments ago, having made the fifteen minute trip from the hospital to my home in under ten, and giving the rampaging taxis a run for their money. I enjoyed the BMW's cocoon, hugged by soft leather seats that lovingly braced me against the G-forces of my lawyer's aggressive driving. Harry would have been conflicted in his feelings about this car, with its luxurious appointments and eager horsepower, and the unnatural ease with which it responded to the driver's commands. The old duffer believed driving was intended to be a struggle, not only against the external forces (poorly maintained roads, the weather, other motorists), but against the machine itself, a match of strength and will, the destination a hard-won victory. Had he witnessed this petite woman navigating the corners without slowing, using only the tips of her fingers on the steering wheel's center pad, and all the while taking a conference call on her cell phone, he would surely have scoffed that the car was doing all the work, which defeated the purpose of driving a car in the first place.

As the car growled through another amber light, Evelyn Wharton snapped her phone shut and dropped it in her lap. "Harry's arriving at the airport tomorrow at two o'clock." She made it sound, perhaps intentionally, as if he were still alive. With minimal effort from her right foot, she overtook a panel van in the narrow right lane, honked a warning at two young boys who were walking their bicycles across the street at a slothful pace, and jolted to a stop in front of Templeton Hardware. "You won't have to be there, though."

"I want to be there," I said. My words seemed too loud, now that the car's engine was idling.

"I've made arrangements for Global News to be here before lunch."

"You're inviting the media? I thought they were the enemy."

Evelyn Wharton smiled at my apparent naiveté. "They're not the enemy, Mavis. They're like a Doberman. As long as you keep it on a leash, you can control it." She saw that I wasn't quite going with her analogy. "Don't worry. They'll ask you a few questions, get a bit of family history that they'll edit out later, nothing too demanding. Basically, all they want is to capture your sad face on tape. Anything else is padding to fill the piece out to ninety seconds. Just remember to work on the hitch. They'll eat it up."

"You're very cynical," I said, more an observation than a reproof.

"You can thank your lucky stars for that. Look, there's nothing to worry about. I'll be here the whole time."

"Who's going to get Harry from the airport?"

"It's all taken care of. After the interview, I'll bring you to the funeral home."

Funeral.

I remembered something. "Do you want your gizmo back?" I was referring to the portable tape recorder she had given me as a means of recording my side of the story. "There's not much more to tell." I proffered the device, electing not to tell her the tape was blank.

"Keep it. I don't think we'll need it, after all."

I shrugged and slipped it back into my shirt pocket, neat as a cigarette packet.

As I was angling out of the car, setting myself up on the crutches, readjusting to *terra firma* after being joggled through the city maze, Evelyn Wharton leaned into the space I had vacated. "It's a good sign, Mavis. If they're sending your father home, it can only mean they're about to drop the whole investigation. Everything's going to work out fine."

"I'm not worried," I said.

And it was true. I was beyond worrying about anything. After all, I had spent my life letting others carry the burden of worry. First were the Valentines, who undertook to raise me as their own—with mixed results, I think I can safely say—and who fearlessly rendered decisions, small and large, as they related to my care and development. And then there was Harry, who was handed the reins and took them unflinchingly, and directed the course of my life for the next three decades, down to the last mundane detail. For most children, it is a rite of passage to shuck the parental bridle, as it were, unhitch from the family wagon and canter blissfully through the willowing pastures of independence. I was one of the few who chomped down on the bit and settled into my role as a dependant. If Harry objected to this arrangement, he gave no sign of it, but I believe he enjoyed the role, enjoyed the position of superiority it put him in. What's the point of making a decision if there is no one around to admire you for it? That was Harry's view. Now Harry is gone, and I find myself orbiting peacefully under the awesome gravitational influence of Evelyn Wharton.

From the moment I first made headlines, way back after my inauspicious entry into this world, I was branded, and forever after regarded, a helpless creature. I don't think I've been needy in my behaviour, but the whiff of neediness swirls invisibly around me. I can't help it. And it's a jacket I'm comfortable wearing. Decision-making, frankly, is not all it's cracked up to be. Look at the brief interval in my life between Harry's death and my introduction to Evelyn Wharton: one disaster after another, smack-ups, injuries, the unnecessary death of a hero. Without Harry's anchor, I was out of my depths in the real world.

If I am anxious about the end of my role in this international brouhaha—which, if my lawyer is to be believed, is assured and imminent—it is for the simple reason that Ms. Wharton will then move on to the next big case, leaving me alone to fend for myself. As I watched the BMW spin off the curb and disappear from sight, a cold wind careened around the corner of Woodbine, circling me, snaking up my pant legs, whipping strands of hair across my face. Winter was coming, and I couldn't help wondering if it will be my last season.

Home again, home again...jiggedy jig.

- - -

There are many smells, and they don't conflict so much as coexist in careless amity. Linseed, sawdust, sour milk, damp fabric, Old Spice, fried potatoes, burnt tobacco leaves, musk, the slightly rancid niff of phantom pets that we never owned. *Home again...*

I move from room to room like a potential leaseholder, examining the familiar possessions: the green corduroy sofa with the fabric worn to a shine, the wobbly maple chair acquired (through mysterious circumstances) from The Pig & Whistle, the vintage kitchenette with the chipped faux-marble laminate, the rosewood bureau in Harry's room (the only piece with any value; it came from the Valentine mansion as a reluctantly-bestowed wedding gift), the first-generation colour television set, the cast-iron kettle that has sat on the stove since Harry's youth, my own bed with the plain blue bedspread. All of it now mine, including the deed to the building and the wares in the shop below. The responsibility also now mine, if I want it. Bills to pay, stock to order, hours to keep, insurance premiums, credit cards, bank statements, the blasted key-cutting machine. And I have no son to pass along my infinite wisdom and knowledge to, no heir to the Templeton empire. I wonder if I should get a dog.

And these possessions, my inheritance, they no longer connect me to life the way they seemed to when Harry was alive. They are mine in the way the memory of a book, read long ago, is mine. I feel like an interloper, a voyeur, an irrelevance—just another thing Harry left behind that no longer has any use, now that he's gone. I run my hand across the bedspread and feel the velvety texture of the fabric. It's not real velvet, of course; the old duffer would say, and I would agree, that spending good money on real velvet would be foolish. This ersatz velvet feels good under my hand. I had been with Harry when he bought it, for less than twenty dollars. *Nice one, Harry.*

Through the closed upper windowpane I hear the front door of the shop rattle. I think at first it is merely the biting winter wind, still seeking me out, but then realize it must be a customer, some local husband in need of a plumber's wrench or Varsol. For sixty-four years Templeton Hardware could be relied upon, if for nothing else, to be open for business between the hours of nine-thirty and six, except on Sundays. While everything else in the modern world changes—and rarely for the better, I will add, cynically—our little shop has been a notable constant. No Templeton ever took a holiday until Harry agreed to drive me to Edmonton. We have been here for our needy and faithful customers, supplying the wire brushes and cotter pins that held their lives together. In two days' time we will have been dark for two weeks, long enough, surely, for the local handymen to classify us as merely part of the ever-changing world, and accustom themselves to the fifteen minute drive to Home Depot. Where there is plenty of free parking. And which is open for business well into the evening, and all day Sunday.

A single profanity wafts up, and the front door falls silent. Had I possessed a head for business, I might have ambled downstairs, thrown open the doors and ushered the customer inside with a neighbourly smile, and proclaimed our merchandise at his disposal—but I possess no such head. The head I am in possession of is beginning to throb. I am vaguely sorry for the customer's flooded bathroom or hardening paint roller, but he will have to seek help elsewhere.

Moving indolently through Harry's former bedroom, I pick up the picture frame on the nightstand, the old black & white wedding photo, the only image of my mother I own. The lovebirds, reunited at last. I carry the picture to the living room and set it on the coffee table. The apartment seems alien without Harry's doleful face looming beside me. Even my living presence doesn't register here. An era has irrevocably passed. I am more convinced than ever that I will sell everything and...do what? I don't know. Thanks to the progression of my disease, long term plans are wasted on me. Perhaps I will acquire a shopping cart and a dog, and move to the treed grounds of the Metropolitan United Church, live according to the whims of Nature, share my last days with the other lost souls who've given up making decisions for themselves. *Go with the flow. No gumption required.*

- - -

When the telephone rings, I open my eyes to darkness. I am reclined on the sofa, feel the weight of a hardcover book in my lap, can't tell if it is late at night or early in the morning. I only know that it is either too late or too early to be telephoning someone, and only Evelyn Wharton is thoughtless enough to do so.

"Hello?"

"Hang on," says Evelyn Wharton. "Got another call." There is a click, and the ambient noise on the line changes. Her audacity makes me smile. She revives in me the belief that Von Daniken was onto something when he speculated that Earth, throughout its short history, has been visited repeatedly by alien life forms. Evelyn Wharton is from another world.

I use this pause to switch on the lamp at my side and look at my watch, but the lamp fails to come on. This, combined with the chill creeping around my shoulders, tells me the furnace is off, which means the power is out. I stare at the grey window and detect a swirl of light snow. The new season has come early this year. I shift the book off my lap, drop it on the coffee table, try—and fail—to recall what the book is called. My memory is not what it once was.

Some minutes later, after watching the snow outside the window build into a squall, there is a click, and Evelyn Wharton's thin voice pulls me out of my trance. I had forgotten the receiver was tucked into the crook of my neck. I put it back to my ear. "The power is out," I say, over Evelyn's gabbling.

"What?" She still isn't used to being interrupted.

"I said the power is out, over here."

"What do you think I've been telling you? The power is out *everywhere.*"

"Well, I don't think—"

"From Detroit to Kingston, and as far north as Barrie. Buffalo is out. Cincinnati is out. New York is out."

"How can that be?" My question is rhetorical. I don't really expect my savvy lawyer to have an answer. But, of course, she does.

"We're all on the same grid," she says. "Or at least the grids are all connected. One of the major hubs went down, somewhere in Ohio, I think. It hasn't been confirmed yet. They're saying it's the biggest blackout in history."

"Who's saying?"

"What?" There is a lot of static on the line.

"Who is saying that?"

"The experts, Mavis. The experts are saying that. By the way, were you awake?"

"What time is it?"

"What? I don't know. Four something."

"You're up early," I say.

"No, I'm up late. Listen, this blackout is a big deal. It's a major problem."

"My furnace is off."

"What? Yes, everyone's furnace is off. Put a log on the fire."

"You've seen where I live. Do you really think I have a fireplace?"

"Listen, listen. If they can't get the power back on, the whole schedule goes out the window. They can't put Harry on a flight in Grand Forks if our airport is shut down. I've been in touch with Global News and put them on standby. And obviously we won't be having a funeral without the body. So—"

"Harry's never been on an airplane before."

"What?"

"He didn't get around much."

She isn't going to let me derail her train of thought. "Okay. So, they say it might be a day or two before the power's back up. That means we'll have to wing it a bit. Don't worry. I have contingency—"

"Why are the phones on?"

"What?"

"The phones are working, but you say the power is off *everywhere.*"

"I don't know. Emergency backup batteries. Something like that. They can't ever let the phones go down."

Not in Evelyn Wharton's world.

"Listen, I only called to give you an update. We'll have to play it by ear."

"Wing it."

"What? Yes, wing it. Right. Oh…sorry, got another call."

The line goes dead.

I hoist myself onto the crutches. I am getting better with them, which is good, because I will need them for weeks to come. Then I will have a cane. Perhaps I will have a permanent limp. It won't make any difference to me.

Bringing my mother's photograph with me, I begin to lurch towards my bedroom. With no power and no heat, my plan now is to get into bed and wait for the power—and my furnace—to come back on. On the way, I stop in the bathroom, brush my teeth in the dark, drink water from the tap. The water still runs, but I can't say why. My bedroom is in back, the window overlooking the alley and the blank brick wall of the Laundromat. I can barely make out the snow, which moves like bacteria under a microscope. Tendrils of ice-cold air reach through the gaps in the window frame and touch me. I am wearing a pair of good flannel pyjamas that Harry bought at Goodwill for just a few dollars. This is the first time I have worn them. The stiff fabric around the collar scratches my neck, but I know that in time it will soften, will chafe no more.

I wonder if this will be the last pair of pyjamas I will own. These days, my life is filled with *lasts*. My last haircut; last bus ride; last toothbrush; last winter; last bowl of green chili; last heart attack; last rites. But who's counting?

It feels good to be in my own bed. There is a depression in the left side of the mattress that fits my body perfectly, and I am grateful for this familiar comfort. Here in this bed, there are no problems. The blankets are warm. I can see little around me in the darkness, although I sense the light outside the window is increasing. Somewhere above this snowstorm, the sun is preparing to rise.

As I lie here and think about Harry and his upcoming funeral, the telephone rings. I ignore it. The telephone is in the living room, and nothing can motivate me to get out from beneath my warm sheets. I feel like a kid, with just enough of a fever to stay home from school. The only thing I need now is a mother.

26

A flawless pale sky stretches over Kingston Cemetery, dispensing unseasonable warmth to those of us at ground level. A brilliant cast of light causes me to squint. I require no overcoat over my new suit, but I could use some sunglasses. My suit, which is such a deep shade of black that the eye wants to slide off it, was given to me this morning by Evelyn Wharton, a gift, her final act of goodwill before she moves on to more pressing cases on her roster. When I offered to reimburse her for the cost of the suit (an expense I wasn't sure I could afford), she thumbed the buttons on her cell phone menacingly and dared me to make a fuss. Being a natural coward, I relented with many thanks and hobbled to my room to change. The suit fits me perfectly, which makes me think Ms. Wharton has been snooping in my closet. She will stop at nothing to succeed.

She stands beside me now on the hard, flat November grass, snugly ensconced in a tailored suit as brilliantly white as mine is invisibly black. She is the Yang to my Yin. Together, in our monochromatic splendour, we represent the entire known spectrum. She holds my arm and makes soft noises, and I know at this moment that this is what a mother feels like. Comfort and protection. I feel safe.

Evelyn Wharton has orchestrated this event, two days after the eastern half of the continent emerged from a thirty-six-hour blackout. From beneath my bed sheets I had heard my neighbours cheering when power was finally restored. An hour later, with the city once again moving, the dump of snow that had amplified the silence of the blackout had melted away, leaving behind a dirty wet stain. And two hours after power was restored, Harry was in the cargo hold of a Boeing 767, making his final journey home.

Because we were "winging it," Evelyn had decided that we both should be at the airport to meet Harry's arrival after all. The media had turned up, too, but not in the numbers I expected.

"There's no news in happy endings," she explained. "They'll put this story to bed with a thirty-second voice-over, right before the first commercial break." I was no longer a person of interest to either the United States or the RCMP. Or the media.

"I hope Harry enjoyed his first airplane ride," I said.

"At least he didn't have to suffer the shoe-leather chicken in tourist class."

"Beats a Mexican Fiesta, any day."

Also present for this sombre celebration of Harry Templeton's life are representatives of the remaining Valentine clan: my cousin David, my Auntie Benz and Uncle Robyn. Absent are Joseph and Irene Valentine. Joseph is resting peacefully under a grassy knoll in Forest Hill Cemetery. Irene had recently suffered a second stroke; she is recovering—permanently, David tells me—in Gainsborough Manor, a posh nursing home only a few blocks from the Russell Hill Road mansion.

"She still has most of her marbles," says my cousin, as we pace the grounds, waiting for the ceremony to begin. "But after two stokes, she sounds like a toothless wino. And she's not too happy about being in the old folks' home." He shrugs, holds out his palms in a helpless gesture. "But, hey, what can you do? It's not as if Mom or Uncle Robyn can take care of her, and I've got the business to run."

"The office on Spadina," I say.

"The very one." He grins mischievously.

"Finally taken an interest in literature, David?"

He gives a small shrug. "The appreciation of art is not the same thing as the business of art."

I understand what he's telling me. He is dismantling Joseph Valentine's magnificent collection. If my heart weren't already broken...

"The old lady's been asking for you. She wants you to come see her."

"More family heirlooms gone missing, I suppose?"

David laughs. Beyond him, I see my Auntie Benz frown. She has not spoken since arriving, but she is listening, and clearly doesn't approve of my making light of that long-ago theft. I have no doubt she still believes I am guilty of the crime her own son perpetrated, and I am not going to disillusion an old woman who already has so many troubling things on her mind. Her dark star has lost none of its power.

Robyn Valentine is using the pre-ceremony time to wander the grounds, towed along by a young black terrier—the evil Scotch terrier Prickles having been the first of the Valentines to go to his just reward, many years ago. "Goo bow," mutters Robyn, perhaps to me.

So here we are, numbered five: the last Templeton, his stylish mouthpiece, the former thug and his black-hole mother, the dimwit uncle. The glare of a potent sun, the undulating hash of traffic noise along Woodbine filling the silent gaps, the nameless terrier squirming at Robyn's heel like a restless child, southbound geese honking their good-byes for another year. I survey the cemetery grounds. The rest of the world churns around us as Harry descends, face-up, into the ground.

So long, you old duffer. So long, Dad!

The Unitarian minister presiding over this event is a cheerful septuagenarian with an easy, gap-toothed smile. "Call me Stacey," he had said to me, as the introductions were made, late yesterday afternoon. "Or Reverend Stacey, if you must. But, to be honest, I'm too old for useless formalities." And he unleashed a hearty baritone laugh that swept away all traces of the grief I was supposed to convey at such a solemn time. How could I feel sad next to this old codger and his holey grin? I had to smile. And I immediately felt a bond with this man who seemed utterly unashamed of his girly name—not only unashamed, but proud enough to shun the other names and titles that might have distracted from its ambiguous gender.

"Call me Mavis," I said, in a moment of emotional brotherhood.

And now the ceremony has begun:

"…It's only natural that we should grieve for the loss of our father or brother or friend," intones Reverend Stacey, to the small group gathered around the rectangular hole in the ground. "Harry Templeton is gone, and we can't help feeling the tremendous loss in our lives and in our souls. But just as we do not mourn the loss of spring as it gives way for summer, nor mourn summer for fall, nor fall for winter, so we should not mourn a life that gives way for death, for that is simply part of the natural cycle of God's great design. Do not feel sad for Harry. Death is not a tragedy, not a punishment for one's sins. It's not an end but a beginning, a God-given gift that should be rejoiced. Harry Templeton has been given the greatest gift a man can receive: that of eternal peace at the right hand of God..."

I am so moved by his words that I briefly consider putting myself up for membership in the Unitarian church, giving myself over, finally and completely, to a legitimate faith, one with a brick-and-mortar foundation. My last chance to earn a ticket that will gain me entry through the Front Gates. *Look, Big Guy, I'm a Unitarian. None of that Trinity nonsense, You're the only One for me.* I envision my debut as the newest member of the Unitarian congregation: the double doors flung wide open, brass horns blaring a regal triad that causes every head to swivel in my direction, and then a meaningful stillness, a pause dripping with anticipation, and as my left foot crosses the threshold, one more miracle to cap a miraculous life: the stiffness and aches of my vile disease lift away from my body, dissipate like an exorcised demon, and I stride forward in a brisk march, one leg in front of the other, arms moving at my side like alternating pendula, head swivelling left/right as I acknowledge the cheering masses, my new family, my adoptive clan, the Unitarians!

But old habits cling like barnacles to my hull. My homeless and unnamed faith asserts itself, pokes me in the ribs, and informs me it will not be so easily usurped. And, in the end, I cannot abandon the only true and familiar brand of comfort I have left.

Standing in the place of honour in this small crowd, I feel my balance waver, until Evelyn Wharton readjusts her grip on my arm. I look down at her timeless face, and she bids me a smile that seems to originate from a more divine source, as if she were merely an envoy, delivering an unexpected message from above. *Thank you, Mother.*

An air horn sounds at the busy intersection over my shoulder, and the spell is broken. I know there are no cheering crowds, Unitarian or otherwise, and I've run out of miracles. As for family...well, what remains of it is with me now, cunning, maudlin, daft, flea-bitten, they are here, with the exception of Irene Valentine, who lords over Gainsborough Manor in paralyzed splendour, awaiting my call. At the thought of seeing her again— my childhood warden—the blood begins to pound at my temples. The tainted blood of a "broomstick vendor."

The good Reverend Stacey is wrapping things up. "…And with acceptance comes Everlasting Peace. With faith comes the knowledge that we are one with God. Harry Templeton may be gone from this world, but he is now part of the One that surrounds us, the One that lives within us all, and in that way he will always be with us."

A helicopter thuds overhead, on a mission to somewhere. A roaming dog barks, and Robyn Valentine's pup answers. *Goo bow!* Life goes on. The official celebration is concluded, and now the real party will begin. We will be making our way to Russell Hill, to send Harry off in grand Valentine style.

"Listen, Mavis," says Evelyn Wharton. "I can't stay. I have another appointment."

The announcement does not surprise me. I knew she'd be leaving me, sooner or later. "Your job here is done. On to the next big case."

She tightens her grip on my arm, unsure of my sincerity. "It's been an honour to work for you," she says. "Don't think it hasn't."

"I only hope my mysterious benefactor doesn't chisel you out of your fee. You've earned every penny."

She smiles. "Don't worry. I know where he lives."

"If you can't find him at home, you can always try his office on Spadina."

She kisses both my cheeks, and, as if on cue, her cell phone chirps. She releases me, flips open her phone and presses it to her ear. As she slowly walks out of my life, I wonder if whoever is on the other end of the conversation is going to give her the answers she needs. Life goes on.

This is the moment that Mercedes Valentine, the black hole, my Auntie Benz, chooses to enfold me in a tight, tremulous embrace. "I'm sorry," she whispers in my ear, clutching my shoulders with her brittle hands. She smells dusty, like a closet that has been shut for years; and although she has me firmly in her grip, I feel she is as light as the black silk shawl that drapes her, that a sudden gust of wind will send her aloft, reduce her to dust and scatter her elemental pieces across the Kingston Cemetery grounds, ashes to ashes...

Before I can blink, Auntie Benz is replaced by Robyn Valentine, who is an old man now, grey and rumpled and soft as the boy in his soul. His embrace is bearish and heartfelt, his great paw patting my back. "My dog's name is Curly," he says. We separate, and both look down at Curly, who at least seems a more sociable creature than old Prickles had been. "He's black," says my uncle.

"Yes," I say.

"Like you."

"Yes, I'm very black today."

David intervenes, shaking my hand and touching my arm. "Ready to go?"

I nod.

"You can sit up front with me."

And so this odd family unit shuffles towards the silver Jaguar parked at the curb. My aunt and uncle, resembling an old married couple who, years ago, had run out of things to say to each other, fold themselves into the back seat, young Curly scampering across their knees as he attempts to look out every window at the same time.

I take my familiar spot in the co-pilot's seat, next to my cousin. "Too bad Harry never got a chance to drive a nice car like this," I say, admiring the walnut trim and leather upholstery. I try to imagine what our drive across the continent would have been like, comfortably ensconced in this fine automobile, instead of rattling around in Harry's old Pinto. There is more than enough leg room for my six-foot frame. No travel cramps from this ride. But we'd still have bickered relentlessly, because that was what we did, and no degree of luxury would have changed that.

We launch into the flow of traffic like the Queen Mary II, silently gliding through the grey asphalt sea. I break the silence. "It was good of you to take care of us—Harry and me, I mean. I don't know what I would have done."

David shrugs. "What's family for?"

Indeed. After corrupting me, and then sending me into a thirty-year exile, this family was there for me in the end. I suppose it could have been worse. I might have remained in that dour mansion, the one we are now en route to, might have spent my life, as David had, under the constant, watchful eye of Irene Valentine, with her *tsk*-ing disapproval and her dinnertime polemics. I might never have known my father, beyond the strange annual visitor who always seemed as if he were trying to climb out of his own skin and slither away. Only god knows what fiendish crimes Bugsy might have pinned on me, had he had the opportunity.

As we roll smoothly into Russell Hill, I say to David, "Can we stop at a corner store? I need cigarettes." For the first time in days, I crave my old drug of choice, nicotine.

"You won't find a corner store around here," says David. "Brings down the tone of the neighbourhood. Irene's legacy."

I should have guessed.

He turns the sedan gently into the driveway. "Anyway, those things'll kill you."

"So I've heard."

I haven't been in the Valentine living room since the day of my interrogation over the missing pendant, back in 1971. The room is arranged differently now, of course, the Queen Anne theme replaced over the decades by Ethan Allen chic; but the gloom is still there, lurking in the corners, an inescapable feature built in to the original design of the house. The old manse still sighs, and cracks its joints with the natural indifference of age. A fire crackles, and I collapse into a plush loveseat angled towards the hearth. Heathcliff, no longer the tatty ragamuffin, warms his November bones, stretches his stiff fingers towards the flames, and idly plots his next move. Which, it turns out, is to get very drunk.

Three glasses of zinfandel later, I realize Reverend Stacey is seated beside me, seemingly taking as much pleasure from a tall Guinness as I am from the wine. He nods once, seems pleased I have finally noted his presence, raises his glass towards me. "Cheers to Harry Templeton."

I tap his beer with my empty wine glass. "To the old duffer."
"Eh?"
"A term of endearment."

I am delighted to discover some kind spook has refilled my wine glass, and we drink to Harry.

"He had a full, rich life," says the Reverend, as if he knew.
"I was a disappointment to him."
"I'm sure he was very proud. You're a good man, Mavis."
"He wanted to go fishing without me. Did I mention that?"

"Well—"

"Sink or swim. Show a little gumption."

"I—"

"I'm not sure he would have gone through with it, though. We Templetons, we lack courage. At least the men do. My mother was brave, but then, she was a Templeton only by marriage. It takes a brave woman to marry a broomstick vendor and be happy about it. And she worked tirelessly to save helpless kittens from total annihilation. And dolphins. And hedgehogs."

"Hedgehogs?"

"All of God's creatures. That's what I'm trying to say, Reverend."

"Stacey."

"She couldn't save herself, though."

"I'm sorry."

"It's not your fault. I'm sure there's nothing you could have done."

I look at the yellow liquid in my glass and wonder if there wasn't something the Reverend…Stacey…might have done, after all. A prayer. Put in a good word with the Man. It always boils down to who you know.

"Stacey, I think I'm having a crisis of faith."

He purses his lips, as if he prefers not to talk shop at parties, but he is a dedicated practitioner, and a professional holy man. "That's not unusual at a time like this, Mavis."

"I can't help thinking that god's laughing at me, that I'm the butt of some joke, and he's up there splitting a gut. I'm the comic relief."

"We have no way of knowing why God does something, but there is a reason, you can be sure, even if you don't understand it, or agree with it. I think if we try to look at it through unselfish eyes, we can see that His motives are always for the greater good of mankind."

"That doesn't really help, does it?"

He has no response to that, so he pokes his stick around the usual platitudes. "I *can* guarantee you that God did not take your father away as a joke."

I can see he is not thrilled with the conversation, and I don't wish to drive this good man away. "How old are you, if you don't mind my asking?"

"Not at all. I'm seventy-six."

"I've noticed that preaching is an old man's game. Young men today aspire to become software programmers or croupiers. They put their faith in science and dumb luck."

Stacey shakes his head at this sad and undeniable truth of modern life. "They don't flock to the calling the way they did in my day, that's true, but sooner or later they will come back to the church."

"Once the countdown begins."

"The countdown?"

"When they hit forty and realize they've passed the halfway mark. When the faux-chrome trim starts peeling off the fenders and the muffler starts making that *noise*. Things start to sag, and important parts begin to fail. Blindness, diabetes, heart disease, kidney stones, gout, arthritis, divorce, depression—then the panic sets in. Science can only do so much, and dumb luck is never doled out fairly. The only thing left is spirituality."

"There is some truth in that, I suppose."

"I've always believed, in my own fashion, you know. I used to think god took a particular and personal interest in each and every one of us, what we did on a daily basis, how we conducted our lives, whether we told a lie or committed a crime. Believe it or not, I used to think that you couldn't get into heaven unless you died face-up. Isn't that the most ridiculous thing you've ever heard?"

"Well—"

"But I see now that god sees us the way we might see grains of sand on a beach. We don't pick out each individual grain, fondle and admire it for its distinctive qualities or beauty. No, we see them collectively, how they come together to make a beautiful whole. Imagine! Each grain of sand, in itself sharp-edged and irritating to the touch, but when gathered in the billions, they make something so wonderful and soft that you just can't resist walking on it with your bare feet, spread a towel and stretch out across it. One grain of sand sitting on the top, glistening in the sunlight, another trod underfoot, compressed by an unspeakable weight, buried beneath the layers, trapped in the darkness, oblivious to the light and beauty above. I feel like that grain of sand."

"I don't have all the answers, Mavis. You have to look for those answers in your own heart. What I can tell you is that if you have faith, true and complete faith, you will find comfort there."

He drained his Guinness and regarded the empty glass with something like regret. "We all have doubts, now and again. And I'll let you in on a secret that has served me well during my own moments of doubt. In order to avoid disappointing answers, I simply avoid asking difficult questions. Works like a charm."

27

I am in my bed, my familiar and comfortable bed, with its form-fitting depression on the left side that fits me perfectly. But there is no rest for me. Any hope of sleep is disrupted by the riot of thoughts rampaging through my mind. My historic reunion with Irene Valentine is concluded, and the only thing I know for sure is that I will never see her again.

- - -

I arrived by taxi.

Gainsborough Manor was a converted mansion on a dead-end street, a five minute drive east of Russell Hill. The colonial façade glowed pearly white under the November sky, its thick columns rising like marble fists towards a pale, distant heaven. The immaculate grounds, with precisely carved flowerbeds and shaped pear trees, were in stasis, battened down for the winter's hibernation. The summer's flowers had receded, and not a single fallen leaf remained on the ground. Some lackey with a gas-powered leaf-blower knew his business, knows his clientele. Every nugget of white pea gravel was in place on the semi-circular driveway.

As the taxi completed the arc and skidded up the road, back towards St. Clair, I realized I was committed to this visit. There was nowhere to go except up the wide steps and through the elegantly carved door. I navigated the stairs with slow, easy motions, the crutches having become a second, almost-natural pair of legs for me. At the summit, I spent a long moment facing the stained-glass panel mounted in the door, reconsidering, for the final time, my decision to see Irene Valentine. But after everything that had happened to me during the past weeks, I refused to be afraid of a feeble old woman. So, with a somewhat flimsy sense of security, I reached for the door handle.

The foyer was a shock of institutional flavour. The open space featured a crystal chandelier of theatrical proportions, which presided over a wide staircase that swept up in a gauche curve to the second floor. Underfoot was industrial broadloom, worn to a darker shade of grey in the high-traffic areas. Arranged along the walls was a mélange of sofas and padded armchairs, skinned with inoffensive browns and beiges. These seats were randomly populated by elderly residents, each fixed in an attitude, it seemed to me, of expectancy, as if waiting for a bus that was due three minutes ago, not yet a worrisome delay. All eyes focused on me as I hinged forward on my sticks, headed towards the main desk. I murmured a general greeting to this ancient group, and my syllables seemed to break their collective spell; I was returned a garbled salutation, in loose unison, tinged with the faint whiff of desperation. Dentures clicked and rosaries clattered in withered fists. Hair nets rustled impatiently as this gang realized I was not there for them.

In the center of the foyer was a glass-and-chrome reception station, behind which sat a young man in a subtle grey suit, who spoke quietly but confidently into the telephone.

"...I understand, Mister Fenchurch. I will pass the message along." He waited for Mr. Fenchurch to add something to the message. "No, of course not. I'm sure she will agree ...Yes, I understand. I'll take care of it...Yes, sir. Very good. We'll see you then." He replaced the receiver and gave me an appraising look.

The first impression I leave is always the same: fear, loathing, scorn, amusement, suspicion, any of the above. I would give anything to experience, just once, what it feels like to hear an intake of breath and know I have stirred in my fellow man a longing that doesn't involve perforating me with the business end of a pitchfork. I may have accepted my lot as Frankenstein's monster, but that doesn't mean I have to like it. And once again, despite the nap of my new black suit, I had failed to impress.

"May I help you?" The young man's voice was a gentle *basso*, rolling my way like distant thunder, polite, utterly professional. But the lightning in his eyes reached me first, searing me with his harsh, unspoken judgment.

"I'm here to see Irene Valentine," I said, brushing some lingering static electricity from my shoulder.

This caught him unaware, and he had to re-evaluate his assessment of me. Was I more courageous than the average man, or a complete fool? Either way, his new look said, ogre or not, I was no match for Mrs. Valentine. The outside corners of his eyes drooped with pity.

"May I tell her who's calling?"

"I'm her grandson."

By the look on his face, he couldn't reconcile this information in any way that made sense in his world. But, like any well-trained monkey, he pushed the buttons he was trained to push, and I was soon being ushered down a rather austere corridor, towards the Great Room, where, I was told, Irene Valentine awaited my call.

How best to describe the Great Room, with its panelled walls and lofty ceilings, hard-back chairs clustered in pairs and quartets, linen-draped card tables, television set roaring in one corner, fireplace roaring in another? How to detail the disintegration of Irene Valentine, who, at ninety, was no more substantial than some clever piece of origami, a fading sovereign who had shrunk to half the size of my memory of her, collapsing like a paper bag with the air sucked out, silk rendered in royal colours willowing over frail bones, white hair rising from the scalp with the same delicate tension as dandelion pollen? Should I mention the obvious effects of her recent series of strokes, the slack shoulders, the lightly drooping eye, the mouth pulled even further into its familiar disapproving arc? I'll say this: we were a couple of old wrecks, the two of us. Intact were two brilliant eyes, diamond-hard nuggets the colour of the North Sea under a tempestuous sky; and I knew that below the surface of the fragile wisp sitting across from me was the same fierce soul that had sent me packing, all those years ago.

Before we could begin in earnest, there were pleasantries required.

Sitting erect—as far as she was capable—Irene presented both cheeks for my dry lips. Her first words to me after all these decades were these: "Come to see the remains?" David had accurately depicted her disabled speech. She sounded drunk, the words staggering from her mouth, weaving and colliding with each other, wet and garbled. To her credit, she still managed to make herself understood. *Come to see the remains?*

"Yes," I answered, because I had already made the decision, before arriving, that I would speak truthfully. I had no illusions about being drawn with open arms back into the Valentine fold, not so long as Irene was alive. No one clung to a grudge with quite the same fanatical commitment as my grandmother. And besides, the race was on to see which of us would give up the ghost first. I had nothing to lose, so I said, *Yes.*

Irene's laughter detonated between us like a small bomb, sending ripples of nervous tension through the smoky, cloying air in the room. It was the mad laughter of the scientist, the howl of elation Dr. Frankenstein released into the rafters of his laboratory when he finally succeeded in cobbling together his homespun creature.

"Good," she said, finally. "Very good, Mavis."

At that moment, we understood each other. And not to be outdone in the pathos department, I added, "Did I mention that I'm dying?"

She gave me a long look, trying to decide whether or not to laugh again. "We're all dying, son. It just takes some of us a long time to fall down and stop moving."

I readjusted my posture in the hard chair. "David tells me you've been asking for me."

"He's turned out all right, don't you think?"

I hadn't quite made up my mind about my cousin, but I was willing to meet her halfway. "He's become a thoughtful and well-mannered thug."

Irene smiled. "He's smart, that boy. Always was."

"Cunning."

"Yes, that's the word."

"I could never get the hang of cunning."

"You lack guile," she said, not by way of compliment.

"A trait I inherited from Harry, I suppose."

"Don't bet on it."

I didn't know how to answer that. Was this another reference to my infamous bad blood? "You've been making ambiguous allusions about Harry."

Irene's head tilted slightly to the left, as if to see me more clearly. "That's why you're here, isn't it? You want answers."

"I guess I'm a little curious. But I'm not exactly sure what I'm suppose to be curious about."

"Another weakness, besides your lack of guile."

I was beginning to wonder if all this truth-telling was such a good idea. "Suppose you give me a question—"

"—*the*."

"I beg your pardon?"

"*The* question. There is only one."

"All right. *The* question."

Her ropy hands rose from her lap, turned upward, as if to receive a blessing. "Who are my parents?"

"Your parents?"

"Don't be a dolt, Mavis. Repeat after me: *Who are my parents?*"

"Who are my parents?"

"Good boy," she said, dropping her hands and slumping slightly. Her physical stamina could no longer keep up with her mind's indefatigable vigour. "Let me tell you."

- - -

History:

1959. Squinting through the small hole left partially unclouded by two devastating cataracts, Walt Porter stabbed a thick finger at the old cash register's keypad. The mechanics inside the ancient device jangled, and a sum total levitated into the window.

"One-hundred-and-forty-nine, seventeen," he croaked.

A recent operation to remove a tumour from his throat had left Walt's voice shattered. Estimated to be in his eighties, he was a physical ruin. He either wouldn't admit, or couldn't recall, his exact date of birth; although he was happy to offer, to anyone willing to listen, his litany of ailments.

The present customer, a young man with a patient face and yellow paint splotched on the sleeves of his work shirt, had watched this mechanical operation with the sort of tolerance one reserved specifically for the very young or the very old. "That can't be right," he said.

Walt squinted through his fuzzy optical tunnel at the young man, then at the tally on the register. "That's what it says," he announced, with a finality that brooked no opposition.

"I can see what it says, but it can't be right. All I've got here is a couple of rollers and some turpentine. It shouldn't be more than a few dollars. Let's see." He picked up the tin of paint thinner and found the price tag. "This here, a dollar-nine." He replaced it on the counter and grabbed one of the rollers. "These are one-seventy-five each, so that's, what…?" He did a bit of mental math. "Four dollars and fifty-nine cents. Plus tax."

Walt tapped an index finger on the glass window of the register. "What does that say there?"

"One-hundred-and-forty-nine dollars and seventeen cents."

Walt looked momentarily perplexed, and then angry. "Ach! That's a lot of money…" He had somehow lost the connection between the tally he was looking at and his current task, which was to accurately ring through the customer's purchases. "You could buy a car for that."

"Not quite," said the young man. "But it'd be a pretty good downpayment."

He looked at the young man, then down at the items on the counter. "I had no idea the prices were so high here."

"The prices aren't high. You just rang it up wrong."

Walt shook his head firmly. "The machine don't lie."

Just then, Harry emerged from the cellar, bearing a cardboard box jumbled with strap hinges and corner braces and barrel bolts. He immediately detected the look of consternation on the customer's face. It was a look he'd grown used to seeing when the customers were being attended to by his part-time employee, Walt Packer.

He'd hired Walt out of a combination of desperation and sympathy. Wally had plucked the 'Help Wanted' sign from the front window and more-or-less demanded the job, offering his fifty years of experience in construction by way of qualification, adding to his credit a fourteen-month tour of Europe during the Great War, and then leaking thick tears from his cloudy eyes, as he detailed the extent of his accumulated medical bills.

"Sir," Harry had said, looking into those cloudy orbs for signs of life, "you appear to be blind."

"Boy, I can count the spots on a leopard at fifty paces, if you ask me."

Harry was non-committal, lacking the steel to turn the man down flat.

The following morning, Walt Porter was waiting outside the front door. "Been here nearly an hour already. You better cut me a key," he said, pushing past Harry.

"Um…" said Harry.

"Where's the broom?" He scooched towards the first aisle and knocked over a display of rakes. "Pick them up, will ya?"

For three months, Walt had been frightening customers with his broken voice and his archaic advice ("Don't need fancy clips, sonny. Here, take this twine and wrap it around a couple of times, Tom's yer uncle."), and Harry was gathering the courage to lay him off, now that the busy season was over.

Now, Harry set down the cardboard box and strode towards the counter. "Everything all right?"

The young man looked relieved to see Harry. "Nothing serious," he said. "This fellow just made a mistake ringing up my items."

"The machine don't lie," said Walt.

"Let me have a look." Harry stepped behind the counter and gently pushed Walt aside. A moment later, the customer was mollified and on his way. "Just call me," Harry said to Walt. "I'll do the cash."

"Think I'm a fool?"

"No. I think you're blind."

"I can count the hairs on a goat's chin at eighty paces, if you ask me."

"Listen, Walt—"

But before Harry had a chance to return the old man to his ailing retirement, the front door open with a crash.

"Ach!" shouted Walt, squinting blindly in the direction of the commotion.

Harry rushed to the door, where a young woman had collapsed, dishevelled, bleeding from her mouth and nose, barely conscious. "Walt, call an ambulance!"

Old Walter showed no sign of having heard the order. "Ach!" he repeated, maintaining his position behind the cash. "Em!"

To Harry's inexperienced eye, the woman might have been twenty. Her light hair was matted with dirt and dry leaves, and she wore a suede jacket, stained with grime and blood. Her white blouse gaped open, the buttons gone from the seam, her brassiere exposed. Her corduroy skirt was torn at the hip, the short zipper twisted and mangled. She wore no shoes. Her left eye was purple and fat, her left ear was red, and seemed to be in the process of swelling.

Harry knelt down and put his palm against her cheek, a gesture of comfort. She flinched slightly at his touch. "It's all right, miss," he said, gently. "You're safe now."

Her eyes fluttered open and found the face of the young man who possessed the warm hand. She groaned—a sound more of relief than anguish. "I..." she began. "I was..."

But Harry was a city boy. He didn't need to be told what had happened, didn't want to believe it, although he did. "Don't worry. Everything's fine." He carefully helped her gain her feet. It was a cool afternoon, and a chill came through the open door. He felt her shiver under his steadying hands. Once they were upright, he noticed she was several inches taller than he was, although she seemed as light as air. After gently manoeuvring her into the store proper, he reached back and locked the front door. Templeton Hardware was closed for the day.

"What's this, eh?" asked Walt, who leaned across the counter, trying to see what was going on. "Who's there?"

"Did you call an ambulance?" Harry couldn't disguise the irritation in his voice. "Did you call the police?"

But the dirt- and blood-spattered woman must have come into the old man's focal range at that moment. All he said was, "Oi!"

The woman turned her face until her mouth was close to Harry's ear. "Help me," she whispered. And then she collapsed into his arms.

- - -

"That was Sara Glynn," said Irene Valentine. "You must have guessed that." She told me that, after that awful day, after Sara Glynn was released from the hospital and recovering at home, she, Irene, had asked Harry to tell her everything he could remember about that day. She needed to know. It was the only way she could cope.

I could imagine only a force like Irene Valentine would be able to pry the details from Harry. He had related to me almost nothing about the day he met my mother, and what he did tell me was a lie. "He said she came into the store, canvassing for some wildlife charity."

Irene nodded. "She had a love for animals that I never could quite understand." There was a hitch in her voice that would have made Evelyn Wharton proud. "She was collecting donations for the SPCA. Sara Glynn was always volunteering for that sort of thing. I was forever reminding her she should be studying for her exams, but she wouldn't listen. She was always ruled by her heart. I don't know how many times I warned her, if she was going to do this sort of thing, she should at least not go into those awful districts. There are plenty of good, safe neighbourhoods, closer to home."

I bristled. "I've lived in that *awful* district for thirty-three years."

She waved a pale hand at invisible flies. "She was *raped*, Mavis, grabbed off the sidewalk, dragged into a deserted laneway and *raped*. Don't expect me to have any sympathy." Those tempestuous eyes grew thick and wet. "She was just a child. Do you understand?"

I was beginning to.

Irene waited for her voice to return. "Harry was kind, I'll give him that. He gave her comfort while they waited for the ambulance, and afterwards he came regularly to visit her, to see how she was doing."

"What about the police? Did they ever find out who did it?"

"Sara Glynn never saw the man's face. They couldn't do anything without a description or a witness. He was never caught." She drew two long, deep breaths. "You can't imagine what it's like to have a policeman standing on your doorstep, telling you your child has been brutally attacked. You just can't imagine it. Only a mother can know that pain."

"Or a father," I offered.

She conceded my point with a nod.

During the brief silence that followed, the main thrust of her narrative coalesced in my mind into something like understanding, and in that moment my world shifted three degrees to the left. A feverish heat raked my face and chest. The wood smoke from the fireplace intensified, filling my lungs with hot ash until I thought I might pass out. The wall to my left was closing in, the ceiling coming down on me. The screech of the television, the *clack* of playing cards as they were shuffled, the scratch of rubber soles on the carpet… This was not the universe I had known, the one that had existed just moments earlier. This was not *my* reality. I rubbed a palm across my eyes and looked again. The room had returned to its normal, serene state. But something in me had changed, and I felt I would never see the world the same way again.

Once I recovered my voice, I said, "You're telling me that Harry wasn't my father."

Irene seemed unaware of my momentary paroxysm. "No, Mavis, he was not." She seemed grateful, if not pleased, to be telling me this, as if the telling had released her from some onerous duty. "It was a bad match. A foolish match. My daughter should have married better."

I remained silent. It had always been my grandmother's pattern to disparage Harry, and it had fallen to me to defend him, if only in my mind. I knew Harry was a better man than Irene Valentine would ever know.

Irene pulled her shoulders up and turned her head slightly to the left, the way she often did at the Valentine dinner table when she was about to launch into another speech about the decline of civilization, or the decrepitude of local politics. That gesture sent me back nearly four decades, brought to my mind images of old Joseph, serenely ignoring his family, lost in his own private thoughts, and poor Robyn, childishly brutalizing the English language while pastry flakes rained down on the linen, and Auntie Benz, swirling in the vortex of her gloom, her young son at her side, interpreting her cosmic messages for the rest of us.

She said, "I will always be grateful to Harry for what he did for Sara Glynn on that terrible day. But, in the end, he took advantage of a vulnerable girl who was incapable of making sensible choices. She was distraught, even if it wasn't outwardly apparent. You have to understand that Sara Glynn was the sort of girl who was not inclined to hysterics. She always strove to appear calm and rational, no matter what she might have been feeling inside. I knew this about her, you see, and I had always considered it an admirable quality, one that enhanced her natural beauty. Before that day, she had many admirers, young men calling on her, taking her out. Bright and promising young men, suitable to her class and station."

Once again I was forced to bite my tongue.

"If you were to ask those young men to describe her, they would say, first and foremost, that she was cheerful. That was Sara Glynn. Cheerful, energetic, thoughtful, and unfailingly grateful. Of course, that was her downfall, in the end. She showed her gratitude to Harry by marrying him."

"Harry loved her," I said. "Whatever you think of him, however low his circumstances, in your view, I know he loved her to the very end."

"Of course he did. Everyone loved her. He couldn't help loving her, but that doesn't mean he should have married her."

"He claimed she loved him, too. I believe him." Or, at least, I believe *he* believed it.

"Don't be a fool, Mavis. Do you want me to continue or not?"

I made a conciliatory gesture.

Irene resumed. "Once Sara Glynn came home from the hospital, she and Harry started spending a lot of time together. I didn't object because I thought he could help her get through the trauma, and her therapist encouraged the friendship because Harry had been instrumental in her rescue, which put him in a powerful position of trust. Naturally, Sara Glynn saw him as her champion, her knight in shining armour. Young women are inclined to hold dear those foolish girlhood fantasies, Mavis. And when she found out she was pregnant by that *rapist*, she didn't know what to do."

"Harry offered to marry her."

"She felt she owed her life to him."

"Maybe she really did love him. Is that so farfetched?" I couldn't stop myself pressing the point.

Irene's tone hardened. "She was a child who had been through a terrible shock. She needed therapy, not some simple-minded fool who couldn't offer her the life she deserved."

"So, your objection was that Harry was poor."

"My objection was that he wasn't good enough for my girl, and neither of them had the good sense to know it. Surely you can see that. You must know that they never would have lasted. If Sara Glynn had lived, she would have left him. Sooner or later, she would have left."

"We'll never know for sure," I said.

"Yes, by God, we do know. *I* know."

We would never agree on the subject. And I now had the additional burden of having to adjust to the knowledge that the old duffer wasn't my father—my *biological* father. My mind reeled in confusion. Why didn't Harry tell me this himself? Was he raising me out of some misguided and over-inflated sense of duty? Could he have truly loved me, knowing I was the product of a violent crime? Is that why he gave me up so easily after I was born? It was easy, now, to see why the Valentine clan, and Irene Valentine in particular, always looked at me as if I were the carrier of a virulent plague. They knew of my dubious origins, and surely were not surprised when I turned out to be of an apparently criminal nature. Bad blood. My real father was a rapist, a nameless and faceless beast who might, for all I know, still be alive and lurking in the neighbourhood I still lived in. We might have passed each other, my *father* and I, on the street a dozen times, over the years, not knowing…not knowing.

At last, Irene said, "I thought you should know about all this, now that Harry's gone."

I nodded. "He was a good man, Irene."

She swallowed her teeth and looked away.

"He loved my mother until the very end."

"We all loved Sara Glynn," she said, quietly.

28

It's not so bad, really. My life, I mean. It hasn't been so bad.

For forty three years I have had a roof over my head, food on my plate. The necessities of life. During that time, a surprising number of people have taken care of me. Some, like the doctors and nurses who rescued me from my mother's dead womb, were merely doing their job, fulfilling an oath. Others, like those unseen church ladies who saw me through the tricky weeks of incubation with their prayer campaign, had no vested interest in me or my life, apart from the commission of a charitable deed. Even the Valentines, who eventually rejected me, even they gave up valuable closet space for a decade, saw to my basic needs with some style, I admit. Kind-faced paramedics, wistful stewardesses, grandmothers of the sweet and not-so-sweet variety, bossy nurses, irritated lawyers—it is the women who have played the leading roles in the drama of my life. They were the ones with all the dialogue, circling, pacing the boards, giving our scenes momentum; me, I was just a prop. And what of the men? Joseph and Robyn Valentine, kind souls, in their own way, were ultimately background players, comic relief. Bullies, rock stars, secret agents, reporters, border guards—so many border guards! To varying degrees, threatening. Except for Harry, who was the real star of my show. *Take a bow, you old duffer.* Harry, who was a like a father to me. No…that's not fair. DNA be damned. My father, Harry Templeton, managed, somehow, to love me. The ogre. Why not? Her Doktor Frankenstein loved his boy, too, despite the bolts in his neck and the lack of civilized conversation at the dinner table.

Now I am alone on the stage. *Time for your closeup, Mister Templeton.*

There is no pain. The aches that have been my crucible for three years have subsided, so much so that I can no longer feel my legs. Warmly ensconced in my bed, I look down at the small tents my feet make beneath the bed sheets. My brain sends the command, and the toes wiggle. A strange sensation—or lack of sensation, as I feel nothing. I wonder briefly if I can walk, but I don't really care. I've got no plans. I'm not going anywhere. I will simply enjoy this respite from the constant reminders of my failing body.

How can I complain when there is warm air coming out of the vent? When there is a thick book on my bedside table, waiting for my undivided attention? Life is good. I am free to stay here as long as I wish, all day, if that's my desire. Templeton Hardware will remain closed, at least for another day. Maybe forever. What does it matter? There is food in the kitchen, in case I want to eat. Which I don't. I can't recall when I last ate, but I feel no hunger—for food, at any rate.

There are many varieties of hunger. The human soul is constructed as a complicated bridgework of hungers: for knowledge, attention, acceptance, restraint (from vice?), compassion, understanding, and especially love. My bridge extends beyond the visible horizon, farther than I will travel during my lifetime. *Walk on, man! Tally ho!* But I have lost my appetite, or rather chosen to set it aside, no longer in *need* or *want*. Nothing matters anymore, except that last and most important hunger: love. It may never really be satiated, that growl in the pit of the heart that calls for more, but every morsel one gets, no matter how small, is a delectation, a mouth-watering treasure. *Love is all you need... Come on, Harry, sing along...*

History:

I was conceived by an act of hate. I could have been abandoned by the herd, or placed in a sack and sunk in the Tiber, but I wasn't. Against the odds, I lived. Not too bad. As for my Faith, I no longer doubt. Anything. Notice the uppercase *F*. Faith. I am one of the *multitude*, now. Legitimate. I'll be going through the main gate, alongside the Unitarians and the Pentecostals and the Baptists. And there are a few faces I'll be glad to see on the other side. *Hello, Mother. Hello, Harry. Father.*

Old habits die hard. I am lying on my back, facing upward. And if my hands are laced formally across my chest, it is because my hands find this placement familiar and comforting.

Was it meant to end like this? I would have to say, yes.